D0247527

We hope you enjoy this boo
renew it by the due date.

You can renew it at www.norfolk.gov.uk/libraries or
by using our free library app.

Otherwise you can phone 0344 800 8020 -
please have your library card and PIN ready.

You can sign up for email reminders too.

NORFOLK ITEM
30129 084 612 788

NORFOLK COUNTY COUNCIL
LIBRARY AND INFORMATION SERVICE

Sophie Pembroke was born in Abu Dhabi, but grew up in Wales and now lives in a little Hertfordshire market town with her scientist husband, her incredibly imaginative daughter, and her adventurous, adorable little boy. In Sophie's world, happy is for ever after, everything stops for tea, and there's always time for one more page . . .

Summer on Seashell Island

Sophie Pembroke

ORION

First published in Great Britain in 2020 by Orion Fiction,
an imprint of The Orion Publishing Group Ltd
Carmelite House, 50 Victoria Embankment,
London EC4Y 0DZ

An Hachette UK company

1 3 5 7 9 10 8 6 4 2

A CIP catalogue record for this book is
available from the British Library.

ISBN (Mass Market Paperback) 978 1 4091 8982 4
ISBN (eBook) 978 1 4091 8983 1

Typeset by Input Data Services Ltd, Somerset

Printed and bound in Great Britain by Clays Ltd, Elcograf S.p.A.

www.orionbooks.co.uk

To the Cannon Family Singers, now more than ever.
With much love.
(April 2020)

MIRANDA

One Friday morning in late July, Miranda Waters paused in her habitual morning run to press the toes of her trainers into the sand of the Long Beach and take stock of her island.

Waves lapping gently against the sand? Check. Puffy white clouds bobbing overhead? Absolutely. The sounds of gulls calling and Albert Tuna singing down by the harbour and the shops on the promenade opening their shutters for the day? Yes, yes and also yes. The smell of salt and fried breakfasts and sun cream and ice cream and doughnuts? Strong.

She waved at Albert Tuna as he appeared on the stone jetty that surrounded the harbour, and he waved back, another part of her morning ritual. At this time of day, there weren't usually too many people around, although that would change now the summer holidays were beginning. Soon the island would be alive with families and tourists, piling in to enjoy a quintessentially British holiday at the seaside.

She hoped.

It had been a long winter on Seashell Island, so named because of its shape, fanning out from the point of the harbour to a long curve along its far side. Easter and the May half term hadn't been as busy on the island as in previous springs, continuing a slow decline that Miranda had tracked over the years she'd worked for Seashell Holiday Cottages.

But things would pick up this summer, she was sure. After all, who *wouldn't* want to spend the summer somewhere as perfect as this?

Miranda turned on the spot, strands of her dark hair escaping from her ponytail in the wind and getting tangled in the arm of her glasses, and smiled at the familiar sights around her. Candy-coloured shops and cottages, all along the seafront. The harbour, right at the end of the promenade, with sailboats bobbing with the waves. The Welsh mainland, just in sight over the water, another world as far as Miranda was concerned. Seashell Island was exactly as it should be at the start of the summer holidays.

Apart from the dog racing across the sand from the harbour, towards her.

Miranda frowned. Dogs weren't allowed on the Long Beach – only on North Beach and the Short Beach. Except, as the animal grew closer, she realised it wasn't a dog. It was too woolly, and its neck was too long.

Wait. Did they have a rule about llamas on Long Beach?

She couldn't remember one in the *Seashell Island Guide and Rulebook*. She'd helped to write the latest version two summers ago, and a rule like that would have stuck in her memory. Perhaps it was time for a rewrite.

Or maybe not. Since the llama *did* seem to be having a lovely time racing up and down the sand, and it wasn't like it was hurting anybody. Well, except for the two poor men chasing after the creature.

Recognising her parents' neighbours Max and Dafydd in pursuit, Miranda raced over to see if she could help.

'A llama, Max?' she asked, laughing, as she joined the chase.

'Seemed like a good idea at the time,' he panted back.

After another ten minutes of chasing the llama, even Max,

twenty years older than Miranda but with more energy than she thought she'd ever had, was starting to look tired. Dafydd, meanwhile, had fashioned some sort of a lasso from seaweed and was chasing after the llama while yee-hawing like John Wayne.

Max and Miranda shared a look, stopped running, and watched.

'So, I take it this is the latest addition to the smallholding?' Miranda said.

Ever since Max and Dafydd had moved into the farmhouse next door to the Lighthouse, her parents' bed and breakfast, they'd been doing it up and adding various animals and a campsite – including a glamping area – where Max ran stargazing courses and Dafydd prepared stone-baked pizzas in an outdoor oven. It was a nice addition to Seashell Island, Miranda thought, and the tourists who wanted to camp weren't usually the same kind of people who'd book the B&B or one of the holiday cottages she managed as part of Seashell Holiday Cottages, so there wasn't even any grumbling about competition.

Max nodded. 'Dafydd thought the kids who visit would like it. So far, it's spat at me and run away.'

'So basically just like the kids, then,' Miranda joked.

Max rolled his eyes at her. 'I'll have you know our guests are always polite and well mannered. Mostly. Anyway, we'll never find out if the kids like the llama if we can't get the bloody thing up to the farm in the first place.'

Miranda squinted against the morning sun as she peered up the beach trying to spot Dafydd and the llama. 'I think he's got him. Or . . . not.'

Even as she spoke, the llama broke away from Dafydd again, this time loping towards the breaking waves, frolicking in the water. Rolling her eyes, Miranda ran towards it.

3

The last thing Seashell Island needed now was a reputation for drowning llamas.

Could llamas swim? She had no idea. Better not to take the chance.

Leaving Max and Dafydd behind, she raced into the water, wincing as the freezing spray hit her bare legs. The sea water would warm up as the season wore on, but right now it was as cold as it had been at Easter, for the charity harbour swim.

'Come here, you blasted creature.' She lunged forward to try and wrap an arm around the llama, but the animal danced away, far nimbler on its feet in the water than she was in her waterlogged trainers.

Miranda darted after it again, and once again it sidestepped her attempts, hopping over the waves.

'Oh God,' she groaned. 'You think this is a game, don't you?'

She wasn't an animal person. She liked Misty, her mother's rescue cat, well enough, but anything bigger wasn't her sort of thing. But here she was, wrestling a llama in the ocean, because that was the kind of thing that happened here on Seashell Island.

Sometimes, she wondered why she loved it so much.

Miranda chased the llama all the way up the shoreline to the harbour before finally cornering it by the stone jetty. Max and Dafydd had followed them along the beach, shouting unhelpful advice and encouragement as they went. Dashing up onto the jetty, Dafydd tossed his makeshift lasso over the llama's head from above, and led the animal out of the water and onto the sand again.

Bending at the waist with her hands on her thighs, Miranda tried to catch her breath. She'd lost feeling in her feet, her legs were splattered with wet sand, and there was a piece of seaweed wrapped around her right ankle. If she hadn't been sweaty enough from her run, she was now. She *definitely* needed a shower before she made it to the office to open up in — she checked her watch — oh. Fifteen minutes.

Then she heard the applause and cheers from the beach, punctuated by laughter. Straightening up, she saw a crowd had gathered on the harbour wall to watch the antics of the llama — and Miranda. Ideal.

Giving the onlookers — most of whom she recognised as amused locals, people she'd have to deal with during the course of her normal week — a weary wave, she headed up to join Max, Dafydd, and that bloody llama.

As she walked closer, she could see the beaming smile of pride on Dafydd's face. Closer still, and Miranda spotted the filthy looks the llama was throwing at his captor.

'Thanks, Miranda,' Max said. 'Sorry you got all wet.' He picked a piece of seaweed out of her hair, showing it to her before tossing it back in the water. 'I'm sure the silly animal will prefer its stall and field to the sea, once we get it up to the farm.'

'Have you named him yet?' Miranda wasn't at all convinced that this llama would be staying on Seashell Island very long — especially given its escapologist tendencies — but she made it a point of pride to know all the names of the island's permanent residents. Including llamas.

'I'm thinking Lucifer,' Max told her, and she snorted with laughter.

'You just don't under*stand* the animals the way I do,' Dafydd told his husband. 'Anyway, she's a girl, aren't you, *cariad*.' He ruffled Lucifer's wool. Lucifer's glare grew more withering. 'So it would have to be Lucy. Lucy the Llama.'

'Lucy it is,' Max agreed easily. 'Short for Lucifer. Now, let's get this demon beast home, OK?'

They waved their goodbyes as they led Lucy the Llama to the truck waiting beside the harbour, Max swearing as she spat at him again.

Miranda turned back towards the beach, still shaking water from her trainers.

'You look like you might need this.' A towel was tossed down from the jetty, and Miranda caught it automatically. Squinting up through the early morning sunshine, she spotted her friend Christabel up above, and smiled.

'You are an angel.' Rubbing the towel over her chilly legs, Miranda asked, 'Don't suppose you've got a hot shower and a change of clothes up there, have you?'

Normally, she ran along the beach then towards the edge of the town, back up to the flat she shared with Paul, always leaving plenty of time to shower, change, and make it in time to open the office for nine o'clock. Today, her morning routine had been swallowed by an escapee llama.

'Afraid not. But I can go fetch the clothes for you, if you're OK with the beach shower.'

Miranda shuddered. The beach shower – a jerry-rigged feature of the Long Beach, set up by the steps from the high street – provided icy cold water in sharp, knife-like droplets. It was fine for rinsing the sand from your feet after a walk on the beach, but you wouldn't want to actually *shower* in it.

Fortunately, she had another option. 'It's OK. I've got a change of clothes at the office, and the holiday let above us is empty this week. I'll nip in and use the shower there.'

Finally, an advantage to not having a fully booked roster of cottages and flats this month.

In the main square, the church clock chimed half past the hour. As Max and Dafydd pulled away with Lucy, the crowd around the harbour began to disperse too, ready to go about their day, just as she needed to. Seashell Island was

6

as it should be again, and it was time for her to get to work.

'So, it's Friday. Can I assume you have wild and wonderful plans for the weekend?' Christabel fell into step with her as she headed towards the office.

'Of course!' Miranda lied. 'I thought I'd go over to the mainland, sing karaoke at a strip bar, gatecrash a stag party then catch a plane to a mystery destination.'

'Sounds like a few weekends in my twenties,' Christabel replied. 'So, same as always then?'

Miranda nodded. 'Friday lunch with Paul, closing the office early, checking in on the B&B for Mum and Dad, then home to bed. We might go to the farmers' market at the church on Sunday, though.'

Christabel clutched at her heart. 'The excitement is too much for me, Miri!'

Miranda rolled her eyes. 'Well, you might not like it. But it's fun for me.'

'Lunch with Paul? Fun?' Christabel shot her a look of disbelief.

'He's a nice guy. And he can be funny, sometimes.' Hmm, that didn't sound particularly enthusiastic, did it? Especially not about the man she was planning to marry. 'And I love him,' she added, belatedly. Not that it made any difference to Christabel.

Christabel had arrived on the island eighteen months ago, planning on staying for a week but loving it so much she decided to stay. That, Miranda understood no problem – she felt exactly the same way about Seashell Island, after all.

It was also the only thing the two of them seemed to have in common, but that hadn't stopped them becoming fast friends. On an island this size, Miranda knew full well that you had to make friends with everybody – and women her own age she got on with were few and far between. Most

7

of the girls she'd gone to school with had settled down and married and were busy with their families, their lives. The one or two she'd actually got on well with, however, had moved to the mainland as soon as they were eighteen – like Miranda's younger sister Juliet had done.

'What about you?' Miranda asked. 'What wild plans have you got this weekend?'

Christabel stretched her arms above her head and reached up towards the sky, her long, lean body strong and at ease with itself in the sunlight. Then she shrugged. 'Actually, very little. You know me, I like to be spontaneous. But it does feel like it might be time for a little fun with a new companion . . .'

Miranda followed her friend's gaze, and found it landing on the figure of a man carrying a box into the Flying Fish Deli and Restaurant.

Rory Hillier.

'Not Rory,' she said, instinctively.

Christabel raised an eyebrow. 'Why not?'

'Because . . .'

Why not? Actually, Christabel's brand of relationship therapy might be good for him, since he'd been moping around the island now for the last ten years.

'Because he's still in love with your sister,' Christabel finished for her, obviously remembering the drunken conversation they'd shared about Miranda's family, around Christmastime.

'Yeah. Poor sod.' Because Juliet wasn't coming back to Seashell Island, certainly not for longer than an obligatory visit. And Rory didn't want to leave.

Just like Miranda.

'Maybe it's time for him to move on,' Christabel said, still eyeing Rory speculatively, as he came back to retrieve another box. Then he saw them watching and waved. Miranda waved back.

Christabel blew him a kiss.

'I know you think you have some magic touch with men,' Miranda told her. 'But I think you'd have your work cut out with Rory.'

'It's not magic,' Christabel said, with a shrug. 'I just like to get to know a guy, have some fun together. And then we get talking and, well, I help them see what they really want from life. Refocus, if you will. Then they're free to go and chase it, and I get to go on with my own life, too. I think it's a legacy from my past life working in the City. I know how to get people where they need to go.'

'Aren't you ever worried that one of them will decide that what they really want from life is you?'

'Hasn't happened yet.' Was it her imagination, or was Christabel's smile just a little sad as she shook her head? 'Anyway, if not Rory, then who? I'm running out of eligible men on this island. Unless you're trying to get rid of me . . .'

'Never!' But she did have a point. Men in the relevant age range, who were also single, straight, and vaguely attractive in appearance or personality, were in short supply on Seashell Island. Which was one of the reasons Miranda was so lucky to have Paul. 'It's a shame my brother isn't here,' Miranda mused. 'Leo could definitely use your special brand of refocusing.' It seemed to her that, since his divorce, the only thing Leo had been able to focus on was work.

'Ha! No thanks,' Christabel replied, as they reached the offices of Seashell Holiday Cottages. 'You've told me too much about him already. I mean, I like a challenge, but even I have my limits. And right now, my body is telling me I'm at my lower caffeine limit. I'm off to fetch coffee. Enjoy lunch with Paul – if you can!'

She pressed a swift kiss to Miranda's cheek and sped off across the road, towards the Crab Leg Cafe.

Miranda smiled, watching her friend dart around the town like she'd always been there. Christabel was a breath of fresh air on the island and, as much as Miranda normally liked things to stay exactly the same, she couldn't deny that life had been a lot more fun since she arrived.

With a last glance back at the town behind her, Miranda unlocked the office door and set about finding her spare clothes, showering in record time, and being behind the reception desk again by 9 a.m. sharp.

Seashell Holiday Cottages had been set up thirty years ago by Miranda's father-in-law-to-be, Nigel, and had been helping families, couples, singletons and friends holiday on the island ever since. Miranda had worked for them since she was fourteen, helping clean properties in the holidays at first, then taking over reception duties once she turned sixteen. Now, she practically ran the place – although she still let Nigel believe he was in charge. He *was* going to be her father-in-law, after all. As soon as she and Paul finally tied the knot. She supplemented her income with some virtual assistant work for companies as far away as London, New York and even Sydney, which helped make ends meet during the slower, colder seasons when the office didn't need to be open full time. But Seashell Holiday Cottages was where her heart was.

It could have grown old, working for the same place all these years, but somehow it never did. When she pushed open the office door and heard the seashells hanging in the window clatter against the glass, she knew she was home. And there was always something interesting to deal with – a new property to photograph and list, a family needing advice on the perfect place to stay, even a nervous boyfriend with a ring wanting tips on the perfect spot on the island to propose.

But, if she was honest, Miranda knew that what kept her going the most was the knowledge that one day, soon, this would all be hers.

She and Nigel had a deal, a plan. Once she and Paul were married, he'd retire, and she'd take over the family business. Just as soon as she was actually family.

Until then, she just ran the place unofficially.

By 10 a.m., she'd dealt with a TV that couldn't get CBeebies in one cottage, found a romantic dinner reservation for a nervous fiancé-to-be, arranged for her favourite photographer to take photos of a gorgeous new cottage she'd just got on the books down by Gull Bay, *and* helped rescue a runaway llama. Miranda was pretty sure she'd earned a coffee break herself, when the phone rang again.

'Seashell Holiday Cottages,' she said brightly, while stretching the office phone cord towards the kitchen and vowing, not for the first time, that when *she* was in charge, they'd go cordless.

'Hey. Are we still on for lunch?'

The sound of her fiancé's voice should make her smile, Miranda knew. Today, the harried tone in his voice – and the yelling she could hear in the background – told her that work was not going well, and that lunch would probably be a chance for him to tell her all about it.

All the same, she forced a smile. She and Paul had been together for nineteen years – since they were sixteen – and she was used to his moods, the same way he was used to hers. And when they finally got married, she'd promise good times and bad, which included a lousy day at work at the very least, she was sure.

She didn't let herself dwell on how many bad days at

work there'd be. Or whether the good days would ever make up for it. Paul and his whole family were a Seashell Island institution, like she'd striven to be. They made sense together, from a purely logical point of view.

However boring Christabel thought he was.

'Absolutely! I'm looking forward to it,' she lied, wishing she could just take a sandwich down to the seafront and enjoy the peace instead. Checking through the front window of the office to make sure no tourists were about to wander in, she lowered her voice and said the words that were guaranteed to brighten his mood, no matter how bad his day.

'The last of the B&B's guests left this morning. So I can stay at home tonight.'

Her parents' trip of a lifetime to Australia had been a bone of contention between her and Paul from the start. Well, not the trip itself – they had both agreed that, since they hadn't had a proper holiday in over three decades, Josie and Iestyn Waters deserved a decent break away. But while Miranda thought the logical extension of that was that she'd move into the Lighthouse B&B while they were gone and manage the early summer bookings, Paul seemed to believe that they should have just closed down for the duration and cancelled any existing reservations.

Miranda had held firm, but she had to admit it had caused some tension. Still, the B&B was unoccupied between now and her parents' return on Sunday, so they could put that behind them and she could move home. Maybe they could even start discussing wedding dates again. They'd been engaged for years, now. It was only sensible to move on with the plans, so Nigel could retire and she could take over the business properly.

'Right,' Paul said, in a distracted monotone. 'So I'll meet you at the office at twelve thirty. OK?'

'That's fine.' She'd tell him again over lunch, when he was listening properly. That would cheer him up. 'Love you.'

'Yeah, bye.' Paul hung up.

Miranda frowned. She might have been with the same guy her whole adult life, but even she didn't need Christabel to tell her that that was not a good phone call with a man who was supposed to love her. Who she was supposed to love.

Outside, a cloud passed in front of the sun, casting shadows through the front window. And suddenly, Seashell Island didn't feel quite as perfect as it normally did.

LEO

'OK, so you're absolutely sure you know what you're doing?' Leo's gaze darted away from the road ahead of him to check the confidence of his assistant's expression.

Tom, sitting in the passenger seat, rolled his eyes. Leo decided that counted as certainty.

Good. At least *one* of them should know what they were doing this summer.

'I'm accompanying you guys to the ferry terminal then, once you're on board, driving approximately three metres to the secure parking garage I booked—'

'It's more than three metres,' Leo interrupted. He'd checked on a map, once Tom had showed him the place he'd booked. After all, he needed to be certain his baby would be safe.

'Fine. Thirty metres to the parking garage, then.' Tom's eyes were basically permanently rolling now. Leo ignored it. 'I'll park your precious car very carefully without dinging it at all, lock it up securely, then catch the train back to London.'

'I wish *we* could have taken the train,' Mia moaned from the backseat. 'Abby doesn't get travel-sick on *trains*.'

'Abby hasn't been sick in the convertible either, have you, sweetheart. Smoothest ride ever.' Leo glanced up at the rear-view mirror to double check that the upholstery of his car was still unstained. All safe. Although he had to admit that six-year-old Abby was looking a little green around the edges. 'Nearly there now, anyway.'

He'd only wanted to drive his pride and joy convertible along the M4 for one last jaunt before he had to say goodbye to it for the summer, with the top down as they reached the coast. Was that so bad? What *was* bad was the ridiculous rules Seashell Island had about cars. No vehicles unless strictly necessary for island work, and even then, they needed special permits agreed months ahead of time.

He blamed his elder sister, Miranda, for that one. The islanders had reviewed the car policy just a couple of years ago, and she'd fought for keeping their arcane and restrictive rules. She'd even started a new bike-borrowing system to make it easier for tourists.

Bikes. Seriously.

This was what happened when a person like Miranda never left Seashell Island. They became institutionalised. That was just one of the reasons he'd been so determined to make his life on the mainland, instead.

'I'm perfectly fine with all the arrangements for the car,' Tom said, continuing the conversation seamlessly. 'The part I don't understand is how you expect to work full time from Seashell Island while also looking after both your kids. I mean, I thought this was supposed to be a holiday.'

'So did we,' Mia muttered. Leo decided to pretend he hadn't heard that.

The girls were just children. They didn't understand the pressures of work. Nobody who ran their own business actually took holidays, right? They were for wage slaves and slackers.

His business was a success because he put everything he had into it. He couldn't stop that now.

'It'll be fine,' Leo said. 'My parents are always saying they want to spend more time with the girls, so they'll take them out and entertain them while I work – and then we can have lots of family time together the rest of the time.' He raised his voice for the last part, hoping it might mollify Mia.

He checked the mirror. She did not look mollified.

When had his little princess grown so difficult? Emily, her mother, would probably tell him she was still processing the divorce. But since even his ex-wife had managed to move on enough to marry someone else in the three years since the decree absolute came through, it seemed unlikely that Mia was *still* being difficult about that.

Maybe she was acting out because of her mum's new marriage. A marriage that, incidentally, had resulted in him being stuck in sole charge of the girls all summer while Emily and Mark headed off on their honeymoon.

Which meant, basically, it was all his ex-wife's fault. Which made for a nice change.

Leo was well aware that *he* was the one who couldn't make a marriage work, couldn't compromise his ambition, his wants, to make everyone happy. He focused on what mattered most, and that, practically, had to be keeping a roof over all their heads and food on the table for the girls. Yes, Emily had worked too, and yes, perhaps they could have managed with less if they had to. But why should they have had to?

Besides, he loved his job. He was *good* at his job.

It was love and parenting he sucked at.

But that didn't mean he couldn't make it work this summer. He'd missed the girls, even knowing that he probably spent more time with them now he only saw them every couple of weekends than he had when he lived in the same house. Still, when he got home from the office at night, not being able to sneak upstairs and look at their sleeping faces still caught him in the chest, sometimes.

Of course, times like this – when Mia was looking like a mardy teenager a good four years before she had any right to – he was glad that Emily still took care of the bulk of the parenting. He got to do fun stuff, like bowling and pizza and movies, and she got to deal with school work and mood swings and fallings out with friends. Fun stuff he could manage. So long as it didn't interfere with work.

Emily had emailed him a lengthy list of rules and regulations for the summer – including limits on how many ice creams Abby was allowed – but Leo hadn't paid it too much attention. What was the point of summer holidays if the girls couldn't stay up too late and eat too much ice cream? Besides, he knew he'd need to provide some treats to make up for all the work he had to do.

Everything would be fine. His parents would deal with the day to day, just like Emily usually did, and he'd be able to do the fun stuff with them like normal.

He definitely had the better part of the parenting deal with Emily, even if he did hand over a serious chunk of cash every month for the privilege. He didn't mind that part. It reassured him that he was taking care of his family. After all, that was why he worked so hard, right?

He frowned, remembering that Emily wanted to talk to him about that when she got back. Now that she was remarried, she'd hinted that Mark would be taking over some of the financial obligation. Which made logical sense, and Leo knew his lawyer and accountant would both be thrilled.

Except . . . Leo wasn't sure he wanted *Mark* taking care of his family, nice as the guy was.

He hadn't wanted to like his ex-wife's new partner, but Mark was one of those guys who was just *likeable*. Laid-back, impossible to offend, and he made Emily happy. He also looked after the girls, including them in stuff he did with his own son from his first marriage.

It had taken a little while for Leo to see all that, of course. But now whenever he felt the irritation rising, he reminded himself of what was really important: he got to do the work he loved, and his family were happy. That wasn't nothing.

It hadn't always been an easy road to where they were now, but one of the things Leo was proudest of in his recent life was that he and Emily had found a way to make separated life as easy as possible on the girls.

That and his thriving business, of course. The business he hoped would continue thriving in his absence over the summer.

'If there are any problems, you will call me immediately, OK?' he told Tom. 'My parents will be there with the girls; I can be back in London in four hours if I'm needed. Maybe five,' he corrected, as the car slid to a halt in the mass of traffic around the tiny ferry terminal that had the only boats that docked at Seashell Island. He'd forgotten how crazy the place could be at high summer. In his memories, the summer days were often overshadowed by the long, empty winters when no one visited at all, and the population of the island shrank down to just the locals, battening down the hatches against the weather and the isolation. He and his baby sister Juliet would hide in the attic at the Lighthouse, planning for the day they'd escape the island and live in the real world for a change.

He'd escaped; they both had. And even now, just the thought of returning for a whole summer was making him edgy. Seashell Island sucked people in, he'd seen it plenty of times before. Visitors who came for a weekend and ended up buying a house there as the island got its grips into them.

His parents had been two of them.

It wasn't that Seashell Island wasn't a lovely place to visit. But after growing up there, Leo was far too aware of its flaws to view it through the rose-tinted glasses that Miranda and his parents wore.

Mia grumbled again in the back seat – about the traffic or the trip to the island where he'd grown up, Leo wasn't sure. He ignored her.

This was how life was. He had a job he loved, and he was going to do it. That didn't make him a bad father.

The thought popped into his head that there were probably plenty of other things that did that. Leo ignored it, too.

Focus, that was the key. That was what was going to get him through the summer. He'd do his job, spend time with the girls, and be back in London before September. It would all be fine.

Quicker than he'd expected, they pulled into the ferry terminal, and Leo parked in the waiting bay, Tom already jumping out to grab the bags from the boot. Leo took a moment to stroke the steering wheel as he said a personal farewell to his beloved silver convertible.

With a last handshake goodbye for Tom, Leo reluctantly handed over the car keys, loaded the girls up with their rucksacks, grabbed the suitcase handles, and headed into the ferry terminal.

As he glanced back one last time, Abby asked, 'Are you going to miss Tom, Daddy?'

Leo sighed. 'I'm going to miss my car.'

But mostly, he knew, he'd miss the freedom it represented. In London, he could go anywhere, anytime – traffic permitting.

On Seashell Island, there was nowhere to go. And he'd just committed himself to five whole weeks there, with his parents telling him he was working too much and Miranda berating him for not visiting often enough, even though she never even left the place to visit *him*.

Steeling himself, Leo led the girls forward to the ferry.

It was five weeks. He'd managed most of his childhood there, he could manage one summer.

Then he'd get back to his real life again.

JULIET

Just tell him.

Sitting in the client chair opposite her boss's desk, Juliet waited for Callum to finish his phone call. In some ways, she was grateful for the interruption – it gave her longer to gather her thoughts. In others, she was seriously narked. She'd told him she needed to talk to him about something important, something urgent, and he'd taken the call anyway, before she'd even had a chance to start.

That told her more than she liked about her place in his mental hierarchy.

If he'd been *only* her boss, she'd probably be OK with that. As it was . . .

Leaning back against the chair as another wave of nervous nausea passed through her, Juliet looked around the office to distract herself. On the phone, Callum was talking about quarterly reports and latest sales figures, while she was remembering how he'd laid her out on that desk and touched every inch of her with his hands and mouth. Or how he'd pressed her up against that glass window, fifty floors above the London streets below, the night skies twinkling above them, and slipped his fingers inside her skirt and—

'Right.' Callum hung up the phone. 'Juliet.' He steepled his hands in front of him, giving her his full attention at last. Juliet frowned, as she took in his expression. Where was the wicked smirk at the corner of his lips he usually saved for her? Or the heat in his eyes that let her know that, as professional as they always were during business hours, later it would be a different story.

Did he already know what she was there to talk to him about?

'I know you said you wanted to discuss something,' Callum went on without giving her a chance to talk. 'But actually, there's something I need to tell you too.'

Her intuition – the one that always told her when a guy was about to be particularly dickish – was pinging wildly. *And I haven't even told him about the*— she broke off the thought, swallowing hard. If she said it, hell, if she even thought it, that made it real.

Far more real than one slim piece of white plastic and a plus sign.

For years, Juliet had made it a personal principle to enjoy life, to wring every drop of excitement and opportunity from it – mostly to make up for the eighteen years spent stifled on an island with no opportunities and nowhere to go. Moving to London, living in tiny flats with housemates of varying degrees of compatibility, getting by on temp wages and spending every penny on Friday nights . . . that had all been part of the fun.

Even getting the job here at Delectable PR, a company specialising in promotion and marketing for food and beverage retailers, had been an adventure to start with. More money, and plenty of evenings spent out in restaurants or exploring food trucks and pop-up eateries. Often with Callum – which was what had led to her current predicament, she supposed.

All those years of doing anything she wanted, regardless of the consequences, seemed to have caught up with her at last.

Miranda would say it was karma. Or carelessness.

Maybe it was both.

But she shouldn't be thinking about her big sister. She needed to focus on the man in front of her.

The man she'd *thought* was in love with her. Until right this moment, when she saw the shifty, awkward look in his eye.

'Francesca and I . . .' Callum started, and Juliet's stomach seemed to drop the full fifty floors to street level.

God, I am such a cliché. The boss and the assistant. How had she ever thought, even for a moment, that this would end differently?

You weren't thinking, that's the problem. Miranda's voice sounded in her head – judgemental and, most annoyingly, right. She hadn't thought, she'd just felt. Gone with the emotion, the moment, and not thought beyond another fun night together.

'You're getting back together with your wife,' she said, flatly. No need to cushion this blow, she'd already felt it.

Callum gave a sheepish nod.

Anger started to rise up in her belly. Was she angry at him for being such a walkover, or at herself for believing he could be anything different? She wasn't sure. 'The wife you told me could never understand you the way I do. The wife who threw you out of your house so you've been living in a hotel for three months. The wife you described as a—'

'Never mind what I said about her before,' Callum interrupted, hurriedly. 'She's my wife. The mother of my children. And whatever happened between us in the past, I never stopped loving her.'

Another twinge, deep in her belly. Perhaps where his *other* child lay, gestating.

She hadn't thought much about his children, until now. Until she was carrying one.

'You told me you never loved her at all.' Was there anything he wouldn't have said to get her into bed? Juliet doubted it. And she'd believed it all because she'd wanted to. She'd wanted the excitement, the thrill of an office relationship that was technically against the rules. Another new thing to try.

'What is love, really?' Callum pontificated, and Juliet wondered why she'd ever thought this man was something special. Right now, he sounded like every other guy who'd ever dumped her. Which was all of them – except the very first. 'Do any of us ever really understand it? Or know how to predict it?' His smile was smug, like he believed he was the only person on the planet who *had* actually figured out those things. Like he knew love better than anyone – and certainly better than her.

Like her opinion, her feelings, didn't matter at all.

Maybe they never had.

God, he was a patronising dick of a man.

'So, just to be clear.' Juliet shifted uncomfortably on the chair as another wave of nausea hit. She had a feeling this one had more to do with the conversation than morning sickness. 'Despite telling me daily for the last three months that you loved me, that I was your future, that your marriage was one hundred per cent over and you wanted to marry me the moment the divorce came through, you're actually now going back to your wife.'

Of course he was. Now she was here, in this moment, Juliet couldn't quite believe she'd ever thought differently. She should know how this story ended by now. Because it never ended with the guy picking her. Even the single ones chose something else.

Only one man in her entire life had ever chosen her over everything else – and she'd picked life outside Seashell Island over him. It wasn't a decision she regretted – she'd had to leave that place or she'd have gone insane. But she did sometimes wonder, on days like this, if her track record with men ever since was punishment for breaking Rory Hillier's heart.

Callum at least had the good grace to look mildly sheepish. 'Juliet, our time together was very special . . .'

Our time together had consequences.

'But I'm sure you knew too that it was more of a . . . temporary escape from reality for us both, rather than a future.' Callum smiled fondly at her. 'Wasn't that what you wanted to talk to me about today, anyway? How we'd grown apart this last week or so, and it was time for us to part?'

You mean how you've purposefully been avoiding me for the last week, hoping I'd break up with you. Which was the whole reason she was having to tell him *now,* and here at the office, rather than somewhere more appropriate.

It was all so obvious now. At the time . . . well, she'd had bigger things to worry about.

She still did. And that problem was literally still growing – inside her.

'No,' Juliet said, flatly. 'I wanted to tell you I'm pregnant. With your child,' she added, in case that wasn't completely and utterly obvious to his deluded little brain.

She didn't get a lot of satisfaction from the way the colour drained from his face, but the slightly green and sickly tinged tone that replaced it *did* make her feel a little pleased. She shouldn't be the only one nauseous and scared by this pregnancy.

Scared. That was such a small, childish word for what she felt.

Terrified was closer. Overwhelmed by fear and uncertainty was even better.

She was pretty sure Callum wouldn't have to feel those

things for the next nine months. Or eighteen years. Or for ever.

'You can't be,' Callum said, his voice a little shaky.

'Trust me, this isn't the sort of thing I'd make a mistake about. Especially now.' She'd taken six tests, just to be sure. All bought from different pharmacies and taken at different times of day.

'You're . . . trying to trap me. Trying to stop me going back to my wife.'

Juliet looked at Callum – *really* looked at him. Saw past the bluster and the confidence and charm that had been so attractive at the start, and saw a terrified man in the middle of a mid-life crisis, who'd tried to have everything and failed.

She'd tried to have everything too, she supposed. But she sure as hell wasn't going to fail.

She just didn't know quite how she was going to achieve it yet.

Juliet shook her head. 'Trust me. Francesca is welcome to you. A baby at twenty-eight wasn't exactly in my life plan either, but it's happening and so we have to deal with it. Like grown-ups.'

She needed to be a grown-up. The one thing no one had ever thought she'd manage to be. Not her parents, who smiled indulgently as she came up with another dream or scheme, anything that would keep her away from festering on Seashell Island. Not her brother Leo, who still insisted on her texting to tell him she got home safely after one of their monthly dinners together. And definitely not her big sister Miranda, who'd made Seashell Island her whole life and couldn't understand why anyone would ever leave, or what Juliet could be looking for over on the mainland that she couldn't find on the island. Even Rory had wanted to keep her safe on the island, with him.

She'd always been the baby to them – to everyone. The one who was indulged, who no one expected too much from. The reckless, unthinking, impulsive one of the family. Seeking her own pleasure and not caring about who got inconvenienced, or even hurt, along the way.

And maybe she'd always been that to herself, too. But she couldn't afford to be that Juliet any more.

Not if she was going to be somebody's *mother*.

Oh God, I don't know how to be a mother. I can barely take care of myself!

'We need to figure this out,' she repeated, as Callum stared at her in horror.

'No,' he said, lurching to his feet suddenly. '*You* need to deal with this. I have a wife. A family. I can't have anything to do with it. You understand?'

He wasn't asking if she could be understanding and forgive him, Juliet realised, horror mounting inside her as he crossed the room to open the door. He was telling her he would deny this to anyone she told. He'd never acknowledge his own child. He just wanted to pretend this wasn't happening at all. That *they* had never happened.

Well. She didn't have that option.

'I understand.' She stood, slowly, her choices running circles in her brain. She had to pick one. Now.

She could demand DNA tests, kick up a fuss, cause him all the trouble in the world.

Or she could deal with this herself. As a grown-up.

Juliet swallowed, her mouth suddenly dry. 'And I'm sure you'll understand, in the circumstances, if I'm not able to work my full notice period.'

She couldn't stay here. Couldn't look at this man another moment longer.

Relief flowed off Callum in waves. 'Of course, of course.

I'll . . . speak to HR. Tell them it was a family emergency or something.'

A family emergency. That had the benefit of being the truth.

She was going to be a family. Alone.

And that was terrifying and unfair and awful. But she was going to do it anyway.

Not just do it. She was going to *rock* it. Somehow.

Juliet nodded stiffly, and picked up her bag as she stood. 'In that case . . . goodbye, Callum.'

She didn't check to see if there was any hint of regret in his eyes as she walked out. Because even if there was, she knew she didn't regret leaving him behind. Not one bit.

MESSAGES

Leo (to Parental Units group): Hi Mum, Dad. Hope your journey home is going OK. Just wanted to check you got my email? About me and the girls coming to stay this summer? We're on the ferry now, so we'll be there when you get home tomorrow. Can't wait to see you!
(Unread)

Leo (to Miranda): Hey, sis. Just in case Mum forgot to mention, I'm setting up camp at the Lighthouse for the summer with the girls, while Emily's away on honeymoon. Is there food in?
(Unread)

Leo (the Waters Wanderers group): Where is everybody? Haven't heard anything from any of you since that photo of Dad with a koala. Great photos by the way, Mum. Sorry I haven't been responding, bit busy at work, you know how it is. Glad you're having fun though, and looking forward to having you home soon. (Btw – check your emails!!)
(Read by Juliet)

MIRANDA

'I'm sorry, I don't understand.' Miranda blinked at Paul over the familiar checked tablecloth at the Crab Leg Cafe. 'Are you actually *breaking up with me*?'

Her engagement ring felt too heavy on her finger, and her heart seemed to be shrinking in on itself, like it was being squeezed and wrung out.

'I think that, after all these years, if it was meant to happen – if we were meant to get married – we would have done it by now.' Paul pulled his napkin tight between his hands, wringing it into a tight spiral. Just like her heart.

Miranda ground her teeth, her jaw tense with frustration. 'We've been engaged for five years, since my thirtieth birthday, and I've been trying to get you to set a date since the day after you proposed.'

'But have you really?' Paul's patronising tone grated, and Miranda only just resisted the urge to grab the napkin from his hand and throw it at his face. 'I mean, if you really *wanted* to get married you'd have—'

'What, exactly?' Miranda asked. 'Saved up thousands of pounds to pay for a wedding? Read every wedding magazine going? Picked out save-the-date cards? Been to three wedding fairs at the venue of my dreams? *Bought my wedding dress*?'

Paul swallowed so hard she saw his Adam's apple bob. 'You bought your dress?'

'Three years ago,' she ground out.

How could he do this? How could he actually be doing this? And how had she not seen the signs? They'd been together since they were sixteen. She'd spent more than half her life with this man. She hadn't ever expected anything to change – just like how nothing ever really changed on Seashell Island. And that was how she *liked* it.

And, in fact, nothing *had* changed. So why was he doing this?

'Let me get this straight,' Miranda said, keeping her voice low, in case any of the tourists eavesdropping from nearby tables were Seashell Holiday Cottages clients. She could already see her childhood friend Becca watching her from behind the counter, curiosity in her eyes. 'After nineteen years together, five of them as my fiancé, you've suddenly decided I'm not the right woman for you after all.'

'Things change, Miri. People change.'

Not on Seashell Island they didn't. That was the *point,* the reason she'd fought to stay there. The security of knowing that every day would be the same as the last, that she could rely on things happening in the proper order at the proper times. The Easter swim. The kite festival on the beach. The end-of-summer festival up at the Lighthouse. The feeble Christmas light switch on where one of the bulbs always blew. She knew this island, she knew how her days, her months, her years would pass.

'*I* haven't changed.'

'Well maybe I have!' Paul's gaze darted out of the window as he spoke.

Suddenly, the awful truth dawned. 'You've met someone else.'

'No! I just . . .' he sighed, and rubbed the napkin across his forehead. 'I got offered a new job. A promotion. Off the island. And I want to take it.'

31

And she'd thought she knew Paul. Known he was steady and reliable and safe, just like her island.

She knew Christabel thought he was the wrong man for her, that she needed someone more fascinating, more exciting. But her friend had always failed to appreciate the most important thing about Paul: he didn't want her to leave Seashell Island.

But evidently she hadn't known him at all.

Miranda stared at him. 'You didn't think about asking me to come with you?' It was more a statement than a question. Of course he hadn't.

'No,' Paul admitted, his shoulders slumped. 'Because I knew you wouldn't. Would you?'

She tried to imagine leaving Seashell Island. *Her* island. The first place she had ever belonged.

Juliet had been too tiny to remember life before they settled on Seashell Island, and Leo never seemed to either, but Miranda did. She remembered moving from school to school, from flat to shared house, never settling anywhere for longer than a couple of terms, never long enough to fit in or make friends. Just long enough to be bullied and teased. Never knowing when they'd move again, or how long they'd be staying. Not even being sure when she went home at the end of Friday if she'd go back to the same school after the weekend.

It had been such a *relief* when her parents had bought the Lighthouse. It had taken a while for Miranda to really believe it, but the fact that they actually owned it had helped convince her that this time, for the first time, she could expect to stay.

Of course, the place had been falling down around them to start with. It had taken months, years of DIY, and even three-year-old Juliet had been wielding a paintbrush by the end, but it had been *theirs*. A place they could stay, at last. A place where Mum could paint and Dad could write – and they could even pay the bills because as soon as they were open they had plenty of guests, because who wouldn't want to stay in the house with the best view on Seashell Island?

This place was home. This *island* was home. It was safe. She couldn't leave it, not even for the man she'd promised to marry.

'No,' she said, softly. 'I wouldn't.'

He looked up, meeting her gaze with his own solemn one, and Miranda knew there wasn't anything else to say.

He wanted to leave, just like Leo and Juliet always had. Just like she never could.

She'd tried once. It had been a mistake, so she came back. But that was her, not him.

She gave Paul a small nod. She wouldn't try to make him stay.

'I guess that's it, then,' he said, after an awkward pause. Miranda couldn't help but notice he didn't seem particularly heartbroken.

'I guess it is.' Nineteen years of her life over, just like that. But her heart seemed intact.

Maybe Christabel was right. Maybe she *had* just stuck with Paul because he was the safe choice.

But what was so wrong with making safe choices?

There were things they needed to sort out, Miranda knew. For a start, all her stuff was still in his flat. She still worked for his father, still hoped to take over that business one day – although, now she'd never be family, would that still happen? She let herself fantasise for a moment about Nigel disowning Paul and adopting her instead. Which, if Paul left Seashell Island for good, wasn't entirely outside the realms of possibility. Nigel and Gwendolyn were as devoted to this island as she was.

But all that stuff would have to wait a while. She couldn't face any of it just yet.

Right now, all she wanted to do was curl up back at the place she'd always felt safest, and grieve for the security and certainty she'd just lost – even if she wasn't sure she'd really mourn the relationship that went with it.

She needed to get back to the Lighthouse.

Dropping her napkin over her untouched plate, Miranda picked up her handbag and got to her feet.

'Goodbye, Paul.'

He jerked up to standing, too. 'Miranda. Don't go. I mean, we can still be friends, right? And we need to sort out the flat and—'

She shook her head. 'Not now. You just broke my heart, Paul, give me a minute.'

'Did I, though?' Paul tilted his head a little to the side as he asked the question, the way he always did when he was talking about something he thought mattered. One of a million tiny quirks she'd memorised over the years, from how he always crammed for exams at the last minute to how he folded his socks. Half a brain full of information she'd never need again. 'I mean, is your heart really broken?'

'Of course it is,' she snapped, even though she didn't fully believe it. It *should* be. 'You dumped me.'

But deep down, she knew she was more angry than heartbroken, more scared at the loss of security than love. More annoyed at the fact her carefully laid plans had been disrupted.

Oh, damn it. Christabel had been right all along.

She'd wanted the wedding, the happy ever after, the certainty of forever on this island. Not Paul. And it had taken him breaking up with her for her to realise it.

34

He gave her a very faint smile. 'I'm sorry, Miranda.'

She didn't want his apologies. Not when he'd stirred up so many unwelcome thoughts in her. She felt like her chest was filled with seawater, crushing her heart and stopping her breath, drowning her from the inside out.

She needed to get away from here.

Turning on her heel, Miranda stalked out of the Crab Leg Cafe, waving off concerned but curious glances from Becca as she went. She didn't need people right now.

She needed her island.

Outside, the fresh sea air filled her lungs, letting her breathe again. She sucked in huge gulps of it, the salt and the tang and the slight chill in the summer breeze. Then, aware that she was probably being watched by half a dozen curious locals and tourists, she started walking.

She should go back to the office, but her feet didn't even try to take her in that direction. She'd call in sick – she couldn't remember the last time she'd taken a sick day, and surely Nigel would understand, in the circumstances.

Right now, she just wanted to go home. Not to the flat over the fish and chip shop she'd shared with Paul for the last four years. But to the first place that had ever really been home to her.

She took the curving path out of the main town of St Mary's up the cliff road towards Gull Bay, and the Lighthouse.

When her parents had first moved there, the building had been abandoned, run down, and basically an eyesore. The parish council had been thrilled that someone – anyone – was willing to take it on, even arty newcomers with no credit history to speak of. But Josie and Iestyn Waters had found their forever home at last, and they'd thrown everything they had into making it perfect, from the whitewashed walls outside, to the cosy, welcoming rooms inside.

35

Miranda remembered those early days, when every wall needed scrubbing and painting, when there wasn't even a cooker to start with, and sometimes there were frogs in the toilet. The building itself had once been home to the lighthouse keeper and his family, and the lighthouse tower still stood at the end of the garden. At ten, she'd been confused by this, sure that lighthouse keepers had to live a solitary, lonely existence on a rock somewhere, not stay in a large, sprawling house with their family. But that had only been her first indication that they did things differently on Seashell Island.

The lighthouse itself was always dark now except for one night a year, when her father lit it for the end-of-summer festival they threw for the whole island. As Miranda groped in her bag for her keys, one hand resting against the duck-egg-blue door of the house, the memory of the summer festivals settled her. Soon, her parents would be home again, and life would go back to normal. Even without Paul.

She was home. That was all that mattered.

Twisting the key in the lock, she pushed open the door and stepped inside, the cool hallway welcoming her and slowing her heart. Misty appeared from nowhere, winding her scrawny body around Miranda's ankles.

Miranda dropped her bag to the wooden floor, crouched down to pet the cat, and let herself just feel safe again for a moment.

Nothing has changed. Not really. Nothing has changed.

She might have lost Paul, but she still had the Lighthouse, and Misty, and her family. That was what really mattered, right? She still had her home, and the certainty that brought.

Immersing herself in familiarity, she picked the reservations book off the shelf by the telephone and flipped through its pages, smiling at her mum's loopy script detailing visitors' names, and her father's more precise hand adding details about their visit. Then, when she reached the last six weeks, it was her own handwriting keeping track of the guests. It had been fun running the Lighthouse B&B while her parents were away, but it would be nice to hand it back to them when they returned.

She turned the next page, deciding to look forward, not back, but it was empty. So was the next.

Miranda frowned. That was unusual. Normally, the Lighthouse was booked up all summer long. She'd been so busy keeping track of all the immediate bookings, she hadn't thought to look ahead. But now, as she paged through the summer months, she saw they were *all* empty.

How could the Lighthouse have no guests this summer?

'Dad must have put them on the computer booking system,' she muttered to herself, as she replaced the book. It would be unusual, she'd admit – her father had always preferred paper to digital, even when it came to writing the first drafts of his essays and articles.

The sharp, shrill ring of the landline echoed off the pale grey walls and, making a mental note to check the online booking system on her laptop, Miranda stretched past the 'To The Beach' arrow sign to answer it before the machine kicked in. After all, if the book was right, they needed all the guests they could get this summer.

'The Lighthouse B&B.' Her voice came out a little hoarse, but hopefully prospective guests wouldn't notice.

'Miranda? Is everything OK?'

Her mother's voice flowed over her like a warm blanket, and Miranda sank down to sit on the stairs and luxuriate in the security of it. The six weeks her parents had been gone had felt like forever to Miranda. They'd all stayed in touch via messages and photos, but even that had trailed off over the last week or so as her parents enjoyed a boat trip down the Great Barrier Reef that took them out of phone reception.

'Mum! Everything's fine. Are you at the airport? It's the middle of the night there! Your flight must be soon. I can't believe you're nearly home!'

There was a long pause on the other end of the line.

'Actually,' Josie said, eventually, 'that's why I'm calling. There's been a change of plan.'

LEO

'Look!' Abby, fortunately, seemed to be as unaffected by boat travel as by train travel. She bounced up and down at the ferry's railings, one small finger jutting out towards the approaching coastline. 'There it is! Seashell Island!'

Mia was beside her sister in a flash, apparently oblivious to the fact that they'd been able to see the island practically since they left the mainland. Most of the time, the small, shell-shaped island wasn't so far from the coast of Wales as to be invisible, even if it did feel a whole world away. Today, the skies were clear, and the cloud or mist that sometimes obscured Seashell Island had burned off in the summer sunshine.

Leo leaned against the railing beside them, alert and ready to reach out an arm if either of them looked like slipping through the metal bars. Their tiny bodies were so slender, they could fit through anything, disappear into the water before he could stop them. He could feel his body tensing at just the thought of the risk.

Shit. Suddenly, it hit him.

He was responsible, entirely responsible for these two little lives for the whole summer. Emily wasn't just around the corner in the house she shared with Mark if he had a problem or Abby had forgotten her favourite bear or if he had to dash into the office and cut short their weekend together. He was Dad this summer, the only parent they had for the next five weeks. It was all on him, and the realisation squeezed his heart tight.

'There's the Lighthouse!' Mia yelled, and some of the pressure on his poor heart retreated.

The Lighthouse. Mum and Dad. Their flight would be landing by this time tomorrow. He wouldn't be on his own with the girls for too much longer.

He wouldn't have to do this alone.

Mia and Abby would probably have far more fun with his parents than with him, anyway. Mum and Dad wouldn't want to follow Emily's list of rules either – they'd never exactly been strict parents. Miranda had been the one to keep them all in line, ensuring their uniform was correct and their packed lunches were healthy. While their parents had believed entirely in free will and spontaneity, Miranda had gone very much the other way.

Maybe he should ask Miranda to watch the girls for the summer . . . except he'd like his daughters to still be speaking to him by the end of it. And he doubted Miranda had become any less bossy over the years when it came to limiting sugar and enforcing bedtimes. Emily managed to do it somehow automatically, as if bedtime was the natural conclusion to the day, and the girls went along with it happily. When he tried – and he suspected when Miranda would try – there was a lot more complaining.

As the tides crashed against the side of the small foot ferry, Leo focused on the town coming into view. With hardly any cars allowed on the island, most boats docked at the small harbour right by the town, and as the ferry powered closer, he could make out the landscape of his childhood and teenage years.

The Long Beach, where he and his sisters had eaten ice cream and built sandcastles. The caves – supposedly once used by smugglers – where he and his friends had hidden out when ditching school or drinking underage at night. And, as they docked, the Crab Leg Cafe, where he'd worked for three summers before leaving the island for good. The ice-cream parlour – the Ice House – where, at the age of fourteen, he'd taken his first girlfriend on their first date.

And yes, there on the clifftop beyond the town of St Mary's, at the tip of one side of the island before the beginning of the long curve around the back, the Lighthouse. Where he'd argued with Miranda, hidden out with Juliet planning their escape, despaired of his parents trying to be cool in front of his friends – but also where he'd eaten homemade cakes and told his dad about his day, where he'd learned to play the guitar (badly), where he'd climbed out of his bedroom window and back in again six hours later to find a glass of water and two headache tablets waiting for him. Where he'd celebrated birthdays and milestones and laughed and sung and cried.

Where he'd lived.

Maybe it wouldn't be so bad to revisit the past, just for the summer. After all, for all his business successes, Leo would be the first to admit that the relationship side of his life could do with some work. And every other side of his life that wasn't work.

Or, as Emily had put it on the anniversary of their divorce last year (which they'd celebrated with a family dinner. Which, now he thought about it, possibly wasn't normal behaviour either), 'Sometimes, Leo, I think you forget that other people exist at all. Or that they're not just supporting characters in your acceptance speech for businessman of the year.'

Juliet, visiting for dinner too, had tried to defend him, citing his insistence on her always texting when she got home safe from a night out. Emily had given him a look that told him this just proved her point – because until they separated, she'd been there on those nights when he'd been woken up by his buzzing phone, having forgotten Juliet completely until the message came through. But at least the thought was there, right?

Seashell Island had formed him as a person – formed all of them, really, even if they'd all turned out wildly different. Miranda, wedded to this place so strongly that she'd never leave; Juliet, desperate to experience everything and everyone outside the island, all at once it seemed – ricocheting from job to job and relationship to fling. And him, trying to have that normal life – career, marriage, family – even if it no longer looked like other people said it was supposed to.

But as the ferry docked, Leo realised he no longer felt like that man, the one who'd been fighting his way through London life. Instead, he breathed in the ocean air and felt more like the eighteen-year-old who'd left this place fourteen years ago.

Was this where he'd imagined he'd be now? Running home to beg his parents for help because he couldn't look after his own children? Not exactly.

'Come on, Dad!' Abby grabbed his free hand, while the other pulled the suitcase behind them as they ran for the exit, Mia dragging the other suitcase alongside them. 'I want to see Grandma and Grandad!'

'They're not back yet,' Mia reminded her, as they joined the queue to get off the ferry. 'They'll be back tomorrow. Remember?'

'I bet they bring presents. My friend Gracie says her grandparents *always* bring presents when they go on holiday,' Abby said, knowledgeably.

Leo didn't answer that. Mum and Dad had never really *been*

on holiday before. He hoped they knew about the expectations of their grandchildren. Mia was definitely old enough
now to notice if the rock they gave them had 'Seashell Island'
through the middle instead of 'Brisbane Australia'.

'Do we get a taxi up to the Lighthouse?' Abby asked, as
they dragged the cases along the stone jetty.

Leo huffed a laugh. 'No cars, remember. We'll have to
walk.' Normally, his parents would be waiting for them
on the jetty, along with Miranda and Paul sometimes too.
Between them, getting the cases up to the Lighthouse had
never been a problem. But he hadn't told Miranda which
ferry he was catching in his text, and Mia didn't look like
she was relishing the thought of dragging her case all the
way up the cliff path.

'We could ride up in that!' Mia pointed to a horse and
carriage, idling outside the Ice House.

'I think that's just for tours of the town,' Leo explained.

'I reckon they might make an exception for the two
prettiest girls on Seashell Island,' a gravelly voice said from
behind them.

'Albert!' Mia and Abby cried, spinning around to hug the
old man.

Leo wrinkled his nose as Albert Tuna and the stench of
his trade invaded his personal space. Emily had met him on
her first trip to the island, twelve years ago, and instantly
befriended the old fisherman. As they'd returned with the
girls, summer after summer, the old man had watched them
grow, watched over them on the beaches, and always saved
the best of his catch for them. Emily called him their 'Fishy
godfather', which sounded about right.

'Here to welcome your grandparents home, are you?'
Albert said, and the girls nodded. 'And I'm sure they'll be
pleased to see you. Now, why don't we go have a word

with Harriet – she's the one with the carriage – and see about getting you three up to the Lighthouse before dinner.'

When he saw the delighted looks on his daughters' faces as they hung off Albert Tuna's arms while he spoke with Harriet, Leo decided he could ignore his natural distrust of wild animals long enough to get home. Harriet had only been running the horse-and-cart rides for the last couple of years, and he'd managed to avoid them so far. He supposed it had only ever been a matter of time.

Harriet flashed him a grin as they all climbed on board, Albert helping Abby up and extracting a promise that the girls would both come and visit him down by the harbour very soon. Leo sat back, eyes closed, but with one hand holding each of the girls', just in case, and waited for the ride to be over.

But as the jolting, clopping motion of the cart started, it was impossible not to peek, to watch the landscape he knew so well passing them by. The waves buffeting against the land, the cliffs falling away to the sea as the path rose, and up ahead, the Lighthouse, in all its whitewashed glory, shining in the sunlight.

'No charge,' Harriet told him when he tried to pay. 'This is my good deed for the day.'

'Thanks.' Leo lugged the suitcases down from the back of the cart, smiled a goodbye, and headed after his daughters, who were already at the duck-egg-blue door of their grandparents' home.

'They're not back yet, remember!' he called after them. 'We'll have to use my key.'

Except then the front door to the Lighthouse opened, and there stood Miranda, her dark curls tangled up into a knot over her shoulder, and her green eyes wide. 'Leo? What are you doing here?'

'We thought we'd come for a visit, for the summer,' he replied. 'I emailed Mum last week. They're not back yet, right?' Something settled in the pit of his stomach, an unease that had nothing to do with the rickety cart or the swaying of the ferry before it.

A feeling that something was very wrong here.

'No . . .' Leaning down, she hugged Abby and Mia – both of whom had wrapped themselves around her legs the moment she appeared. 'Do you girls want to go check your bedroom is still upstairs?'

'Where else would it be?' Mia asked, rolling her eyes – but she ran after her sister all the same.

'What's the matter?' Leo asked, the moment they were out of earshot. 'What's happened?'

Miranda's eyes were huge as she met his gaze. 'Mum and Dad just called. Leo . . . I don't think they're coming back.'

JULIET

The tube ride back to her tiny flatshare was horrendous. Her stomach rolled the whole way, there were no seats – of course – and she couldn't even wear a Baby on Board button to shame people into giving up their seat for her, because then people would know she was pregnant.

And nobody could know she was pregnant.

You need to deal with this. I can't have anything to do with it.

With it. With her. With their baby.

She had no idea how to do that. She'd never been the responsible one, the one who took care of things. No one had ever expected her to be.

Until now.

Because having a baby . . . that was the point when you *had* to grow up, right? Her parents told all these stories about the wacky adventures they'd had when they were younger, but by the time Juliet came along they had settled down and grown up like everybody else. Hell, they were stalwarts of Seashell Island now, respectable and dependable.

Unlike her.

I'm on my own.

She'd always planned for that. Planned to head out into the world on her own and make her own way, without being watched by people she'd known her whole life, or having those people report back on her antics to her parents, or gossip about her behind her back. Growing up, Seashell

Island had been stifling in its monotony – same people, same places, nothing ever new.

She'd wanted to explore the world, find new people, her people, her place. Instead, she'd found . . . *Callum*.

Right now, the idea of the kind of familiarity Seashell Island offered – of knowing there was always someone around the corner who would smile and help her, even if they would gossip about it obnoxiously later – made her heart ache.

More than anything, she realised, she wanted her mum.

Even if that meant going back to Seashell Island.

She wanted to curl up in her mother's lap and have her stroke her hair and tell her everything was going to be OK. She *needed* to believe that everything was OK.

Because right now, everything felt anything but.

She'd sworn when she left Seashell Island she'd never return without an exit strategy. But since right now she had no strategy at all for anything, she decided to forgive herself for the breach of faith. This wasn't a failure. It was just . . . regrouping. Figuring out what she did next. If nothing else, the boredom of Seashell Island had to be good for thinking, right?

It was time to go home.

'What do you mean you're going *home*?' her flatmate, Tanya, asked incredulously when she found Juliet packing her small suitcase.

'Family emergency,' Juliet said, not really lying, not completely. 'I need to get back to Seashell Island.'

Tanya had started out as the friend of a friend of a friend, but it hadn't taken long for them to become friends in their own right, falling into each other's lives until Juliet could barely remember *not* knowing her. In a decade of living in

London, Tanya was by far the very best flatmate she'd ever had. She kind of regretted leaving her.

'Back to the place you said you'd happily never set foot on again?' Tanya asked, eyebrows raised. 'The place you said stifled your very soul?'

Juliet winced. She *had* said that. Was this how Callum had felt when she'd reminded him of all the stuff he'd said about his wife? 'It's just for a visit. I've visited before.'

'Always under duress and with your brother practically packing your suitcase for you.'

'Yeah, well. This time it's important.' Even if she couldn't tell Tanya *how* important.

Tanya knew about her and Callum. Knew he was her boss, knew his wife's name. If she found out about the baby . . . Tanya was also the sort of person who would stalk over there and tell Callum exactly what she thought of him. In front of the HR department.

Juliet paused, halfway through shoving her favourite comforting jumper into her case. Would it be such a bad thing if she told Tanya, and Tanya caused a scene?

Objectively, yes, because Callum would hate her, her career would be ruined, everyone would be staring at her just like they did on Seashell Island the day after the Year Eleven prom when everyone knew she'd drunk half a bottle of vodka, tried to start a conga line, then thrown up all over the headteacher.

She didn't want to be looked at like that again. But at least if everyone knew the truth, she wouldn't have to hide it. And if she told Tanya, she wouldn't be alone . . .

Juliet shook her head. No. Tanya would tell her she told her so, she'd think it was her own stupid fault for being gullible enough to believe she might be different. That *this* guy really would leave his wife, or at least stay left. That *her* office romance could end anywhere that didn't involve a disciplinary procedure for one or both of them, or her walking out of her job.

Again.

This wasn't the first job she'd walked out of, or even the fifth. But it was the first time she had no idea what she was going to do next.

Except go home to Seashell Island.

It wasn't much of a plan. But she needed to retreat and regroup. Seashell Island would give her the chance to do that.

'Is it your parents?' Tanya asked. 'Is someone sick?'

Juliet shook her head. 'No. It's nothing like that . . . I just need to get back.'

She could have invented a mystery illness for someone, she supposed, but that would be another lie to keep track of, and she didn't think her foggy brain could manage it. Instead, she grabbed another handful of underwear and shoved it into her case, hoping it would fit long enough for her to figure out her next moves, at least. There were no lingerie shops on Seashell Island. Well, if you didn't count the ancient Shells Department Store, which Juliet definitely didn't.

'Then I *really* don't understand.' Tanya reached out to still her hand as she shoved her bras into the case. 'Juliet, stop. Just . . . slow down and talk to me. Obviously something's happened. Is it Callum?'

'No!' Juliet said, too loudly. 'No. We're over anyway. Ages ago. I think he's going to go back to his wife.'

Tanya looked a little smug. '*I've* thought he'd go back to his wife for months.'

'Yeah. Well, I think maybe you're right. So I got out of that one before I could get hurt.'

Just not before I got knocked up.

'You did the right thing, babe.' Tanya wrapped both arms around her and hugged her tight, which had the unfortunate side effect of sending Juliet's stomach rolling again.

God, how am I going to cope with the ferry if a hug makes me feel like this?

It would be worth it, though. Once she was there. She hoped.

'I just don't see why that means you have to go home to Mermaid Island, or whatever that inbred backwater of yours is called.'

'*Seashell* Island.' Juliet bristled at hearing her friend talking down her home, even though she knew she'd said far worse herself. In fact, everything Tanya knew about Seashell Island came from Juliet's own mouth.

Maybe it was the hormones, but suddenly she was seeing the island in a whole new light.

It was – or could be, hopefully – a *sanctuary*.

She just had to get there without throwing up all her internal organs.

'Whatever the place is called. Why go there?'

Juliet cast around for an explanation, one that Tanya would buy, that wasn't too close to the truth.

'I, uh, might have been a little indiscreet when I dumped Callum,' she said. 'So the whole office will be talking about it, and I hate that. So I gave in my notice. And now, well, I kind of just want to lie low for a while, lick my wounds, you know?'

Tanya squeezed her close again, her perfume overwhelming Juliet's delicate senses. 'Babe, you're talking to the woman who sent her boss a "Fuck Off" cake but managed to get it delivered the day *before* I handed in my resignation. If anyone gets it, it's me.'

Juliet couldn't help but smile at that. 'True. Things could

be worse.' At least she hadn't just sent Callum the positive pregnancy test through the notoriously leaky internal mail, like Tanya probably would have done.

'But even so. Seashell Island? Really?' Tanya pulled away just enough to give Juliet the full impact of her disbelievingly concerned look.

'It's not forever,' Juliet told her. 'I just need . . . an escape. Just for a bit. I'll be back before you know it.'

'I hope so.' Tanya suddenly looked more serious than Juliet thought she'd ever seen her. 'Because babe, if life has taught me one thing, it's this: you can't run away from your problems forever.'

Juliet nodded sagely in agreement, even though a small voice inside her was screaming, *Just watch me.*

After all, it wasn't like anyone was likely to chase her all the way to Seashell Island. In fact, it would be the perfect solution – if only she wasn't taking her biggest problem along for the ride inside her.

MESSAGES

Juliet (to the 'Rents group): Good news! I'm coming home for a little visit. Just for a bit. Nothing to worry about. See you soon!

Juliet (to the 'Rents group): Just realised you won't even be there yet. Hope the inflight entertainment system is good, and I'll see you when you get there!

Juliet (to Miranda): Coming back to the island for a few days but can't find my key. Can I borrow yours?

MIRANDA

'What do you mean they're not coming back?' Leo hissed, as Miranda ushered him into the kitchen, far away from where her nieces were squealing with excitement to be back in their turret bedroom, bouncing on the narrow twin beds. 'They're our *parents*. They have to come back. We need them.'

'We're grown adults, Leo,' she reminded him, quashing the same feeling of panic that had risen in her stomach at her mother's words. 'I think we can cope.'

'You, maybe! I needed them to help me with the girls.'

Miranda rolled her eyes. 'You can't manage to look after your own children for a week of the summer holidays? Leo, really.'

'It's not a week! Emily's away *all summer* on her *honeymoon*. And I cannot afford to take a whole summer off work. I have clients depending on me out there in the real world, you know.'

Like her existence on Seashell Island wasn't real. Like her job didn't count. Five minutes her brother had been back on the island, and they were already having the same old argument.

'I think that might be a record,' she muttered under her breath, before returning to the much more important issue at hand. 'I checked the reservations book. There's no guests scheduled for the rest of the summer.'

'You think that's why they're staying away longer? Because they knew the B&B would be empty?' Leo asked.

'Or did they keep the B&B empty on purpose so they could stay away longer?' Miranda rubbed a hand over her forehead. 'We've never *once* not been booked up in August, not since the year we opened.' She remembered it so clearly: laying soaps on carefully folded towels on the pristine beds; Leo welcoming their first guests with a wide smile showing off his missing front teeth while Miranda handed them a basket of treats as a prize for being the inaugural visitors to the Lighthouse B&B. The guest book that sat open on the front table in the hall, dutifully signed by all their delighted guests.

That first guest book had taken pride of place on the sitting room bookshelf for almost twenty years, since its last page was filled. It was hard to imagine that the latest one – a silver and aqua Coptic-bound book that Miranda had sourced for them from a local amateur book binder – might not have any more entries this summer.

Or ever.

Oh God, what if it was *ever*?

Leo raked a hand through his chocolate-brown hair, so like their father's, down to the touch of grey already starting at the temples, even though he was barely into his thirties. 'Look, what did Mum say, *exactly*.' He was already pulling out his phone, presumably to message their parents and ask them the same questions. Not that Miranda imagined that he'd get any answers for a while, if they were travelling. Or having too much fun to be bothered by phones.

Miranda sighed. 'She didn't have time to say a lot. They were rushing to catch a plane.' One to anywhere but here, apparently. 'They made some new friends over in Australia who invited them to come back to stay with them for a while. I think she said something about a yacht.'

'A yacht?'

'You know, you sounded like Abby just then,' Mia said, from the doorway. 'Your voice got all high and squeaky.'

Miranda made herself smile as she turned to face her nieces, loitering and eavesdropping just like their father and Auntie Juliet used to do whenever she was trying to have a private conversation with one of her parents.

'Was your room missing?' she asked, eyes wide with pretend panic.

Abby laughed, a joyous, tinkling sound, while Mia, too world-weary already at almost ten, rolled her eyes in a way that Miranda had to admit was familiar from her own reflection.

'Of course not, Auntie Miri! It was right where we left it last summer.' Abby hopped through the doorway and perched up on the kitchen table, swinging her legs and looking for all the world like Juliet had at the same age.

'And this year we get to stay *all* summer,' Mia added, looking between Miranda and Leo. Miranda wondered how much she'd heard.

'Your dad said! That's so exciting! And you know, I'll be staying here at the Lighthouse this summer too, so we can hang out together lots when I'm not at work!' Of course, when she'd originally planned hiding out at the Lighthouse until she figured out what to do about Paul, she hadn't imagined sharing the space with her brother and nieces, but maybe the distraction would be a good thing. It was hard to be heartbroken and sad when she could bake cakes with Mia or make daisy chains with Abby.

And honestly, without her parents there, Miranda figured she could use a little help with keeping the B&B side of things running, too. If they got some guests.

No, *when* they got some guests. The Lighthouse B&B

wasn't going to fade into obscurity on her watch. So that meant they'd all have to pitch in. She and Leo – and even Juliet – had all had their own chores around the Lighthouse when they were kids. It could be a sort of game for Mia and Abby, perhaps. And Leo could *definitely* pull his weight if he expected her to entertain the girls while he worked all this summer.

'It's good that Auntie Miranda will be here actually, because . . .' Leo crouched down in front of Abby, and motioned Mia closer, wrapping an arm around her waist. 'I'm afraid I have some bad news about Grandma and Grandad, sweethearts.'

Mia yanked herself away, her face a picture of horror. 'What happened? Was it a plane crash? No, a *yacht* crash! Are they dead?'

'What? No!' Leo said, but it was too late. Abby was already in floods of tears, and Mia was ranting about all the people who said that travel was good for you.

Clearly, *Emily* had thus far been responsible for all the important conversations in their kids' lives. And most other stuff, as far as Miranda could tell. Damn it, it wasn't as if she was any better a substitute than their father, but she supposed she'd have to do her best.

'No, Mia, Abby, honey, Grandma and Grandad are just fine. Look!' She yanked her phone from her pocket and pulled up the last photo her mum had sent her, of the two of them standing too close to a koala. 'See? They're fine.'

Abby hiccupped a last sob, then took the phone from her, stroking the koala in the image.

Mia was more suspicious. 'That could have been taken before the crash.'

'There was no crash!' Leo yelled. 'I was just—'

'Terrifying them half out of their minds?' Miranda finished for him, and Leo shot her a glare.

'Trying to explain that Grandma and Grandad won't be back tomorrow like we thought,' Leo corrected her.

'Because they're dead,' Mia added, sending Abby into another wail and making Leo throw up his hands in defeat.

'Because they're having too much fun on holiday to come back just yet,' Miranda said, taking pity on her younger brother. 'They're on a plane right now to the next part of their holiday, but we'll Skype them tomorrow so you can see them, OK?'

Mia still looked sceptical, but Abby nodded and threw herself into Miranda's arms. Leo, she realised, had stepped away, putting physical distance between himself and his daughters' emotions.

That wasn't going to be able to last all summer. Especially without Mum and Dad there to pick up the slack for him. But right now, Miranda welcomed the distraction from her own problems.

'Come on,' she said, scooping Abby up into her arms. 'Let's go find your swimsuits and shorts and we'll go take a walk on the beach.'

That perked the girls up, at least, and Leo looked profoundly grateful.

'Are you sure?' he asked. 'I've got some calls and emails I need to return . . .'

Miranda rolled her eyes again. Nope, no idea where Mia got that from. 'Yes, it's fine. I've got the afternoon off anyway.'

Then she hustled the girls upstairs before Leo could ask *why* she wasn't working that afternoon. Or why she was staying at the Lighthouse. She far preferred the story where she was saving him from disasters of his own making, rather than his daughters saving *her*.

The girls skipped happily enough back down the familiar road to Long Beach, Miranda following behind at a statelier, grown-up pace. As the sands came into view, she sighed to see so few families and kids playing on the beach. There wasn't even a queue for Terry's ice-cream van. Surely it hadn't been this quiet last summer?

The afternoon sun warmed her skin and loosened her muscles as the salty breeze washed over her, filling her lungs with a welcome freshness. Mia came racing back as Terry played the van's tune, and Miranda automatically handed over a five-pound note.

'Thanks, Auntie Miri!' she shouted back over her shoulder as she ran back to buy the ice creams.

'Recovered from your adventures with llamas?'

Miranda turned to find Christabel standing up on the jetty behind her, fastening her bike to the railings.

'Would you believe me if I told you that was the highlight of my day?' Miranda asked her friend.

Eyebrows raised, Christabel hopped down onto sand. 'What happened? And how did you acquire those two cuties?' She nodded in the direction of Mia and Abby, who appeared to have ordered ginormous ice creams with flakes. Or maybe Terry was just so grateful for some customers he was being over-generous.

'First? Paul dumped me – don't smile!'

'I'm not!' Christabel lied. 'I'm really not.'

Miranda sighed. 'I know you thought he was wrong for me. And you were probably right. But he was . . . safe.'

'A ringing endorsement for a passionate romance,'

Christabel deadpanned. Then she put an arm around Miranda's shoulder and hugged her close. 'But I *am* sorry. Because even if it is the right thing in the long run, it's hard now, and I'm sad that you're hurting.'

'Yeah.' Giving a small, sad smile, Miranda stepped out of the hug and towards her nieces. 'Anyway. Even *that* wasn't the low point.'

'Look at the size of this ice cream, Auntie Miri!' Abby cried, half of it dripping down her face.

'It's huge!' Miranda said, appreciatively. 'Girls, this is my friend Christabel. She runs a bike ambulance service here on the island.'

'Cool!' Mia said. 'Maybe Dad will take us out on bikes this summer.'

'Maybe,' Miranda said, trying not to sound too doubtful. 'Now, shall we walk over to the rock pools at the end of the beach?'

The girls nodded enthusiastically and, despite still eating their ice creams, outpaced the adults in seconds with their excited steps. The rock pools sat in the cliffs and rocks at the opposite end of the island's fan shape to the Lighthouse, and Miranda figured the walk would give her plenty of time to fill Christabel in on everything that had happened that day. As they crossed the beach, she detailed it all – her mother's call, discovering the B&B had no bookings, and then Leo's unexpected arrival.

'Sounds like your brother is going to have to think about something other than work this summer after all,' Christabel commented, her eyes on the girls as she spoke.

'Hopefully,' Miranda agreed. 'I know he was counting on Mum and Dad looking after the girls for him, but they're not here, and I have an actual job at Seashell Holiday Cottages, plus my VA work, so he's going to have to step up.

And I'm going to need his help with the B&B. Assuming we ever get any guests.'

'Do you want some?' Christabel asked. 'Wouldn't it be easier to just let the place stay empty until your parents *do* get back?'

'Probably.' But the thought made her feel uneasy, unsettled. It was summer. The Lighthouse was *always* full at summer. 'I guess I'm worried that if there aren't any guests over the summer holidays, there might not be again. My parents . . . they don't always think things through before they do them. I don't even know if they've considered the financial implications of this.'

'You're worried the Lighthouse could go under without more guests?' Christabel asked.

Miranda nodded.

'Hmm.' Christabel looked thoughtfully towards the mainland. 'Well, only to enhance my reputation as a problem-solver, of course, but I have some friends of a friend who posted on social media last night that they were looking for a place to hole up this summer and write some music. I'll mention your place to them.'

'That would be . . . great. Thanks, Christabel.'

Christabel shrugged, and slipped an arm through Miranda's as they hurried to catch up with Mia and Abby, who had finished their ice creams and found a crab. 'Hey, that was the easy part. *You've* got to persuade your brother to stop working and engage with his kids this summer.'

'Don't suppose you fancy doing that too?' Miranda asked, hopefully. But Christabel just grinned and shook her head.

LEO

'Emily? I need you to call me back the minute you get this. You have good travel insurance, right?' She could cancel the honeymoon, take it at another, more convenient time. One when his parents were here to help. Easy.

Leo hung up on his ex-wife's voicemail for the third time, then remembered Mia jumping to the worst possible conclusion earlier, and dialled it again. 'The girls are fine, by the way,' he added, after the beep. 'Just . . . call me.'

Some of his friends hadn't been able to understand how he'd been able to maintain such a good relationship with his ex after the divorce, but then, they'd never been married to Emily. Emily was a force of nature – had been since the moment they met. She'd decided he was the one for her, and so he had been. Until she'd realised he was the one thing she couldn't change, couldn't bend to her will. Then she'd decided to move on.

But as for staying friends . . . she hadn't really given him any other option and now, three years down the line, he was glad about that. It definitely made his life easier, having her in his corner, even if they weren't married any more.

Until now, when she was obviously having far too much fun on her honeymoon to call him back when he needed her.

Even after three years, he still felt a small pang imagining Emily happy with another man. But he was honest enough with himself to know it was more because he *hadn't* made her happy, than because of jealousy. He loved Emily dearly, but as part of his youth, his family, his past. They'd been nineteen when they got together, their first year at university, and twenty-nine when they'd divorced. He figured that ten years of Emily was probably more than most people deserved anyway.

They weren't the same people they'd been when they'd met. They wanted different things. All the usual clichés.

And normally that was all fine. But right now, it posed one hell of a problem.

Leo was used to making the most of his time at work, but he was also used to that time being as much of his day – or night – as he wanted or needed it to be. Right now, that wasn't the case. Checking his watch, he figured he had at least an hour or so before Miranda and the girls made it back from the beach. Which meant he needed to use that time wisely.

Grabbing his laptop rucksack from the hallway, Leo headed up to what had always been his dad's study, ignoring the nagging sense in his gut that he was trespassing just by opening the door. He needed a place to work, and there had only ever been one quiet space in the whole of the Lighthouse – Dad's study. Besides, it wasn't as if Dad was there to object.

He'd sent them both texts to the message group he'd titled 'Parental Units', asking what the hell was going on, but there'd been no response so far. Part of him still hoped that was because they were on a plane home, but Miranda seemed to think that was pretty unlikely.

Dealing with just the most urgent emails – including two from Tom on the train home – took over half the hour Leo had allotted himself. Now he was down to thirty minutes, and he still hadn't done any of the actual creative work that clients paid him for.

This wasn't going to work. His business focused on branding, online marketing and social media management for small, local businesses, which could technically be done from anywhere – except that Leo's unique selling point was that he knew the area, the customers, the feel of the place because it was his home too. And all his clients were local to his little corner of South London, not to Seashell Island.

Most of all, he couldn't run a business on the odd hour here and there in the day when the kids were occupied, plus whatever time he could steal back after bedtimes or before wake-ups. It wasn't enough.

Which meant, if his parents weren't here to help him out, Miranda had her own job to go to, and Emily *still* wasn't returning his calls, he needed a new plan.

Pulling up a new internet tab, he searched for childminders on Seashell Island, holiday clubs, anything. He fired off three or four hopeful emails then, crossing his fingers, called Tom.

'Is this about the McMullin proposal?' Tom asked, the second he answered. 'Because I'm still on the bloody train and the Wi-Fi is terrible so just *emailing* you has been a challenge, never mind accessing the company cloud. Plus there's a hen party sitting behind me. Say hi, girls!'

A loud whoop went up from the hen party. Leo winced.

'It's not about the McMullin proposal,' he said. 'I need you to come to Seashell Island. I'm expanding your duties.'

'Last time you said that I ended up dog sitting for your ex-wife's Labrador for a fortnight,' Tom pointed out. 'And you still owe me the promised raise for that.'

'This time is different. No dogs, I promise.'

'Then what?' Tom asked. 'Do you need my help to

win the annual sandcastle-building competition? Because I admit, I am a dab hand with a bucket and spade. Or, ooh, no! Your parents want to launch a new marketing campaign for the B&B and you're giving me the project as my first solo campaign?'

'What have the hen party been giving you to drink?' Leo asked.

'Half a sip of pink prosecco. I didn't even know it was a thing, did you? So, not the solo campaign for your parents, then?'

'No. Not least because my parents have decided to extend their bloody holiday and aren't even here. Which is why I need you.' Part of his rational mind knew that he should have spoken to his parents about his plans for the summer beforehand; if they'd known he needed them, surely they'd have come back immediately? But he'd kept hoping that Emily would change her mind, that the wedding wouldn't go ahead. And then when it did . . . well, he hadn't actually believed that she'd leave the girls with him for the *whole* summer. Until she showed up with them on her way to the airport, and left them and their suitcases in his hallway with a kiss goodbye and a promise to call.

Which was what had prompted his sudden desire to decamp to the island for the summer.

Anyway, what was done was done. Now he just needed Tom to agree to the next stage of his plan . . .

'No,' Tom said, before Leo had even had a chance to tell him about it.

'What do you mean, no? I haven't even told you what I need you to do yet.'

'You want me to come to Seashell Island and babysit your children all summer, while also doing my actual job.' Which was . . . scarily accurate. 'I'm not doing it.'

Leo stared up at the ceiling where his mother and Juliet had, long ago, painted tiny constellations to provide his father with inspiration. Time to employ the boss voice, clearly. 'You do remember which one of us pays your salary, correct? And exactly how that boss—employee relationship is supposed to work? I tell you what to do, you do it.'

'Leo, you hired me as a personal assistant and marketing admin. Not a childminder. Incidentally, have you heard of them? They're people you can hire to look after children. Marvellous invention.'

'And I have emailed two of them, plus the local holiday club,' Leo said. 'But it's Friday afternoon. Even if they get back to me, it might not be until after the weekend and I was planning to work on the McMullin proposal this weekend.'

'Whereas I was planning on having an actual *life* this weekend.' Tom sighed. 'Leo, even if I head straight back after I get home and pack, I won't make a train or a ferry to the island until tomorrow at the earliest. And I'll have to head back Sunday afternoon because you wanted me to meet with the Posie Plants people about their Instagram feed first thing on Monday morning. Plus, I am terrible with children and I'll do something awful by accident and they'll end up in therapy for years, which I will be duty-bound to offer to pay for because of my guilt complex and you do not pay me enough for me to afford that.'

'You are terrible with kids,' Leo admitted. Of course, so was he. That was part of the problem.

He loved his daughters, dearly. He just never seemed to know what to do with them without Emily there to prompt him.

'The McMullin proposal can wait until Monday,' Tom said. 'Take the weekend off. Build a sandcastle with your daughters. Then hunt down each of those childminders and holiday clubs on Monday and beg them to take your kids.'

'Maybe you're right.' It wasn't that he didn't *want* to spend time with his kids. He just didn't really know *how* to. Emily had always been so fantastic at it – building dens and planning picnics with friends and finding out what events were on locally that they'd enjoy – that he'd never had to. Even now she always left him with a list of possible activities when she dropped the girls off for the weekend.

But not this summer.

This summer, she'd left him orders. He pulled her email up again on his laptop for inspiration, but mostly it just looked like a lot of boring rules. *Make sure they eat actual vegetables every day. Abby MUST be in bed by eight. No more than one pudding a day.*

Yeah, that kind of rule definitely wasn't going to help him get through the summer. If he didn't have ice cream as a bribe, how was he going to cope?

'I'm definitely right,' Tom replied. 'Now, if that's all, boss, a lovely young lady in a sash has just handed me a gin in a tin and, since it's well after knocking-off time, I'm going to go and drink it. I'll call you on Monday after the meeting. OK?'

'Yeah, OK. Have a good weekend.'

Leo hung up, and pushed the chair back from the desk, stretching out his legs in front of him. Tom had a point; it wouldn't kill him to spend the weekend with the girls. And they were used to spending some of the summer at holiday clubs and so on, while he and Emily worked. But all the ones they used in London had been booked up months ago, and there was a solid chance the same would be the case here on Seashell Island, he supposed.

Plus . . . the girls were looking forward to a whole summer here, and everything that contained. This could be his chance to finally step up, to be the dad they needed him to be. To show Emily – and the perfect Mark – that *he* could parent too. He didn't need their lists of fun activities, or Emily's schedule and rules, reminding him of their bedtimes and mealtimes and what they liked to eat. They weren't babies any more; they could discuss those things with him. And when he was in charge, he got to decide bedtimes anyway, right?

He shouldn't be panicking about this. He could parent *and* work – millions of people did, every day. He was an intelligent, accomplished businessman. If he couldn't manage two kids and a job, what was he even doing here?

It would all be fine. He just needed a proper plan.

Reaching for his laptop, Leo pulled up his project management software and started a new file.

Project Summer.

JULIET

The ferry ride across to Seashell Island was every bit as awful as Juliet had expected it to be. She passed the time by scrolling through her social-media apps, catching up on the lives of all the school friends who never left the island in the first place, and skipping past the few who'd made themselves perfect lives on the outside.

She needed to be reminded that at least she *had* left, for a time. That she'd been more than this stupid tourist trap, for a few years. She'd followed her dreams, just like she always told everyone she would.

Even if she was back here now, her life merrily falling apart around her.

It wasn't just her family she had to face on Seashell Island. It was everyone else she'd left behind. All the people she'd told, over and over again, that Seashell Island wasn't big enough for her. That she was destined for bigger, better things – the implication being that they weren't. That she was *better* somehow, even if that wasn't what she'd meant.

Of course, as a teenager she hadn't grasped how insulting she'd been. She'd only meant that she'd felt so hemmed in on that island she might scream. But now she cringed at the memory, as she realised what people must have heard.

Her school friends. Her parents' friends. The council, the shopkeepers, the fishermen. Miranda. Rory.

She'd basically told him straight to his face that he wasn't enough, that she didn't love him enough to stay on Seashell Island with him when his dad got sick a month before they were both due to leave and start their new lives on the mainland.

Was there anyone on Seashell Island she hadn't offended before leaving? Talk about burning the bridges she might have to walk back over.

When looking at the screen of her phone started to make her feel even sicker, she switched to staring out over the waves, imagining how she was going to explain her unexpected arrival on the island to her parents.

Mum, Dad, I have some news . . .

Mum, I did something stupid . . .

Hey, great news, you're going to be grandparents again!

Dad, I know you're going to be disappointed in me, but . . .

Yeah, there was no good way to break this news.

She hoped she could talk to her parents without Miranda being there. Disappointment and upset from Mum and Dad she could weather – she certainly had before. But Miranda's rolling eyes and total lack of surprise would finish her off. Hadn't she always said that Juliet was too flighty, too flaky, not to get in trouble once she was out in the real world alone? And heaven knew Miranda *loved* being proven right. Especially when it came to her siblings.

Whether it was the 'I told you so's when Juliet got caught drinking underage in the local pub, or the warnings that if she didn't study she'd fail a test, Miranda had always been the one telling her how she should live her life. Or how *Miranda* would have lived her life, more accurately. Their parents had a much more laissez-faire attitude to parenting, letting them make their own mistakes and learning from them. But Juliet guessed that Miranda had always felt like she had to make up for that when it came to bossing her younger siblings around.

Or maybe it was just the age gap. With seven years between her and Miranda, by the time Juliet had hit her teenage years Miranda had been an actual adult. Leo was sandwiched between them, closer in age to Miranda but nearer in temperament to Juliet, and he had usually made an effort to keep out of the way when the girls clashed. But it was always Juliet he came to find afterwards, to make sure she was OK.

Juliet wished she could have spoken to Leo before she left London, but with Emily away on honeymoon she knew he'd be busy with the girls. If anyone could possibly understand how she was feeling, it would be Leo. After all, if Emily hadn't got pregnant when they were both twenty-three, they probably wouldn't have got married so young. Although it had worked out for them, until it hadn't.

But at least they'd had each other. That was the part that no one back home was going to understand – how she'd got herself into this mess without having anyone to stand by her side while she dealt with it.

Actually, maybe her father would be happier with some sort of immaculate conception story. For all his liberal-mindedness, Iestyn Waters had always preferred to believe his daughters were total innocents. Maybe he still did, although since Miranda had been living with Paul for years it might be stretching credulity a little by now.

Of course, if anyone could manage it, it would be perfect-child Miranda. *Miranda* would never get pregnant by accident while sleeping with her boss. Not least because her boss was her almost-father-in-law and that was just too nauseatingly disgusting to even think about.

While her mind had wandered, Seashell Island had come

into focus, closer and closer, until the ferry bobbed to a halt at the small stone harbour. From the boat she could see the island stretching out in both directions, away from the point of the harbour. To the left, Long Beach – nothing but sand all the way to the cliffs and rock pools where the island turned and curved back to meet the other side. Above the beach, the town of St Mary's – the candy-coloured houses, the church clock tower, the cobbled streets. Even if she couldn't see them from here, she only had to close her eyes, and she was there again.

And on the right, the North Beach, shorter and rockier, with cliffs jutting up from the waves. Beyond them lay Gull Bay, out of sight for now, but just around the bend. And above the cliffs . . . Juliet looked up and saw the white of the Lighthouse in the distance.

Home. She was home.

This was what she wanted, right? She'd wanted to be somewhere safe and supportive.

So why did she still feel like she wanted to turn and run? Maybe if she just stayed on board then the ferry would take her straight back to the mainland . . .

Except she'd caught the last boat of the night. And now, as the summer sky began to darken to deep oranges and violet pinks overhead, Juliet knew she had nowhere else to go except the Lighthouse.

The walk up the cliff path to the family home was steep, familiar, and full of dread. With each step, Juliet's overactive mind came up with more ways this could all go horribly wrong. But when she tugged her suitcase over the last step and stood at the front door, she still felt the wave of *home* that told her she'd made the right decision coming here.

The Lighthouse didn't look as bright and pristine as in her memories. The white paint was dirty grey these days, and the duck-egg-blue paint of the door was peeling. But it was still home. The place where, when you had nowhere else to go, they had to take you in – right?

Miranda hadn't answered her text about her key, so Juliet hoped she was there – she was supposed to be running the B&B while their parents were away, so it seemed likely. But before she could knock the door swung open to reveal six-year-old Abby, clutching an enormous teddy bear in a wedding dress. The bear also had a white towel attached to its head, held on by hairclips in the shape of bees clamped to its ears.

'Auntie Juliet!' Abby grabbed her hand. 'Come on. We're playing weddings. You can be the bridesmaid!'

Bewildered, Juliet followed. 'Isn't it a little late to be playing weddings?' She only had the vaguest idea about child-rearing – something she supposed she was going to have to address sooner rather than later – but she was pretty sure that approaching ten o'clock at night was past bedtime for six-year-olds.

'Daddy says bedtimes don't exist on holidays!' Abby replied gleefully, leading her down the back hallway towards the sunroom that served as a playroom for any kids staying at the B&B.

'I'm sure that will end well,' Juliet muttered. 'When did you guys get here, anyway?' Leo hadn't mentioned visiting the island that summer, but now she thought about it, it made perfect sense. Of course he'd want Mum and Dad to help look after the girls while Emily was away.

'Today!' Abby sang. 'Auntie Miranda is here too.'

'Oh good,' Juliet said, her voice flat. Luckily, Abby didn't seem to notice her lack of enthusiasm.

'Not Grandma and Grandad, though,' Abby went on. 'Their plane crashed, but we can talk to them tomorrow!'

Juliet froze. 'What?' she whispered, just as Miranda appeared in the doorway to the sunroom.

'OK, the groom is starting to think the bride is never going to show up and— Juliet? What are you doing here? Did Mum call you?'

'Mum and Dad's plane crashed?'

'What? No!'

'Abby said—'

Miranda sighed, and shot an exasperated look at their niece. 'Abby, go get Big Bear married before your maid of honour falls asleep in there. And after the ceremony it's time for bed, I don't care what your dad says. OK?'

With a resigned nod, Abby walked into the sunroom, humming the wedding march loudly, and slightly off key.

'What on earth has been happening here?' Juliet asked. 'Are Mum and Dad all right?'

She'd only thought about how *she* might disappoint them. It hadn't occurred to her that they might not be here to be disappointed.

'They are having the absolute time of their lives,' Miranda said, flatly. 'Come on. Let me put these two to bed then we'll go grab Leo and have a drink and I'll fill you in.'

A drink. Yeah, that was something she couldn't do any more. There were probably other things she couldn't consume, right? Like . . . maybe cheese? She needed to find out. But first, she needed to figure out what the hell was going on around here.

Rehearsing her excuses about a dry July in her head, Juliet dragged her suitcase up the stairs to her childhood bedroom. One step at a time. That was the only way she was going to get through any of this.

MESSAGES

Josie (to the Waters Wanderers group): Having a brilliant time living life out on the ocean wave! Hope you're all having fun together on the island, too. Here's a photo of Dad pretending to be a pirate. I think we might buy a parrot . . .

MIRANDA

Miranda shut the girls' bedroom door softly, then opened it again a crack when she remembered how much Abby hated the dark. She'd have to remind Juliet and Leo to leave the landing light on tonight.

Juliet. And Leo.

Both her siblings home under one roof, neither of whom she was expecting or, quite honestly, had the patience to deal with right now. All she wanted was some peace and time to process everything that had happened with Paul. And instead she got a family reunion – without the two people she imagined they'd all come to see.

Miranda was under no illusion that either Juliet or Leo would have come to Seashell Island just to see her.

Some siblings she knew were closer than friends, and most of the family groups on the island at least *liked* each other. Miranda didn't expect to have the former relationship with her brother and sister any time soon, but it would be nice if they could at least manage the latter.

She loved them, of course she did. And she hoped they loved her too. They were family.

They were just all so very different.

Maybe it was the age difference. She was only three years older than Leo, but seven older than Juliet, and sometimes it felt like so much more. They'd never been in the same place in their lives at the same time – perhaps until now.

Did age gaps fall away when you reached adulthood? If they had, it didn't seem to make much difference to their ability to relate.

Maybe it was their personalities. She craved order from chaos. Needed to know what each day was going to bring. Juliet would choose chaos and spontaneity over organisation every day of the year. And Leo . . . he was too focused on his job to notice whether he was surrounded by chaos or order.

That had surprised her when, one Christmas four years ago, she'd sat with a tipsy Emily while Leo took a business call late on Christmas Eve when they were supposed to be hanging the stockings. She hadn't realised how single-minded he'd become. But perhaps it was just a natural extension of who he'd been as a child. Back then, his focus had been on different things – making the football team, dating a particular girl. Then passing his exams, getting to the university he wanted – clear on the other side of Britain from Seashell Island.

'At university I thought his focus was a sign of dedication. I thought he'd have the same dedication to me, too. And he did, to start with . . .' Emily had trailed off, and suddenly Miranda could see exactly what had happened.

When he'd got on the football team, he'd wanted to be captain. When he'd been captain he'd wanted to win the league. When his team had won the league . . . he lost interest and moved on to tennis.

Same with everything else in his life. While their parents had drifted from one interest and one place to another for the first nine years of Miranda's life, that shifting unsettledness had shown up differently in Leo. But it was still there.

It was more obvious in Juliet, of course. She'd never settled on one thing, or one place, ever. The closest she'd come was when she was dating Rory, but even that hadn't lasted.

While Miranda had stuck with the same man for almost two decades, long past the point when it was obvious to everyone – except, evidently, herself – that he was never actually going to marry her, just because he was familiar and safe.

She had nothing in common with her siblings. It was that simple – and that depressing.

What *were* they doing here anyway? Leo she could understand – clearly he'd realised too late that he couldn't do a full-time job *and* look after his kids at the same time, so had come to beg Mum and Dad to help him out. Well, he was going to have to figure that one out for himself, because she'd done her auntie duties already tonight, and she had work on Monday same as him.

Juliet was a bigger puzzle. Normally she had to be dragged kicking and screaming back to the island for family occasions, usually by Leo. Their brother had always looked forward to the day he could leave the island and pursue his own bigger dreams and ambitions, but for Juliet it had been an obsession. It wasn't about what she wanted to do off the island – it was about being anywhere but here.

Another difference. Miranda's sanctuary was Juliet's hell.

Maybe Leo would be able to get to the bottom of what had brought Juliet back – the two of them had always been closest out of them all. Miranda suspected that only some sort of personal crisis or disaster would have driven her sister back to the island – both of which she'd managed to have with alarming regularity while still *on* the island, as a teenager. And every time it had been Miranda who'd had to be the practical one. To find a way to fix whatever had gone wrong – speak to Juliet's friends' mothers, talk to the policeman who brought her home, clean up the mess and pay the bills. *She'd* had to be the responsible one – the parent, almost – while their mum persuaded Juliet to meditate with her, and Dad made notes for his next book.

For them, as for Juliet, life was one big adventure, meant to be lived to the full with no regrets.

For Miranda, it was a series of obligations, all of which had to be fulfilled to keep things calm and steady.

Juliet didn't believe in calm and steady. And Miranda wasn't sure she had the energy to deal with another one of her crises right now.

It could be Leo's turn. That was only fair.

She had enough to deal with.

Turning down the last bend in the landing, Miranda rapped on the door to their father's study, then opened it without waiting to be invited in. After all, it wasn't like it was Leo's workspace anyway. He was just borrowing it – or hiding out in it.

'Your daughters are asleep, and your sister has just arrived.'

Leo looked up, blinking in the greenish light from the accountant's lamp Iestyn had kept on the desk for decades. 'Thanks, Miri, that's great. I really needed to finish this proposal so I can spend tomorrow with the girls.' He frowned. 'Wait, Juliet's here? Why?'

'I have no idea. I'm making it your mission to find out.'

He looked resigned to that, which was good. Then he turned his laptop towards her. 'Speaking of finding out what's going on . . . remember I set up that cloud drive for Dad, last summer?'

'Yeah. What about it?'

'I logged on to it this evening. Wanted to check if there was anything about bookings in there, or on the online system.'

'And was there?'

'No. But I did find this.' He clicked an icon and a document opened. Miranda squinted at it, trying to figure out what she was looking at.

There was a picture of the front of the Lighthouse, a blurb about the building . . . and a price.

'They're putting the Lighthouse up for *sale*?' Miranda squeaked. 'No, they can't be. They'd have talked to me first, to all of us. Wouldn't they?'

'Maybe not, if they thought they had no choice,' Leo said. 'I've been thinking about this. There are no summer bookings, and I can't find the accounts from this year at all, anywhere. What if they're in real trouble? What if they *have* to sell?'

'They've just extended their trip of a lifetime, Leo,' she pointed out, as all the variables turned over and over in her brain. 'They can't exactly be broke if they're doing that.'

'Can't they?' Leo leaned back in his chair, arms folded over his chest, and met her gaze. 'They have credit cards, Miranda, and you know as well as I do that Mum and Dad have always been a bit . . . woolly with money.'

That was true, she had to admit. They'd never gone short, exactly, but their parents' attitude had always been that money was for spending, not saving. The Lighthouse had done well in the past, but Miranda had no idea if that had declined with the fortunes of the rest of the island over more recent years – it seemed likely it had. And as for their parents putting aside money for the bad times during the good times? Well, she wouldn't want to bet the house on it.

Or the Lighthouse.

'We need to message them. Ask them what's going on.'

'I already did,' Leo replied. 'All I got back was that damn picture of Dad in a hat and an eyepatch.'

'Time difference?' Miranda tried, weakly.

'Avoidance,' Leo countered. 'I reckon they're having one last hurrah before they sell this place and retire on the proceeds. If they can get enough for it.'

Oh God, this was a disaster. Miranda sank onto the cushioned window seat to process what her brother was saying. The Lighthouse was a great property but, the way things were going on the island, she couldn't believe that it would earn them enough to live off for the next twenty, thirty years – or longer. Unless there was something else they weren't telling them . . .

'Do you think one of them is sick? Like, really sick?' she asked.

A shadow crossed Leo's face, but he shook it away quickly. 'Don't think that. We don't know anything until they tell us.'

'I know, but—'

'I mean it, Miranda. You're going to do what you always do and start catastrophising. Telling us all the ways things can go wrong until we're all worried stupid. We don't know anything, so we have to wait until Mum and Dad are ready to tell us what's going on.'

'I don't do that,' Miranda said, but there was no force behind her words. Because she did, she knew she did. She just couldn't help it. No one else in the family ever seemed to see the canyons they could fall into, so she had to. That was her role.

'Mum gave you no hints what was going on when she called?' Leo asked.

Miranda shook her head. 'She was barely on the phone more than a few minutes. I figured she'd call again when they landed wherever they were going next and we'd sort out the details. I'd only just realised then that there weren't any summer bookings, and I didn't have time to ask her about it. I assumed it was a mistake. It just made no sense.'

Not unless they'd known from the start that they wouldn't be coming back when they'd planned.

She'd assumed their decision to extend their trip had been a spur-of-the-moment thing – the opportunity arose and they took it. But what if it *wasn't*? What would that mean for the Lighthouse? For their family?

'They *are* still planning on coming home, aren't they?' For a brief, flash of a moment, Leo looked so like the twelve-year-old boy who'd still looked up to his big sister that Miranda's heart ached.

But he wasn't that boy any longer. None of them were kids any more, and they had to deal with life on their own terms.

Still, the Lighthouse was *home*. And it was meant to be filled with people. Because if it wasn't, her parents had no income, and they were giving in to the general decline of Seashell Island – *her* island. Unlike her parents, that wasn't something she could ignore while she hopped around the planet having fun.

'I don't know, Leo. But I guess we're going to find out.' She got to her feet. This day seemed to have been going on for years, and it wasn't over yet. 'Come on. Juliet will be waiting for us.'

Just another thing to worry about.

Brilliant.

LEO

Leo followed Miranda down the creaking stairs of the Light-house, having fallen a little behind while he checked in on his sleeping daughters. They both looked angelic, even Mia. Abby had fallen asleep with the new bride – Big Bear – tucked under her arm, most of her body resting over the enormous teddy. Leo vaguely remembered Juliet winning it by shooting bottles when the fair came to the island, late in the summer, many years ago. He was surprised it hadn't been given away before now – but now that Abby had found an old white bridesmaid's dress of Juliet's that fitted the damn thing, he suspected they were stuck with it. She'd be marrying it off to various toys all summer long.

Abby's obsession with weddings had begun at almost precisely the same time Emily and Mark had announced their engagement. While Mia had moaned about having to wear a pretty dress, Abby had fallen head first into the magic of the wedding industry. Even Leo had been dragged along to a wedding fair at a local hotel one weekend, where all the vendors had been utterly charmed by Abby's intense knowledge of wedding favours, and blissfully unaware of Mia's accompanying black mood.

Unlike Leo, who had been required to make it up to her in the form of overpriced takeaway pizza ('And you have to get the cookies, Dad, they're the best bit') and letting his eldest stay up late to watch Harry Potter, which she cried at.

Even after nearly ten years of parenthood, Leo wasn't sure he had a clue exactly what he was doing or what was happening.

Which was basically how he felt now, heading downstairs to the Lighthouse kitchen, to sit down with both his sisters and try to figure out why one of them was there – both of them, actually, since he'd seen Miranda's empty suitcase sitting on her bed. With no guests booked in, there was no reason for her to stay, was there? Why hadn't she gone home to Paul? Leo found it hard to believe it was because of him and the girls.

And of course that was just part of the bigger mystery – what exactly his parents were playing at. Leo wasn't at all sure they'd solve that one tonight between them. Wasn't sure he even wanted to try.

Like he'd told Miranda: whatever his parents were doing, it was their problem. They'd tell them when they were ready. Until then, he needed to keep his focus where it mattered. On his business, and his girls. That was more than enough to be going on with anyway.

And as for Juliet . . . well, she'd talk if she wanted to, and he'd listen. But he was under no illusion that he'd be able to fix whatever was going on with her. That was OK, though. With Juliet, trying to fix things just made her madder. It was better to listen, and pour more wine when needed.

Juliet, he realised, was possibly the one relationship in his life he *did* have figured out.

'This is a surprise,' he said, smiling at Juliet as he entered the kitchen. He opened his arms and she fell into his hug.

'You too,' she mumbled against his shoulder. 'Girls running rings around you already, so you had to come for backup?'

'Something like that.' Which was worse? Letting people

83

believe that he couldn't manage his kids alone, or admitting he'd been so sure his ex-wife wouldn't actually go through with her new marriage that he hadn't bothered organising childcare for his working hours while she was away on her honeymoon?

Juliet wouldn't care either way. It had been him and her against the world for too long, back when they were kids, for her to judge him that way. Besides, he knew all her teenage secrets – even the ones that Miranda never uncovered.

He pulled back from Juliet and held her at arm's length to study her. She looked exhausted, red rings around her eyes and her skin pale even in the middle of July. Her blond waves were flat and almost greasy. She looked nothing like the vibrant, excited Juliet he'd seen in London just last month.

'I'm guessing whatever it was you were hoping to tell me soon didn't come off?' he murmured, low enough that Miranda couldn't hear.

Juliet gave him a sad smile and a small shake of her head, and stepped away.

'Why don't we take these out on the terrace?' Miranda suggested, holding up three bottles of beer.

Leo grabbed his bottle and raised it in a toast. 'Sounds like a plan.'

Juliet followed more slowly, and Leo noticed that the smile she gave them never met her eyes.

The Lighthouse terrace spanned the back of the bed and breakfast, stretching out into the garden with space for a wooden swing seat at one end, and a bistro table with four seats at the other. The rails looked out over the neighbouring farmland that stretched inland, with sheep dotted around and hedgerows glowing in the fading summer sunlight. Leo squinted at a long-necked sheep-like creature in the distance, wondering what the hell Max and Dafydd were breeding over there these days.

Juliet curled up onto one end of the swing seat, while Miranda took the other, so Leo dragged one of the other chairs over to sit beside the railing opposite them.

'So,' Miranda said, after a swig of beer. 'This is unexpected. All of us here together, I mean. Without any threats of disinheritance or anything.'

'And without Mum and Dad here to appreciate it,' Leo added. That part still rankled – especially now it looked like a deliberate plan on their part.

Although they couldn't have predicted that all three of them would end up here at the Lighthouse, could they? Leo didn't fully understand it himself.

'Nowhere better to be on a summer evening than this terrace though, is there?' Juliet said with a soft smile.

Miranda raised an ironic eyebrow, and even Leo had to hold back a laugh.

'That's not a sentiment you've ever expressed before,' he pointed out when she glared at him.

Shrugging one shoulder, Juliet placed her beer on the boards beside the swing. 'That's not entirely true. I spent a lot of my teenage years on this swing. It's basically one of about five things on the island that I liked, and most of them were on this terrace.'

She shot Miranda a quick pointed glance as she spoke, but their big sister didn't seem to notice. Beside her, Miranda was staring out into the distance, perhaps in the direction of the weird sheep.

'What were the other four?' Leo asked, mostly to fill the silence that followed Juliet's words. Miranda didn't even seem to be aware they were there. Like she was in a different world to the two of them.

But then, she always had been, in some ways.

When had they stopped being able to talk to each other? Or maybe they'd never really started. The age difference, the personality difference, the . . . distance. Maybe it had always been there, and him and Juliet moving away from the island had just made it grow.

'Like . . . lunches out on this terrace after we'd spent all morning swimming down at Gull Bay and raced back still damp and covered in sand.' Juliet tipped her head back to stare up at the stars as they twinkled into life, and Leo couldn't help but do the same.

Maybe Juliet was right. All he knew was that nothing in the world looked like the skies above Seashell Island on a summer night.

Something in his shoulders started to relax, and Leo knew it wasn't because of the half bottle of beer he'd just drunk.

'Or the birthday parties Mum and Dad would throw us out here. With the fairy lights and the millions of candles,' Miranda added. Leo hadn't even been sure she'd been listening.

His own memories started to kick in. 'Or sitting here on the swing, fixing the kites for the Seashell Island Kite Festival.' Straightening the strings, tying on the bows, fixing the handles and bending the sticks. Listening to his dad talking about the fighting kites he saw flown in India, years before. Hearing Mum tut as she leaned over to fix a knot that Dad had missed, or tighten a bow Leo had tied.

'Or getting ready for the Lighthouse Festival!' Miranda said, just as Juliet said, 'And our festival!'

The girls laughed, smiling at each other. Leo thought it might be the most in sync they'd been in years.

Then Juliet frowned. 'Mum and Dad *will* be back for the festival next month, right?'

Leo and Miranda exchanged a look. The Lighthouse Festival was an annual tradition, started the first year the B&B was open. When it began, it had just been Josie and Iestyn and a stall full of homemade cakes and homebrewed elderflower wine, plus a couple of their friends from earlier days playing guitar and singing. It had grown over the years, although Leo hadn't made it back for the last five or six to see it for himself, despite his mother's entreaties. Life had been too full, too busy, and before his divorce there had been other holidays in other places to take with Emily and the kids or with Emily's family or their friends. They'd managed the odd long weekend on Seashell Island, but never timed it right to be there for the festival.

And since his divorce, he'd never wanted to be there, without the girls.

But this year, they were all there to enjoy it – to see the old-fashioned fairground rides his dad had raved about, and taste the apple cider brewed across the island.

If it happened at all.

'We don't know, Jules,' he said.

'Mum and Dad haven't taken any bookings for August,' Miranda explained. 'And we're *always* booked through August. I think they knew they weren't coming back this weekend. I think they *planned* it.'

By unspoken agreement, they didn't tell her the rest – the missing accounts, the sales listing for the B&B. Perhaps it was habit. Juliet was the baby and, whatever else happened, they'd all always tried to protect her. From hard truths, from secrets – and from herself.

They'd have to tell her eventually, Leo knew. But not yet. Not when she actually seemed happy to be here for the first time since those long-ago days of swimming in Gull Bay and fixing kites.

Juliet's eyes were wide in the starlight, her face pale and small. Folded in on herself on the swing seat, she looked like a small child again. Like she'd been when they all lived here, the two of them dreaming of escape.

Had any of them ever really grown up?

'Then we have to keep the Lighthouse open for them,' Juliet said suddenly, the look in her eyes turning to determination in the twinkle of a star above. 'We have to keep the lights on.'

JULIET

Juliet knew that her siblings were looking at her like she'd been taken over by a pod person, but her words were true. Yes, maybe she'd never be ready to be an 'island person', but she still belonged to this island in the way that anyone who'd grown up there did.

It had turned out that when the chips were down, it was still the place she thought of as home. The place she ran to when she was in trouble.

Like now.

She'd planned on confessing everything to her parents the moment she arrived, transferring the horrible burden of knowledge to them. She'd longed to make this . . . not someone else's problem, but to share it, at least.

Now, she knew that wasn't an option.

She loved her brother and sister, of course she did. But Miranda would make judgey eyes and even Leo, who could normally be counted on to take her side in most things, wouldn't understand getting pregnant by another woman's husband, by her boss, and losing her job and her relationship because of it. Hell, she hardly understood how it had happened herself.

She couldn't face the disappointment. This wasn't like the time the police brought her home after some guys she was hanging out with tried to steal a boat. It wasn't like the time she threw a party in the cottage on the edge of their property and absolutely trashed the place. This wasn't something that could be fixed with some of Miranda's sweet-talking and a lot of cleaning.

This was something she needed to figure out on her own.

Maybe if she went to her family with a plan – told them not just everything that had happened, but what she was going to do next, how she was going to fix her life – they wouldn't give her *that* look. The one that said, 'Here we go again: Juliet screwing up her whole life despite every advantage she's had and everything everyone has ever done for her.'

She *hated* that look.

She needed to prove to them that she wasn't the baby any longer. She needed to prove to them that she was responsible enough to deal with the consequences of her actions. Responsible enough to be a mother, to look after another living being as well as herself.

Maybe she needed to prove that to herself, as well.

But for now, she needed another reason that they'd buy for why she'd want to stay, since it seemed they weren't totally buying nostalgia. Another something to focus everyone's attention away from her rapidly growing middle. How fast did that happen, anyway? Would she need to go clothes shopping soon? She'd need to see the doctor, or a midwife before too long. There were scans and things, weren't there? At the very least, she needed to download some sort of app to tell her what was happening to her body, and what she should expect beyond the exhaustion, constant low-level nausea, and the fact that just the smell of the bottle of beer Miranda had handed her made her gag.

Focus, Juliet.

She needed to stay here while she figured things out. And if she was working hard to save the Lighthouse then no one would question that, right? It gave her a purpose – and a chance to prove that she wasn't the flaky little sister they remembered. She was a grown-up now too – one who could take control, get things done, and not collapse into a puddle at the slightest setback. Like the small matter of an unplanned pregnancy.

Miranda sighed, kicking the floor so the swing seat bobbed back and forward again. 'You're right.'

Juliet blinked in surprise. 'Really?' Because she was pretty sure Miranda had never, not once, said those words to her before.

'Yeah. I have to save the Lighthouse.'

Oh, right. Of course Miranda thought *she* had to be the one they all relied on. That she had to take charge and take over and boss them all around until they did things her way. Like always.

'Actually, I meant—'

'I can probably funnel some bookings through from Seashell Holiday Cottages – we're always getting last-minute calls for cottages that are all booked up. I can add the Lighthouse to our alternatives list and talk it up a bit. Plus, Christabel said she might have some friends looking for somewhere to stay this summer – that could buy us some time while we figure out what to do next.'

Of course, the problem was that was exactly what they needed. And Miranda, who seemed to know every person who stepped on the island, was the best placed to do it. How was Juliet supposed to argue with that?

'Glad you've got it all in hand,' Leo said, sounding relieved that this didn't seem to be his problem. 'But who is going to run this place when all these hypothetical guests start flooding in? You already have a full-time job, and I have two right now, between the kids and my business. I think we should at least talk about not doing *anything* until Mum and Dad get home.'

'That's ridiculous,' Miranda said, dismissively. 'Of course we need to do something.'

Juliet's shoulders straightened a little as she realised that even if they needed Miranda to find the guests in the first place, there was still plenty for her to do. She'd spent almost her whole life until the age of eighteen at the Lighthouse – she knew what running a B&B took, even if that was only because she'd usually avoided having to do any of it.

'I could do it,' she said, before Miranda could come up with any other ideas that made her unnecessary.

Miranda and Leo shot her matching looks of disbelief.

'For the weekend, maybe, but you'll be running back to London soon, right? We need a longer-term solution than you.' Miranda dismissed her offer without further thought, and Juliet's shoulders slumped again. 'I could call Mum and Dad's friends, the Warburtons, see if they could come and run the place for the summer? They've done it before, for odd weekends and such. Mum and Dad have to be back by the autumn, right?'

They all looked at each other, and Juliet could almost hear the same thought echoing around the terrace. *What if they're not?*

She knew there had to be more to their parents' absence than the others were telling her, but that was just par for the course. No one ever told her anything. Either they thought she couldn't be trusted with the information, or they were trying to protect her, the baby, as usual.

Well. She had her own secrets this time, and she wasn't going anywhere. She'd get to the truth sooner or later.

She swallowed, hard, and pushed her fears away, ready to

try again. 'I'm not planning on heading back to London for a couple of weeks at least. Maybe even longer. I'd like to see Mum and Dad before I go, apart from anything else. So, um, really. Why don't I take over running this place for a little while? Just to keep things ticking over?'

This time they didn't dismiss her offer out of hand. That was something.

Or that's what Juliet kept reminding herself through the barrage of questions and objections that followed.

'Are you sure you're really up for that, Jules?' Leo asked.

Miranda jumped in. 'Because if you take on the B&B you can't just dash back to London because someone is throwing a party or something.'

'And it means a lot of early mornings. No lie-ins or late nights. Or hangovers. You have to be up and smiling before the guests.'

'And you have to be nice to guests, however odious they are. It can't be like that time when that American couple stayed and you told them that cake was not a breakfast food and they could have eggs instead.'

'Plus there's all the cleaning and tidying and making up of beds – you always hated doing that.'

'You'd have to be here, on call, all the time. No running off because you fancied doing something else for a change.'

'And we're not going to be able to bail you out if you decide it's too hard. We've got our own jobs and responsibilities, you realise.'

Patience. That was what she needed right now – something she'd sadly been lacking for most of her life so far. Her parents always joked that she'd spent her childhood desperate to catch up to Leo and Miranda, leapfrogging whole stages of child development because she didn't have the patience for it. She'd started school able to read and do some of her times tables, but never learned to play with other kids her own age.

But mothers needed patience, didn't they? They needed to stay calm and not shout too much even when any reasonable person would want to, like when a baby wouldn't stop crying.

So she was going to have to learn.

With a deep breath, Juliet prepared to answer their objections – which would have been a lot easier if they weren't all reasonably based on her past behaviour.

'Firstly, I said I'm staying a couple of weeks and I mean it. I won't just up and leave without warning.' Partly because returning to London would mean running the risk of bumping into Callum and his wife, living happily ever after. 'Secondly, I'm used to early mornings. I mean, I have to get up at six in London to make my train in to the office. Here, my commute is just down a flight of stairs.'

Miranda and Leo might not look completely convinced, but they were listening. Encouraged, Juliet pressed on. She couldn't tell them exactly why she wouldn't be going to parties or staying up drinking for the next however many months, but she could remind them of one vital fact they seemed to perpetually overlook.

'Most importantly, I'm not a teenager any more. I'm a fully functioning adult who understands the concept of responsibility. I know it's hard for you to stop seeing me as the baby of the family, but I can do this. And until Mum and Dad come back, I'm your best option, OK? Especially since this is my home too.' Even if she hadn't always appreciated that until now.

Miranda and Leo exchanged another look, and Juliet sighed. It still wasn't enough. *She* wasn't enough. Like always.

She gave it one last shot. 'I know running a place like this is a lot of work. And I know I won't be able to do it entirely by myself – we're all going to have to pitch in, like we always did. But if we work together . . . I can coordinate it all. I can take charge this time, I promise. Just let me try, OK?'

She needed this. She needed to prove to them – and to herself – that she could do it. She could be responsible and patient and competent and reliable, and everything else she'd need to be every day once this baby was born.

If she could mother the Lighthouse and all its hypothetical guests for the summer, she could manage a child, right?

If they'd just let her try.

'OK,' Miranda said, after a long pause, and Leo nodded his agreement. 'If you're sure you want to do it.'

'I really do,' Juliet said, fervently.

Even if it meant staying on Seashell Island all summer and facing up to all those old ghosts she'd left behind. It could be good for her.

Maybe this time, when she left, she'd be moving on for real. Ready to start her proper new life – as a mother.

MESSAGES

Miranda (to Mum & Dad group): Hope you're having lots of fun on your adventures. I wouldn't cuddle too many koalas though, they tend to be a little bit . . . diseased, according to my research. Also, if you want to get a parrot I'd wait until you get home to avoid issues with quarantine and pet passports etc. Speaking of which . . . do you know when you are coming home yet? Only there's quite a lot going on here. Would be good to talk to you about it all if you could call, next time you're in port?

Dad (to Mum & Dad group): Your mother thinks all parrots have to be called Polly. I'm thinking Persephone. What do you think?

Mum (to Mum & Dad group): Glad you've got everything in hand! Off to sea for a week or so now, but will call when we're on land again. And OBVIOUSLY a parrot has to be called Polly.

MIRANDA

By first thing on Monday morning, three things had happened – two unexpected, one sadly not.

Firstly, Juliet had fully taken on the role of Lighthouse B&B manager, with a clipboard and pen, and fresh sheets for all the guests they didn't have yet. That was the most unexpected thing, because Miranda had fully anticipated Juliet coming down to breakfast on Sunday morning and telling them both she'd changed her mind, she didn't want to do it, and actually this fun opportunity had just come up in London or Edinburgh, or Australia, for that matter, and she was off to take advantage of it.

At least she came by her flakiness honestly. Just look at their parents.

Secondly, Leo had taken the girls out for a bike ride. That was unexpected because Miranda couldn't remember the last time she'd seen her brother on a bike, and given the way Abby and Mia had stared wide-eyed as he'd wobbled up and down the drive, neither could they. She'd half expected him to beg her or Juliet to look after the girls while he worked, but instead he'd packed water bottles and snacks, loaded the girls up onto the ancient bikes from the shed round the back, found helmets that just about fitted them all, and headed off to explore the island.

Miranda did wonder, though, if they might be back

sooner than expected when Leo realised how little of Sea-shell Island had 4G reception.

The one, totally expected – and dreaded – thing, came about as Miranda walked to work that morning. In fact, she'd barely made it to the high street before she was enveloped in the strongly perfumed embrace of her ex-mother-in-law-to-be.

'Miranda, *cariad*!' Gwendolyn Stone was a cuddly and loving, if slightly overbearing woman, who had welcomed Miranda into their family life – mostly, Miranda suspected, because she gave Paul a reason to come home to Seashell Island after university and stay there. 'What's all this non-sense Paul has been spouting about moving to the mainland?'

Miranda forced her mouth into a smile, although she was sure it looked more like a grimace. 'I really don't know, Gwen. You'd have to ask him. I was as astonished as anyone when he told me.'

Gwen's self-satisfied expression made her look like a small child tattling to the teacher. 'I *told* Nigel this wouldn't be your doing. You're a sensible girl. What would you want to go leaving Seashell Island for?'

'I don't,' Miranda confirmed. 'But apparently Paul does, so . . .'

Gwen gasped. 'Oh, but *cariad*, you have to talk him out of it! He'll listen to you. He always has! When he wanted to go work for that company in the city after graduation it was you who persuaded him to move back here and go to work for Barry's firm instead. I'm sure you can persuade him again, can't you?'

'I'm afraid I don't think Paul wants to listen to me any more, Gwen,' Miranda said, gently. 'That's why he broke up with me.'

Gwen's eyes widened to take over half her rounded face.

'Oh, but he didn't! He told me that you didn't want to move to the mainland so you ended it!'

Of course he did. 'I think Paul had already made the decision that we were over before he told me about the new job. He didn't even ask me to go with him.'

Because he knew I wouldn't go. And because he wanted to.

That was a thought that had been bothering her all weekend. How long had Paul been wanting to leave Seashell Island, and her? Had this been festering ever since she convinced him they should stay on the island? Was he already thinking about leaving when he proposed? Or the day after his university graduation when he came home at last? Did he always hope she'd change her mind about staying here?

Or had the reality of the future ahead of them – one looking very like his own parents, she supposed – eventually got too much for him?

Either way, she understood now why they'd never managed to agree and set a wedding date. There had always been something else going on: *Not next summer, there's a big work trip I'll need to take. Not the spring, that's my busiest time. Not autumn, it'll rain. Christmas weddings are so tacky, don't you think?*

All those excuses had meant the same thing: Paul didn't want to commit to this life, in this place, with this woman. Her.

'I can't believe he'd do this.' There were fat tears running over Gwen's cheeks now, firing off like a sprinkler system as she shook her head with violent disbelief. 'You two have been together forever! It was meant to be!'

Yeah, that's what I thought, too.

But had she? Miranda stopped, her thoughts suddenly swirling, coalescing around a strange new idea. Had she really believed that they were meant to be? Or had she *made* them inevitable, because their relationship gave her what she really wanted: a reason to stay on Seashell Island?

Had she ever really given Paul a say in it at all?

No, that wasn't it. Maybe he'd gone along with her plans because that was easiest, because it involved the least conflict. But if he wasn't happy with them then it was on him for not speaking up.

Until now. When he was apparently shouting his unhappiness to the world.

'Miranda! Is it true?' Becca, wearing her work apron, rushed across the road from the Crab Leg Cafe. 'I thought there was something wrong when I saw you two at the cafe on Friday, but then I spoke to Paul in the Anchor last night and he said you'd split up and I just couldn't believe it!'

'Believe it,' Miranda said, sending Gwen into a fresh fit of sobs. 'He dumped me.'

Becca raised her eyebrows. 'Really? The way he told it, it was more of a mutual decision.'

Because he doesn't want to look like the bad guy. Island politics were complicated, but if it came down to picking sides, Paul must know that a man who dumped his fiancée and left the island to run off to the mainland was never going to get as much sympathy as the heartbroken guy who just couldn't bear to stay on Seashell Island after the demise of a long-term relationship.

She didn't want to cause trouble for Paul, not really. Not when she was finally seeing clearly that he was right – that she had only stayed with him because it was easy. But the truth was he *had* dumped her, whatever he was saying now.

She was just trying to come up with a version of events that suited everybody, and might make Gwen stop crying, when Christabel appeared behind her and blew that plan out of the water.

'Nope. He blindsided her in the Crab Leg Cafe with the news that he was moving to the mainland for a new job, and he didn't even ask her to go with him.' Christabel put an arm around Miranda's shoulder. 'Can you believe it?'

'Wow.' Becca looked gratifyingly astonished. 'And you're just going to—'

'Go to work, yes,' Miranda interrupted. She could see another small group of people across the road talking and glancing over in her direction. She wasn't sure she could face any more questions this morning. At least at the office, she was more likely to be bothered by people complaining that the Wi-Fi in their cottage wasn't working than locals wanting to know the ins and outs of her love life.

'Are you sure you don't want to take some time off?' Gwen sniffled. 'I'm sure Nigel would understand. And maybe you and Paul could talk some more—'

'I think Paul and I have been talking in circles for long enough,' Miranda said, decisively. Five years of being engaged without ever setting a date. Not to mention the years of dating before that.

She was done. She didn't know what happened next – and that kind of terrified her – but with so much else on her plate right now, rehashing things with Paul wasn't on the agenda.

'Now, if you'll both excuse me . . .' With a last smile for Gwen and Becca, Miranda let Christabel lead her past them towards the office, ready to get on with her day. Starting with hopefully finding some guests for the Lighthouse.

See? She had more important things to focus on than the wedding dress mouldering in the Lighthouse attic bedroom anyway.

'You OK to make it all the way to the office?' Christabel asked, once they were out of earshot.

'I think I can make the length of the high street alone,' Miranda assured her.

'Good. And remember: if anyone asks, you're excited about the new opportunities ahead of you!' Christabel backed her way across the road, ignoring the oncoming traffic. 'Oh, and you might have a visitor later this morning!'

'What? Who?' But Christabel was gone, in a chorus of car horns and seagulls, heading towards the Long Beach. 'Great,' Miranda muttered. 'More surprises.'

She had to fend off two other concerned island citizens before she reached the Seashell Holiday Cottages' office. Apparently, Paul's campaign not to be the bad guy was in full force, as both of them asked if she might not reconsider in order to keep Seashell Island's favourite son at home.

'A wife is supposed to support her husband's career, you know,' Mrs Kendle said, sagely, and Miranda only just about managed not to point out that Mrs Kendle's own husband had worked overseas for their entire marriage before coming home to retire and spend all his days on the golf course. 'I'm sure he could commute from wherever his new office is back to Seashell Island if you gave him a good enough reason to.'

And that was what it would all come down to in the end, Miranda knew; no matter how hard she fought the accepted narrative: *she* hadn't worked hard enough to make him want to stay.

Never mind that *he'd* decided to go, that *he* wanted to live somewhere other than Seashell Island, that *he* was the one who'd postponed a wedding for five bloody years. Somehow, this would all be *her* fault.

She loved Seashell Island, really she did. But in the same way that everyone there would be thrilled to see Leo and Juliet home for the summer, Paul would become the prodigal son who everyone would miss the most.

And she'd be the one who stayed. Again.

Wrenching open the office door after finally getting rid of Mrs Kendle, Miranda flipped the kettle on angrily before taking a breath and deciding that maybe a green tea might be best this morning.

'Ah. Miranda . . .' She jumped, and spun round to find her boss, Paul's father, hovering awkwardly in the doorway. Of course. Who else would be here so early? And who else would have opened up the office? She'd been in such a rush to get away from Mrs Kendle she hadn't even registered that it was unlocked.

'Nigel! You surprised me.' Hand on her chest, she felt her heart rate start to slow again. 'Do you want a coffee?'

'Ah, actually . . . I was wondering if I could have a word.'

Miranda tried not to groan out loud. 'You and half the town. I assume this is about your son deciding to leave Seashell Island?'

'Um. Not exactly.' Nigel shuffled from one foot to the other, and Miranda realised for the first time that he was sweating. What was going on here?

She put down the mug she was holding. 'OK. What is it?'

'I'm sure you've noticed that we, ah, haven't been as busy this season as in previous years.'

'The same goes for the whole island,' Miranda pointed out. 'Everyone is struggling.' That made her think of the Lighthouse again, but she forced the thought away. One problem at a time. And right now, she needed to focus on the fact that her boss looked as if he might have a heart attack any minute.

'I'm . . . I'm so sorry to do this, Miranda, especially after what's happened with Paul, but I should have spoken to you about it weeks ago. You see, the thing is, once this summer is over . . . I think I'm going to have to close the office for the winter season. Maybe even give it up altogether. Gwen thinks we can run it from the house, you see, and, well, she might be right. Even if she isn't, I can't afford to keep renting this prime real estate without the numbers to back it up. And I can't afford, well, you.'

Miranda blinked. 'You're firing me.'

'No! Well. Sort of. But you're welcome to work out your notice over the summer, if you'd like.'

'You're firing *me*.' It hadn't sunk in yet. She wasn't sure it ever would; she'd worked for Nigel since she was sixteen. 'But I'm the only person who does any work around here!'

'Yes. Well. I suppose that Gwen and I will have to learn to take care of things ourselves.'

Good luck with that. 'Right.' She picked up her mug again. Then her handbag. 'Well, I guess you'd better start now, then, hadn't you?'

'You . . . you don't want to stay to work this summer?' Nigel asked, a little desperately.

Miranda considered. In the past few days, this family had taken away everything she took for granted: her relationship, her career, her future.

If ever she'd needed a sign that it was time to find a new path, this was it.

'No,' she said, and walked out of the kitchen – only to find a tall, well-built man with his back to her leafing through the tourist information leaflets, his reflection in the shop window showing her the most incredibly good-looking man she'd ever seen in real life.

'Hi,' Miranda said, struggling to remember how the English language worked. 'Um, welcome to Seashell Holiday Cottages. The boss will be out in a moment.' She picked up

104

the photo frame on her desk – then put it back again, as she realised it held a photo of her and Paul.

The man turned, even better-looking from the front than he'd looked in the reflection, with his hazel eyes and his dirty blond hair pulled back from his handsome face.

'Are you Miranda? I'm Owain. Christabel sent me.' He smiled, and said the magic words. 'She said you'd be able to help my friends and me find somewhere to stay this summer. Preferably somewhere a little bit out of the way?'

Miranda thought of the fifteen-minute walk up the hill to the Lighthouse, glanced back at the kitchen, where Nigel appeared to be having a nervous breakdown on the phone to Gwen, and beamed.

'I have just the place,' she promised. 'Follow me.'

LEO

There really was nothing to this multi-tasking lark, Leo decided. Yes, the 5 a.m. start had been a bit of a killer, but at least the coffee machine he'd insisted Mum and Dad buy for the Lighthouse was working and fully stocked with those pods Juliet said were killing the planet, so that helped. Well, three of those, plus the pre-made pain au chocolat Juliet dug out of the freezer as an attempt at the breakfast part in B&B. Caffeine, sugar and carbs: that was what was going to get him through this summer.

And since he'd spend most of it chasing around the island with the girls, he wouldn't even have to worry about gaining a dad-bod in the process.

Now it was mid-morning, he was careening down the path towards Gull Bay on his old bike he'd found at the back of the shed, Abby and Mia were laughing and singing as they followed him, and if he could just get some goddamn 4G signal it would be an actual Julie Andrews movie moment.

Seashell Island hadn't changed at all, as far as he could see. Same candy-coloured buildings along the high street, and stripy beach huts on Long Beach. Same smell of candyfloss and sea salt and fish and chips and ice cream all rolled into one. Same white clouds puffing along in front of the sun every few minutes. The gorse and grasses still grew on the hills, running into and then giving way to the sand as the land sloped down towards the sea. Gulls cawed overhead as they approached their bay, on the lookout for a stray piece of battered fish, or even an ice cream. Leo smiled to himself as he remembered losing a fish-and-chip supper that way when he was smaller. Maybe even that first summer after they arrived on the island, back when everything still felt so magical.

He supposed it had never stopped feeling that way for Miranda. That must be why she'd stayed.

And right now he could see that same magical feeling in his daughters' eyes when he glanced back at them, hear it on the wind as they laughed. Why hadn't he and Emily brought the girls here more? Life had always just seemed so busy, and the island such a long slog away. A drive of five and a half hours just to the ferry, and then there was still the crossing to contend with.

And the lack of internet signal.

Leo raised his hands from the handlebars of his bike to lift his phone higher in the hope his email might finally ping and tell him he had the dozens of new messages he knew must have arrived since he closed down his laptop as the girls finished breakfast that morning. God only knew how Tom was coping. Or how the meeting went. Or—

The path dipped suddenly under his front wheel, and Leo grappled to control the handlebars while still keeping hold of his phone, failing on both counts. As his phone flew through the air, followed by his body, followed by his bike, wheel over handlebars, Leo finally spotted something new about Seashell Island.

The old-fashioned ambulance he flew into the side of.

Abby screamed as his shoulder hit the vehicle, and even Mia called, 'Dad!' as he sank to the sand and gravel of the path, his whole body vibrating from the hit.

Then he heard another voice. A woman's voice. Swearing loudly and creatively from inside the ambulance.

'Dad! Are you OK?' The girls brought their bikes to a much more orderly halt beside him, scrambling down to crowd around him, patting his aching body with more concern than gentleness.

'I'm fine, I'm fine,' he lied, as his shoulder started to throb. His leg stung too, and when he looked down he winced at the blood pooling on his torn skin.

Abby followed his gaze and gasped, her eyes wide and her face pale as she clapped one hand to her mouth. Mia, meanwhile, scrambled around to find his phone, holding it up triumphantly despite the cracked screen.

'We need to call an ambulance!'

Leo, dazed, looked up at the strange vehicle he was leaning against. 'I think we've already found one.'

He blinked again, as darkness started to fill his vision. His last thought before passing out was, *But vehicles aren't allowed on Seashell Island*.

The first thing Leo was aware of as he came round was that he was much more comfortable. The second was that his daughters were laughing, and apparently completely unconcerned about his plight.

The third was that they weren't alone on the side of the road any longer.

'You're awake.' A low, melodious voice spoke – last heard cursing like a sailor from inside the ambulance, unless Leo was mistaken – moving closer with each word. 'That didn't take long. We only had time for a couple of hands of gin rummy.'

'Are you teaching my children to gamble?' he asked, blearily, as he forced his eyes to open.

'Well, somebody had to. A shocking gap in the girls' education.'

The voice was very close now, and as Leo finally managed to get his eyes open he saw why: the bad-influence woman was leaning right over him, studying his face. She lifted one of his eyelids higher, peered in, then let it drop.

'He'll live,' she called back to the girls, who whooped with delight. Which was fairly gratifying.

Struggling into a sitting position, Leo bumped his head on the ceiling.

'Careful,' the woman said, sounding amused.

He shot her a look as he sat more carefully and took in their surroundings, trying to make sense of what he saw. The girls were sitting on miniature armchairs around a small, circular table that was attached to the floor by a metal pole. They had cards set out in front of them, along with a china teapot and cups that looked to be full of blackcurrant squash. The walls behind them housed a rainbow of fitted cupboards, each door painted a different colour, with a small curtained hatch in the middle. The third wall beside them was missing completely, sunlight pouring in from outside and the sea lapping against the shore in the distance. He frowned. How could a wall be missing?

Then the small curtain blew aside in a sudden breeze, and revealed the steering wheel and front seats beyond it, and suddenly his bashed brain caught up.

'We're inside the ambulance,' he said, in wonder. An ambulance that was also a tearoom. Or a living space, he supposed. And sleeping space, given that he was lying on a surprisingly comfortable single bed, covered in a crocheted blanket made of soothing green, blue and aqua wool, with flashes of white like surf spray on waves.

'Are you always this slow, or should I be worried about

brain damage?' the woman asked, in a whisper. 'Only I just told your daughters you'd be OK, so that would be kind of embarrassing.'

There was a slight hint of concern behind her laughing eyes, but only slight. Her smile danced over her lips like the whole world amused her, and him in particular. Her short, black and purple hair dipped over one eye, and she shook it out of the way.

Mindful of his head, he swung his legs round and slipped off the bed, which was raised off the ground by a good metre. The room didn't spin, which he took as a good sign.

'Not brain-damaged,' he assured her. 'Just confused. Tourist vehicles and motor homes aren't allowed on Seashell Island.'

'Dad had to leave his car on the mainland with Tom,' Mia explained, helpfully. 'He's still in mourning.'

'I am not,' Leo lied. 'Anyway. I was wondering how you managed to persuade the council to allow this converted ambulance off the ferry.'

'How do you know I didn't smuggle it on in the dead of night with the help of pirates? Maybe I'm a rebel.'

She looked like a rebel, Leo decided. Or maybe that was just the swirly purple and blue vest top she wore that read 'Winging It' over an image of a bird flying free.

'Christabel isn't a rebel. She's Auntie Miri's friend,' Mia said. Which on the one hand made perfect sense – any friend of Miranda's was unlikely to be trying to overthrow authority or what have you. But on the other . . . the woman in front of him definitely didn't look like anyone his sister would be friends with.

'We met her on the beach the other day when we went rock-pooling. And her ambulance isn't just a caravan,

Daddy,' Abby piped up, putting down her teacup of squash. 'Come on, I'll show you.'

It wasn't until he took Abby's little hand and stepped down from the ambulance that he realised his leg had been cleaned and bandaged. 'Are you running an actual first-aid service from this ambulance then?' he asked Christabel. 'And thank you, by the way.'

'You're welcome. But the first-aid thing is incidental to my actual purpose. Come on.'

Christabel led them around to the back of the ambulance, and threw open the rear doors, revealing – along with a mini generator and water tank – two pink and purple bikes, and rack upon rack of tools, tyres, inner tubes and other bike paraphernalia hanging on the inside of the doors.

And across the top ran a sign that read: 'Bike Ambulance'.

'So, how about it, mister?' she asked. 'Like me to fix your bike?'

JULIET

By Monday, Juliet thought she was starting to get the measure of the Lighthouse again, this time from a proprietor's point of view, rather than that of a reluctant guest. She'd always known that a lot of work went into running the place – she'd had her own share of it to do on the chores rota, for a start. But only now was she starting to see how many details went into making the place run smoothly.

Figuring all this out would have been a lot easier if her parents had left comprehensive notes or operating procedures, like the ones for making the printers at work actually print rather than just beep alarmingly. Working for Callum, Juliet had *almost* got used to the constraints of having a standard operating procedure to follow for every tiny task that needed doing, right down to the clients' coffee preference chart in the office kitchen.

Here, on Seashell Island, everything seemed a lot more free-form.

Determined not to be put off at the first hurdle, she decided to tackle it like a project at work. For all that she was technically Callum's assistant, in reality she knew she'd done a lot more work than most of the admins – partly because it gave them an excuse to stay late and work together. Something that, now she thought about it, probably wouldn't have been necessary if his marriage had been quite as over as he'd claimed.

Still, it had given her plenty of experience of setting up and managing projects. Running a B&B couldn't be all that different to running a street-food event, could it? Both started as a list of things to be done to achieve the right outcome. Then she just had to split the list up into who would do them and when.

From the records on the computer, the scrawled lists stuck inside cupboard doors, and the stacks of sheets and towels in the linen cupboard, Juliet was able to gain a pretty good idea of what needed to be done, whenever they finally got some guests. To begin with, she decided on the most important tasks – the ones that, if a new guest arrived tomorrow, they'd need done – and tackled them first.

She started by making up the rooms, ensuring that each had a full set of the mini-soaps and lotions made locally in a nearby farmhouse. She updated the local information file that still seemed to contain fax numbers rather than email addresses, and put a mini-printout of all the most important details in each room. She cleared out the fridge and freezer of any out-of-date or dodgy-looking food and drinks.

And she ignored the amused looks from her siblings.

She knew what they were thinking – that this was another fad, something she'd take on for a few days before losing interest. Well, they were wrong. Because losing interest was no longer an option.

She felt like she had when Miranda had tried to talk her out of getting her first tattoo. 'Don't you know they're painful, expensive and *permanent*?' Miranda had said, as if Juliet had no common sense at all.

She'd got the tattoo anyway – a small sunflower on her shoulder. And now she was about to become the proud owner of something else that was painful to get, expensive to keep, and terrifyingly permanent.

Still, she'd never regretted the tattoo, even if she had given it considerably more thought than the baby growing inside her before it happened.

By the time she'd finished her most urgent tasks, her siblings had both disappeared – Miranda to work, she assumed, and Leo wobbling on a bike with the girls following behind laughing. Juliet took in the rare peace and quiet, and got planning.

Sitting at the kitchen table with a cup of sadly decaffeinated coffee, Juliet looked at the notepad in front of her, tapping her biro against the paper until it left a smattering of freckles across the page. Would her baby have freckles? Callum was a redhead; it was definitely possible.

His other kids did. She'd seen photos.

Focus, Juliet.

She couldn't think about Callum, or the siblings her baby would never know existed, or the future she'd thought she might actually be heading towards.

She had a new future now. And she was bloody well going to make it work.

So. The rota.

Writing the list had been easy enough – but knowing what needed to be done was just the start. With the immediately urgent actions ticked off, now she had to turn to the bigger problem: how to keep the place running.

She'd never been much of a list maker before she started working for Callum. That was always Miranda's domain. But right now, with her thoughts scattered far and wide and her rolling stomach making it hard to focus, writing down the vital next steps for the B&B was helping. Everything else – like telling her family she was pregnant, for instance – would have to wait until they reached the top of the list. Possibly around the time she was the size of a house and calling for the ambulance, if she had her way.

And she was wool-gathering again.

Growing up, there had always been a rota stuck with a magnet to the fridge door – the one area in which her parents showed some level of organisation. On it, each family member was assigned tasks that needed doing on different days of the week. Making the beds, clearing up the breakfast plates, cleaning the bathrooms, everything was on the rota – and they all had to do their part.

Juliet didn't see why it should be any different now.

So, with her list of essential daily and weekly tasks on one side of the table, and her decaf on the other, she drew up a large timetable on a piece of plain paper and started assigning tasks.

Abby and Mia weren't old enough to do some things, but they could definitely help with others – emptying the bins, for instance, or loading the dishwasher with supervision. And Miranda and Leo were *definitely* both old enough to do everything, however much they complained.

The big advantage of setting the rota was that she got to pick and choose the jobs she liked, although she made sure she did a reasonable share of the ones everyone hated too. Juliet assigned herself breakfast cooking duties six days out of seven, and smiled at the thought of feeding crowds passing through the Lighthouse this summer.

She'd always enjoyed cooking, even before she'd moved away and had to start fending for herself. Back when she lived at the Lighthouse, her days on the breakfast rota were always her favourites. And working for a company promoting and helping start up food businesses had only exposed her to more interesting possibilities in the food world.

Her stomach rumbled at the thought. Well, with the rota done, she supposed her next job was figuring out the breakfast part of the B&B equation. She'd cobbled together pastries, porridge and cereal, along with toast and home-made jam (found at the back of the cupboard), for the family the last couple of days, but she knew that couldn't be all that her parents usually offered. In fact, the in-room information she'd just printed mentioned locally sourced sausages, bacon and eggs. As did the website.

Which meant she should probably get sourcing, she supposed.

Until Miranda found them some proper customers, Juliet intended to treat Leo and the girls – and Miranda, until she went back to the flat she shared with Paul – as paying guests. Their parents had left Miranda access to the B&B's accounts, and she'd reluctantly handed the business credit card over to Juliet for 'Essential spending only, absolutely nothing else, OK?', which meant she had the funds to get started. And if she was the one running the place, Juliet figured *she* got to decide what was essential, not Miranda.

It had been years since she'd spent any real time exploring the town of St Mary's. Normally, in an effort to keep her visits to the island short, she headed straight up to the Light-house and stayed there until it was time to catch the ferry back again. Since it was usually Christmas when she visited, most of the shops would have been shut anyway.

But not today. Today the high street, while not exactly bustling, boasted open shop doors, brightly coloured awn-ings, and cafe tables and chairs on the pavements.

Juliet started her exploration at the small craft centre at the far end of the high street, where she stocked up on sea salt and summer-scented candles for the bathrooms and bedrooms. She ticked 'candles' off her list with a sense of accomplish-ment, before spotting a beautiful patchwork quilt that would look perfect on the back of the sofa in the day room.

It had clearly been a long time since her parents had made any real updates to the Lighthouse, she reasoned. A few fresh touches would make all the difference.

She added 'quilt' to the bottom of her list, then ticked it off as she paid.

By the time she'd made it to the far end of the high street her bags were bulging with locally sourced everythings – except the food she'd actually come out for. Already wondering how she was going to get all her purchases back up to the Lighthouse without dropping them, she finally spotted a deli/restaurant she didn't remember from the last time she visited this end of town.

The Flying Fish was nothing like the Crab Leg Cafe, Juliet realised as she pushed open the door. There were no plastic chequered tablecloths here, or tomato-shaped ketchup dispensers. And it wasn't like the Smuggler's Inn, either – the nicest pub in town – or the Anchor (not quite so nice), yet it also wasn't as pretentious and stuffy as the Yacht Club across the water on the mainland, with its dress codes and its membership fees.

In fact, the Flying Fish looked kind of like the sort of place she'd have liked to hang out with her London friends, if she could have found it in the city. Scrubbed wooden tables were laid with mismatched crockery, and with painted wooden chairs around them. Pendant lamps in shades of aqua and cream hung over each table, giving them the feel of a private dining space. And behind the long, wooden bar – complete with comfy-looking bar stools – was a full array of spirits, wines, beers and non-alcoholic drinks. Through a large, open archway, Juliet could see another counter, this one with glass covering cured meats, dishes of olives, and a huge selection of cheeses.

It was still early enough that the few people sitting at the tables in the restaurant half of the building were lingering over morning coffee, or polishing off a late breakfast before the lunch crowd came in. Juliet hovered between the two spaces, torn between the impulse to sit down and order another decaf coffee and maybe one of those pastries in the glass cloche on the counter, or head through to the deli to see if they also stocked local meats, breads and eggs.

The decision was made for her when she heard a voice behind her. A very familiar voice.

'Did you want a table, miss? Sorry, our head server has just run out on an . . .' the words trailed away as she turned around and he saw her face. 'Juliet.'

'Hi, Rory.'

Rory Hillier. Her best friend since reception class. And the love of her life for almost eighteen whole months at the impressionable ages of seventeen and eighteen.

She suspected he might not remember her *quite* so fondly, though, after the way she left.

'Back for the weekend?' he guessed, in a neutral, almost friendly tone. 'To welcome your parents home?'

If she hadn't known him so well, once, she might have believed the tone. As it was . . . she couldn't help but notice the tightness of his jaw, the slight narrowing of his eyes.

Or the fact that the eyes were the only part of him that had narrowed at all. As a teenager, he'd been slender to the point of scrawny. Now, his broad shoulders caught her attention and held it, all the way down to the narrowing of his waist, and the incredibly good fit of his jeans over his thighs . . .

Stop it. You're practically a mother.

She dragged her eyes back to his face and her mind back to the conversation.

'Um, actually I'm here for a little while. Mum and Dad

aren't coming home yet, so I'm running the Lighthouse while they're away.'

Ah, that look of shock at least was familiar. It was identical to the ones Miranda and Leo had given her at the suggestion.

Rory at least covered it better. Schooling his expression back into polite disinterest – something that just looked wrong on a face she remembered as showing his every feeling, every thought, with those intense blue eyes under black eyebrows – he gave a small nod.

'Right. In that case, you'll be here to discuss the meat order? Come on through.' He turned and walked through the archway, calling over to the bar to another staff member to cover walk-ins until Debbie got back.

'The meat order. Yep. That's why I'm here.' Setting up the Lighthouse for the future. Becoming the person she needed to be for *her* future.

Even if it suddenly felt like she'd walked into her past.

MESSAGES

Juliet (to the 'Rents group): Hi guys! Definitely think you should get a parrot for the B&B. Speaking of, I was thinking of emptying out the back two rooms to set them up as singles for guests . . . what do you think?

Juliet (to the 'Rents group): Full disclosure, I already started sorting through the boxes. Do you realise you've kept every single one of our school books?

Juliet (to the 'Rents group): And Mum, you didn't want that bag of clothes, right? I mean, they all look like they date from the nineties. And not in the good, *Friends*-revival way.

MIRANDA

'Christabel didn't mention the no cars on the island rule,' Owain said, as Harriet's horse and cart jolted him, his friends, and a surprising number of musical instruments up the hill to the Lighthouse. 'Sounds a bit of a pain.'

Miranda winced, and decided not to mention that she'd been on the committee that upheld that rule at their last meeting. 'There are exceptions for local businesses,' she explained instead. 'Mostly it just affects the tourists, but a lot of them come here for the peaceful atmosphere, so it seems to work.'

'And this B&B of yours never thought of investing in a shuttle bus?' Owain's redheaded friend, Suzi, stuck her head back into the cart from where she was sitting next to their driver. 'Not that I'm complaining about our ride, of course,' she added, with a flirtatious smile at Harriet, who blushed.

Interesting.

Everything about Owain and his friends seemed interesting, actually. For starters, they were all absurdly good-looking, which had made sense when Owain had explained they were a band. 'We're called Birchwood,' he'd said. She had to admit, they seemed like the kind of cool kids Christabel would be friends with.

After she'd told him about the Lighthouse, he'd nodded, said it sounded perfect, and disappeared off to collect his mates. He'd returned with three other people, plus apparently an entire orchestra or something, as there were *definitely* more instrument cases than there were people.

The other members of Birchwood, however, seemed nice enough. As well as Suzi there was Robyn, a tall and willowy blonde, and Ryan, Robyn's twin brother, who was equally tall, if rather less willowy. They all seemed relaxed and happy to be on Seashell Island, which was just how Miranda liked her tourists, and nobody had asked too many questions about the Lighthouse B&B, barring the shuttle bus one, which was good.

Miranda had fired off a thank-you text to Christabel while they were loading up the instruments. Her response had been an indecipherable row of emojis, but from the winking face and the aubergine emoji she got the basic sentiment. Clearly, Christabel thought she hadn't just sent her some guests, but also an opportunity.

And looking at Owain, Miranda almost wished she was right. But moving away from safe and familiar was one thing. Skydiving off into the new and scary was a whole different level – one way beyond her capabilities.

'Do you really think this place we're staying will be OK with us practising?' Robyn asked, as they bumped up the hill. 'I mean, we were really thinking of a secluded, self-catering cottage sort of place.' She shot a glare at Owain, who shrugged. Miranda took this to mean that Owain wasn't great at taking instructions. And that Robyn felt that she had the authority of position to give them to him. Also interesting.

'Full disclosure?' Miranda gave what she hoped was a disarming smile. 'It's my parents' B&B. They're away travelling at the moment, so my sister and I are running it. The only other people staying there are my brother and his kids, and trust me, they're more likely to get the noise control people round than you are.' Conscious that this wasn't the best selling point, she hurried on. 'There's an old cottage on the edge of the property that you can set up as a rehearsal space, if you like? Give you some privacy?'

It had been her private space, once. When Leo and Juliet were both preparing to leave, she'd made that cottage her own nest on the island. Close enough to home, but with some privacy and autonomy too. She'd thought about moving back into the cottage herself, now she was no longer living with Paul, but it had been easier to put up at the Lighthouse than air out the cottage, and she needed to be close in case of guests anyway. And now . . . well, if it meant they had a full house, she could give up a little privacy for a while.

'That sounds perfect,' Owain said, shooting Robyn a smug grin. She rolled her eyes good-naturedly.

'How long were you guys planning on staying?' Owain had mentioned a week or so, but she suspected that Robyn might have more concrete plans.

But Robyn just sighed. So did Suzi, and even the taciturn Ryan.

'Until the album is finished,' Owain said firmly. 'Which could be a week—'

'Or could be all summer,' Ryan finished, in a dull voice.

'Yep!' Owain, for one, didn't seem too disappointed at the prospect. His slow, lazy smile was aimed directly at Miranda, and she couldn't help but smile back. 'And can you think of anywhere better to spend the summer?'

Suzi flashed Harriet another of those meaningful looks. 'I certainly can't.'

Harriet, to her credit, kept her eyes on the road, but even from her seat in the cart Miranda could make out the small smile on her face and the pinkness in her cheeks.

123

'What sort of music do you all play?' Miranda asked, already wondering how she could delay album making. Keeping the band there all summer would certainly solve their Lighthouse occupation problems.

'Sort of folk, sort of rock,' Owain said, with a shrug. 'Sort of whatever we fancy at the time.'

'Sounds . . . interesting.'

'You'll have to come listen to us rehearse,' Suzi said, turning around from the front seat again. 'Or come along to one of our gigs on the mainland later in the summer. We always love a good groupie.'

She looked meaningfully at Owain as she said the word 'groupie' and Robyn rolled her eyes again, and Miranda started re-evaluating everything she'd assumed about the group's relationships.

Finally, the whitewashed walls of the Lighthouse came into view, along with the tower of the old lighthouse itself. Suzi jumped up in her seat, making Harriet grab her hand to pull her back down – then let go in a hurry, blushing again. Miranda smiled. She'd never seen so much emotion from the usually reserved Harriet as she had in this trip.

'This place looks amazing!' Suzi announced, from a seated position. 'Can you go up the old lighthouse tower?'

'We only open it once a year,' Miranda explained. 'For the end-of-summer festival. If you're still here, I'll get my dad to take you up after they light it.'

If they're back by then.

No. She wasn't thinking about that. She was thinking only about the next week. Once she'd got through that she'd worry about the one after, and the one after.

And the rest of my life, since all my plans for that have apparently gone up in smoke too.

Just this week. This day. This hour, even.

Harriet tugged on the reins and brought old Smokey the carthorse to a halt. Miranda jumped down and helped the band unload their instruments, then went to get the door open – surprised to find it locked.

'Everyone must be out,' she explained, fishing for her keys. Except Juliet was supposed to be here getting the rooms ready. She'd tried to call to warn her about the impending arrivals, but Juliet hadn't answered, so she'd left messages on the B&B voicemail and Juliet's mobile. Surely she'd picked at least *one* of those up by now?

She'd taken all the details she needed from Owain on the way from the office, so Miranda went straight into the tour as they all traipsed in after her.

'So, this is the hallway, obviously. Through here . . .' She opened the large, bleached wood door on her left. 'This is the main lounge and bar; feel free to use it. There are games, books, plus a stocked bar. We run an honesty box on the top if no one is available to serve.'

She saw Robyn and Ryan exchange an incredulous grin at the idea of an alcohol honesty box, but it had worked for her mum and dad for years, and Miranda had no reason to believe it wouldn't work now. From the serious nod Owain gave her, she had a feeling he'd make sure the box balanced by the end of their visit, even if no one else did.

'The family spaces are back there,' she said, motioning further down the hallway. 'And the kitchen is in here. We're fairly relaxed, so if you need anything, help yourself.' She led them into the bright and airy farmhouse kitchen, and showed them where the coffee machine was, since that always seemed to be the first thing guests needed to know.

Then she spotted the new addition to the fridge.

Juliet had made them a chore chart. A rota, like the one they'd had as kids. Apparently, she really was on a nostalgia kick this week – but it showed more organisational skill than she'd expected from her sister, so that was something.

'Everything OK?' Owain asked, as the others fiddled with the coffee machine.

She turned back to him with what she hoped was a reassuring smile. 'Absolutely. Come on, I'll show you the bedrooms.'

She didn't like to presume about who would be sharing with whom, so she just showed them all the rooms the Lighthouse had to offer that were not currently occupied by her own family and let them pick their own. Suzi grabbed a room with a sea view on the first floor, Robyn and Ryan took the two single rooms the next floor up. Owain, she noticed, waited until all the others were settled, then took the next room they saw, the small double by the stairs to the attic rooms where the family slept.

He dumped his bag on the bed, then turned to Miranda. 'While the others are getting settled – and probably acquainted with your honesty box – how about you show me this cottage we can use for practice space.'

Miranda nodded and smiled, wondering so many things. Like where Juliet was. Like what the relationship between Owain and Robyn was. What Christabel had been thinking sending him here. What she'd told him about her, and if it explained the looks he kept giving her. The ones that made her feel warm and as if something exciting might happen any moment . . .

And also, how he managed to make 'honesty box' sound as dirty as he did.

She led him back down the stairs to the front door, still wondering about all those things. Until she opened the door to find Paul standing outside it with a box of what she recognised immediately as her own belongings.

LEO

Leo leaned back against the ambulance and watched as Christabel expertly removed the wheel from his bike and set about seeing if it was possible to make it wheel-shaped again. Apparently, he'd hit the ambulance with some force; the fact that it barely showed a scratch while his entire body hurt said more than he'd like about their relative levels of sturdiness.

Sipping the tea she'd made him, he listened to Abby and Mia playing in the sand dunes nearby, just about within sight, and smiled. OK, so the day hadn't gone *exactly* how he'd planned, but he had to be racking up Super Dad points, right? He'd brought them out for an adventure, met a *very* interesting woman, and let them play on the beach.

Surreptitiously, he pulled his phone out of his pocket and winced at the cracked screen. He'd have to call his phone insurance people and get a new one sent out. It wasn't like Seashell Island had phone shops, and he wasn't living with a spiderweb of a screen for the rest of the summer.

'So, Miranda mentioned that you're on the island for the summer?' Christabel said, reaching for another tool Leo couldn't identify.

'Yeah. We came to stay with my parents, except they're not here.' He shrugged, hoping it wasn't immediately obvious how much that had derailed his plans. It had been a long time since Leo had enjoyed a flirty conversation with a beautiful woman – one he couldn't quite believe was

Miranda's friend – but he was fairly sure that letting on that he'd come running home to his mum and dad when life got difficult wasn't exactly a good first impression.

'I heard about that. I say, good on Josie and Iestyn! More people should take the chance to follow their dreams and explore when they get the chance.'

Leo raised his eyebrows. 'Are you *sure* you're a friend of Miranda's?'

Christabel laughed. 'I'm trying to corrupt her.'

'She needs it,' Leo replied. 'Do you realise she's not left this island in years? Not even to go to the mainland?'

'I'm working on it,' Christabel said, airily, as she tightened something or another on the bike. 'I have a bit of a reputation around here, you know.'

'I can imagine.'

She swatted him with a spanner. 'Hey!'

'Oh God! I didn't mean like that!' Leo put up his hands, horrified. 'I just meant . . . you're not like the normal boring folks on Seashell Island. You're more . . . interesting. Fun. That's the sort of thing that usually gets people around here talking.'

Christabel looked vaguely mollified at his explanation, which was all he could really hope for. Emily was right. He was *hopeless* with people, outside a business context. Small talk was definitely not his forte.

'What I was saying was, I have a reputation for helping people find their path. To help them see what they really want from life and go after it. Miranda is just proving . . . more of a challenge than most.'

'So you're some sort of life coach, as well as a bike mechanic?'

Christabel shrugged. 'I don't really use labels any more. I had enough of that in my past life.'

He raised his eyebrows, unsure whether she meant she used to be Cleopatra before being reincarnated, or something else.

'I used to be a hedge-fund manager,' she clarified.

'Really?' Leo wasn't sure that was any less surprising than Cleopatra would have been.

'Really.' She hung the spanner back up and reached for a pump for the new tyre she'd added to his bike. 'For years, I did nothing but work, make money, and talk to people who could help me make more money.'

'What changed?' he asked, curious.

She didn't look up. 'I did.'

Huh.

'So, the girls were telling me that their mum is away on honeymoon this summer.' She shot him a sideways look. 'How do you feel about that?'

How do you feel? Who asked that kind of question? Even his mum had only asked 'Are you OK?' Not 'How do you feel?' Nobody had expected him to articulate the strange muddle of feelings in the pit of his stomach over his wife's remarriage. Everyone just accepted that it wasn't something that could be put into words. They just wanted to know that he was still functioning, still coping, and that was enough.

But not for Christabel, apparently. Because she was still looking at him, waiting for an answer. Did she want to fix him too? Well, she'd be disappointed. He didn't need fixing, or refocusing. He already knew what mattered to him.

'Mark, Emily's new husband, is . . . a good man.' Better than he was in the ways that mattered to Emily, anyway. Ways like not working at weekends and remembering to come home from the office in time for dinner. Ways like remembering important conversations about their planned future together and not making alternative work plans instead. 'He'll be a good . . .' he swallowed, before he could say the words. 'He'll be a good stepdad for the girls.'

'And you hate that, right?' Christabel asked, one knowing eyebrow raised.

'Of course I don't!' That was crazy talk right there. 'I want what's best for my girls. And a happy Emily is what's best. A stepdad who will love them and appreciate them is what's best.'

'And what's your place in that?' Christabel, not even looking at him as she asked the question, tightened something with a tool Leo thought might possibly be a wrench.

'I'll . . . I'll be their dad. I'll always be their dad.'

She flashed him a smile. 'Good. Don't forget that.'

What was she talking about? Of course he wouldn't forget that.

'I mean, I'll see them most weekends. Well, at least every other. I'll bring them here in the summer, if that's OK with Emily. I'll be their dad.'

'Oh, so you're going to be *that* dad.' She was back to focusing on the bike again.

He blinked, watching her. 'I just met you today. Are you really critiquing my parenting style?'

Christabel shrugged. 'I don't usually stay in one place very long, so I don't have time for being subtle. Eighteen months here on Seashell Island is basically a record. But, you know, ignore me if I make you uncomfortable.'

She did make him uncomfortable, Leo realised. It was those disturbing eyes, he decided. The way they seemed to look right inside him and read him as easily as a novel. No, as easily as one of Abby's reading books from school. Like she'd digested everything meaningful about him in the first few moments of their meeting.

Maybe she had.

Or maybe his sister had been telling tales about him. That would make sense.

'What sort of dad do you think I should be?' The question was out before Leo could think through why he was asking it, let alone if it was a good idea.

Christabel put down the maybe-a-wrench she was using, looked at him for a long moment, then shrugged. 'What do I know? It's not like I even have kids. I already told your sister I wasn't getting involved in your issues. *She* thought I was exactly what you needed, by the way.'

That surprised a laugh out of him. But underneath his amusement, he was thinking. Hard.

She'd seen something. Something in him or in the girls that had made her ask the question about Emily's remarriage in the first place.

And suddenly, deep inside the pit of his stomach, something was burning, making Leo need to know what it was.

'I want to know what you think,' he said, leaning closer. Over the dunes he could hear the girls squealing with laughter as whatever they were constructing in the sand apparently worked – or possibly failed again. It was hard to tell. 'I mean, you saved me from a ridiculously embarrassing bike crash. I feel you're already invested in my life.'

Her lips twitched into a smile, gone in a second as she put on a mock serious expression. 'That is true.'

'So?'

Sighing, Christabel picked up the actually-maybe-it-was-another-spanner again. 'My dad wasn't exactly a role model. He wasn't even a part of my life for most of my childhood. But that didn't stop me imagining what my relationship with him *could* have been, if he'd stuck around. Probably because the relationship I had with my mum was kind of tense anyway.' She shrugged. 'Your kids adore you. You have the opportunity to spend all summer with them on this incredible island. I guess I'd just hate to see you waste it because you haven't decided it's important enough to focus on.'

Leo blinked. Had he ever, even for a moment, thought of this summer as an *opportunity*? Probably not.

'You think I'm wasting it?' he asked, not wanting to linger on that thought. 'I'm here taking my kids for a bike ride, aren't I?'

'And what were you doing when you crashed?' She gave him a knowing look, and Leo's hand instinctively went for the smashed phone in his pocket.

'I have to work,' he said, knowing he sounded defensive. 'Just like my ex-wife does. More than that, I *love* my work, and that doesn't mean I love my kids any less.'

That earned him a brilliant smile, for some reason. 'Of course it doesn't. I'm not saying you shouldn't work. Just . . . don't hide behind it.'

'Hide? What do you mean?' Work was just work, wasn't it?

'Just . . . OK, this is way overstepping the mark for someone who just met you. Even for me.'

'I've already passed out in your bed,' Leo pointed out, with a grin. 'I think we've left the mark far behind.'

'OK, then. And I'm only doing this because you're Miranda's brother.' Turning, Christabel faced him, giving him every bit of her attention. Those violet-blue eyes were strangely compelling as they met his. 'Your girls, they know they're an inconvenience this summer. They know you'd rather be working. So you need to show them that you're happy to be here with them too. That you're listening to them. Understanding them.'

'Of course I am!' Leo said, defensively. 'I love them.'

'I know that. They're great girls – happy, secure and loved. I knew that in the first five minutes of meeting them on the beach with Miranda.' A shadow passed across Christabel's face. Leo suspected she knew that by contrasts. She knew what little girls looked like when they *didn't* have that. Somehow, that only made him more determined to listen to what she had to tell him. 'But knowing you love them isn't the same as being a part of their lives. Every other weekend out, presents and trips . . . that's great, for now. But the time goes fast. And before you know it those little girls will be tweens, teenagers, leaving home . . . and then, what they'll really need is someone they can call when they're in trouble, someone they can tell their worries to at night, someone they trust more than anyone else in the world.'

'Their mum,' Leo said, automatically. 'They'd call Emily, they'd talk to her. They always have. They have her and now . . . now they have Mark, too.'

It hit him, exactly what Christabel had been trying to show him.

He'd thought he'd been doing so well, accepting that Mark had his place in his marriage now – and he had. He was happy that Emily was happy. He was happy that his kids would have a stepdad who loved them.

But what if that meant they didn't need him any more at all?

'They're lucky to have them,' she said, softly. 'But . . . don't you want them to have you, too?'

Do they need me? Maybe not. But I want them to.

'Kids can never have too many people who love them.' Christabel turned her attention back to the bike for a moment while he processed everything she'd said. This strange, wise woman who seemed to be younger and older than him both

133

at the same time. She didn't know him, or his family – but it felt like she did.

Suddenly, he felt like he had new purpose on Seashell Island that summer.

Or maybe purposes, plural. Because as much as he wanted to build his relationship with his daughters, he realised he wanted something else, too.

He wanted to see Christabel again. To have her look at him with those violet eyes and talk to him in that melodic voice. And to fix his bike when he crashed it.

'Done.' Christabel stowed away the last of her tools – Leo had given up even trying to guess what they were – and lifted his bike frame. 'Ready to give it a try?'

Leo nodded. 'I'll go fetch the girls. But I might need you to ride with us. Just to make sure I don't injure myself again.'

Christabel's smile was warm with understanding. 'I'll consider it my public duty.'

JULIET

In the hierarchy of mortifying things she'd done lately, or ever, sitting with her ex-boyfriend discussing breakfast sausages wasn't even up there. But, Juliet had to admit to herself as Rory patiently explained the ordering system he'd set up with her parents, her lack of knowledge was a little bit embarrassing. When they'd been together, she'd been the leader, the one who decided what they were going to do, the one with the big ideas and the ambition to make them happen.

Having to take advice on bacon – or, more precisely, being told how to do the job she'd blithely volunteered for – was not how she pictured the reunion between the two of them.

Not that she'd pictured it over the last ten years. Much.

OK, fine, so she had. She'd imagined coming back to Seashell Island, wildly successful in her chosen career – when she had finally chosen one. In her head, she'd been impeccably dressed, confident, secure in herself and her future.

She hadn't been pregnant, unemployed, and unable to understand the sausage-to-guest ratio. She knew how to cook, how to feed people. Just . . . not in bulk.

'So. Do you think you're OK with everything we've discussed?' Rory asked, looked doubtful.

'Absolutely,' Juliet lied. Then she gave an emphatic nod for good measure.

Rory did not look reassured.

She sighed. 'Look, this is just until Mum and Dad get back. If you can help me keep the place going for the next few weeks, I promise someone competent will be back in charge again by the end of the summer.'

Where *she'd* be, she had no idea. But he didn't need to know that.

Rory shook his head. 'I never said you weren't competent enough to run the Lighthouse, Juliet. I was just surprised that you even wanted to.'

You and everyone who's related to me.

'It's just a short-term thing,' she said, with a shrug. 'I'm not *staying* or anything.'

'I never imagined for a moment that you would,' Rory replied, looking straight into her eyes, and she knew what he was thinking: *If you couldn't stay last time when I needed you, why would you stay now?*

Juliet's gaze darted away. 'Anyway. I should probably get back to the B&B. Miranda was going to try to drum up some customers for me today, so I need to make sure the place is ready. At least now I know I can feed them in the morning!'

She grinned at Rory, but his answering smile was weak. 'I'll finish packing up this week's order for you, then I can give you a lift back to the Lighthouse with it.'

'You don't need to do that.' The refusal was automatic; the thought of spending even more time with Rory, driving up to the Lighthouse together, just like they used to in his dad's butcher's van, made Juliet shiver. It felt too much like falling back into old ways, her old life.

Like being trapped on Seashell Island again.

I'm not staying, she reminded herself. *I chose to come here, and I can leave any time I want. Just as soon as the outside world stops being scarier than the island one.*

'Juliet, the bags will be heavy, and it's a long walk in the hot sun. Just take the lift. I won't read anything into it, if that's what you're worried about.'

Juliet's eyes widened in surprise. 'I wasn't worrying about that.'

'You honestly weren't thinking that I might have spent the last decade here mooning after you, waiting for you to come home, and now I was going to try and trap you here again, like you accused me of when you left?' Rory's voice was calm and even, one eyebrow raised sardonically, but she still sensed this was something he'd been waiting ten long years to say to her.

'I . . . no. I wasn't thinking that.' Because she hadn't been thinking about him at all. She'd been thinking about what it meant for *her* to be back on this island, carrying her secrets within her. She hadn't even asked what had led to him working here, what had happened to his dad's butcher's shop, or anything. Juliet swallowed, sinking her fears at the same time. 'And a lift would be great, thank you.'

He gave her a nod. 'Right then.' He disappeared back behind the counter to put together the order he'd made for her.

Juliet watched him as he worked, his words echoing around her brain: *Try and trap you here again, like you accused me of when you left.*

She had done that. She'd known it was unfair, even then. Now . . . now it made her squirm, and not just because she needed the toilet *again*. Seriously, how could a tiny embryo already have so much influence on her bladder?

Back to the point, Juliet.

The point was, she'd been unfair to Rory when she broke up with him. And probably most of the time they were

137

dating, too. She'd been the one always talking about leaving, about them escaping together. She'd never thought how much harder that would be for him – it was just him and his dad and the family business, and there were expectations on him. She didn't even know if he'd have wanted to leave the island if it hadn't been for her, going on about it all the time.

She'd wanted him to be more, to want more. To want *her* more than he wanted to be here.

And then, when his dad had got sick and he'd told her he needed to stay, she'd yelled accusations at him – that he was using his dad as an excuse, that he was just like the others and never really wanted to leave the island at all, not even for her – and left anyway.

Honestly, how had she *ever* believed that they might work out, long term?

Behind the counter, Rory wrapped meat and packed eggs, all while answering questions from other staff members and customers. His patient expression never faltered; his precise hands moved efficiently about his work. He'd grown up in the last ten years – not just physically. He was a man, now.

While she still felt like a teenager disappointing her parents.

Finally, Rory stopped to talk to a dark-haired girl wearing a navy Flying Fish shirt who listened attentively then nodded and said 'Yes, boss' loud enough for Juliet to hear at a distance.

Boss. Rory was in charge of this place? Well, of course he was, she realised belatedly. That was why he'd known all the ins and outs of her parents' orders. She'd assumed he was still like her – someone who took orders and made coffees and never got taken seriously.

But he wasn't like her at all. He never had been.

'Ready?' Juliet looked up and found Rory standing over

her. She nodded, and got to her feet. She held out a hand to take one of the bags he was carrying, but he shook his head and led her out the back door to the van.

That, at least, was familiar. It wasn't the exact same butcher's van he'd used to drive when working for his dad – one of the few vehicles allowed on the island, and only then because they made deliveries – but it was pretty close. The Flying Fish logo was emblazoned on the side, and the seats were more comfortable in the new model, but otherwise Juliet could have slipped straight back through time to ten years ago.

'The Flying Fish looks like it's doing well,' she said, eager for some neutral conversation as Rory put his hand on the back of her headrest to look over his shoulder as he reversed out of the space. Ten years ago he'd have stolen a kiss while the van was still moving. Today, he was entirely focused on the road.

'It is.'

Not exactly the full and informative response she'd been hoping for with that leading statement.

Juliet tried again. 'How long have you been working there?'

That, at least, earned her a look. 'Since I bought the place three years ago.'

'You own the Flying Fish?' She shook her head. 'Of course you do. Sorry. That's what you said. I'm just . . .'

'Surprised?' Rory guessed, as they pulled out onto the high street and headed up towards the Lighthouse.

'Impressed.' She should have known, from the way the rest of the staff deferred to him, respected him, that he was more than just a shift manager. But he was only twenty-eight, like her. Owning a successful business in his twenties was quite something. And not something the Rory *she'd* known would have even dreamed of.

As if he'd heard her thoughts, Rory turned his attention back to the road and muttered, 'Yeah, well, maybe some of your ambition rubbed off on me after all.'

'Glad it was useful for one of us, then,' she said, staring out of the window.

They drove in silence for another few minutes, until Rory asked, 'How is Miranda coping? I meant to stop by and see if she needed anything, but the restaurant was packed this weekend and, well, turns out you were here anyway, so she didn't need me.'

'Leo too,' Juliet replied. 'Seems we're all home for the summer for once.' Then she frowned. 'And how's Miranda coping with what? You mean Mum and Dad being away?'

'I meant her and Paul splitting up.'

'What?' Juliet jerked up straighter in her seat. 'They split up? When?'

'On Friday.' Rory shot her a frown. 'You didn't know? It's basically the only thing anyone in town has been talking about all weekend.'

'I haven't been into town since I got back. And Miranda didn't tell me.' Apparently, she wasn't the only sister keeping secrets this summer.

'Huh.' Rory didn't elaborate, and she knew that if she wanted the details she should really talk to Miranda. And yet . . .

'Do you know what happened?'

He shrugged. 'Depends who you ask. You know what this town is like. Everyone has a different version of the story.'

'And probably none of them are more than forty per cent true.' Juliet sighed. Looked like a sibling heart-to-heart was on the cards after all.

Rory pulled the van off the main road and on to the

Lighthouse driveway, slowing down as they approached the main house.

'Thanks for the lift, and for all the advice,' she said as she opened the passenger door before Rory even had the handbrake on. 'I'll, uh, be in touch about the next order.' Maybe by email. Or seagull post, if that was what it took. Being this close to Rory made her remember all the reasons she *almost* hadn't left the island in the first place. Made her feel like eighteen-year-old Juliet again.

That couldn't be good for anybody.

But Rory was already climbing out of the van, grabbing the bags for her from the back. Without a word, he carried them towards the front door of the Lighthouse. Juliet followed mutely.

The silence meant they both heard the laughter from inside the B&B – female voices, plus a lower male one – and the sound of a guitar strumming.

'Sounds like you have guests,' Rory said.

Juliet's heart pounded against her chest. Actual guests. And she hadn't even been here to check them in. Miranda was going to murder her – or at least use it as evidence that she was wildly incapable of looking after the Lighthouse for even a week.

Well, she'd just have to prove her wrong.

If Rory could own a successful restaurant, she could manage a B&B. Right?

Pasting on her biggest smile, she took the bag of sausages from Rory and pushed open the front door to see what Miranda and Seashell Holiday Cottages had delivered her. 'I hope they're hungry.'

MESSAGES

Emily (to Leo): Landed safely here in the Maldives after our stop in Dubai. How are the girls? I'll Skype tonight to see them. Don't forget to make sure Mia eats more vegetables than sugar, and that Abby goes to bed on time!

Leo (to Emily): They're on holiday, Em. And so are you. Stop worrying. I know how to parent too, you know.

MIRANDA

'Here it is!' Miranda smiled brightly as she motioned towards the small cottage on the edge of her parents' land. But Owain wasn't looking at the cottage. He was looking at her. The same way he had been since she'd grabbed the box from Paul's hands outside the Lighthouse, shoved it onto the shelf inside the front door without even a thank you, and sent him on his way. With faint curiosity and amusement.

It probably wasn't helped by the way Paul had called her name after them as she'd hurried Owain down the path to the cottage, or how she'd steadfastly ignored him even as his shouts got louder. Or the way she'd babbled constantly ever since about anything *but* the ex-boyfriend yelling her name.

'It looks great,' Owain said, still not looking at the cottage.

Miranda fished the key from her pocket and worked it into the lock. 'There should be plenty of space in here. I mean, it's a while since I've been down here, but—'

She pushed open the door and the memories hit her before she even stepped inside.

This had been *her* place. Her sanctuary. The place she'd decorated herself, her first step outside the family home. Those were her books on the shelves, filled with adventures she'd read but never taken. And now . . . now she was back up at the Lighthouse, right back where she started – or worse. She hadn't even come back to the cottage when Paul left her. She'd run straight back to her parents' home, like a sobbing child.

Except her mum and dad hadn't been there to give her a hug or kiss it better.

'Is there a problem?' Owain asked, behind her. Shaking her head, Miranda stepped aside to let him pass.

She stayed by the door as he explored the three-room cottage, taking in the space, the quiet, the views. Everything she'd loved about it. Even from here she could see the map wallpaper she'd chosen for her bedroom peeking through the open door, and the ocean theme of the bathroom.

The girl who'd lived here hadn't been reliant on Paul, or a relationship for her independence or for her future. She'd designed her future herself and made it true in this cottage. She'd been safe here.

Why did that girl seem further away than ever right now?

'This place should work great,' Owain said, returning from the far end of the living room. 'Plenty of space to set up here, a kitchen for the required tea and coffee – and beer. Too far from anywhere to bother people—' He stopped, right in front of her. 'Hey, are you OK?'

'I'm fine,' Miranda sobbed, and realised that tears were streaming down her face. God, how *embarrassing*. 'Honestly, ignore me.'

She *was* fine. So why was she crying?

Placing a tentative arm around her shoulder, Owain led her over to the sofa and sat her down, perching awkwardly beside her as she stared out at the woods beyond the window.

'I take it this has something to do with the guy screaming your name at the house?' he asked.

Miranda nodded. 'Paul. He's my . . . *was* my fiancé. He broke up with me on Friday. He's leaving the island and doesn't want me to go with him.'

Owain raised an eyebrow. 'Did you want to go with him?'

'I don't want to leave the island. Ever.' Miranda pulled the sides of her cardigan tighter around her, hoping he wouldn't question that. 'Paul knows that.'

She didn't look up at him, but she could feel the curiosity coming off Owain in waves. Of course he'd want to know why she stayed so tied to this place.

She knew the next obvious question – when was the last time she *did* leave? And she didn't want to answer it. She had *been* to the mainland, naturally – she'd been born there. And in the first few years after they moved to the island, she'd been back a few times with her parents for hospital visits or shopping trips. Then that one time she'd been to Cardiff for the university open day . . . even the memory of that one made her shudder. And since then, since she'd been an adult, able to make her own choices . . . her world had grown smaller and smaller, until every bit of it fitted into the safety of Seashell Island.

Christabel was the first person to break through that forcefield the island had provided her with. Other people came, of course, and left again. But Christabel had stayed, and made her think about the world differently.

She dreaded to think how she'd have coped with Paul dumping her if it wasn't for Christabel shifting her world-view over the last eighteen months.

But *thinking* about the outside world, and letting people *in,* wasn't at all the same as going out there into the real world. Leaving.

And now Owain was here, bringing more of that outside in, and she knew he wanted to ask her why she wouldn't leave the island. One question would lead to another, she knew. He'd want to know how she managed to live her whole life on the few square miles of Seashell Island. He'd say all the things her siblings had been saying to her for years, and she didn't want to hear it all again. Not now, not here, and not from him.

But to her surprise, all Owain said was, 'He seemed awfully keen to talk to you for someone who's leaving you behind.'

She managed a watery chuckle at that. 'I imagine that's because his mum got to him. Or one of the locals.'

'Is dating usually a community activity around here?' He sounded entertained by the idea. She supposed the whole island was a curiosity to him – her included.

'Basically, yes.' Miranda sighed. 'Paul and I . . . we've been together for ever. After university, he could have moved away, but he came back to Seashell Island to be with me because he knew I loved it here. And his mum was thrilled – she didn't want him to move away either. Since then, he's been the sort of golden boy of the island, because he came back and made his career here – he's a lawyer, you see. He works for all the local businesses, helps everyone out when they're in a jam . . .'

'And now he wants to leave.'

'Yeah. Which doesn't seem to have gone down well with anybody. I think he was hoping to spin it as a "I'm too heartbroken to stay now that Miranda and I have split up" thing. But I might have ruined that by telling his mother that he broke up with me rather than ask me to go with him.'

'Ah. I see.' Owain frowned. 'At least, I think I see. He was trying to put the blame on *you* for him leaving? What a dick.'

That made her laugh for real. 'Yeah, I guess he is.'

'So. Are you crying because you really loved him and are heartbroken because he's leaving, or because you wasted so much time on a dick?' She looked up at his question, and saw his eyes sparkling with something almost like amusement.

'I'm sure this is hilarious to you, but this is my actual life falling apart here, you realise,' she snapped. Her boyfriend, her parents, her home . . . would there be anything left for her on this island by the end of the summer?

'Trust me, I'm not finding anything about this funny,' Owain said, wryly. 'Just familiar. I wasted a lot of years on . . . whatever the female equivalent of a dick is.'

'A dick-less?' Miranda guessed, her anger fading.

Owain grinned. 'Let's go with that.'

'So which were you?' she asked. 'Heartbroken or annoyed at the wasted time?'

'Both, for a while.' He shrugged. 'Eventually the heartbreak faded. I'm still annoyed about the time, though.'

'For me . . . it's not just losing *him*,' Miranda explained, thinking it through as she spoke. 'Christabel . . . she was right.'

'She usually is,' Owain said, sympathetically.

'It wasn't really Paul I was in love with. It was what he represented . . . my whole future. Everything I imagined happening for the next fifty, sixty, even seventy years . . . it's just gone. It's all blank now. I mean, I even had my wedding dress ready to go the minute he finally agreed to set a date.' She sighed. 'I should have known – and I'm annoyed at myself for that too. For not realising he was never going to go through with it.'

'You had faith. There's nothing wrong with having faith in a person.'

'Even the wrong person?'

'How can you know if they're right or wrong if you don't have faith in the first place?' Owain asked.

'True.'

His arm was still around her shoulder, she realised. Instinctively, she leaned back into it, soaking up the warmth of closeness even with a virtual stranger. He smelled good, too – all salt and spice, in the best sort of way.

She thought about Christabel's string of emojis, and understood them just a little bit more. Christabel had given her many things since she arrived on Seashell Island – apparently Owain was just the latest. She'd assumed he was just there to help with the Lighthouse's lack of guests problem. Now, she wondered if Christabel had been hoping for more . . .

'How did you get past it?' she asked Owain. 'The heartbreak, I mean.'

She wasn't heartbroken, exactly. Maybe heart-sprained. Or heart-cracked. A greenstick fracture of the heart she hoped she could bounce back from. Now the initial shock had faded, it didn't feel like the end of her world. More like she'd been thrown into a new one she couldn't quite see yet – as if she'd woken up in a new place and not put her glasses on yet, so everything was still blurry and indistinct, waiting to come into focus.

Owain chuckled. 'I wouldn't necessarily suggest my methods for dealing with it. I was a lot younger then.'

She shifted to look up at him. 'Sounds interesting. I definitely want to hear it now.'

'Well, my recovery plan had three stages. The first was tequila.'

Miranda laughed. 'I'd probably go for beer or wine, but I can definitely do that part.'

'The second was people. The band – Suzi and Robyn and Ryan – they're the people I'm closest to in the world these days. We know each other, understand each other. They're my . . . my safety net, I guess. They looked after me, and never complained when we spent most of the next year on the road gigging. I mean, that was what got us our record deal, so it wasn't exactly a bad move, but still. I don't think I'd have made it through without them.'

'Hmm.' She'd thought Paul had given her security, but now she thought about it, she realised that it was only the island that gave her that. Owain had found security in people, rather than a place. But otherwise they weren't so different. 'So tequila, a lot of nights on the road with the band . . . what was the third thing?'

He smirked. 'A lot of rebound sex.' His gaze met hers on the last couple of words, and suddenly the warmth of comfort turned into something considerably more combustible.

Yeah, Christabel had known *exactly* what she was doing sending Owain her way. Showing her everything else that was out there in the world. Damn her.

'Rebound sex, huh?' Her mouth was so dry the words almost wouldn't come out. She licked her lips, and tore her gaze away from his. 'Yeah, I wouldn't have thought of that as a cure.'

'It's not a cure,' Owain admitted, shifting away slightly. 'More a distraction. And like I said, I wouldn't necessarily recommend it as a healthy way of processing emotional stuff. Or the tequila either.'

'And the nights on the road with the band?'

'Oh, those I'd definitely recommend.' He smiled, and got to his feet, reaching out a hand to pull her up too. 'Good friends and great music? Can't be beaten as a cure for most things.'

'Just as well you guys are here to provide the music for me, then.' She was still holding his hand. Why was she still holding his hand? *Because it feels good. And you're still thinking about the rebound sex.*

Miranda tugged her hand away with a small smile.

'Yep. Music to mend a heartbreak, that's us. Maybe we'll even change our name. Suzi never really liked "Birchwood" anyway.' Owain opened the cottage door and stepped back out into the sunshine. 'Come on, I'd better go check on the rest of the band, before they start raiding that honesty bar of yours.'

Miranda fell into step beside him as they walked up to the Lighthouse together. And somehow, she couldn't shake the feeling that this new world was starting to sharpen up around the edges, just a little bit.

LEO

Leo had been pretty sure that waking up in a converted ambulance was the most surreal thing that was going to happen to him that day. Twenty minutes after he and the girls – and Christabel, tagging along to make sure no one fell off their bikes – returned to the Lighthouse, he had completely re-evaluated that assessment.

Finding the Lighthouse occupied by what seemed to be a folk-rock band waiting for an audience, and neither of his sisters anywhere to be seen, had only been the start. Soon, they'd all been out on the terrace tuning up, joking and laughing as they picked out melodies.

Then, as Abby and Mia settled in to beg for songs, and Christabel hugged the band like old friends before picking up a random tambourine that was lying around to join in, Juliet had arrived with Rory Hillier, of all people, and started cooking breakfast food for dinner as the music went on. Finally, Miranda had returned with a guy whose appearance gained cheers from the band as he picked up a guitar and started singing.

'Do you have any idea what's going on here?' he asked, sidling over to his big sister.

Miranda shrugged. 'I found us some guests. Well, Christabel did. And is someone cooking . . .' she sniffed. 'Pork and apple sausages?'

'How can you tell that they're the ones with apple in?

Never mind.' He shook his head and tried to focus, which would have been easier if it wasn't for the foot stamping of the beat shaking the terrace. 'Juliet's cooking the sausages. With Rory.'

Miranda's eyebrows went up at that, which Leo took to mean that at least *one* other person remembered the absolute shit show that had gone down when Juliet and Rory broke up. What the hell the guy was doing hanging around again now Leo couldn't imagine. He'd never seen a man so cut up. Well, not until Emily left him and he looked in a mirror, anyway.

But if Miranda had thoughts on that subject, she didn't share them. Instead, she nodded towards the band, as the tall, blonde woman picked up her fiddle and started to play. 'When did Christabel get here?'

Leo looked over at where Christabel was bashing the tambourine against her thigh, her hips moving to the rhythm of the guitar, her smile wide, the purple streaks in her hair flashing in the sunlight as she nodded her head to the music.

'She came back with us,' he explained, knowing even as he started that he was going to get teased mercilessly about this. That was what family did, right? 'The girls and I met her on our bike ride, and they introduced me – I understand you guys went rock-pooling the other day? Anyway, since she owns that bike repair ambulance thing, she was able to help us when I . . . had a few problems with my bike.'

Miranda shot him an innocent look. 'What sort of problems?'

Damn her, she was going to make him say it. 'I crashed. Into her bike ambulance. Because I was looking at my phone.'

Miranda's lips twitched as she obviously tried to hold in a smile. 'Poor baby. Did Christabel kiss it better for you? Because I'll be honest, I have warned her off you.'

'That's not what she said. She said you said she was perfect for me.'

'Yeah, but for Christabel that's the same thing. Tell her she should do something and she instantly does the opposite. So no kisses better?'

'Sadly not. But she did fix my bike.'

'I should probably warn you off her too,' Miranda mused. 'I mean, I love her and she's a brilliant friend, and actually I *do* think she'd be good for you. But she doesn't stay, and I'd hate the girls to get all attached and think she was going to be around for ever.'

'Don't worry,' Leo said, his mood souring slightly. 'I am under no impression that anyone would want to stick with me long term.' If he couldn't make it work with Emily, who he'd loved more than anything, then what chance did he have with anyone else?

Leo turned his attention back to the performance on the terrace, although he didn't bother watching the actual band. Not the guy with the guitar, singing about heartbreak, or the gorgeous, tall blonde with the fiddle, or even the cute redhead with some other stringed instrument he didn't recognise.

He just watched Christabel, and how she came alive in the music. And he watched his daughters, watching her and beaming, wiggling where they sat until Christabel pulled them up to dance with her, twirling in the afternoon sunlight.

Who *was* she? An ex-hedge-fund manager who decided to fix bikes for a living instead? Who lived in an *ambulance*? Who did that?

Whoever she was, Leo knew he wanted to get to know her better. And, watching Abby and Mia spin under her arms as they danced, he knew they'd enjoy that too.

Emily had Mark, and the kids loved him. Maybe it was time he found someone his girls loved being with, too. Someone who could help him show them he was still a real, important part of their family. Still their dad.

'You're staring,' Miranda said, pointedly. 'A lot.'

'I'm watching my girls dance,' Leo objected.

Miranda rolled her eyes. 'Sure you are.'

'So wait. *You* rented these guys rooms?' For some reason, he'd figured this had to be Juliet. It was such a Juliet thing to do — let a band take over the whole B&B — and she'd been so adamant about looking after the Lighthouse in their parents' absence.

'Christabel knew they were looking for a place to stay, somewhere out of town so they could practise in peace. It seemed made to be. So she messaged them and they came.' Miranda shrugged. 'Hey. Speaking of our little sister, want to go check how Juliet's getting on in the kitchen?'

'No.'

'Please.'

Leo gave her a sideways look. 'You do it if it matters so much to you.'

Miranda huffed an impatient sigh. 'What are we? Twelve again?'

'You're the one asking me to do your chores for you.'

'I am not! I was asking you to check on our sister, who clearly has something going on she's not telling us about or she wouldn't be on Seashell Island in the first place.'

There, at least, Leo had to admit Miranda had a point. 'She hasn't told you why she's here yet?'

Miranda shook her head. 'You?'

'Not even a hint. Well, maybe one,' he amended, remembering that strange, secretive but excited conversation with Juliet in London, a month or more ago.

'What did she say?' Miranda pressed.

'Nothing, just . . . when I saw her in London last month, she said she'd have something exciting to tell me soon. Then last night I asked if this meant it hadn't come off and she kind of shrugged and nodded.'

'You don't know what it was, though?'

'No idea.' Leo shrugged. 'I guessed it was maybe a promotion?'

'Or a new boyfriend.' Sighing, Miranda leaned back against the terrace railing. 'But whichever it is, you know she won't talk to me about it.'

Which Leo had to admit was a fair point. 'She might not talk to me about it either, you realise.' It had to be something pretty bad for Juliet to decide to hide out on Seashell Island.

'So you won't even try?'

'I didn't say that.' Although, if he was honest, he didn't really want to. Not because he didn't love his sister, or because he didn't want to help her. But because he'd had the same conversation so many times already. There were only so many times he could tell her that there'd be another opportunity around the corner, or that the right person would come along eventually.

Not to mention that it would mean walking into a kitchen with Rory and Juliet in it, and he was still mentally scarred from the last time he did that.

At least this time the odds were better on them both being clothed.

Miranda sighed. 'Maybe it's better to wait until the morning, when there's less going on around here.'

'The morning sounds good.' Or never. Never sounded pretty good too.

She gave him a sceptical look, like she'd heard the second

half of his thoughts, then pushed away from the railings and headed towards the terrace. As she drew closer to the band, he saw Christabel grab her arm and say something that made his sister laugh in a way he didn't remember seeing for years. What was it about this woman that brought out things in people they'd thought were hidden?

Whatever it was, Miranda said something back and then headed towards the kitchen, still smiling, and sharing another snatched conversation he couldn't make out with the band's frontman on the way. He wondered if the fact Christabel had sent the band to them meant that they were part of her big plan to help Miranda find her focus and path in life. Probably.

'Daddy! Come and dance!' Abby twirled across the terrace and caught his fingers, trying to drag him over to where Christabel was still dancing like no one was watching, even though he really, really was. Mia, on the other hand, hung back.

'Daddy doesn't dance, Abs,' she said, taking her sister's hand. 'Come on.' She led her back across the terrace, to where Christabel was dancing with the guitarist.

Leo stared after them. Mia was right: he didn't dance. Emily had always hated that he'd never dance with her, not at weddings, parties or even in bars and clubs. She'd danced with her friends, but never with him. He just didn't have the rhythm.

But suddenly, a strange, new part of his heart wanted to dance. With his daughters.

With Christabel.

For a moment he stood, torn between clinging to the terrace rail and the cool detachment he normally cultivated — which, to be fair, had already been ruined by his bike crash that morning — and giving in to the impulse to move to the beat.

Then, before he could decide, his back pocket started vibrating and he whipped out his phone automatically.

Tom, the screen read.

With a last, apologetic smile in the direction of the dancers, he stepped down off the terrace and onto the grass below, searching for a quiet spot in which to take the call.

There'd be other chances to dance, anyway.

JULIET

'You don't have to stay, you know.' Juliet cracked an egg into the pan, then held her hand out for another one.

Rory passed it over bang on cue, like they'd been doing this for years, rather than minutes. 'And you don't have to cook breakfast for your guests at dinner time, but here we are.'

Juliet shrugged. 'Miranda, Leo and the girls need feeding anyway. And, as much as it might surprise you, I actually *like* cooking. When I get the chance.'

That made him raise his eyebrows. Probably because the girl he'd known had complained endlessly about everything she had to do at the Lighthouse – even the parts she enjoyed, like cooking. Admittedly, when she'd left the island, a full English was about the only thing she *could* cook. But she'd had to learn, out in the world by herself and not wanting to live on bacon and eggs, especially when she was starting out and couldn't afford takeaways or ready meals that didn't taste like cat food. So she'd actually *used* the cookery book for students Miranda had given her when she left – not that she'd ever admit it – and learned the basics. Once she realised that she could feed herself better and cheaper by making meals herself, it had become a bit of a hobby, even before she started working in the industry.

But usually, she'd only been cooking for herself, or maybe her current boyfriend or flatmate too. Never breakfast for nine. Ten, if she counted that woman who'd arrived with Leo. Eleven if Rory stayed, too.

'Do you think we have enough sausages?' she asked. She'd picked the pork and apple ones, because she knew they were Miranda's favourite, and it meant she could save the more traditional breakfast ones for actual breakfast another day. Maybe she'd do pancakes in the morning, with crispy bacon and maple syrup, or blueberries and yogurt.

'You have plenty,' Rory assured her. 'And I'll bring more in the morning.'

She glanced up from the egg frying perfectly in her pan. 'You don't have to do that.'

'I know,' he said, simply. 'And I think that egg's done.'

He was right. Juliet hurriedly flipped it out onto the waiting plate and put it back in the warmer, then reached for another to fill the space in her pan.

'Why are you?' she asked, after a moment of nothing but the sizzle of frying fat. 'Helping me, I mean?'

She didn't look at his face as he answered. If she was honest with herself, she was almost afraid of what she might see there. 'Because it's you.'

She bit her lip. Rory had told her he wouldn't get any ideas, right? She risked a glance. There was no lust, no hope in Rory's expression. No slight leer of suggestiveness, like she'd have expected in Callum's.

Instead, he looked . . . resigned? As if this was just the way the world worked, and he was going along with it against his better judgement.

'Well . . . thank you.'

She wanted to say more, although she had no idea what. And even if she'd been able to find the words, there wasn't the time because at that moment the kitchen door swung open, letting in a blast of music, laughter, and Miranda.

'How are things going in here? Are those the pork and apple sausages? They're my favourite.'

'They are! And they're just about ready,' Juliet said, sliding the last egg onto the sausage bap waiting for it.

'Brilliant! I'll help you take them out.' Miranda crossed the kitchen and gave Rory a hug, leaving Juliet looking on in astonishment. 'Hey, Rory.'

Since when had her sister been on hugging terms with her ex-boyfriend? Not that she'd have noticed, Juliet had to admit. She always tried to avoid the town when she was on the island. Her visits were always so fleeting, it was easiest just to head straight up to the Lighthouse and stay there until it was time to catch the foot ferry. It wasn't even Rory in particular she was avoiding, just everyone. Everyone who'd want to know how life was on the mainland, who'd judge her based on who she'd been when she lived there, and everything she'd said she wanted to achieve and then hadn't.

Not having to face Rory had just been a blessed side effect. But of course Miranda would have seen him. His restaurant was only a stone's throw from her office. And in winter, the population of Seashell Island contracted so much that if one person started ignoring another they'd lose a significant proportion of their human interactions.

She just hadn't thought about it. Hadn't thought about how Rory's life would have gone on without her. But it obviously had. And far more successfully than hers had gone without him.

It was a thought that occupied her mind as they took the food out onto the terrace, and the band stopped playing long enough to demolish it. Given the way they'd been hitting the honesty bar, Juliet had to admit providing them with food had been self-preservation.

Suzi, the redhead who played what Juliet had learned

tonight was called a bouzouki, sidled up with a mouthful of dinner to thank her. 'Pretty sure supper wasn't in the B&B tariff Owain agreed with your sister. But it's appreciated all the same!'

Juliet shrugged. 'It's nice to see the place full of life again.'

And it was, she realised as she said it. Over the last few years when she'd visited, guest numbers had definitely been dwindling. Growing up, she remembered the place packed with visiting families and holidaymakers bringing tales of the outside world – or so it seemed to her – and other kids to play with. Kids who went to schools with thousands of other pupils, not less than a hundred. Kids with trains into the city or huge concert arenas or actual *things to do*.

Those were the visitors who had inspired her to leave in the first place.

Her gaze roamed around the terrace, taking in the new life they'd brought to the Lighthouse. Leo was nowhere to be seen, but Abby and Mia were having a brilliant time chatting with the band and Christabel. Robyn and Ryan seemed to be competing for who could eat the most sausages in a bap, which seemed particularly unfair given their slender forms. And Miranda and the band's lead singer, Owain, were leaning companionably on the terrace, heads close as they chatted.

Maybe, Juliet thought, as she watched Miranda laugh out loud at something Owain had said, bringing life back to the place could be good for all of them.

Not drinking had its benefits, Juliet decided, when she awoke first the following morning. While it took a moment for her to start feeling human, it wasn't anything like the full day procedure a hangover required. Later, the erroneously named morning sickness would kick in, probably around mid-afternoon, but for now she felt pretty good.

And hungry.

It had been long after midnight when they'd all finally crashed into their beds. Rory had stayed and chatted to Leo when he'd returned from wherever he'd gone to take some vital phone call, then disappeared without saying goodbye, leaving Juliet feeling vaguely out of sorts for the rest of the night.

It wasn't as if she'd imagined she'd slip back into Rory's life after a decade away. But at the same time, it was unsettling to feel almost like a stranger – or, at best, an acquaintance – of someone who'd been such a big part of her childhood and growing up.

Resolving not to dwell on the Rory situation, Juliet decided to focus on something she *could* fix. In this case, breakfast.

Pancakes. That was the answer to everything this morning. With bacon and syrup and fruit and fresh orange juice. If that didn't wake people up, nothing would.

She hummed to herself as she bustled around the kitchen, sifting flour and breaking eggs and setting the old-fashioned coffee-maker, the one without environmentally unfriendly pods, bubbling away. In fact, she was so focused on the task at hand, she didn't hear the footsteps on the stairs, or her sister arriving in the kitchen.

'I had no idea you liked cooking so much.'

Juliet jumped at the sound of her voice. 'God! When did you get here?'

'Just now.' Filling her coffee cup, Miranda leaned against the table watching her. 'You make pancakes as well as a full English now?'

'And many other things.' Juliet tried not to sound annoyed. 'I mean, food, cooking . . . it kind of went with the job.'

Miranda frowned. 'With temping? How?'

'I haven't been temping for three years, Miri,' Juliet said, frustrated. Although, given how little attention she'd apparently given to what had been going on here on Seashell Island, perhaps she shouldn't feel so resentful that her sister cared so little about what went on off it. 'I worked for a company that specialises in promoting up-and-coming food brands. I was in charge of organising all sorts of street-food events and stuff.' She caught herself and stopped, hoping Miranda wouldn't have noticed her use of the past tense.

'That sounds fun.'

'Yes, it is.' Or it had been, until she screwed it up by screwing the boss. 'I got to sample all sorts of world foods, as well as talk with chefs and cooks from around the globe. Plus it turns out I'm actually pretty good at the organising side of things. Making sure things get done.'

Miranda waved her coffee mug towards the fridge. 'I guess that explains your sudden conversion to the way of the rota.'

'It all needs doing.'

'It does.' Miranda peered closer at the rota. Juliet tried to pretend she wasn't watching her, but she was. She wanted to know what she thought. After all this time, apparently she was still desperate for her big sister's approval. 'And it looks good. I notice you've given yourself most of the breakfast cooking duties.'

Juliet shrugged. 'Like I said, I enjoy cooking. It's soothing.'

She'd meant it as an innocuous comment, but Miranda gave her a sharp look.

'And there's something going on in your life right now that you need soothing about? That's why you're here on the island, and not in London organising street-food festivals?'

Damn.

Juliet considered her answer carefully. Odds were, whatever she'd said Miranda would eventually twist it round to her motivations for coming home. It wasn't like she hadn't known this conversation was coming. And she'd deal with it the same way she'd always dealt with Miranda – by attacking, not defending. But not like she had as a moody teen, with ranting and yelling. Like an adult, who deserved to be part of the conversation.

Because she *was* an adult now, even if she didn't always feel like it.

'Speaking of things going on in our lives, why didn't you tell me you and Paul split up?' she asked, as neutrally and calmly as she could.

Miranda tensed and froze. 'Rory told you?' she said after a long pause.

Juliet nodded. 'Apparently it's all anyone in town is talking about.'

'Of course it is.' Miranda swore under her breath, and Juliet's eyes widened. Had she ever heard her perfect older sister swear before? She wasn't sure.

'What happened?' Juliet asked. 'I mean, if you want to talk about it. Rory said there were a million different versions going around.'

'Yeah.' Sighing, Miranda put down her cup and hopped up onto the kitchen stool beside her.

Turning down the hob as the last of the bacon finished frying, Juliet flipped the pancake in the second pan – and then reached for the jug of fresh orange juice in the fridge, pouring her sister a large glass. Vitamin C was important, and always helped with a hangover.

Miranda smiled gratefully and took a large gulp.

'You don't have to tell me if you don't want to,' Juliet said, suddenly feeling guilty for putting her sister on the spot. 'I know we're not the girly-talk and secrets kind of sisters.' She'd always had her friends for that. And Miranda had had . . . well, Paul, she supposed. Miranda and Paul had got together when Juliet was only nine or ten. She barely remembered a time before Paul was joining them for Sunday lunches and summer barbecues.

But if Miranda didn't have Paul any longer, she was going to need someone else to talk to. Why not her sister? Especially if listening to Miranda meant that Juliet could avoid spilling her own secrets for a little longer.

'There's not really much to tell,' Miranda said after another sip of juice. 'We wanted different things. He got offered a job on the mainland. He wants to take it. And he knew I wouldn't leave the island to go with him, so he broke up with me instead.'

Juliet winced at the matter-of-fact description of the evaporation of a nineteen-year-long relationship. 'Did you think about going with him?'

'Not for a moment.' Miranda's smile was sad as she answered. 'Oh, and I lost my job, too. Just to round out a really rubbish few days.'

'Oh God! Miranda!' It looked like Juliet wasn't the only Waters sibling getting screwed by life right now.

'It's OK. I mean, it would have been weird, still working for Paul's dad. And I've been doing a lot of VA work on the side. I can step that up, build up a real business there. Plus moving back home means no rent payments.' Miranda shrugged. 'Things could be worse.'

Of course she had a plan. Had Miranda ever not had a plan? But Juliet knew that the one thing you couldn't plan for was matters of the heart.

'Are you . . . I mean, never mind the job thing. You and Paul had been together for ever. You must be heartbroken.'

It took Miranda a few moments to answer. Then she said, 'My friend Christabel – you met her last night, right? – she says I was only with him because he gave me an excuse to stay here.'

And wasn't that how it had always been, Juliet mused as she slid the perfectly cooked pancake onto a plate with the others and ladled another spoon of batter into the pan. She couldn't wait to leave, and Miranda couldn't be dragged away from Seashell Island. No wonder they'd never been able to find any common ground; they were just too different.

Juliet remembered Christabel, dancing in the moonlight the night before. 'Huh. She sounds like a good friend.'

'She is.'

'I'm glad. Everyone needs good friends.'

Although, right now, Juliet wasn't sure who she'd count as hers. Tanya, back in London, she supposed. But here on the island, who did she have to confide in? Rory had been her closest friend since she was a child, but of course there was too much distance and history there now. And all her school friends had drifted away, lost touch, as they made their own lives on the island.

Or, in truth, she'd pulled away from them. They didn't fit the new, exciting life she'd planned for herself in London, so she'd dropped them and left them behind.

But she *did* have her siblings. Miranda had talked to her, told her what was going on in her life, like she was a fellow adult for maybe the first time. Was it just because she'd come home to Seashell Island at last? Had she just never spent enough time here before to try and build this kind of grown-up relationship with her sister?

Was this summer finally her chance to try?

MESSAGES

Miranda (to Christabel): I thought you were staying well away from my brother . . . ? Also, you could have given me a heads up about Owain!

Christabel: I know, I know. But you know me and hopeless cases . . . why do you think I've stuck with you for so long?

Miranda: And Owain?

Christabel: He's another hopeless case. You two are a perfect fit.

MIRANDA

Miranda woke on Friday morning to sun streaming through her open curtains, her head pounding from Juliet's generous glasses of wine over a delicious seafood paella dinner the night before, and music still ringing in her ears from the impromptu concert they'd had afterwards. It seemed that every night was a party at the Lighthouse these days. And even the days were more exciting – there was always something delicious cooking in the kitchen, and the sound of laughter and music coming from the other rooms. The place felt *alive* again, in a way it hadn't since her parents left.

She smiled.

Last night had been fun – from the band playing to Juliet cooking and the silly guessing game Suzi had insisted they all play in pairs or threes once the girls were in bed. She'd been on Owain's team, and they'd smashed the competition. Yes, it had been lots of fun, all the way to the moment, right at the end of the night, when she'd said goodnight to Owain at his bedroom door before climbing the stairs to her own, childhood room. For a moment, he'd swayed forward towards her, and all she could hear in her head was *rebound sex, rebound sex*, on a loop. Then he'd smiled that slow, lazy smile of his and wished her sweet dreams, before disappearing behind his door.

It had taken a full ten minutes for Miranda's heart rate to return to normal. And even now, remembering it made her feel warmer than the blanket and sunshine really warranted.

She should get up. She needed to get to— no. She didn't.

Almost a whole week into her new routine and she still wasn't used to it. Maybe because things had been so busy at the B&B, and she'd been throwing herself into developing her VA business, while also helping Leo with the girls. Every morning, her new reality still took her by surprise.

She didn't have to go to work. She didn't have to put on her former personal uniform of skirt, top and cardigan with trainers that she switched for heels when she got to the office. She didn't need to follow the same morning routine she'd honed and adhered to for too many years now. She didn't have to think about the office email inbox, or if there was milk in the fridge for Nigel's coffee.

She could do whatever she wanted.

And so, for a moment each morning, she lay back and revelled in that fact all over again.

Then, usually, she realised she should probably get up and help Juliet with the breakfasts for the band, and see what else she was on the rota for today. It wasn't like her days had got any less busy since she left Seashell Holiday Cottages – just more fun.

Slipping out of bed, she crossed to the window, the same way she had every morning she'd spent in this room, to take in the view of her island. From her attic room at the top of the house, she could see all the way across to the sea, sparkling in the early morning sun. Next to that, the high street, with only the roofs of the candy-coloured buildings on show, and the harbour, with the boats bobbing at high tide. Then up through the houses of the town, some holiday cottages, some for locals, all the way to Max and Dafydd's farm next door, right to the gardens of the Lighthouse, with their seat swing, rose beds and—

Miranda squinted, even though she already had her glasses on.

Llama?

There definitely hadn't been a llama in the garden when she'd gone to bed. She hadn't had *that* much wine.

Washing and dressing hurriedly in jeans and a T-shirt, she made her way downstairs to find Juliet stirring her delicious breakfast muffin mix in the kitchen.

'Did you look out the window yet this morning?'

Juliet looked up from her bowl, wooden spoon still in hand. 'No. Why?'

Miranda pointed to the nearest window. Juliet put down the bowl and crossed to it, dripping muffin batter from her spoon the whole way.

'Oh! Is that an alpaca?' Juliet beamed. 'He's gorgeous!'

'She,' Miranda corrected. 'If I'm right, that is Lucy the Llama from Max and Dafydd's farm. She has form on the escaping thing.'

'Lucy! That's a lovely name.' Juliet smiled soppily at the creature through the glass.

Lucy stared back, impassively.

'It's short for Lucifer,' Miranda told her, but Juliet didn't seem to care.

'We should take her some food! Do you think llamas like muffins?'

'We should take her back to the farm,' Miranda said, firmly. Unfortunately, her firmness was undermined by Abby and Mia running in, still in their pyjamas, and squealing.

'Oh my gosh, is that a llama!' Mia, for the first time since her arrival, seemed truly excited. Joyous, even. Miranda had been sure that Mia was taking her mother's remarriage badly, given her recent moods, but apparently a llama was a universal cure-all. Even Juliet seemed to have forgotten whatever it was that had driven her to the island – although Miranda hadn't forgotten that her sister had distracted her from that question once already with the knowledge of her own current issues.

'How lovely!' Miranda turned at her brother's overly jolly tone. Surely *Leo* wasn't enamoured with stinky half-camels too? 'Why don't the two of you go outside with your aunts and meet Lucy?'

Over their heads, he held up his mobile and pointed towards the office, miming taking some calls and then typing.

Of course. He was going to work and leave her with his daughters, their sister and a llama to deal with. Never mind that *she* had work to do too. She'd realised pretty quickly that if she wasn't going to have the income from working at Seashell Holiday Cottages any longer, she definitely needed to start hustling on the virtual assistant side of her business. Not to mention getting the Lighthouse back up to speed with Juliet, who had many grand plans for the B&B and would probably want to start all of them at once if Miranda wasn't there to plan things sensibly with her.

She opened her mouth to object, but Leo was already gone, the girls were halfway through the door, and Lucy was just staring at them all, as if this was totally normal.

'Right. Let's go get this llama home, then.'

Of course, it wasn't as simple as that – not least because Abby and Mia were desperate to keep it for ever, and Juliet wouldn't let it go until she'd given it some blueberries. Miranda overruled her on that one, at least until Max and Dafydd could confirm what llamas ate.

'If we take her back now, I'll ask Max and Dafydd if we can go visit her sometime soon, OK?' Miranda said to the girls and a disappointed Juliet. 'We'll take the right food and everything.'

There were a few mutinous grumblings, but the girls were eventually lured back inside by the promise of Juliet's savoury muffins with a side of sausages. Miranda descended from the terrace and looked Lucy in the eyes.

'OK, so here's what's going to happen, Lucifer. You and me are going to take a little walk back through the fields to your nice warm . . . stable? I don't know. Your own field, anyway. And before you destroy my mum's flowerbeds.'

'Are you talking to the llama?' Owain's voice was warm and amused in the morning air.

Great. Because what this morning needed was an extra layer of embarrassment to add to the madness.

'I'm trying to persuade her to go home,' she explained, turning to face him.

Owain shrugged, like that was a perfectly reasonable thing to do on a Friday morning, then hopped down from the terrace to join her. 'Want some help?'

It took a lot of cajoling, but eventually between them they managed to get Lucy moving, just as Miranda finally got hold of Max on his mobile and told him what was going on.

'Max and Dafydd – the llama's owners – are going to walk over and meet us.' She shoved her phone back in her pocket. 'Let's see how far we can get her before they find us.'

'So, does this sort of thing happen often on Seashell Island?' Owain asked, as they shepherded Lucy in approximately the right direction.

Miranda laughed. 'Definitely not. Well, not until last week, when I had to help Max and Dafydd catch her on the beach when she arrived.'

'Understandably, she seems to have taken a shine to you.' Owain gave what Miranda could only think of as a flirtatious smile, and she couldn't help but return it.

They walked in companionable silence through the fields and the early morning sunshine for a few minutes, before Owain said, 'You know, I think one of the things I like most about Seashell Island is how many unexpected things have happened to me since I arrived.'

'Honestly? I like it for the exact opposite reason,' she admitted.

'Nothing unusual ever happens to you?' he asked, disbelief in his voice. 'Not even llama-walking before breakfast?'

She laughed. 'Fine. Nothing unusual ever happened to me until Lucy arrived on the island.' *And you.*

Because since she chased that damn llama across the beach, everything about her life seemed to have changed. But it was Owain arriving with his band, making every night a party and saying *rebound sex* that had seemed to open a hundred new possibilities on the island for her.

They made it halfway across the field before Miranda spotted her neighbours waving madly over the low stone wall that marked the boundary between the properties. Relief seeped through Miranda's body. She hadn't relished the idea of trying to get Lucy all the way to the farm – even if she *was* enjoying Owain's company while they did it.

'Thanks, Miranda,' Dafydd said, as Max slipped a harness around Lucy's neck. 'I don't know how she got out. Unless she's learned to open gates with her hooves.'

'I wouldn't put it past her,' Max muttered, darkly. Harness on, he handed the reins to Dafydd, and turned to Miranda. 'Actually, I was going to pop over to talk to you this morning anyway.'

'Oh? What about?' Generally, Max and Dafydd kept to themselves – when they weren't retrieving llamas. Unless they had friends who wanted to hire a holiday cottage, or stay at the B&B, Miranda couldn't imagine what they might want from her. And given the size of the farmhouse they lived in, and how lovingly they'd restored it, that seemed unlikely.

'I spoke with my mate Tudor over on the mainland, this last week – you know, the one with the hog-roast stall? He said that he was sad not to have been asked over for the Lighthouse Festival this year, and it got me thinking. The festival's still happening, right? I mean, Josie and Iestyn will be back for it? Only, if you want to have the best stalls and such there, they really should have been booked by now. Tudor's already booked up through until Halloween, you know.' Max looked anxious and apologetic. And suddenly, Miranda wondered how many other locals were asking the same questions.

The Lighthouse Festival was an island institution, marking the end of the summer season and the slow slide towards winter, when the locals mostly only had each other for company and entertainment. One last hurrah before the nights drew in. And one last chance for them all to make money from the extra tourists it brought in, not ready to say goodbye to summer yet.

She dreaded to think of the island's reaction if it didn't happen this year.

'I'm sure Mum and Dad are on top of it,' she lied, smiling reassuringly. She'd text them when she got home, check what plans they'd made. Surely they wouldn't have just *forgotten* about it, would they?

'So, tell me more about this Lighthouse Festival,' Owain said, as they started back to the B&B, leaving Max and Dafydd to wrangle Lucy the rest of the way home. 'Because it sounds like it might be another unexpected thing to add to my list. Does it feature a petting zoo? Because if so, I know just the llama. Hardly spits at all, except when you put a harness on her.'

Miranda laughed. 'No petting zoo. At least, not so far. But then it's been growing every year . . . well, until now.'

Owain took her arm to help her over the stile across the low stone wall. 'Then this year it clearly needs a petting zoo.'

'Maybe.' If it happened at all. Time to change the subject, she decided. 'So, how's the album-writing going, anyway?'

Owain groaned, and launched into a long and involved monologue about artistic differences, broken strings, and whether or not every album needed a protest song that had her in giggles all the way back to the Lighthouse.

LEO

Just over a week later, Lucy the Llama had appeared in the Lighthouse garden nine times, Juliet had cooked what had to be a million breakfast muffins and pancakes, Miranda had got a bee in her bonnet about something to do with their parents' traditional end-of-summer festival that Leo was hoping he could ignore, and Leo had 127 emails flagged for urgent response in his inbox.

He'd been trying to make inroads into them that morning, while the girls ate yet more pancakes for breakfast and watched Miranda and Owain try to return Lucy all over again, but even those things were losing their ability to hold his daughters' attention. Soon, they'd need entertaining again, and he was running out of ideas of how to do it.

They'd been out on bikes, again, and he'd managed to stay on this time, which was just as well as they hadn't seen Christabel that day. Most other days, though, she seemed to find a reason to join them – or he and the girls sought her out. She'd come over for a jam session with the band one evening, regularly turned up in time for one of Juliet's delicious dinners, and even ended up playing French cricket in the garden with them on Wednesday. They'd played board games when it rained, been for ice cream at the ice-cream parlour in town (whose Wi-Fi was *not* all it was advertised to be). They'd even built sandcastles and gone rock-pooling.

Not that Abby and Mia seemed to appreciate his efforts

– and he knew that Tom and his clients didn't. That nagging red spot on his email icon on his replacement phone with its 99+ reminded him every time he looked at the uncracked screen. And the girls, well, they cheated mercilessly every time he had to go take a phone call during Monopoly, and he kept coming back to find himself in jail. They'd even looked morose eating their ice cream when he'd looked in through the window from the call he was taking. And Mia had almost knocked his phone into a rock pool on the beach.

No, summer was not going exactly as he'd hoped, no matter how late he let them stay up, or how much sugar he gave them.

It didn't help that Christabel's words about building a relationship with the girls kept echoing around his head. It was all good in theory, but how was he supposed to do it in practice – without letting his business collapse?

A rapid knock on the door made him look up, to find Juliet hanging on the doorframe. She looked better than she had done when she arrived, Leo decided, if not quite back to her normal sparkling self. Hopefully, whatever disaster had befallen her in London would pass without them even having to talk it out.

'Are you coming?' she asked, a little breathlessly.

'Where?' Leo frowned. 'If this has to do with that damn llama again—'

'Miranda and Owain are taking her back right now, much to Mia's disappointment. I think she was hoping we could take Lucy down to the beach with us for the kite festival.'

The Seashell Island Kite Festival. 'That's today?' How many festivals did one tiny island need? Still, if the girls were watching the kites, he might manage to answer some emails on his phone without losing it in the sea . . .

'Starting now,' Juliet confirmed. 'Miranda's meeting us

down there, everyone here's been fed and the girls have helped me make up the rooms – which was *your* job on the rota, incidentally – so we're all ready to go. Come on!'

One surprising thing, Leo thought as he changed into shorts and grabbed a couple of beach towels from the stack in the airing cupboard, was how well Juliet had taken to running the B&B. Given how much she'd always despised it growing up – complaining about having to make the beds, about having strangers in their house, about how it meant they could never go away – she seemed perfectly happy to be trapped there with a whole band's worth of strangers plus a lot of beds to make this summer. He brushed away the possibility that maybe that meant whatever was going on in London was worse than he thought, and headed down to find the girls.

The beach was packed with people and kites. At one end, a large section had been roped off for displays, with a team currently showcasing several of a special sort of swallow kite that dived and rose and danced in synchronicity with each other, all in time to the music blasting out from the speakers on the harbour. Further down the sand were food vans, stands selling kites, charity stalls and a few small rides for the kids. Families and groups had laid out picnic blankets to sit and watch the kites while having some lunch. At the other end of the beach were the amateur kite flyers – a whole sea of strings stretching up towards the blue sky, blotted with kites in the shape of birds, fish, dragons, ghosts, or just the traditional diamonds and triangles.

'Can we buy a kite?' Mia asked, as they made their way past the stalls to find a place for the picnic blanket Juliet was carrying.

'Of course!' Juliet said, before Leo could say no. 'It's not a kite festival if you don't fly a kite.'

So apparently he was buying a kite today. Who knew?

Juliet lay out the blanket in the fifth space they found, although Leo had no idea what had been wrong with the other four. As they all settled down to watch the kite display, Leo took in the crowds around them. He recognised hardly anybody – probably because the locals were all working, and the people attending the kite festival were tourists. Like them, he supposed.

Maybe that was why Juliet had always liked the kite festival. Only people who didn't plan to live on the island attended.

'This is incredible,' Mia said, leaning back on her hands as she took in the festival.

'It's fun,' Leo agreed, fishing his phone from his pocket to check his emails.

Suddenly a new voice added, 'It is. But nothing compared to the Lighthouse Festival your grandparents throw every year.' Beside him, Juliet froze. Leo looked up to find Rory Hillier smiling down at them, holding a plastic tray full of burgers and hot dogs. 'Thought you guys looked hungry,' he said, placing the tray on their picnic blanket.

'Thanks,' Leo said, since Juliet clearly wasn't going to. 'What do we owe you?'

'On the house,' Rory replied. 'Since the Lighthouse B&B is my best customer right now. Guess that band of yours love a full English, right?'

'Thanks.' Leo nudged the girls and they both echoed the sentiment. Juliet still said nothing.

'My pleasure,' Rory said, pointedly not looking at Juliet. Then he headed back to a food stall named 'The Flying Fish'.

Juliet, Leo noticed, watched him go. And suddenly things started to make sense.

179

'What's the Lighthouse Festival?' Abby asked, around a mouthful of hot dog.

'Grandma and Grandad throw this big party for everyone on the island at the end of summer,' Mia told her younger sister knowledgably. Then she shot a glare at Leo. 'We're never allowed to stay for it.'

'That's because your mum always said it was too close to the end of the summer holidays, or sometimes even after you'd started back at school,' Leo explained, throwing Emily to the wolves for a change. Finally, something that wasn't his fault. 'It's not until the first weekend in September.'

'Mum's not here this year,' Mia said, her gaze suddenly calculating.

'And the first of September is a Saturday,' Juliet added, unhelpfully.

'Grandma and Grandad aren't even on the island this summer,' Leo stalled. 'And I'd planned to be back in London before September.' His words did nothing to stop the beseeching looks his daughters were giving him. Juliet, a smile hovering around her lips, copied the look.

Leo knew when he was defeated. 'Fine. If the festival happens this summer, we can stay for it.' Miranda had been muttering something about having to cancel it, he was almost sure, so the odds were good he wouldn't even have to make good on his promise. It was a win–win. Especially given the way the girls squealed with excitement.

Finally he'd done something they liked.

'Can we go watch the kites?' Mia asked, shoving the last of her hot dog into her mouth.

Leo glanced over at the barrier to the display ground. Not too far away, easy to see . . . what would Emily say?

'Just make sure you stay where we can see you,' he

decided. Mia grabbed her little sister's hand and pulled her up, still holding her hot dog.

'Come on, Abby!'

Leo craned to watch them weave through the picnic blankets, before stopping right by the display ground, in full sight. Good.

And then it was just him and his sister.

Juliet reached for a burger from the tray, not catching his eye. And Leo was almost certain that he knew why. Maybe Miranda was right. Maybe it was time to talk to his baby sister about what was going on with her this summer. Even if it was only to do a little light teasing.

'So. Rory.' Leo raised an eyebrow. 'Bringing us free food. And he's been up to the Lighthouse every other day for the last couple of weeks, making deliveries . . . He wouldn't happen to be the reason you're back on Seashell Island, would he?'

Juliet's eyes widened. 'What? No! He delivers the food because that's his job, Leo.'

'Are you sure? I mean, he must have staff who could do that for him,' Leo pointed out. 'And besides, I can't think of any other reason you'd want to come back here, to be honest.' Not that he'd given it a huge amount of thought, in between everything else.

'Unless I was so desperate for a boyfriend I decided to trawl the graveyard of terrible teenage relationships that is Seashell Island?' she shot back.

Leo winced, as he saw that Rory had come up behind her. 'Just . . . came for the tray. I'll come back.'

'Shit.' Juliet spun round looking for him – rather proving Leo's point, he thought – but he was already halfway through the crowd, heading back to the Flying Fish stall.

'You're not strengthening your argument,' Leo pointed out.

'You think I don't know that?' Juliet muttered.

'Lucy the Llama is back on the farm. Again.' Miranda dropped to sit on the edge of the picnic blanket, and motioned to Owain, who was standing beside her, to do the same.

'I really should get back to the guys. We're supposed to be working on a new song Suzi's written . . .' Owain said, but Leo could tell he was wavering. What hold his sister had over this guy he had no idea, but he had to admit that Christabel might have been on to something, introducing the two of them.

'We have burgers.' Juliet pointed to the tray, where a couple of cooling burgers remained. 'Courtesy of the Flying Fish.'

'And Rory,' Leo added with a meaningful look in Miranda's direction.

Miranda's eyebrows raised, and she turned to look at Juliet. 'Really.'

Owain, bandmates apparently forgotten, sat and took a burger. 'Who's Rory?'

'Juliet's first love,' Miranda explained, still staring at her. 'Whose heart she completely and utterly trampled on when she left, to the point where he didn't date for three years.'

Juliet winced, which Leo thought was the least she could do. God, the guy had been a mess.

'He's the guy over at the Flying Fish stall who is blatantly staring at Juliet right now,' he added cheerfully. 'The one with the big, sad eyes.'

'Do you have any siblings, Owain?' Juliet asked.

'Thankfully, no.' He gave her a sympathetic look. Juliet looked like she'd decided she liked Owain better than any of her relatives, right now. Leo thought that it was about time they got some payback for all the times they'd bailed her out of trouble in the past.

'All we're saying is, be careful with Rory,' Miranda said, in her best big sister voice. 'You really hurt him last time.'

'I know,' Juliet whispered, not looking at any of them.

'Auntie Miri! Did Dad tell you? He's going to let us stay for the Lighthouse Festival this year!' Mia and Abby threw themselves back down onto the picnic blanket with more glee than Leo thought he'd felt all year. How did they still have so much energy? How were they not as exhausted as him? Although, now he looked at them, Mia was looking a little pale.

Miranda shot Leo a panicked look and he shrugged apologetically. 'Did he? Right.'

'It is happening, isn't it?' Abby asked, her voice plaintive. 'Even if Grandma and Grandad don't come back in time?'

Sitting behind the girls, Leo shook his head, safe in the knowledge they couldn't see him. Miranda looked between them for guidance, but Juliet just shrugged.

Owain, meanwhile, smiled and said, 'Sounds to me like the festival's a big deal here – for your family, and for the island. Be a shame not to uphold the tradition.'

'It would,' Miranda said, thoughtfully. 'It would take some planning at this late notice, though. Mum still hasn't responded to my messages, but it doesn't seem like anything's been put in place for it.'

'We'll help!' Mia yelped, volunteering her sister alongside her. Abby nodded her agreement. Well, he supposed that would at least keep them busy . . .

'In that case, how can we fail?' Miranda asked.

So apparently they were throwing a festival.

Miranda would make it happen, Leo had no doubt at all. His big sister always achieved whatever she set her mind to – with the possible exception of marriage to Paul, although Leo hadn't ruled that one out completely yet, either. And now she wasn't working for Paul's dad any more, she probably had some time on her hands.

But it seemed to him she was kind of ignoring the inevitable. Their parents were selling the Lighthouse. Miranda could pull one more festival out of the bag, but by this time next year the Lighthouse would be gone, so what did it matter?

Not that anyone else seemed bothered by a little thing called reality.

'Brilliant!' Abby bounced up and down a little, as the air was punctuated by the familiar tune of the ice-cream van, sited up by the kite stalls. 'Dad! Can we have ice cream?'

Leo handed over a five-pound note without even trying to argue, and Abby dragged Mia with her to the ice-cream van.

'So, we're definitely doing the festival?' Juliet asked, as the girls left.

'I think we have to,' Miranda replied. 'The island needs it – the revenue, as much as the mood boost. Owain's right – it's too big a deal on Seashell Island to just drop it like that.'

'Don't you think we should wait to hear from Mum and Dad?' Leo craned his neck to watch the girls as they queued – and a familiar figure with purple streaks in her hair joined them. Christabel. He smiled, despite himself. Maybe this day was about to improve.

'Mum and Dad are too busy arguing about what to name a hypothetical parrot.' Miranda rolled her eyes. 'They're not here, and they're not even thinking about here. If we want this to happen, *we* have to do it ourselves.'

'Well, good luck with that.' Leo knelt up on the rug, ready to go join the girls as they returned with Christabel and their ice creams.

'Wait. You're not going to help us?' Juliet's eyes were huge and disappointed.

'You don't need me. You two between you could shift this island to a different ocean if you put your minds to it. And I've got other stuff to do.'

'More important stuff?' Miranda asked. 'Or just work?'

'Both.' Over by the ice-cream van, Christabel had one arm around Mia's shoulder. Leo frowned. Was she OK?

'So you're just going to leave it all to us.' Juliet said. 'This is like the chores rota all over again.'

'No, this is me listening to Christabel and focusing on what really matters to me this summer.' And not getting swept up in a nostalgia last-stand project. Getting to his feet, Leo shaded his eyes from the sun and watched his daughters slowly approaching.

'I don't think this is what she meant,' Miranda was saying, but Leo wasn't listening. Instead, he strode out across the sand towards Abby and Mia and Christabel.

'Hey. Is everything OK?' he asked, as soon as he got close.

'Mia's not feeling so well,' Christabel said.

Leo crouched down in front of Mia. 'What's the matter, sweetheart?'

Mia gave him a miserable smile, then threw up all over his shirt and his lap.

'Too much sugar,' Abby said, wisely, as Leo resisted the urge to swear out loud.

JULIET

Some mornings, pregnancy was just the worst. Well, some afternoons and evenings, too. But on Sunday morning, the day after the kite festival, Juliet woke feeling worse than ever – nauseous, exhausted, and done with everything.

Or perhaps some of that was just because of her realisations the day before.

She needed to talk to Rory. Apologise for what he overheard, if nothing else.

God, she hated apologising.

By the time she dragged herself out of bed and downstairs, the place was deserted – apart from Lucy, staring in at her through the kitchen window. The dishwasher was running with breakfast things, so Juliet knew everyone must have eaten. Miranda had been on the rota to make breakfast today – and people must have been hungry, she realised, as she checked the fridge and found the last of the eggs and bacon gone.

More reasons to head down to the Flying Fish. Supply run.

There was a note on the kitchen chalkboard telling her that Miranda had taken the girls for Sunday sundaes at the ice-cream parlour in town – which seemed a risky choice, given Mia's sugar sickness yesterday, but who was she to judge? It was signed with a 'Mx', so she hoped that meant her big sister wasn't too angry with her for abandoning her duties.

She probably just thought it was par for the course. Maybe she was right.

Blinking away the ridiculous tears that formed at the corners of her eyes, Juliet tried to pull herself together. What had come over her this morning? Discounting the pregnancy hormones, which she was learning were a law unto themselves.

She needed a plan. Baby steps, so to speak. She wasn't a planner by nature, unfortunately, but Miranda always swore by them. And working her way through a list was the only way to keep her brain on topic at the moment.

Grabbing the magnetic pad from the fridge door, she started writing.

1) Talk to Rory.

She needed to convince him that she wasn't the soul-sucking, heart-breaking Juliet he seemed to remember, whatever he'd overheard yesterday. She'd been treading on eggshells around him ever since she arrived, unsure whether it was better to try and be friendly or stick to an arm's length acquaintance, or even just a business relationship. But clearly that wasn't working, so she needed a new approach.

Maybe she needed to show him that she remembered their time together fondly, hoped they could be friends again, but wasn't about to try and trap him into a new relationship because . . . well, maybe she could leave off the because, for now. She needed him friendly, and without the rest of the town talking about them. That shouldn't be too hard, right?

2) Buy breakfast food.

That one, at least, she felt confident she could manage. Maybe not without throwing up, given how the nausea seemed to have taken over her entire body, but she'd get it done.

3) Talk to Miranda and Leo.

This was where the trouble started. She needed to tell them about the baby. About why she'd come home. Mum and Dad clearly weren't coming back soon, if their messages to the family group about all the fun they were having were anything to go by. She couldn't wait for them to come and fix things for her. She needed to do it herself.

Starting with what was happening inside her body.

Three things seemed plenty to be going on with for now, especially given number three, so Juliet tore the list off the pad, grabbed a couple of shopping bags, and set out the front door towards the high street, hoping the fresh sea air would help her fend off the overwhelming attacks of nausea.

It didn't, much, but at least being outside was distracting – taking her mind off the sickness and her problems.

Until she reached the Flying Fish.

'He's not here today,' Debbie, Rory's assistant manager told her. 'I can help you with your order though?'

'Thanks.' Juliet smiled weakly and handed over her shopping list.

Debbie scanned it quickly. 'No problems. It'll be ready for you to pick up a little later, if that's OK?'

'That's fine.' Because coming back again later and *still* not apologising to Rory was just ideal.

Still, as the door closed behind her and she strolled down the sunny cobbles, Juliet reasoned that she'd at least crossed *something* off her list. Miranda and Leo were both busy, so she couldn't talk to them. And if Rory wasn't there to be apologised to then apologising would have to wait. She wasn't rostered on to do anything at the Lighthouse until dinnertime, so she might as well make the most of her day off.

Rather than heading towards the Long Beach, where they'd been yesterday for the kite festival, or back towards Gull Bay and the Lighthouse, Juliet headed further into the town proper. It had been years since she'd explored these areas of St Mary's, and it was as if she saw them all with fresh eyes.

The holiday cottages, with jaunty nautical names on plaques beside their doors, looked sweet rather than corny. The primary school she'd attended looked so much smaller than she'd remembered; even the secondary school was just another set of buildings – not the prison she'd always imagined it as.

It was, she realised, just another town. No different to any over on the mainland, really – and prettier than most. The water all around it was just water – not bars. She could leave any time she wanted.

Except . . . she didn't want to, for now, at least. She was having *fun* up at the Lighthouse, keeping things ticking over. She'd forgotten how enjoyable things like the kite festival could be. She *wanted* to work with Miranda to organise the Lighthouse Festival, too. Not least because she wanted to spend time with her sister.

God, she'd never imagined she'd even think those words.

Maybe it was the pregnancy hormones talking, that would make sense. She wasn't herself right now – in fact, she was two people.

And she was absolutely blaming the baby for the fact she was permanently starving. And the fact she was craving cheese on toast with plum chutney was *definitely* its fault.

As she turned another corner, Juliet found herself heading back towards the town centre, along a different path to the one she'd taken out of it. This road led her past the church, she knew – the scene of countless nativity plays and carol services and egg hunts around the graveyard, something she'd only realised was *deeply* weird once she'd left the island for good.

But as she approached, it became clear that there was something different going on there today. Pausing at the entrance to the churchyard, she took in the banner hung over the noticeboard.

Farmers' Market, today!

Maybe they'd have plum jam. And good cheese.

She went in.

The stalls were arranged around the grassy area in front of the church, more usually used for wedding photos and the Christmas live nativity with actual donkeys. Juliet wondered if Lucy might stand in for a camel this year.

She moved easily between the stalls, sampling some of the offerings, chatting with the sellers about their farms, dairies, their processes. Many of them were from Seashell Island themselves, although a few had popped over from the mainland, and most were sole traders, making their wares in their kitchens or smallholdings. For a short while, it almost felt like she was back at work again, talking with traders about their wares and how to get more people aware of them.

'We've been talking about trying to set up some sort of collective,' one of them told her, as she sampled chutneys. 'But none of us really have the time or the experience to make it happen. You know, all the promotion and social-media stuff. It's a mystery to me!'

She understood it, Juliet thought, as she chewed. She could help them. If she stayed.

But she wasn't staying.

Still, she could still help in some small ways. 'Well, I'd definitely like to stock your preserves at the Lighthouse B&B,' she told the stallholder. 'And if you've got business cards I can take a few for anyone who wants to buy some to take home?'

'That would be brilliant! Thank you.' The stallholder

handed over cards – and a jar of plum chutney, no charge.

She turned to a cake stall next, thinking she'd stock up on some treats for afternoon tea – the band often got hungry when they were working, she'd discovered – only to blink as she recognised the woman behind the cake-laden table.

'Mrs Norris?'

The older woman looked up with a smile. 'Yes, dear? Can I interest you in sampling a bit of cheese scone? It's a new recipe, using— goodness me, Juliet Waters?'

Juliet smiled. 'Yep, it's me. It's lovely to see you again.' It was funny, Juliet reflected. When she'd been a ten-year-old in Mrs Norris's Year Six class, her teacher had seemed middle-aged already, if not older. Now, eighteen years later, she didn't seem to have aged a single day.

'You too! Gosh, I don't know that anyone was expecting to see you back on the island, especially with your parents still away. Are you here long?'

'Been here two weeks already,' Juliet replied, totting it up in her head and amazed at the total. How had it gone so fast? Two whole weeks and, while she'd been busy the whole time, she hadn't done anything about her biggest problem. The ticking timebomb inside her womb. 'It's actually a nice break from the city.'

'I'm sure.' Mrs Norris gave her the kind of look that had always terrified her as a child. One of those that made it clear that she could hear all the things Juliet wasn't saying. Sometimes, she'd been afraid her teacher could read her mind. 'You know, Juliet, there's never any shame in coming home. That's what home *is*. A place you're always welcome.' She handed her a cheese scone. 'And I, for one, am glad to see you back.'

'Th-thanks, Mrs Norris,' Juliet stammered, taking the scone.

'Call me Ellie,' her old teacher said, as she turned to serve the next customer. 'And I hope we'll see you here again next week.'

'Definitely,' Juliet promised, stepping away.

By the time she'd made a full circuit of the stalls her reusable bags were fully loaded – although she was still short of some of the essentials she'd need for breakfasts that week until she'd gone back to collect her order from the Flying Fish.

As if conjured by the thought, Juliet turned away from a cheese stall – after acquiring some pasteurised local cheese to go with her chutney – and saw Rory crossing the churchyard towards her. She saw the moment he spotted her, too – because his steps faltered, just briefly, before he squared his shoulders and kept walking.

She didn't want to do this here, like this, laden down with bags and with half the island's small businesspeople – plus her ex-teacher – watching. But here was where it seemed to be happening.

'Rory.' She forced a wide smile as she stepped towards him. 'I was hoping I'd see you today. I wanted to, well, apologise.'

His expression remained completely bland as he replied, 'For telling your brother you'd never come back to Seashell Island to "trawl the graveyard of terrible teenage relationships"? Or for walking away ten years ago when my father was dying and I needed you?'

Ow. Every word hit her hard in the heart. 'Both, I guess.'

'Great.' He gave a sharp nod. 'Glad we cleared that up.'

Then he walked right past her towards the chutney stall, leaving Juliet staring after him.

MESSAGES

Miranda (to Mum & Dad group): Hi! Everyone missed you at the kite festival yesterday. We've got some new guests at the Lighthouse too, which is fun. Um . . . people were asking about the Lighthouse Festival, though. I couldn't see anything in the files. Did you have anything arranged yet?

Miranda (to Mum & Dad group): Guessing you're probably out at sea, since I haven't heard anything back yet. Juliet and I thought we'd help out and get the festival planning started at least, before you get back. Any suggestions on where to start? Or who to contact?

Miranda (to Mum & Dad group): Assuming you're still out of signal range, Juliet and I will just make a start, yeah? Let me know if you have any advice!

MIRANDA

On Monday morning, Miranda came downstairs to find
Lucy the Llama staring through the kitchen window for the
umpteenth time.

'Ready?' Owain asked from behind her. She jumped at
the sound of his voice.

'Just let me make the teas.' As the kettle boiled, she put
teabags into the travel cups they'd been using for the last few
days, to make their early morning llama walks a little more
bearable.

Although, she had to admit, spending time with Owain at
the start of every day was a bit of a treat, too.

Every morning, as they walked across the fields, a reluctant but resigned Lucy trotting beside them, she and Owain
talked about anything and everything – from the llama
beside them—

'I think she thinks this is her morning constitutional.'

'I think she just hates me.'

— to their lives, hopes, dreams and futures.

Miranda had managed not to sob on his shoulder again,
which she was counting as a victory, and she'd learned some
interesting things about the members of Birchwood. Like
the fact that Suzi had run away from home at fourteen and
lived on the streets and taught herself to play the guitar
while keeping warm in music shops. Or that Owain had a
degree in medieval studies, 'Which has proved pretty much

useless in my chosen career.' Or how Robyn and Ryan had a weird twin telepathy thing. 'Which is actually *really* useful on stage, when you're trying to keep everyone in time.'

He'd kept her entertained with anecdotes about their tours, and updates on how the new album was going – slowly, apparently, although she'd heard Robyn mutter that it would be faster if Owain wasn't so distracted. Miranda only allowed herself a small smile at the idea that *she* might be what was distracting him. After all, Robyn probably meant Lucy anyway.

Miranda had shared plenty about herself and her family too – about growing up on the island, her worries about her siblings, and frustration with her parents.

They'd had a pretty good brainstorming session about the Lighthouse Festival the day before, bouncing ideas off each other. Miranda planned to write up action lists for them all – although she imagined Leo would ignore his the same way he seemed to be ignoring the chore rota Juliet had stuck to the fridge.

At least Owain seemed willing to help, with the festival as well as the llama.

'You'll definitely still be here for it?' she asked, as they tramped across the fields again.

Owain gave her a secret sort of smile. 'For sure. Turns out this album is going to take some time to get right – so we'll just have to stay on Seashell Island until it's done.' Then he frowned. 'Although we do have some gigs on the mainland the week before. We'll have to go back for them. But I promise we'll be back well before the festival.'

'Good. That's good.' Not least because she was already finding it hard to imagine the island without Owain on it.

Or Lucy, come to that.

Still, the idea of him leaving, even for a short time, weighed on her over the next few days. Because after the festival, after the album was done, of *course* he'd leave. It wasn't as if they'd even reached a point where she could talk to him about staying. They were friends, she hoped, but that was all.

If she was anybody else, she'd make plans to visit him, once he left. See if there really was something between them.

If she was anybody else, they'd have options.

But she was Miranda Waters, and this island was all she had.

By Saturday, she was fed up of even thinking about it. And as she came down the stairs and saw Lucy through the kitchen window once again, a realisation hit her.

This was her life. The only one she had. And right now it consisted of her VA work, helping Juliet with the B&B, playing with her nieces so Leo could work, organising a festival she wasn't responsible for, and enlisting the help of a guitarist to ferry a llama across two fields. And while at least half of that wasn't all that bad, it wasn't exactly what she'd dreamed of as a child. And none of it, she realised suddenly, was actually for *her*.

Apart from the spending time with Owain bit. That, she admitted, was a definite bonus to the llama situation. But spending time with him without an animal chaperone would be even better . . .

Not that he'd more than hinted at wanting that, since that first mention of rebound sex that still reverberated around her body at inconvenient moments. Like whenever she looked at him. He was gorgeous, a musician, temporary . . . perfect for getting over her ex, right? And since he'd given up his mornings to act as a sheepdog to a llama, he couldn't be *completely* uninterested. He'd even joined them at the kite festival, entertaining Abby and Mia by helping them fly their new kites with Leo. And he said he wanted to stay for the whole summer. Was he just being cautious, because he knew she'd just come out of a relationship? Or because Christabel had told him what a hopeless case she was?

If she asked him out – or even just asked him to bed – might he say yes?

But while that might be an everyday kind of request for Juliet or Christabel to make, for Miranda it felt a lot more complicated. Apart from anything else, she'd been with Paul since she was a teenager. How was she suddenly supposed to restart that romantic part of her that she locked up into one relationship at sixteen?

Plus . . . what would people say? Miranda didn't exactly want to be the sort of person who cared what people thought, but on an island like Seashell it was hard not to. One wrong move and she'd be hearing about it for ever. Or at least all winter long.

She was the good girl, the girl next door – and that kind of local status was hard to come by on the island. She'd won it fair and square, used it to get voted onto the island council, to give back to the place that had become her first real home. She had a *reputation* here, a position. One she wanted to protect.

And it wasn't the sort of reputation that led to holiday flings with touring musicians.

Owain would leave at the end of the summer. She'd have to live with what she did here for ever.

Half the island was waiting for her to get back with Paul and stop him leaving. Hell, that half were probably hoping for a surprise wedding ceremony at the Lighthouse Festival, as if she'd have time to organise both. The other half seemed to expect her to wear widows' weeds and mourn him until he saw sense and came home again. And still organise the festival to keep people's spirits up.

Miranda really didn't want to do either of those things. But it was *expected*.

But what if she just . . . did something else? Saw this as an opportunity to reset her place on the island, to become whoever she wanted to be next?

She'd have to really, really want it, to take that kind of risk. That risk of becoming a different sort of person. But maybe the island would cut her some slack right now, because of her apparently broken heart. If she was ever going to make a change, now was the time. Even her parents weren't here to disapprove . . . and her siblings, well. They'd never really liked – or at least understood – who she was anyway. They'd probably be thrilled.

Mug of tea in her hands, she stared out of the window and met Lucy's eyes.

'What do *you* want, Lucifer?' It seemed only right to give the llama her full name when she was asking such a personal question. 'What would make you happy? Fulfilled?'

And then she realised that Lucy had been telling her exactly what she wanted, for two full weeks.

Miranda bit her lip. Who was she now? Was she the sort of person who fulfilled the dreams of a runaway llama?

Apparently she was.

Pulling her phone from her pocket, she called Max, who sounded half asleep as he answered.

'Lucy there again?'

'Of course.'

He sighed. 'Right. Let me just get Dafydd up and we'll come and get her.'

'Actually . . .' Miranda took a breath. 'I was thinking, she clearly wants to be here at the Lighthouse. What if we just . . . let her stay?'

Stunned silence. Then a rustle of bedsheets and the pad

of footsteps on floorboards, as if Max were sneaking away from his husband to discuss this with her – which Miranda suspected was exactly what was happening.

She heard a door close, then Max said, softly, 'I mean, I would love that. The damn animal clearly isn't happy here, although Dafydd won't see it. I'll have to work on him but . . . why don't you hold on to Lucy while I talk to him? Then, if it works, I'll bring over her stuff this afternoon.'

'Sounds like a plan. And of course, Dafydd can come visit her whenever he wants.'

Max clicked his tongue. 'Ah, he'll be on to a new big idea soon enough. But yes, it'll be nice to keep up with her. What is it you think she loves about the Lighthouse so much?'

Miranda thought, trying to imagine what might have brought the llama to them. *She* loved it because it was safe, a refuge, but Lucy already had that at the farm.

Then she heard the clatter of footsteps on the stairs and figured it out.

'I think it's probably all the people here. Leo's girls adore her, Juliet's besotted, and I even found a few of our guests serenading her the other afternoon.'

Max laughed. 'Yeah, that'll do it. They're pack animals, I suppose. Like company. Just don't tell Dafydd, or he'll be shipping over a whole herd of them for the farm.'

She hung up in time to see Abby and Mia burst into the kitchen. 'Is Lucy here today?' Abby asked, breathlessly.

Miranda inclined her head towards the window. 'She is. And it looks like she might be staying. You guys can go give her the good news.'

With twin whoops of excitement, the girls raced out the back door to pet the devil llama. Leo, she noticed, was nowhere to be seen. And neither was Juliet, for that matter. She frowned and set about getting the breakfast things out before the band came down – only to find Owain helping her to reach the top bowls moments later.

'You're up early,' she said, as they set the table together.

He shrugged. 'Couldn't sleep last night, so I went down to the cottage to work on some new songs. Looked up and it was morning, so I thought I'd come grab some breakfast before I get some sleep.'

'The erratic creative life, huh?' It wouldn't suit her. She liked routines and order and checklists.

But then, she'd never really tried staying up all night . . . and watching Owain's hands as he laid out cutlery she could think of some circumstances in which she might be willing to give it a go. Especially if those long, clever, guitarist's fingers were involved . . .

'So, I hear from the very excited girls outside that you've acquired a llama,' Owain said, oblivious to the direction her thoughts had wandered in. 'Guess that means our morning strolls across the fields are over.'

'You sound almost disappointed,' Miranda replied, a thrill of something new and exciting blossoming in her chest.

'I am, a little.' Owain's smile was soft and warm and just for her. 'I'd got used to spending time with you first thing in the morning.'

I can think of other ways to make that happen.

But that was too forward, even for New Miranda. So instead, she smiled back and said, 'Well, if you're looking for ways for us to spend time together, I could definitely still use your help getting the Lighthouse Festival together, if you're up for it?'

'Absolutely.'

She wasn't sure if he saw it for the excuse it clearly was,

but it didn't matter. He'd said yes, and that meant she could move on to the next stage.

'In that case, how about we try spending time together in the evening, instead? Go out for dinner, maybe. Once you've got some sleep, of course.'

This time, his smile was blinding, lighting up his hazel eyes and his whole face under his dirty-blond hair. 'I'd like that very much indeed.'

'Then I'll call the Flying Fish and see if I can get us a table for tonight. And get out my planning notebook.'

Just like that, Miranda Waters was the sort of woman who asked a guy out, and even made reservations. At a restaurant where the whole island could see her.

And she didn't even care.

LEO

'What do you mean you can't open the file? Hang on, I'll send it again.' Balancing his phone between his shoulder and his ear, Leo lifted his laptop to the one spot in the office that got a consistent Wi-Fi signal, pressed send, and hoped to God the file reached Tom in a reasonable state this time.

This was getting ridiculous.

For all Dad's office was technically set up to run the business, it wasn't fit for purpose for what he needed. He needed to be back in London, visiting clients, doing his actual job, not flying kites, battling to be heard over weird stringed instruments, and praying for Wi-Fi.

Although the kite-flying had been pretty cool. Apart from Mia throwing up, anyway.

'OK, got it,' Tom said. 'Right, I can deal with this now. Or on Monday, when I get to the office, because it's Saturday, in case you haven't looked at a calendar recently. The weekend. A time to relax. You should go and build a sandcastle, or whatever.'

'What? No. We need to talk through our approach. If you're going to present this to the client you need to understand—'

'Leo, I *do* understand,' Tom said, with what was clearly mounting impatience. 'We've been through it. I get it. You know . . . you hired me because you believed I could do this job. At some point you're going to have to let me actually do it.'

'What do you think I've been doing all summer?' Did Tom really not know how much it was killing him to be away from the office? From the one place where he knew what he was doing?

Tom sighed, a burst of air down the phone line. 'OK. What do you want to go through?'

Slumping lower in his father's office chair, Leo pulled out the file for the client presentation in question. It was a big one; a client who'd brought them in for a very small tester project and had been impressed enough that they now wanted their input on a major, city-wide marketing campaign.

'Right. Let's start at the beginning.'

They'd barely even made inroads on the presentation itself when the office door banged open.

'Dad! Dad! Auntie Miranda's keeping Lucy here at the Lighthouse for good!' Abby's fluffy blonde hair bobbed in excitement as she threw herself into his lap. Mia, only a little more reserved, followed behind, beaming.

Leo, trying to drag himself mentally back from London to Seashell Island, frowned. 'The llama? This is about the llama?'

They want to know you care about what they care about. Christabel's advice echoed in his mind. The only problem was, he didn't care. Not about the llama.

He cared about landing this commission, about making sure Tom didn't screw up in the meeting. *That* was what he cared about right now.

Abby nodded, squirming in his lap. 'She's going to live here and we can help look after her and feed her and take her for walks – do llamas go for walks?'

Leo screwed his eyes up and tried not to scream.

'I think llamas mostly graze,' Tom suggested, on the other end of the phone, sounding far more amused than Leo liked.

Didn't anyone take his business, his work, seriously?

'Tom, stop thinking about llamas and start thinking about this presentation. Girls, I'm doing something that actually matters right now, and that stupid llama keeps spitting at me anyway. Why don't you go tell Auntie Juliet?'

Abby stopped squirming. Mia's expression turned solemn, her brows low over her dark eyes as she reached out to take her little sister's hand. 'Come on, Abby. Dad doesn't care about Lucy.'

They were halfway through the door, and Leo was about to sigh with relief, when he heard her add, almost a whisper, 'Or us.'

The sigh caught in his chest, choking him, and he struggled to catch his breath as the door swung shut behind the girls.

I'm doing this all wrong. And I still don't know how to fix it.

'Leo?' Tom's voice echoed down the phone line, filling the suddenly empty study. 'You still there?'

Leo swallowed hard, trying to find his voice again. 'I'm here. But, uh, you're right. It's Saturday. You should go build a sandcastle.'

'That was more a suggestion for you,' Tom said, drily.

'Whatever. Just— I'll call you on Monday. OK?'

'Fine by me! See ya.' Tom hung up promptly, and Leo let his phone slide down from his shoulder to his lap.

I need to fix this. Before Emily and Mark get back.

I need my daughters to know they matter to me.

But I need to do my job too.

Were the two mutually exclusive? Emily seemed to manage it well enough. But how?

He considered phoning his ex-wife and asking, but since she was on her honeymoon he didn't imagine it would go down well. Besides, wasn't this one of the reasons she'd divorced him in the first place? If she'd been able to fix it, she would have. Emily could fix anything. Except him.

He needed help from someone else. Someone who could think outside the box, and find a way for him to have *everything* that mattered to him.

Someone who'd seen the problem long before he had.

Someone who'd had the same problem and fixed it herself.

Someone who had only laughed a little bit when Mia threw up all over him because he'd thought Emily's rules about her sugar intake were more guidelines than actual necessity.

He needed to go and find Christabel.

And this time, he needed to listen to her.

By the time Leo made it downstairs, the girls were already distracted by the llama, and were feeding her with Miranda. He caught his sister's eye and beckoned her over.

'I need to pop out for a bit. Do you think you could look after the girls for a couple of hours?'

Miranda raised an eyebrow. 'They already told me you're too busy working to help them with Lucy today.'

Leo winced. 'I know. I . . . screwed up. Am screwing up. Will probably continue to screw up. But I'm trying to fix it.'

'You could start by playing with them, like you did with the kites at the festival.' Miranda sounded slightly more sympathetic at his confession. 'I mean, once Mia got cleaned up and less nauseous, they both seemed to really enjoy that.'

'I could. But then I'd be worrying about work, and I'd stay up too late trying to fix this presentation, then snap at them in the morning because I haven't slept enough and—'

'OK, OK. So you're saying the problem's a little deeper than not caring about Lucy the Llama.'

'Yeah.' Looking over at his daughters, Leo let out a deep sigh. 'I don't know how to be their dad any more, Miri. I mean, clearly I wasn't doing a great job when I was still married, or Emily wouldn't have left me. But now . . . I don't even know where to start. Christabel was talking about being the kind of dad they can come to when they need someone to listen, someone they trust to help not shout when they're in trouble . . .' And he'd just let her take over playing with the girls whenever she showed up because it meant he could get some more work done. Probably not what she'd intended.

'Christabel's really made an impact on you, huh?' Miranda's smile was a little smug. 'I *said* she'd be perfect for you.'

'It's not like that,' he said, although it kind of was. In his head, Christabel was mixed up with everything he wanted. Someone who knew how to work hard but also how to stop. Someone who could dance when the music played. She made him want to dance with her – and he *never* danced – and to dance with his girls, too.

She showed him another way. And while he wasn't about to go careening about the countryside in a converted ambulance anytime soon, he had to admit that some things about the life she advocated did appeal to him.

'From the moony look in your eye I'd say it's *exactly* like that,' Miranda crowed. 'And thank God. Have you even been on a date since Emily left you? Leo, life is bigger than just your job. You have to make room for the other stuff, too.'

'I know, and I've tried. I just . . . can't seem to make it work. I'm hoping that Christabel can help me with that. I mean, she seems to have it all together. Which for a person who lives in an ambulance and fixes bikes for a living seems kind of absurd, if I think about it,' Leo admitted. 'But she does. Like, she knows what really matters in life. And I think . . . I think I need some reminding.'

'So you want to go and find her now and ask her how to fix your life?'

'Basically.'

Folding her arms across her chest, Miranda turned to him with the 'I'm your big sister, and that means I'm the boss' look he remembered so well from their childhood. 'Promise me this isn't just an excuse to go and find a better Wi-Fi connection, and I'll watch the kids for a while. But you need to be back by four. I have a . . . planning meeting tonight. For the Lighthouse Festival.'

Something in the way she said it raised his suspicions. 'A planning meeting? With who?'

Miranda's cheeks turned pink. 'Owain.'

Leo bit back a grin. 'I see. So not just me looking a little moony, then? How do you think Paul will feel about this?' If Miranda's ex-fiancé even noticed, now he'd decided to up and leave. It seemed to Leo that Paul hadn't really noticed Miranda since they were about twenty. Longer, if he didn't know her well enough to know how much this island meant to her.

'It's none of Paul's business any more, is it?'

'Are you sure? I mean, you guys were together a long time, and not that I like to give in to island gossip, but Albert Tuna is running a book down at the docks that you two will be back together before Halloween.' Plus, Leo knew his sister. She liked things the same as always, predictable and routine. And it was hard to think of anyone in the world more predictable and routine than Paul – at least until now.

But apparently Miranda felt differently. 'I'm sure. Paul's

made his decision and I can't see him changing it. And I can't see me changing mine either.'

'OK then.'

Lucy snaffled the last of the food Mia and Abby had taken out for her, and they both laughed in delight as she licked their hands looking for more. Then Mia looked up, spotted Leo, and settled her face into a glare that looked so much like her mother's Leo shivered.

'Yeah, you'd better go,' Miranda said, catching the look. 'But be back before four, OK? I need to get ready for my—'

'Planning meeting,' Leo finished with a grin. 'Will do.'

MESSAGES

Juliet (to Tanya): Do you reckon you could pack up some of my clothes for me and post them to me here?

Tanya: You're never coming back, are you?

Juliet: Of course I am! I've just eaten far too many ice-cream sundaes. I need my fat jeans. And some more dresses.

Tanya: Date-type dresses . . . ?

Juliet: Just dresses. Whatever sort you think.

Tanya: Knowing you? Date dresses.

JULIET

Rory had been avoiding her for almost a week.

Juliet knew that, realistically, there was no reason why they should have seen each other – but on an island the size of Seashell Island, it wasn't hard to know when you were being actively avoided. And Rory was actively avoiding her.

She'd been to the Flying Fish twice since their encounter at the Farmers' Market, and each time as she opened the door she'd seen him ducking into the back room as Debbie came forward to take her order. Yesterday, he'd even crossed the street to talk to Gwendolyn Stone, Paul's mother, rather than bump into her.

And she got it, she did. She'd treated him horribly all those years ago, and hadn't really done much better since she got back. He was totally right to avoid her. And she'd let him do it, would actually stay out of his way, if it wasn't for two small things.

One, the Flying Fish served the best Welsh rarebit in the world, and it was the only thing she seemed to want to eat these days. Often with plum chutney. So she couldn't stop visiting his restaurant or she'd starve.

Two, Rory had been her best friend since childhood, long before he'd been her boyfriend. This morning, she really needed a friend – and he was the only person on the island who still held the title.

Juliet looked down at her body – at the boobs that seemed

to have ballooned over the last few weeks, and most of all, at the stomach she suddenly couldn't fasten her jeans over. Surely this was too soon? All the apps said she shouldn't be showing until at least three or four months along — and she was only nine weeks. She'd thought she had time — to make the booking appointment with the midwife that she apparently needed before her twelve week scan, to tell her family, and *definitely* to go clothes shopping. But here she was with no fitting jeans and bras that cut into her breasts.

She needed to talk to *someone* about this. Needed to tell someone.

Juliet sank down on the bed, pushing her hands through her hair and thinking it through.

Miranda was the obvious choice, or Leo perhaps. Except that telling her family made it too real, too soon. She needed to talk through all the angles before she confessed to her brother and sister.

If her parents had been there it would have been different. They might have struggled with the news, but they had never judged her, had always supported her unquestioningly.

Miranda, she knew, would have questions.

And Juliet needed to work out the answers before she asked them.

Growing up, whenever she'd had to talk through problems or possibilities, she'd talked to Rory. He'd listened to her frustrations with her family, her dreams of escape, her ambitions, everything she'd hidden in her heart. For ten years, most of that stuff had just had to stay inside her, without a Rory to listen. Maybe it had been too much, or too long, because now it was all fighting to get out.

And now, back on Seashell Island, despite everything, he was still the only person she wanted to talk to about what was happening to her.

Plus, if she went to the Flying Fish to find him, she could have some Welsh rarebit for lunch.

So, switching to a looser dress she hoped didn't highlight the bloating in her belly, she checked on the rota – Miranda had been on breakfast again, since it was the weekend – and the llama in the garden, who was apparently now a permanent fixture, and headed out down the path towards town.

As she approached the Flying Fish she could see Rory behind the counter of the deli half through the front windows. He hadn't spotted her yet, or he'd have run, so she took advantage of the moment to take him in all over again.

He wasn't the boy she'd known as a toddler, child and teenager, she knew that. But in so many ways, he still was exactly that. Still the one she'd spilled her heart to, over and over. Whose heart she'd broken.

He looked up, those wary eyes in that older face, and she knew the second he saw her because his shoulders tensed. Then he turned back to the customer he was serving, and Juliet took a deep breath and entered, hoping he wouldn't run away this time.

She waited, killing time by examining the jars of local chutneys and jams, until the deli was empty and the buzz from the restaurant next door became background noise as people finished off brunch.

'Do you have a few minutes?' she asked, when they were alone.

'You need to place another order?' Rory turned towards the restaurant. 'Let me get one of my colleagues to take it for you.'

'No!' Too loud, too desperate, she knew, but she didn't care. Gathering her composure, she said, 'I need to talk to you. I mean, yes, I also need to order food. But mostly I just need to talk to you and I can't because you've been avoiding me. Understandably.'

His gaze stayed steady on her face, like he was reading her mind, and she tried to meet it openly and honestly.

Finally, he nodded. Unwrapping the black apron from around his waist, he tossed it under the counter, and disappeared to talk to someone in the back room. Then he returned, walked straight past her towards the door, saying over his shoulder, 'Come on, then. Let's get this over with.'

Well. That boded *really* well. And also meant she wasn't getting her Welsh rarebit.

She caught up with him just as he was taking the steps down to the beach, two at a time, the sea breeze ruffling his hair.

'So,' he said, as his feet touched the sand. 'You wanted to talk. Talk.'

She'd rehearsed this in her head on the way over. She knew exactly what she'd intended to say. Apologise again first, then confess. So why wouldn't the words come?

'I just wanted to . . . apologise again,' she started, uncertainly. She hadn't expected the anger in his eyes, that was the problem. Even though she'd expected him to be furious. 'For everything, of course. But especially for what you heard me say the other day. I know you must be angry with me, or else you wouldn't be avoiding me.'

He barked a laugh at that. 'Angry with you?' Shaking his head, he stopped walking and turned to her, grabbing her hands as he spoke. 'Juliet, I'm angry with myself. For ever letting myself believe . . . let's just say that your nicely timed declaration that you hadn't come back here for me punctured any self-delusion I'd been operating under.'

Letting her go, he stalked away up the beach, shoving his hands in his pockets and leaving Juliet to puzzle out his meaning until she realised he was halfway to the steps back up to town and if he took them she'd lose him.

She couldn't lose him. Not before she'd fixed things between them.

Chasing after him, she grabbed his arm and made him stop. Glancing up, she saw a couple of locals she recognised watching them curiously from the street above, and cursed inwardly. This was going to be everywhere, no matter what she did next.

People would be talking about her, just like they always had. She was scandal-worthy – even more so than normal, right now.

She might as well live up to her reputation.

'Here's the thing,' she said breathlessly, as Rory turned to face her, his expression steeled for disappointment. 'I didn't come back to Seashell Island for you, I came for me. And I didn't come planning to stay, and I probably won't. All the reasons I left the island still stand, but I need you to remember that *none of those reasons were you*. I loved you, Rory, more than I've ever loved anyone, it turns out. But I couldn't live my life out here, and you—'

'I needed to stay, for my dad,' Rory finished for her. 'I remember.'

'Leo was teasing me at the beach. That's why I said what you heard. But honestly, he seemed more worried about you than me.'

That brought a half smile to Rory's face. 'That's because he left to go back to university a week later than you that last summer. He saw the mess you left me in. And Miranda and your parents . . . they put up with me showing up drunk and morose to moon around the Lighthouse gardens, missing you for months afterwards.'

'That's . . . kind of pathetic,' Juliet said, trying to not

sound unkind but, knowing her track record, probably failing.

Rory laughed. 'It was. Very. And I got over it. I moved on with my life. Worked with dad at the family business then, when he got too sick to manage, I took over. Started the Flying Fish, which became a successful business, rather than just scraping by. And I'm glad he got to see that before he died.'

'I'm sorry, Rory.'

He shrugged. 'We knew it was coming. It is what it is. The point is, I managed very nicely here without you after the first little while. Even started dating again. Living again. Until this summer.'

Juliet froze. 'What changed?' she whispered, although she already knew the answer.

'You. You came home, and suddenly I was eighteen again. Stumbling over my words, struck dumb every time I saw you. Finding excuses to deliver your orders to the Lighthouse instead of letting Kieran do it like he normally would. Ready to be humiliated by you over and over. And it didn't matter. I still wanted you, after all this time.' He looked down at the sand, and gave a small, self-deprecating chuckle. 'Nothing had changed. When you are here on the island, you're still all that I see. You walked into my restaurant and . . . the tides stopped for me. You were still so . . . you. Beautiful and vibrant and—'

'Pregnant,' Juliet blurted out. 'I'm pregnant. That's why I came home.'

Why had she said it like that? That definitely hadn't been the script for how this conversation was meant to go. But he was being so open, so honest . . . didn't she owe him the unvarnished truth?

Plus, all her insides were squirming at the way he described her. At how she affected his world, when she'd only ever been thinking about herself.

She didn't deserve someone like Rory even acknowledging her presence.

'You're . . . what?' Rory blinked at her in obvious bafflement.

'Pregnant,' she repeated, softer. 'I . . . it's a long story. Basically, the father isn't in the picture but, because he was someone I worked with, I had to leave my job, too. So I came back to Seashell Island to throw myself on my parents' mercies because apparently I'm still a teenager and incapable of looking after myself. Only they weren't here, and I couldn't tell my siblings and I can't go back to London, so now I'm running the Lighthouse B&B and I have no idea what's going to happen next in my life.'

Rory stared at her for a long, long moment. Behind her, Juliet heard the sea crashing against the sand and counted the pause in waves. *One, two, three, four, five . . .*

'OK,' Rory whispered eventually, raking a shaky hand through his already windblown hair. 'OK. We're going to the pub. I'm going to have a drink and you're going to tell me everything. OK?'

Juliet looked up into his blue, blue eyes and burst into tears.

MIRANDA

Leo was back at four o'clock, as promised, with Christabel in tow, so Miranda handed over two sandy and only slightly sugary girls and headed upstairs to shower and try and find anything in her wardrobe that said 'flirty planning meeting'.

Obviously, nothing she owned managed that. She settled on a pale blue sundress she'd always liked and stuck with flat sandals because the cobbles in town were ridiculous in heels, and anyway, they might want to walk on the beach afterwards.

Owain was waiting for her by the front door when she descended the stairs, A4 folder and notepad in hand.

'Looks like you're ready to work,' he said, nodding towards her stationery supplies.

'Of course. What else could tonight be about?' She couldn't help the smile that fluttered around her lips as she said it, and from the way Owain stared at her mouth he didn't miss it, either.

'I can't possibly imagine,' he said. But the heat in his voice told her he was imagining it every bit as much as she was.

As they walked into town together, Miranda gave him a fuller version of the history of the Lighthouse Festival than he'd heard so far, starting with the summer they'd moved to the island, and how they'd been outsiders, trying to find their place on Seashell Island.

Owain shook his head at that. 'Kinda hard to imagine that

now,' he admitted. 'Ever since I've been here, every time we've gone anywhere together – even just dragging Lucy across those damn fields – you've bumped into someone who knows you.'

'Mostly people who want to ask me about the Lighthouse Festival,' she pointed out. 'Or ask when Paul and I are getting back together.'

'Perhaps. But the point stands. You're like the True North of this place. The backbone of it. I think the whole place might fall apart without you here to keep it together. You're the locals' local, these days.'

'I wasn't once, though,' Miranda admitted, with a wry smile. 'To start with, this was just another new school, more new kids to make fun of me. I guess I assumed that it would be like every other place Mum and Dad took us. We'd stay a while and then move on. It was only at the end of our first summer, when they threw that first festival and invited everyone on the island for barbecue and music up at the B&B, that I realised this was it. We were really staying. We had a proper home, at last.'

'You moved around a lot before that?' Owain asked.

Miranda nodded. 'Every year or so. Creative parents, you know. Always seeking the next inspiration.' She looked out over the sea, towards the mainland, and was surprised to find she didn't shudder at the very sight of it, for once. 'You must know how it is. I bet you travel all over with the band.'

'We do,' he admitted. 'And I love it. But then we go home again, and I love that too.'

'That's North Wales, right?' It was hard to imagine Owain in one place, not adventuring the world with his guitar on his back.

'Right. I inherited a little cottage from my grandparents, up in the hills. I used to go stay there with them as a kid, in the holidays. It's good for holing up and thinking, but a bit cramped when the band's all there together. Plus the nearest pub is a five-mile walk away. That's why the band insisted on settling somewhere else this summer, to work on the new songs. And since we had a lot of gigs down this end of the country anyway, when Christabel sent us the link to the Lighthouse website, it made sense.'

'Well, I'm glad you decided to come,' Miranda admitted, smiling up at him.

'Me too.' For a moment, he just held her gaze, and Miranda realised she could read anything she wanted to in his eyes. Did she really see the heat she hoped for, or was that just a reflection of her own desire? Owain seemed determined to hold back and let her set the pace for anything that happened between them. Which she applauded in the abstract. But right now . . . she just wanted a sign.

'So, tell me more about the festival,' Owain said, as they continued walking. 'What was last year's like?'

Miranda talked about candyfloss stalls and vintage fairground rides and country dancers and so on until they reached the Flying Fish. Inside, Rory was nowhere to be seen, but his restaurant manager took them swiftly to their table.

'How are things coming with the festival?' Debbie asked, as she handed them menus and a wine list. 'Rory said to let you know that of course the Flying Fish stall will be there.'

'Brilliant,' Miranda said. That was *one* stall at least. 'I'm still, ah, confirming the details with the other stallholders.'

'Well, let us know if we can do anything to help,' Debbie said. 'Summer's not complete until we've all enjoyed the Lighthouse Festival.'

Miranda gave her a wan smile as she walked away, then turned her attention to her menu. She'd barely made it past the starters, though, before someone else came up to the table.

'Miranda! I just wanted to check in about the arrangements for the festival.' Dottie, from the island's WI group, whipped out her diary and put it on the table. 'When would be a good time for us to meet and discuss?'

Um, any time I'm not on an actual date? 'How about you give me a call tomorrow?'

Dottie wrote it down in her diary. 'I have lots of ideas.'

'Oh good.' Last year, the WI had run a flower-arranging stall, which had been much more successful than the naked husbands of the WI calendar venture from the year before.

Before Miranda could return her attention to the menu, though, the door opened and the restaurant went bizarrely quiet. Which she liked, because it meant she could decide what to eat.

But then Owain cleared his throat. 'Um, Miranda?'

Damn it. She was going to have to look up. And she just knew, in her gut, that she didn't want to see whatever was going on behind her.

Still, she turned, hyper-aware that everyone in the Flying Fish was staring at her. Which made sense when she realised that Paul had just walked in with Becca from the Crab Leg Cafe hanging off his arm.

Right. Of course.

Miranda did a quick check on her heart and found it still unbroken. She and Becca hadn't been close in years, and she couldn't exactly berate Paul for moving on while she was out on a date herself. So she smiled, waved at the pair, then turned her attention back to the menu.

'Nicely done,' Owain murmured, across the table. 'Now, what are you having? I'm thinking maybe the duck.'

'The duck is really good,' Miranda agreed. 'But I quite fancy the chicken pie.'

Conversations began to start up again around them and, the next time Miranda glanced around, she saw that Paul and Becca had been seated at the far side of the restaurant, and no one was paying them any attention any more.

Good.

Of course, that didn't stop another two locals stopping by to ask about the festival arrangements while Debbie was trying to take their order. But since that wasn't as bad as everyone gossiping about her personal life, Miranda smiled nicely and promised to keep them updated.

'This festival of your sounds like quite the important event for the whole community,' Owain said, after they'd finally ordered. 'Maybe even more so than your love life.'

Miranda sighed, and decided to ignore the love-life dig. 'Usually, yes. This year . . . probably not. I've emailed all the usual people Mum and Dad get in for it, and every single one I've heard back from has said they're already booked that weekend, sorry. The others . . . I don't know if they'll even bother replying.'

Owain leaned back in his seat, arms folded across his chest. 'Well, maybe you need to think outside the box this year. Try something different.'

'How do you mean?' The Lighthouse Festival was an island *tradition*. People expected certain things. Like candy-floss stalls and carousels, neither of which she'd been able to source so far.

'Well, from what you've said, it sounds like the festival has grown every year, right? So maybe it's time for the next big evolutionary growth for the Lighthouse in general.' The waitress brought their drinks, and he took a long sip of his pint after saying thanks. 'What would have happened with the B&B this summer if we hadn't come to stay? I heard you talking to Juliet about it that first night,' he admitted with a sheepish look.

'Honestly, I don't know.' Miranda reached for her wine glass, toying with the stem, turning it round and round as she considered. 'Mum and Dad . . . they were supposed to be home by now, but when they extended their trip, they didn't have any bookings in place for the whole of August. We're *always* booked up in August.'

'Suspicious.'

'And that's not the only thing.' Suddenly, all the strange things she'd been noticing over the past months started to pour out of her, like they'd reached critical mass and couldn't help but overflow. 'They've basically abandoned the online booking system; everyone who has stayed with them this year were past visitors who contacted them directly. In the past, Mum was always religious about repainting rooms the minute they started to show any wear and tear, but I don't think they've decorated *any* of the Lighthouse for the last two years. And then this sudden trip of a lifetime they decided to take when they've barely left the island since we arrived, years and years ago.'

'You sound worried,' Owain commented.

'I am.' Miranda sighed. 'Leo and I . . . we found a sales listing for the Lighthouse. Photos, descriptions, guide price, everything. And the most recent accounts are missing, too. What if they're planning on selling? They're not that old. But . . . what if it's all getting too much for them? And . . .' She bit her lip, reluctant to name her biggest fear, in case it made it real. 'I'm scared one of them is sick and they won't tell us. You know. Really sick.'

Dying.

The word echoed in her head. She'd been avoiding even

thinking it, for strange, nonsensical, superstitious reasons. But now it was out there . . . she couldn't avoid it any longer.

Owain reached across the table and took her hand in his. 'Have you spoken to Leo and Juliet about that?'

Miranda shook her head. 'No. I'm probably just catastrophising, anyway. And I'm the one who has been here, who should have noticed before now that something was wrong. It's just . . . I don't understand how they could leave Seashell Island.'

He gave her a strange look. 'It's a holiday, Miranda. People take them.'

'Not my parents. Not ever. Not since we moved here.' They'd been like her: committed to the island. Happy enough there that they never needed to go anywhere else.

Until this summer.

'Then they were probably due,' he pointed out, with annoying reasonableness. 'What about you? When was the last time you left the island?'

This was it. The moment he realised she was so crazy he would definitely not want to sleep with her, even for rebound sex. Juliet had told her often enough how insane her obsession with this place made her. Now Owain would know it too.

She took a breath, and confessed. 'Never. I've hardly left Seashell Island at all if I could avoid it. Not since the summer we moved here. And not once since I've been an adult.'

His eyes widened. 'Not even for . . . I don't know? A day trip? To go to a gig? Nothing?'

'Nothing. I . . . this is my home. And for the first ten years of my life I never had that, so once I found it, I refused to let it go.' She shrugged, and reached for her wine. 'Sounds crazy, I know.'

'Not crazy.' But the thoughtful look he was giving her suggested otherwise. 'It just explains a lot.'

'The last time I left . . .' She paused. Did she really want to share this with him? Mostly, she tried to pretend it hadn't happened. But she could see that Owain didn't understand, and she wanted him to, at least a little. 'I went to this university open day in Cardiff, when I was seventeen. I didn't want to, not really, but Mum and Dad were talking a lot about opportunities and seeing what the world had to offer.'

Even now, she could feel the same panic and uncertainty rising up in her that she'd felt then, taking the ferry to the mainland alone, facing the world outside Seashell Island again.

'What happened?' Owain asked.

She smiled down at the table, the concern in his voice warming her more than the wine. 'Juliet got into trouble, of course. She was ten, and she decided she could swim out to the rocks past Gull Bay. Only she got caught in a current . . . search and rescue were out and everything. She claimed it was dare with Rory, but I suspect she just wanted to do it, so she did. And he covered for her, like always.'

'She was OK, though,' Owain said.

'Yeah. But I didn't know that at the time. Mum was in pieces, and Leo called and begged me to come home and fix things, so I did.' She shrugged. 'And that was the last time I left Seashell Island.'

She didn't tell him what a relief it had been to be safely back home, where she knew how to manage life – rather than lost in a maze of newness and unfamiliarity on the mainland. He looked like he had more questions, but Miranda didn't want to discuss it any more. It was done. What difference did it make now? So she'd never gone to university. Never visited Paul when he went, either, however much he asked

– just waited for him to come home instead.

She stood by the choices she'd made about her life. Everything had worked out fine.

Until this summer, anyway.

'Anyway.' Miranda dragged her files up onto the table and opened them, mostly just to have something else to look at. 'Back to the festival. You said I should shake it up a bit, then you asked about the B&B. What were you getting at?'

He shrugged, apparently unconcerned by the change of subject. 'I figured that maybe the Lighthouse was in financial trouble. I know that you said the festival was normally for the locals, and the last of the holidaymakers who'd be here anyway, but . . . well, I reckon people would pay to attend an exclusive festival on a special island like this. Plus you'd boost visitors for that first weekend after the proper summer ends.'

'It would have to be more than just the usual stuff, though,' Miranda said, thoughtfully. 'I mean, no one would come all this way for candyfloss and a carousel. They'd want—'

'Music,' Owain said, succinctly. 'They'd want a music festival.'

She stared at him. 'Do you *honestly* think I can throw together a full-blown music festival in three weeks and get people to travel all the way to Seashell Island for it?'

'No,' Owain admitted. 'But I think *we* could. If you'll let me help.'

LEO

The girls hadn't looked particularly happy to see him when he returned, but they'd been thrilled that he'd brought Christabel, so that was something.

Convincing her to help him had been easier than he'd expected. He'd found her ambulance down by the dunes again, knocked, and basically begged.

'I don't know what I'm doing.'

'I could have told you that,' she'd said, putting down the bike she was mending.

'You've done this before, right? I mean, fixed your life when you realised it was off track.'

'Well, yes.' Christabel had frowned at that. 'I suppose so. I mean, I realised that I wasn't happy, so I found a way to redesign my life so I *was* happy.'

Happiness. It had never been the key component Leo had worked for in his life. He'd wanted success and security, to know that he could take care of his family. A hangover, he supposed, from those early days before the Lighthouse had enough guests to keep the heating on in the winter.

Emily had always sought happiness – and found it with Mark.

He'd found satisfaction instead, and personal pride. But for his daughters? He wanted happiness, as well as that security he'd always longed for.

'I want to make Mia and Abby happy, and secure. So I need you to help me. Please.'

It was probably the please that had won her over. In any case, she'd dragged him into town to buy supplies, and lectured him along the way. And he hadn't been able to stop himself arguing back, even though he knew he'd asked for this.

'All they want is for you to see them, Leo. To know that they matter to you.'

'Of course they do! I've put my whole summer on hold to spend it with them—'

'Have you, though?' she'd interrupted. 'Or have you been trying to keep them entertained while also running your business from your mobile phone?'

'You want me to completely abandon my business for five weeks? Because I don't think the girls will like it much if my company collapses and I can't afford food.'

She'd rolled her eyes. 'You're catastrophising – just like you complain about Miranda doing. And that's not what I'm saying, anyway. Come on, we've got supplies to buy.'

'Supplies for what, exactly?'

'For your apology,' Christabel had said. 'First you're going to make it up to your daughters. Then, you and I are going to figure out a new plan for the rest of your summer that can make *all* of you happy.'

To be honest, that still seemed pretty much impossible to Leo, but he'd gone along with it because it wasn't like he had any better ideas.

Now, back at the Lighthouse, he let Christabel entertain the girls in the front lounge with a rousing game of Monopoly (in which she seemed to be bending the rules considerably to encourage bartering, shared ownership, and working together for the greater good, which he was pretty sure wasn't how Monopoly was supposed to work), while he got to work in the back garden.

The basic plan was simple, as he understood it, after Christabel had explained it to him in bullet points, ticked off on her fingers in between adding items to his shopping basket.

'First, you want to show them that you care about their happiness. Then you want to show them that you've been listening and know what *they* care about. And thirdly, you want to make them a promise to do better in the future.'

'I *do* care about their happiness, and I *do* want to do better,' he'd said. 'So, what do they care about?'

Christabel's smile had been downright smug. 'You tell me. Prove to me that you really *do* listen to them even when they think you don't. What is the biggest issue in their little worlds right now, this second?'

And that was how he'd found himself throwing a 'Welcome Home!' party for a llama.

Leo strung a final rope of lights through the trees around the terrace and looked around to judge his handiwork. The barbecue was smouldering nicely, ready to cook burgers – Mia's favourites. The firepit was laid ready to be lit for marshmallows after the main course. Suzi had brought out one of her many stringed instruments and was happily strumming it from the terrace swing seat, while Harriet sat beside her, horses abandoned for the day, looking pretty besotted, as far as Leo could tell. And the guest of honour, Lucifer the Llama, was wearing the party hat Christabel had insisted on for the occasion, even if she had spat at him as he tried to tie it on. He got the feeling that Lucy wasn't any keener on this plan than he was.

Hopefully his sisters would show up and join in sooner or later, too. Miranda was out at her 'planning meeting' with

Owain, and he had no idea where Juliet had got to.

Straightening the last of the chairs and outdoor beanbags around the firepit, Leo nodded to Suzi and Harriet, then headed in to interrupt Monopoly.

'Girls? When you're done, I've got something outside to show you.'

Mia didn't even turn around. Abby just said, 'Not now, Daddy. Christabel and I are setting up a collective to provide housing for the poor.'

He shot Christabel a glare, and she returned an unapologetic shrug.

'Maybe I can play?' he suggested.

Mia gave him a dark look. 'No. We're already halfway through a game.'

'We'll be done soon,' Christabel promised, and Leo sat and tapped his fingers against his knee as he waited.

He should be checking his email. Using this time profitably. Doing *something* useful.

But Christabel had set down one very firm rule for him that afternoon. 'Just one,' she'd said. 'But if you ignore it, I'm out. OK?'

'OK.'

'For the rest of the day, you don't get your phone out where the girls can see.'

'That's it?'

'That's it. But I think it'll be harder than you think.'

He'd been certain he could do that easily. He'd just check in with Tom before and after spending time with the girls. Or when they were distracted, or busy with their aunts, or whatever. Easy.

Except now, with Christabel watching him as he waited, he knew she was remembering that rule. If he walked out of the room now, she'd know exactly why, and some perverse part of him wouldn't give her the satisfaction.

She thought he was addicted to his phone; that much had been obvious from her sceptical look when he'd said how easy it would be to follow her rule.

She was wrong. He just had to prove it.

So he sat, and he drummed his fingers on his knee, and he thought about all the emails he could be sending and—

Christabel cleared her throat meaningfully, and Leo looked down to find his phone in his hand, email app open.

'Just checking the time,' he lied, shoving it back in his pocket. He realised they were packing away the Monopoly board. 'Are you done? Who won?'

'We all won,' Abby replied. 'It's more fun that way.'

'I suppose it is,' Leo agreed doubtfully. 'Now, come on. I've got a surprise for you outside.'

That, at least, got their attention. As they raced outside, Christabel came alongside him and held out a hand. 'Why don't you give it to me to look after. Then you won't have to worry about it.'

'I think I can manage to control myself,' he said, drily. Christabel looked unconvinced, but he ignored that and hurried after the girls instead.

Summer was still lingering, but they were well past the longest day now, and since bedtime had been slipping later and later since they arrived on the island, the sun was just starting to dip lower in the sky towards the sea as they emerged outside. The lights he'd hung through the trees – actual old-fashioned lightbulbs glowing in the growing gloom – looked magical around the terrace. Suzi was still playing – something light and fun and tuneful that made even Leo think about dancing. The girls skipped down the stairs towards the firepit, Abby clapping her hands together with glee.

For a second, Leo caught a similar look on his older daughter's face – until she saw him looking and replaced it with her usual scowl. Ten going on fifteen, that's what his mother would have said. Juliet had been just the same at that age.

He just wished Mum was there to give him some advice on how to handle it.

Maybe Juliet would remember . . .

'It's a party!' Abby said, hopping around to hug his legs. 'It is a party, right?'

'It is,' Leo confirmed.

'But what for?' Mia asked. 'I mean, it's not even anybody's birthday or anything.'

Right on cue, Lucy gave a long-suffering moan, and everyone turned to look at her as she trotted over, party hat miraculously still in place.

'It's a welcome party for Lucy,' Leo explained, trying not to feel like a total idiot. 'To celebrate her coming to live at the Lighthouse. I thought we'd have a barbecue for dinner, then toast marshmallows for pudding, and Suzi and her friends said they'd play us some music so there can even be dancing . . . you seemed to like that the night they [The musicians weren't at the Lighthouse the night Leo and the girls arrived.] arrived, so—'

'It's brilliant!' Abby bounced up to hug him, and he caught her in his arms. 'Thanks, Dad.'

Relief flooded through him as he hugged her back. He'd done something right, at last.

Mia, however, was still looking at him speculatively. 'Will you dance?'

He *hated* dancing. He glanced over at Christabel, but she just raised her eyebrows as if to say, you're on your own now.

'If that's what you want,' he told Mia. 'Of course I'll dance with you.'

She nodded. 'Let's start with the burgers then. I'm starving.'

There were far too many burgers − not least because Miranda and Juliet never did show up − but Ryan and Robyn ate twice as many as he'd expected, so it all seemed to work out. And even without their front man, the band played up a storm − fast and fun stomping folk reels that had both girls spinning in circles between toasting their marshmallows. (Leo watched Mia closely for any signs of greenness, but with her stomach lined with burger and salad veg, she seemed OK tonight.)

Now, the music had calmed to more gentle tunes, the band laughing between themselves as they played snatches of melodies back and forth. Leo sat back by the firepit, a last, lazy marshmallow toasting for Abby, and watched his daughters spin anyway, arms wide, staring up at the night sky and the lights.

'You did good today.' Christabel, sitting next to him, raised her beer bottle for him to clink his against. 'Are you happy?'

'You know, I am,' he admitted. 'I mean, tomorrow all my problems are still going to be waiting for me. But right now I am honestly happy.'

'It's a start,' Christabel said. 'I mean, nobody is happy all of the time, right? We wouldn't want to be, or we wouldn't appreciate the really good times. But moments like this? They're the magic in the everyday. They make the lonely days and the hard days more worthwhile.'

Leo turned to her at that, surprised to hear something in her voice he'd never heard before. Regret. 'Are *you* happy? Here on the island, I mean?'

'I have been.' She flashed him a quick smile. 'And sitting

here, right now, with you? With fairy lights and good music and a llama? Yeah, I'm happy.'

'But longer term?'

She considered, longer than he thought the question would have needed if the answer was yes. 'When I came here, to Seashell Island, I'd been on my own, detoxing from the city, living wild and free for about six months. I'd promised myself I'd never stay in one place longer than a week. That I'd keep moving, keep living. But when the time came to leave Seashell, I just . . . didn't. I stayed and I stayed and I made friends and I kept learning.'

'Learning?'

'Always. The day I realised I couldn't keep working in the City, I learned something important about myself – that money and prestige aren't enough for me if they can't buy me anything I really want. And, I mean, I'm about the billionth person to realise that this week, right? But knowing something and believing it are different, and that day I believed it. And so I walked away.'

'What made that change?' Suddenly, it felt like something he needed to know. To learn. To believe. 'What made you believe?'

'I'd love to say it was when I missed something important in a loved one's life, or when I fell in love, or something really profound like that. But it wasn't. I kept working through love affairs, and I missed birthday parties – and even a funeral, once.' She winced at the memory. 'But the day I realised I needed to leave? It was just like all the other ones. And that was what did it. There was nothing about that day – nothing I did, no one I talked to – that really mattered to me. And as I walked out that night . . . I knew I had to make a change.'

'And you did.'

'And I did.' She twisted on the bench seat around the firepit, close enough to him that Leo could see the flames of the fire flickering in her eyes. 'What about you? Are you going to make a change?'

'I hope so,' he said. He wasn't sure if that unwavering belief she seemed to feel about the world was in him yet, but he wanted to feel it. And that counted, right?

'Good.'

She was so close, he could kiss her now, if she let him. And the smile lurking around her lips made him think that she might.

But then the music turned fast and furious again and Abby and Mia were at their sides, grabbing their arms and pulling them up to dance with them.

'I thought you didn't dance?' Christabel asked, amused.

'Only with my daughters,' Leo explained, and let them lead him out onto the grass below the terrace.

And as he held his daughters' hands and danced under the starlight, Leo felt for the first time in years that he was finally getting something right.

MESSAGES

Leo (to Siblings): Guys, you're missing burgers, dancing and a llama party. Don't say I didn't warn you!

JULIET

She'd told him everything.

It had taken hours, several drinks (for him) and a couple of portions of chips (for her), but she'd brought Rory up to date on everything that had happened in her life since she'd left the island – and got a much better idea of what had been going on in his, too.

Until, sitting in the quiet back room of the Anchor pub, talking in whispers, she'd reached recent events, and told Rory the whole sordid story of her relationship with Callum, the pregnancy, and that horrible last morning in London.

'No wonder you came running home,' Rory said, giving a low whistle. 'That is one hell of a special kind of London bastard.'

Juliet's answering chuckle came out sort of soggy. Was she still crying? She hadn't even noticed.

'You say that like nobody on Seashell Island has ever cheated on their wives, or got pregnant by accident, or screwed up in some other terrible way. And I know for a fact that isn't true.' She could recount half a dozen such scandals from her teenage years. She'd always liked to keep track of people who were in more trouble than her.

'Maybe not. But none of them did it to you.'

She couldn't help but meet his gaze at that, and remember how they'd been as a couple. Their first times together – fumbling and awkward but funny and sweet. And they'd got a lot better, very quickly, learning together.

He'd been so careful with her, always. She wished now that she'd been as careful with his heart.

'No,' she whispered. 'You never would.'

He pulled away at her words – not obviously, but his gaze slid from hers, and suddenly, somehow, there was a few more inches between them on the bench seat they shared. Enough that she got the message.

'So. What are you going to do now?' Rory asked. 'I mean, you've decided to keep the baby, yes?'

Picking up her glass of lime and soda, Juliet nodded. 'That part was weirdly easy. I mean . . . I know it's crazy, and I know it'll be hard, but I never questioned that I'd have the baby. I don't know why.'

'I do,' Rory replied, not looking directly at her. 'It's because you'll be a brilliant mum and you should definitely have the chance to do that, however it happens.'

She looked up at him in surprise. 'You are the only person in the world who would say that.'

'I doubt it. But either way, it's true.' He gave her a lopsided smile and she knew, without question, that this was why she'd started her confessions with Rory. He'd always had more faith in her than anyone else. 'You love fiercely, Juliet, and you have ambition. I know you'll love and want and do the best for your child.'

An unfamiliar warmth began to fill her, from her heart outwards. It felt like . . . confidence.

She *could* do this. She could do this alone, and she could do this on her own terms.

But it would be a hell of a lot easier with her friends and family behind her.

'I want to do this right,' she whispered. 'I want to do this *one* thing in my life perfectly.'

Rory laughed. 'I don't think anyone does parenting perfectly. I know my dad didn't – and my mum was a perfect example of what not to do.'

'My parents were pretty perfect, even when I was a nightmare child for them.'

Rory's expression was unreadable. 'I'd ask Miranda if she agrees with that assessment, when you tell her about the baby.'

Juliet's head dropped to the table with a painful thunk. 'Oh God. I really have to tell Miranda. She's going to be so disappointed in me.'

'Juliet, you're twenty-eight. You're allowed to live your own life without worrying about disappointing people. You're doing something brilliant here – and I think your sister loves you enough to support you in it. In fact, I think the whole island will. You're one of our own, even if you've been away.'

'Do you really think so?'

'I really do.' Rory's words were genuine, but Juliet still felt the distance between them in a way she hadn't before. She was sure there were still a lot of issues they needed to work through between them if they wanted to recover their friendship. But she hoped today had gone a way to doing that – rather than putting another, more permanent issue between them in the form of the baby growing inside her.

'You look exhausted,' Rory told her.

'Long day,' she admitted.

Juliet picked up her phone to check the time, and spotted a number of missed notifications. Frowning, she swiped open the app to read them – then pulled a face.

'Something's going on at home.' She held up the phone so Rory could read Leo's text. 'Goodness knows what a llama party is, but I'd better get back there and find out.'

'And get some rest.' Rory was already standing. 'I'll take you. Come on, the van is round the corner at the restaurant.'

They walked along the high street back towards the Flying Fish, only to see Miranda and Owain appearing out of the restaurant. Together.

Juliet raised her eyebrows as she realised her big sister was wearing actual make-up, not to mention her best frock. And, if she wasn't mistaken, even her contact lenses.

This was a date. Juliet grinned. Good for Miranda.

'Did you get Leo's message?' Miranda asked.

'Just now. I . . .' she glanced up at Rory. 'We were busy talking.'

'Us too.' Miranda didn't look back at Owain, but her cheeks turned a slight pink that Juliet was sure had nothing to do with the sea breeze. 'Is he honestly throwing a party for Lucy?'

Juliet shrugged. 'Apparently. I was just heading back to find out.' And because she was about to fall asleep standing up, otherwise.

'Come on,' Rory said. 'I'll take us all in the van – as long as you and Owain don't mind the bench seats in the back.'

They reached the Lighthouse long after daylight had faded. When had the summer days grown so short? Or had she and Rory spent far longer hashing out the mess that was her life than she'd realised?

They heard the music, and the laughter, the moment Rory cut the engine and they all tumbled out of the van.

Miranda and Juliet exchanged looks, then hurried out to the terrace – where they found Lucy the Llama glaring at them from under a party hat.

'How did he even get her to wear that thing?' Juliet asked, baffled.

Christabel crossed the terrace from where she'd been

sitting with Suzi and Harriet, a beer in her hand. 'Persever-ance. We're having a Welcome to the Lighthouse party for Lucy,' she explained. 'Leo had some making up to do with the girls, so he went all out.'

'So I can see.' Juliet took in the strings of lights, the fire-pit, and the decorations. No way Leo had come up with this all on his own – it had to have been Christabel's idea.

'And where is our darling brother?' Miranda asked.

'Putting the girls to bed,' Christabel replied. 'Abby half fell asleep while she was dancing with him. It was very cute.'

Miranda and Juliet shared a look. 'Leo was dancing?'

'Apparently he only dances with his daughters,' Christabel explained, but the grin on her face told Juliet she understood what a step forward this was for him. 'Come on, we've got beer over here. Come join us.'

While the others went to get a drink, Juliet left them to it and went to welcome Lucy personally instead.

'Why, exactly, do you guys now own a llama?' Rory asked, following her. 'I mean, I'm not even going to ask why it gets its own party—'

'She,' Juliet corrected him, stroking Lucy's head. 'Lucy is a girl llama. And she chose us. She likes us better than the farm.'

'Mia and I looked it up earlier,' Miranda called from the swing. 'Llamas are herd animals. They're used to being around others. I think she got lonely on the farm.'

'Well, she'll certainly never be lonely here.' Juliet looked around at the party – Miranda and Christabel handing out drinks, Owain and the rest of his band tuning their instru-ments for another impromptu concert, Leo upstairs with his girls . . . and Rory.

Rory, who'd listened to the whole saga of screw-ups that

made up her life since she'd left him and hadn't flinched. Instead, he'd offered to help.

'Are you OK?' he asked now.

'I think I need to go to bed too,' she admitted, reluctantly.

Rory laughed, a low, warm chuckle that she felt somewhere deep in her belly. Or maybe that was the baby. Nine weeks was too early for that, though, according to her new favourite app. So probably it was just Rory.

'Come on. I'll see you to your room.' He was standing so close to her now. Closer than he'd been in the pub. And for a second, as they stood there, watching the llama, only a sliver of night between their bodies, she wondered what would happen if she stretched up and kissed him. Just once. Just to see if it was as perfect as she remembered.

But she didn't. Because she'd be leaving Seashell Island again, and his life was here. Because she'd already broken his heart once, and she knew he hadn't forgiven her for that. Because she had a new life growing inside her, and couldn't afford to make mistakes any more.

It wasn't just her life she was screwing up now.

So instead, Juliet let herself be led towards the Lighthouse back door, up the stairs to her attic room. And then she smiled, and said thank you, and good night, and shut the door on Rory before she was too tempted to do anything else.

MIRANDA

The party was dying down. Even Lucy had wandered off to snooze in the little shelter they'd made for her, with some help from Max and a slightly tearful Dafydd. Miranda leant back in the swing seat and watched as Suzi and the twins packed up their instruments, low conversation passing between them and Owain as they said their goodnights. Rory had already led Juliet back towards the house, and hopefully bed. Juliet had clearly been working flat out keeping them all fed and happy, and she looked exhausted.

What was going on between Juliet and her ex-boyfriend was another question, but one Miranda didn't intend to try and answer tonight.

She had another, more urgent, query she wanted answering.

She got the first part of her answer a few moments later, when Owain came and settled beside her on the swing, even as the others disappeared inside. He had a beer bottle in his hand, and lifted it up to his mouth to drain it before he spoke.

'So.'

'So,' she echoed.

He turned his head where it rested against the back of the swing, until he was looking right at her, suddenly incredibly close. Even in the weak light from Leo's strings of bulbs, she could read a lot in his eyes.

She just hoped she wasn't writing what she wanted to see there.

'This planning meeting of ours didn't end exactly how I'd hoped,' Owain said.

'Oh? How were you hoping it would end?' Because she knew what *she'd* been hoping for. *Us, naked in my bed.*

'With you admitting it was a date.'

Miranda's stomach tightened, her breath catching at his words. 'There were certain date-like qualities to it, I suppose.'

A warm smile spread across his lips. 'Nice restaurant, good wine, great company. Romantic lighting.' He glanced up at the bulbs in the tree.

'Can't beat some string lights from old Myrddin's hardware store,' she agreed. 'So, if it *had* been a date . . . what do you think would have happened after dinner? Once we'd dealt with all the locals who needed to urgently discuss festival matters or my love life with me?'

Owain slouched lower onto the swing seat, his hips almost at the edge as he stretched his long legs out in front of him. One arm snaked around her shoulder, and Miranda sank into him, resting her head comfortably against his chest as if it were the most natural thing in the world.

'I think I'd have taken you for a walk along the shoreline. You'd have kicked off those shoes and let the waves flow over your feet. And we'd have talked some more, of course – not about the festival, but about you and about me and our lives. What matters to us. Who we really are. The sort of conversation you can only have in the dark.'

'Sounds kind of serious,' Miranda said. Possibly, she was incredibly shallow for jumping straight to the naked-in-bed part of the evening. But in her defence, he was *impossibly* good-looking, and he wouldn't be here very long. She had to take her chances where she could.

'Yeah. But then we'd have stripped off all our clothes and gone skinny-dipping,' Owain finished, with a wicked grin she could feel against the top of her head as he kissed it. 'Then rushed back home together and fallen into bed.'

'For rebound sex,' Miranda clarified, not wanting to admit how her whole body had tightened at his words. God, she wanted this man. Naked in the water, just like he'd described.

'If that's what you wanted,' Owain replied.

She pulled back, just enough to look him in the eye, for him to know she meant every word she said. 'I want it all. The swimming and everything that comes after.'

He held her gaze for a long moment before nodding, just once.

'Let's go then.'

The water was freezing, even in August.

She'd led him down to Gull Bay, because it was closest to the Lighthouse, and hardly anyone went there in the daytime, let alone at night. Plus, she knew it like the back of her hand, pale in the moonlight. She felt safe there.

And she felt safe with Owain, even if she'd only known him for a few weeks. Which was weird, but something to worry about another, less interesting time.

They'd skipped the deep-and-meaningful conversation part, but Owain didn't seem to mind. Maybe they'd get to it later, maybe they wouldn't, but Miranda knew she wouldn't be able to concentrate on any of it right now anyway. Not when she was imagining him naked and inside her with every breath she took.

Stripping off their clothes, they left them behind the pile of rocks that marked where the staircase up the cliff started. The moonlight gave her courage, Miranda decided, as she pulled her dress over her head. The darkness blurred boundaries, hid edges and imperfections, and the pale white light was more flattering than any Instagram filter.

More than that, it seemed to give her power. Strength.

She paused, before unhooking her bra, and realised *she* wanted to know what she looked like in this place, in this light. Wanted to know who this new Miranda was, who could even agree to doing such a thing. Needed to know how far she could swim from the shore – inching away from her island, wave by wave.

Juliet would be so proud.

Not that she'd ever actually tell her sister, of course.

'God, you're gorgeous.' She'd looked up to see Owain, still half dressed, staring at her.

She'd smiled back with a recklessness she didn't even recognise in herself. 'Your turn.'

He'd dropped his pants and, seconds later, they'd both been running naked into the freezing water.

'In my imagination, this was warmer,' Owain gasped, as they came up for air.

'Mine too,' she admitted. 'Although at least this way we get to keep each other warm.'

'Works for me.'

The water was shallow enough that they could stand, even a decent way out from the beach. She looked back at the shore, seemingly slipping further away with each wave that crashed against her bare skin. And for the first time, she wondered if maybe she could go further. Keep walking into the water and find out what happened . . .

Owain wrapped his arms around her waist and pulled her close, and Miranda's feet left the sand of the ocean floor as she moved with him. The water lapped against them, pushing them closer, until she could feel every inch of his body against hers. Every impressive-even-in-the-freezing-water inch.

She shivered, but it wasn't because of the cold this time. It was pure desire, coursing through her naked body.

Owain seemed to take the hint, as he brought his mouth down to hers at last, his hands sliding over her wet skin as he kissed her deep and desperately, and it was everything she hadn't known she needed until this moment.

He was like the water itself, an adventure away from her everyday life, baby steps away from the security and familiarity she'd prized and prioritised for so long. Owain wasn't staying on Seashell Island past the end of the summer. He wasn't offering her anything more than a few weeks of fun, and she wasn't asking for more. She had no idea what would happen next . . . but she was ready to take another step into these unknown waters and find out.

'Bed?' he murmured against her lips.

'Definitely,' she replied, between kisses.

They parted just long enough to swim back to shore, grabbing their clothes and throwing them on over their wet bodies. Then Owain took her hand and they both raced up the narrow staircase, trying not to slip in their haste.

'The cottage,' Miranda panted as they reached the top. 'It's closer.'

More private, too, which helped. She wanted to hold on to this wild and free Miranda she'd found tonight, and somehow she knew that being back in the Lighthouse, with her siblings in the neighbouring rooms, wouldn't make that possible.

The cottage, secret in the woods, was perfect.

Owain nodded and obediently changed course, heading for the edge of the Lighthouse property, never letting go of her hand for a moment. Miranda felt like moonlight and magic combined, like she might explode if she couldn't kiss him again soon. Like she could fly, above Seashell Island and to places she'd never dreamt of.

The cottage door fell open for them as Owain pressed her into the wood and kissed her hard. Stumbling backwards, Miranda laughed, and now it was her leading him, back towards the bedroom and that wide, soft bed she'd chosen all those years before when she'd first moved out. And he followed, smiling and wanting, his touch everywhere even as they moved. And Miranda thought this was the happiest, the freest, and the most *herself* she'd felt since before she could even remember.

Then the door shut behind them and they fell onto the bed, and Miranda didn't try to think any more at all.

LEO

Finally, the girls were both in bed. Maybe it had been the excitement of the party, or just the sugar in the marshmallows, but they'd wanted to talk and talk tonight – even though he'd have sworn Abby was ready to crash while they were dancing. Questions about everything from llamas to folk music to tide times to bicycles to the Lighthouse Festival, to when Grandma and Grandad were coming back.

That last one had been from a drowsy Mia, after Abby had finally succumbed to sleep, her new favourite stuffed toy – a llama Juliet had found for her in the local toy shop, which Leo imagined would feature in a wedding soon enough – curled up close at her side.

'Grandma and Grandad are coming back, right, Dad?' Mia had murmured, her eyes hardly open.

He'd already answered eighty-four random questions that evening, mostly from Abby, but somehow Leo knew this was the one that mattered the most. The one that showed that Mia trusted him to tell the truth. To answer difficult questions. To stay and talk when she needed him to.

This, he realised at last, was what Christabel had been talking about. How he was supposed to do it when also running a business instead of throwing parties for llamas was another matter, but one he'd save for later.

Right now, he was focused on his daughter's question.

Sitting back down on the edge of her bed, Leo brushed

the hair out of Mia's closing eyes and smiled softly at how young she looked all of a sudden. Less the almost tween, more the little girl he remembered.

'Of course they're coming back,' he told her. 'This is their home, remember? They wouldn't leave it. And they wouldn't leave us.'

'You left,' Mia whispered, so quiet he wasn't sure if she was even awake any longer. 'I hope you're coming back.'

He froze, one hand still stroking her head, as her words ricocheted around his head. *You left.* Then her breathing evened out and he knew she was truly asleep.

But he'd never felt more awake.

With one last kiss to each of the girls' heads – and after tucking Lara the stuffed toy llama more securely into Abby's embrace – Leo took the stairs back down to the ground floor two at a time.

He found Christabel in the kitchen, making tea in the proper old teapot his mum never used any more.

'You missed Juliet and Miranda,' she said. 'I think Juliet's gone to bed, and Miranda disappeared again with Owain. I think you're in for a lecture about throwing parties without them tomorrow.'

Leo winced. 'Excellent. Suddenly I'm glad bedtime took so long.'

'The girls wanted to talk tonight?' she guessed.

Leo nodded, watching as she poured the dark, steaming tea into mugs. 'They have *so* many questions.'

'But they wanted to talk to *you* about them,' Christabel pointed out, and he couldn't help but smile.

'Yeah. They did.' Then he remembered Mia's last words before sleep, and the smile fell away.

Placing two mugs of tea between them on the kitchen table, and retrieving a packet of chocolate digestives from who knew where, Christabel sat down opposite him. 'What happened?'

'Mia. She said something . . .' He reached for his mug, then paused. 'What happened to the beer?'

Christabel shook her head. 'It's time to talk now. Talking requires tea.'

In his experience, talking – the real, things that matter kind of talk – needed strong liquor, but he didn't argue with her. Instead, he sipped his tea – scalding his tongue in the process – and told her what Mia had said.

'Hmm.' Christabel took a biscuit, and dunked it in her tea. 'Well, on the positive side, she hopes you're coming back.'

'I suppose.' It wasn't much, but it was hope. For both of them. 'Tonight . . . it worked. The girls loved the party, they forgave me, and they talked to me for ages at bedtime. I felt like we were close again, like we used to be when they were tiny.'

'So that's good,' Christabel said. 'Why aren't you smiling?'

'Because it's not real.' Leo sighed. Any enthusiasm he'd felt about rebuilding his relationship with his daughters while he'd been dancing in the starlight with them had drained away step by step as he'd walked away from their bedroom. 'This summer . . . it's an anomaly. And even tonight was a moment out of time. Anyone can pull it together for a special occasion. But that's not every day.'

'Why can't it be?' Christabel asked. 'Why can't every day be special?'

'Christabel . . .' he groaned. 'You said it yourself – we can't be happy all the time.'

'No, but that doesn't mean we can't work *towards* happiness.' She leaned forward across the table, and he made a point of keeping his focus on her face, not the curves she presented him with as the neckline of her top draped low. Well, after the first few seconds, anyway. *Focus, Leo.* 'I truly believe that every single day is a special occasion, deserving of celebration and joy. And that's how I live my life.'

'Which might be possible if I lived in an ambulance, travelling the country, going wherever I wanted and making my living fixing bikes,' Leo pointed out. 'But I don't. I have a business to run, employees relying on me – well, just one employee right now, but he's demanding. Not to mention the fact that I don't even *see* the girls from one week to the next back in London. Seashell Island isn't real life, I've always known that. Why do you think I left? I wanted the real world. Except it turns out that in real life, most days are just something you have to get through to get to the next one.'

Christabel's eyes were sad as she watched him across the table. 'That's not the only way to live life, Leo. That's what I've been trying to show you. But you have to be willing to see it.'

He wanted to believe her, really I did. But what did she know? Her life was so free and easy, with no responsibilities, no obligations. Nothing that even vaguely resembled his own.

'What if it is for me?' he asked. That deep fear that lived down in his gut.

She shook her head. 'I won't believe that. You got a glimpse of what your relationship with your daughters could be tonight—'

'If I threw them a party every day and gave up work.'

'No. If you listened and focused on what is important.'

'My work is important too,' he pointed out. 'Maybe not to you, but it matters to me.'

'I know that.' She tilted her head and looked at him

curiously. 'What is it, exactly, that makes it so important? I mean, besides the money to live on and stuff. I know that matters – it mattered to me too. But I realised the job I was doing wasn't who I was, who I wanted to be. But you, you *love* your job, so it must mean something to you. So, why do you do *this* job? What made you start *this* business?'

Leo blinked. 'Um . . . because I'm good at it?' He always had been. He'd had an eye for figuring out how to tell the stories that got people to do what companies wanted them to – buy their product, visit their attraction.

He knew how to manipulate and make people think something was their idea in the first place.

But for some reason, it didn't work on his children. It had stopped working on his wife, too. And he had a feeling it would never work on Christabel.

Actually, he liked that.

She was still waiting, apparently not satisfied with his answer. Leo tried to dig deeper, to find the words she wanted to hear. Or maybe even the ones he wanted to say.

'I . . . my business is something that *I* control. I'm in charge, and things only happen if I say they happen.' He looked down into his mug, as if the tealeaves might provide some answers. 'That makes me sound like a control freak, and I'm not. It's just that . . . so much of what happens in this world happens *to* people, whether they like it or not. And there are elements of that in business too. But at least I can steer my company, guide it in the direction I think it best, or safest. One that gives us all security and comfort. Like I . . .' he swallowed, as he realised the truth. 'Like I always wanted to do for my family, in my marriage. But it turned out I wasn't any good at that. I *am* good at this.'

'But you are good at being a dad,' Christabel said gently. 'Look at how your daughters responded this evening.'

'Because I threw them a party,' he grumbled. 'I can't just buy their love with parties every time I screw up.'

'Because you knew what was important to them.' Christabel reached across the table and placed her hand over his, small and smooth and cool. 'It wasn't that it was a party. It was that it was a party for Lucy the Llama. A party where you were all together. That's what won them over.'

'Oh.' He might have screwed up when they told him about Lucy, but he'd remembered that she mattered to the girls. He'd remembered that Mia loved marshmallows, and Abby adored fairy lights. He'd noticed how they'd both loved the music when Birchwood played on the terrace.

He knew his daughters. He loved his daughters. He just needed to show them that more.

'I still don't know how I'm going to keep that up *and* work, though.'

Christabel shrugged. 'So that's phase two. And I don't have the answers for you. But I'd suspect it has something to do with not trying to do two things at once.'

'But two things – or more – always need doing.' Usually about fifteen by the time he'd phoned to check in with Tom in the mornings.

'But not at the same time. Your girls are intelligent enough. Set expectations. That's what I do with myself when I'm working but I'd rather be cycling.'

'How do you mean?' It was hard to imagine Christabel ever doing anything except exactly what she wanted at that moment.

'Well, I tell myself that if I do one hour of mending bikes, I can go out for an hour on *my* bike afterwards.'

'Like personal bribery.'

'Like setting my expectations,' she corrected with a scowl. 'Nobody can spend all their time doing *exactly* what they want, Leo. But when you spend enough of it on the things that really matter to you, I find you don't mind the other bits so much. So, if what matters to you is the important work of your business that only you can do, and your daughters, set aside time for both those things and forget about the rest. They'll usually take care of themselves.'

She made it sound so easy. As if a person could just *choose* how they spent every moment of their day. In his experience, it seldom worked out that way. There were too many unpredictable factors, too many opportunities not to be missed. Too many daughters asking for snacks while he was trying to send emails.

'Maybe.' Leo wasn't sure it would work, but it wasn't as if he had any better ideas. 'I'll talk to Tom in the morning.'

'Good.' Christabel smiled, slow and warm. 'Now, next question . . . the girls are asleep, everyone else is occupied, it's too late to do any work . . . so what do *you* want to do now?'

Warmth flooded through him as he realised *exactly* what he wanted to do. He wanted to stop worrying about everything else and cut loose, relax.

And he wanted to do that with Christabel. 'I have some ideas,' he admitted.

'Good. Because so do I.'

She leaned across the table to kiss him for the first time, and Leo hauled her closer, into his lap, losing himself in the embrace.

Now, *this* was the sort of dream following and happiness seeking he could definitely get behind.

MESSAGES

Josie (to the Waters Wanderers group): Your dad decided to go swimming with sharks! I watched from dry land and took photos.

Miranda: Sharks?! What was he thinking!

Iestyn: It was perfectly safe. You all fuss too much.

Juliet: Dad, you're scared of the jellyfish on the Long Beach. Sharks are a bit of a stretch!

Iestyn: You only live once, Juliet!

JULIET

On Friday, Juliet served breakfast, made the beds, cleared up the kitchen, and took a nap.

It was her new routine, one that had been serving her well since Lucy's llama party. Annoyingly, it hadn't even been her idea – it had been Rory's.

When he'd left her after their evening in the pub, she'd still been unsure how he felt about her revelations. There was so much history between them, it was hard to tell how much of his reticence was due to her past behaviour or their break-up, and how much was caused by the baby. Likewise, their long-standing friendship meant that she couldn't be sure, when he was kind to her, how much was misplaced affection from their romance, and what was just automatic defence of someone he'd known as an accident-prone toddler.

The island looked after their own. But after the first couple of days – days when she assumed he was processing all she'd told him – *Rory* seemed determined to look after her.

'You need to rest more,' he'd told her, when he arrived on the doorstep with a bag full of what he told her were essentials. She was grateful that everyone else had gone out – to work, to practise, or on another bike ride. 'Your body is doing something miraculous. You need to give it time and space to do that.'

She'd pulled a face at him as he stood on the step. 'You read that in a book, didn't you?'

He'd blushed, and later, she'd found that exact same quote in one of the three books he'd included in the bag.

Also included were: pre-natal vitamins, a water bottle, ginger sweets, pregnancy magazines, a baby name book, bubble bath, and a multi-pack of ready salted crisps.

'You shouldn't really have too much salt or fat,' Rory had told her, frowning, as she unpacked the last item. 'But Mrs Hibbert the pharmacist said they were the only thing that helped her daughter control the nausea, so I thought they might help.'

'You told Mrs Hibbert I'm pregnant?' Juliet had shrieked.

'Of course not!' Rory said, looking offended. 'I just said it was a friend.'

'Right.' Except, of course, everyone in town knew that *she* was the friend he was spending time with most these days. She didn't know how the Flying Fish was coping without him, but Juliet was pretty sure he hadn't worked a full shift all week. Not since he got over finding out about the baby and decided that she was his latest project.

The point was, if Rory had a friend who was unexpectedly pregnant, there were limited candidates for the role. All it would take would be Mrs Hibbert innocently mentioning it to the wrong person, and the news would be around the island like wildfire. In Juliet's experience, locals just couldn't *wait* to spread gossip about her misdeeds.

And this was definitely the best gossip she'd ever offered them.

Why had she come back here again?

Because staying in London was even worse. And that's saying something.

'Mrs Hibbert is a pharmacist,' Rory had said, sounding

suddenly uneasy. 'She's bound by some sort of confidence rule of secrecy or something, right?'

'You'd better hope so,' Juliet had muttered darkly. And when he'd pushed her to make that midwife appointment she'd been putting off, she'd called a clinic on the mainland, instead of Dr Parson's surgery, on the island.

But now it was nearly a week later and, so far, she hadn't heard any outlandish rumours about herself, so maybe Mrs Hibbert really could keep a secret. She'd be the first person on this island who could, but all the more credit to her for that.

Then there were the text messages. Even when Rory wasn't able to check on her in person, he still managed to nag her into looking after herself over the phone.

Like today, when she woke up from her late morning nap to a message that read: *Have you taken your pre-natal vitamins today?*

Rolling her eyes, Juliet had swallowed the damn things just so she could reply, *Yes. And I ate my vegetables like a good girl.*

Rory's response was almost immediate. *Good. Also, I was reading that you need to stop wearing underwired bras.*

Juliet blinked at the screen. She wasn't awake enough yet for this. On the other hand, she couldn't resist the urge to tease him, just a little. *Um . . . how much attention have you been paying to my bras over the last week, exactly?*

Even the dots on the screen that told her he was typing somehow looked flustered. *I haven't! Well. Not much. Anyway, you know what I mean. You need to do what's best for the baby, right? So buy some new bras.*

Juliet slumped back down into the bed as she tapped out her response. *Trust me, doing what's best for the baby is basically why I'm here at this point.*

As long as it didn't involve, well, actually telling her family about the baby.

The fact was, summer was almost over, and she still hadn't figured out answers to the two most important questions on her mind.

One, how to tell Miranda and Leo she was pregnant.

Two, what to do about Rory.

OK, fine, three questions.

Three, what the hell to do with her life now.

But for now, she was focusing on the first two.

She knew she had to tell her siblings sooner or later, she just couldn't figure out *how*. How was she supposed to start a casual conversation that led to 'Also, I had an affair with my boss and now I'm pregnant and unemployed and I don't know what to do with my life.' As if everyone in her life wasn't disappointed enough in her already.

But she had to do it. Before long they were really going to start raising questions about why she was still on the island, not in London. September was only a week or so away; even Leo and the girls would be leaving as soon as the festival was over. Mum and Dad would come home, and there'd be no reason for her to stay any more.

Of course, if Mum and Dad came home she could tell *them,* and then maybe they could tell Miranda. And Leo. And everyone else, while Juliet hid out in her attic bedroom, grew fat and ignored everybody. Rory would send her care packages, she'd be fine.

Which brought her to question number two. Rory.

She didn't know what his game was. On the one hand, he was acting like a doting father-to-be, a loving boyfriend. And he was categorically neither of those.

On the other, he *wasn't* acting that way. Because he never tried to touch her stomach, or talk about the baby, or discuss names, or even mention the future or what the baby would be like. His only interest in her breasts was to do with whether the underwires in her bra would stall her milk production, for heaven's sake. He was completely focused on her, and her well-being. Like she was a problem to be solved.

There was still an unfamiliar distance between them, as if for all his help, he wouldn't let himself too close. This wasn't a romance or a relationship, for sure. But then what was it?

He was basically being the best friend anyone ever had, just like the old days, and it was making her nervous. Especially because she knew she didn't deserve it, after everything that had happened between them.

Since she obviously wasn't going to nap any more, not now her head was filled with such questions, Juliet got up again. The band were down in the cottage, packing up for some gigs they had on the mainland that weekend, and over the next week. It looked like they'd be coming back, though – at least, Owain would be, if the basically pornographic smiles he'd been giving Miranda lately were anything to go by. Juliet had caught them both doing the walk of shame up from the cottage the morning after the party – although neither of them had looked particularly ashamed, which she applauded.

Miranda had been too tied into what she thought the island expected of her for too long. It was far past time she cut loose a little bit.

Maybe it would even make her a little more understanding when Juliet told her the truth.

Probably not.

Pottering downstairs, she found the place quiet. Miranda was probably with Owain, she assumed. And Leo had taken to working first thing, while she fed the girls and they helped to look after Lucy. Then, when she went for her nap, he put his laptop to sleep and put his phone in the bowl by the front door, before taking the girls out on some adventure or another – usually with Christabel. (Juliet had her smutty assumptions about what was going on there, too, but that might be her own frustrations talking.)

He was usually back by late afternoon, when the girls settled down with a film, or a board game, or got their drawing stuff out while he got back to work for a couple of hours before dinner. Juliet had taken to joining the girls for film afternoons, and hoping no one noticed that she slept through them more often than not. Although Leo was probably hoping that none of them noticed Christabel sneaking back in after bedtime, either, but they all totally had.

Today, she realised with a frown, his phone was missing from the bowl. And she thought she'd heard him talking in the study on her way downstairs. Poking her head outside the back door, she saw the girls and Christabel playing some game or another down at the bottom of the garden. Which meant that, whatever Leo was up to, Juliet had time to get on with some of her projects without interruption.

Turning the back rooms on the top floor, which had mostly been used as storage for as long as she could remember, into functioning guest rooms was taking her a lot longer than she'd expected. Mostly, that was because her mum and dad seemed to have kept everything that ever came into the house over the past couple of decades in these two rooms, and going through the boxes had taken weeks.

Still, now the rooms were clear – with the important keepsakes stored safely in the attic – she could start scrubbing down the walls and the floor ready to decorate. *Nesting,* a small voice whispered at the back of her mind. Juliet stopped, looked around the pale-yellow room, and couldn't help but imagine a cot in one corner, maybe a rocking chair in another . . .

No. These rooms were for guests. She'd be long gone from Seashell Island before she needed to worry about cots, anyway.

She threw herself into cleaning as a distraction from thinking for the next couple of hours, until her hands and her back were sore. A warm shower helped her feel more human again, but by the time she was out she could still hear Leo in the study, and Christabel and the girls were now playing board games in the sunroom.

With nothing she really needed to do – other than read the rest of Rory's pregnancy books, which she was still avoiding – she headed outside to check on Lucy.

Pulling on her old trainers, ones that had been living at the Lighthouse since she left home but looked exactly right with her ratty fat jeans that Tanya had sent, which only just still fastened up, and the long, loose T-shirt she was wearing under one of her mum's cardigans, she then opened the front door—

And stopped, staring, at the sight in front of her.

Harriet's horse and carriage, decked out with ribbons and flowers like she did when there was a wedding, was standing on the driveway. And stood beside it, in what had to be his best shirt, was Rory.

Oh God. What the hell is this?

'Juliet.' He stepped closer, smiling, and held a hand out to her.

'What the hell is this?' Ungrateful and difficult, that was her. Pregnancy really was bringing out her best qualities.

But Rory's smile never faltered. 'I was hoping you'd take a ride with me. I have some things to show you, if you'll let me.'

Juliet looked down at her tatty old clothes, thought about the bird's nest her hair must be since she'd let it dry without brushing it after her shower, and decided they didn't matter. Because they were friends, right? Friends didn't care what the other one looked like.

And if this was something more . . . well, she couldn't have that now anyway. So what did it matter what she looked like?

With a tentative nod, she took Rory's hand and let him help her up into the carriage.

And prayed this wasn't a huge, huge mistake.

MIRANDA

'You could come with me, you know,' Owain said, one arm at her waist, his mouth warm against her ear as he hugged her goodbye. They'd said their first round of goodbyes in bed that morning, preparing for Owain to disappear to the mainland for a week with the band for a round of gigs. She'd thought she'd made her peace with him going.

And yet she'd still snuck out back down to the cottage during a break from her VA work – and yet more festival phone calls – to say goodbye again.

The others were loading up Rory's van, loaned for the occasion, with their equipment, ready to drive down to the ferry, and not so subtly giving them space to make their farewells.

'You don't want me there cramping your style,' she muttered against his chest. 'What would all your groupies say?'

He laughed, and she felt it vibrate against her cheek. 'I don't have groupies.'

'That's not what Suzi says.' Miranda didn't tell him what Suzi had *actually* said, though. *'You're not like his normal groupie flings. We actually like you.'*

'I could sneak you backstage, show you the bright lights of Bristol after the gig,' Owain offered. 'You'd be back on the island before you knew it.'

'You'll be gone a whole week, Owain. Between my VA

work and organising the Lighthouse Festival, I'm swamped here as it is.'

'Just come for tomorrow's gig, then,' he suggested. 'I'll make Ryan get his own hotel room for a change.'

'You know I can't.' Miranda shook her head. 'They need me here. Besides, you know I won't leave my home.' But right in that moment, she wanted to. For the first time in her memory, she wanted to be somewhere else. Just for tonight. Just with Owain.

Frustration surged through her at the realisation. Before now, staying on Seashell Island had been a deliberate choice, a relief. It was her sanctuary.

What had changed that now it felt more like a prison?

Owain. Owain is what changed. Because suddenly, when she thought of sanctuary, she thought of lying in his arms instead. Because he'd shown her that the world outside the island had more in it than she'd believed. That sometimes you had to dive into the freezing water and take a chance, rather than just living safe – that nothing at all would ever change if she didn't.

But . . . what might change here if she left, even for a night? Last time, Juliet had almost drowned. This time, she dreaded to think what might go wrong if she wasn't there to look after everybody.

God, that was an exhausting thought. Would she always feel this responsible?

'Miranda . . . you realise that Seashell Island will always be home, right? Even if you go away, you can always come back again. That's what home *is*.'

He made it sound so simple. But Miranda knew that it wasn't. She knew how it felt to not have that safe place at all. How could she give it up now? Even for that feeling she got in her Owain's arms?

Not now. Not when her parents were gone, and Juliet was trying to keep the B&B running for them, and Leo . . . God only knew what Leo was doing. Trying to persuade Christabel to play some sort of pornographic Mary Poppins, perhaps, given the noises she'd heard from his room last night. The point was, this place was her home, yes, but so were the people, she was realising.

Her family needed her. And so did her island.

So she'd stay, and she'd be safe, and so would everyone else. And if part of her heart was leaving with Owain, well, that was her problem.

It was only rebound sex, after all. Right?

'Look around you,' Owain said, suddenly spinning her around to face the cottage bedroom, the place they'd first made love. 'Look at the wallpaper you chose for this place – all those maps of places you'll never go. Look at your bookshelves – filled with stories of adventures all around the world. Don't you want to step outside and see some of those places for yourself, instead of just imagining them?'

Yes.

The thought was so sudden, so unexpected, Miranda swallowed it down fast before it could find its way out of her mouth.

Owain sighed as she shook her head. 'Just . . . think about it, Miri. That's all I'm asking. OK?'

Somehow, she had a feeling she'd be thinking about nothing else.

'I'll be here when you get back,' was all she said, in the end. Because what else was there to say?

Owain's smile was just a little bit sad. 'We'll be back in good time to help with the festival. Maybe we'll even bring some fans along, play an after-dark set or something.'

'Maybe,' Miranda said, non-committally. She wasn't sure

Seashell Island understood about after-dark sets or things like that. That didn't sound like the usual Lighthouse Festival.

'Owain?' Suzi called, from over by the van. 'We need to go if we want to catch the ferry.'

'Want to ride with us into town?' Owain asked, and Miranda nodded, not ready to say goodbye just yet.

'I've got some errands to run, anyway.' She could probably come up with some, on the way.

Suzi drove, with Robyn and Ryan crammed into the bench seat in the front with her, so Miranda could sit in the back with Owain and all the equipment in privacy. They didn't say much, though. They'd said it all already.

He'd be back in a week, and Miranda knew it was ridiculous to miss him. But one week was about as long as they'd had together in the first place, in the relationship sense, anyway.

Except this wasn't a relationship. It was rebound sex.

And she knew she wasn't really worrying about missing him this week.

It was just that this was a precursor to the real thing.

At the end of the summer, Owain and the others would leave for good, and she might never see him again. Better to get used to missing him this week, to remind her heart that this was only temporary now, than be destroyed by him leaving then.

He had his own life, off the island. And she had nothing beyond its watery borders.

Different worlds. And Miranda knew better than to imagine they could meet in the middle, any more than they had done for one, magical summer. She'd do far better to be grateful for what she'd had, rather than hoping for anything more. They hadn't even *talked* about what would happen at the end of the summer.

So why was her heart hurting so much?

The van pulled in behind the Flying Fish, and the back doors opened to let the others in to unload. Owain did his share, then pulled Miranda aside, the August sun warm against their faces even as the sea breeze ruffled her hair.

'I know you need to get back to work,' he said, holding her hands against his chest. 'And I know you can't come with me now. But . . . one day, you're going to have to leave this place, Miranda. Even if it's only for twenty-four hours.'

'Maybe,' Miranda said. But deep inside, she was suddenly afraid that she wouldn't. How ridiculous, to be sad to lose something she'd never even wanted until this moment.

Owain sighed, and pressed a last kiss to her forehead. 'I'll see you next week.'

'See you soon.' She gave him what she hoped was a brave smile. It didn't seem to work, though, because it only made him swoop in and kiss her properly – deep and long and everything she needed – until Suzi started whooping behind them, and he broke off to give her the finger.

'Bye,' he whispered. And then he was gone, away with his bandmates, all of whom seemed to be teasing him good-naturedly.

Away to a world she was too scared to visit.

She watched them go for another moment, then turned to walk the other way back to the Crab Leg Cafe for a pick-me-up latte – and slammed straight into her ex-boyfriend.

'Paul! What are you doing, just standing there?'

'Who was that?' he asked, staring at Owain's retreating form. 'He was with you that day at the Lighthouse, too. And at the Flying Fish.'

Miranda felt a blush hit her cheeks, and sternly ordered it away in her mind. She had nothing to be embarrassed about.

She might not be able to leave the island, like everyone seemed to want her to, but she wasn't the same Miranda who'd hung around for years and years, waiting for Paul to set a date, either. She'd had a fling with a musician, she'd swum naked in the sea, she'd adopted a llama, for heaven's sake.

Maybe she was still a work in progress. But she felt like she'd made more progress over the last month spending time with Owain, and Juliet, Leo and Christabel, than in five years of stagnating as Paul's fiancée.

'That's Owain,' she said, simply. 'He's been staying at the B&B this summer.'

'He's in the band you have staying? And he's your new boyfriend?' Was that jealousy she heard in Paul's voice? She honestly thought it might be. Huh.

'He's my rebound fling,' she said, with a broad smile. 'We're having lots of incredible sex. Now, if you'll excuse me, I need to get going.'

She brushed past him, heading towards the cafe, but he quickly spun around and scampered after her.

'I was looking for you, Miranda,' he said, falling into step beside her. 'I think we need to talk, don't you?'

'Not really.'

He ignored her. 'I know you needed space – that's why I didn't bother you after I came to the Lighthouse before.'

'And here I thought it was because we'd actually split up and you were getting on with your life. Like I am.' That day he'd come to the Lighthouse had been the day Owain had first said the words 'rebound sex'. She'd almost forgotten that Paul had been there at all, even though they'd never have had the conversation otherwise.

In fact, she'd pretty much forgotten Paul completely since Owain walked into her life. And that was a good thing.

Except now he was here, walking beside her, his hands in his pockets the way he always had. And Owain was gone, for now, and soon forever. Miranda could almost feel herself slipping back towards the person she'd been before this summer.

She couldn't let that happen.

'The thing is, Miranda, *you* were my life for so long,' Paul said, and Miranda thought, *No, I wasn't.* She'd just been comfortable, familiar, background noise. 'The world doesn't seem quite so friendly without you by my side.'

By which she assumed he meant, *My mum's on my back and people keep glaring at me and telling me I've lost a good thing there.*

'Paul, you were right. If we really wanted to get married, we'd have done it by now.' They were nearly at the cafe. Reluctant to have him follow her in and carry this on over coffee, Miranda paused outside the bucket and spade shop next door, and hoped this might be the end of it.

No such luck.

'But I've been thinking about that.' Paul grabbed her hand, his expression earnest. 'I think having this time apart, it's helped us see what we really want from life.'

Miranda narrowed her eyes. 'Did your mother tell you to say that?' It definitely sounded like something Gwen would say.

'No,' Paul said, but his gaze slid away from hers, and she knew he was lying. 'I've been watching you this summer, working so hard for the festival, for this island and everyone in it. It reminded me what an incredible woman you are, and how much this place means to you.'

She sighed. All the right words, and yet she didn't believe any of them. 'Look, I know your life would be easier if you could tell everyone we'd made up. But how would that even help? You're going to be moving to the mainland for this new job as soon as you've worked your notice, right? New opportunities, new people . . . like Becca, for instance. I bet she'd move to the mainland with you.'

'I haven't asked her,' he said, quickly.

'You didn't ask me either,' Miranda pointed out.

'Because you wouldn't go! And anyway, I could come back on the weekends,' Paul said, but even he sounded doubtful. 'Look, the bottom line is: you won't leave this island, right? So who else do you think you're going to find here to marry you? You've known everyone who lives here for decades. And it's not like your musician guy is going to stick around, is he? So we make up, my parents are happy, you're happy, I can still go work on the mainland and have you to come home to. It's the best of both worlds.'

She blinked. Gwen must have really done a job on him if he honestly thought that was the best outcome either of them could hope for.

'Paul, you wanted to move away from this island. Why would you come back every weekend?'

'Because . . . it'll make my mother stop crying. Because this is my home, too, and right now people here hate me, especially after I took Becca out that night. Because I've never lived away from here since I was twenty-one.' He looked tired, defeated. 'And because I love you, of course,' he added, an obvious afterthought.

'No you don't. And honestly? I don't think I love you either. Not any more. I did, once, but I guess love is one of those things that fades away when you don't feed it. When you take it for granted, like we did. Because we knew there was no one else on this island for either of us.'

'And now? You really think your musician is going to give it all up and live on Seashell Island for the love of you?'

Paul asked, sceptically. He didn't question the love part though, she noticed.

'Honestly? No. We haven't even talked about . . . that's not what we have, or what we're doing. But being with him . . . it's made me think about what I want. Who I want to be.'

'And that person can't be with me?' There was a hint of sadness in Paul's voice for the first time.

Miranda felt a small pang, somewhere in the vicinity of her heart, as she said, 'No. I don't think she can.'

LEO

By five o'clock on Friday afternoon, Leo was done. With work, family, good intentions, everything. Just done.

It had all been going so well. He should have known it would fall apart at any moment. Good things didn't last; just look at his marriage.

He'd managed almost a full week of juggling childcare and work without anyone getting annoyed with him. Mia had only had two epic sulks the whole time, and both of those were unrelated to him and his work and more to do with her little sister – who had been sunshine and delight for days, beaming with happiness at all the fun things they'd been doing. Well, apart from when losing at Monopoly. Without Christabel there to supervise, it turned out they both liked winning after all. But Mia hadn't been sick again due to too much sugar, and Abby had been happy to go to bed at her assigned bedtime, knowing there was more fun around the corner the next day. They both loved a routine far more than he'd expected, and they were all happier for a decent amount of sleep and some vegetables.

Even Tom had seemed happy with the new arrangement. Leo had checked in with him first thing every morning, gone through the most important stuff of the day, and then left him to get on with it. He'd check in again in the late afternoon, pick up any new stuff that needed working on, then got it done after the kids were in bed – but before

Christabel slipped into his office and pushed his laptop closed and everything became a whole lot more fun again.

To be honest, there'd been a lot less that he'd really *needed* to do for work than he'd anticipated. Mostly because it turned out that Tom was more competent than he'd really given him credit for.

'You're doing a great job, Tom,' he'd informed him, just last night.

Tom had scoffed. 'Told you so. I've been waiting to pick some of this stuff up from you for *months*. It's way more interesting than picking up your dry-cleaning and getting your car valeted.'

So it had been working. It had been working *well*. Leo had even felt relaxed enough to ask Christabel out for dinner that evening, giving up his work time and enjoying a Friday night out while Juliet watched a movie with the girls at the Lighthouse.

Christabel had been firm, the first morning they'd woken up together, that this was Just For Now. No great love affair, no strings, no obligations – just something for them both to enjoy until the end of the summer. And Leo was fine with that; he was still figuring out how to work and be a dad – throwing boyfriend obligations into that mix could only make things more complicated.

Still, they'd spent every night together for the last week – time when he could switch off and just feel, enjoy, *be,* rather than trying to juggle and balance all the things he had to keep moving. She'd helped him find his path and his balance *and* she'd made his nights exciting and fun too. The very least he owed her was dinner.

More than that, he wanted to spend some time with her outside bed but without the kids. Miranda had been making too many Mary Poppins comments, and the last thing he wanted was Christabel thinking he just kept her around to help him with the girls. He enjoyed her company, was endlessly fascinated by her unexpected world view, and he thought she was sexy as all hell. It was past time for an actual date. So he'd called the Flying Fish and booked a table, and asked Juliet to watch the kids. Maybe afterwards he and Christabel could even go back to her ambulance for a while. He'd never had sex in an ambulance . . .

Anyway, the point was, he'd had it all perfectly planned. Which should have been the first sign that it was going to be a disaster.

Things had started going to hell just after eleven o'clock that morning, when Juliet handed the girls over after breakfast and chores and went to do whatever it was she did with her days instead. He'd finished up his morning call to Tom, sent a few urgent emails, cast an eye over the final version of the proposal Tom was presenting to an old client that morning and approved it, then shut down his laptop, put his phone in the designated phone bowl by the door and gone to find the girls to find out what they wanted to do that day.

The consensus was a beach picnic. 'Can Christabel come?' Abby asked, so Leo had grabbed his phone and fired off a text to ask her to meet them down on the beach, if she was free.

He'd almost made it. Almost put the phone back in the bowl and hurried the kids out of the door with the picnic supplies. But then it rang.

'Tom?'

By the door, Mia and Abby groaned, and he heard Mia mutter, 'Should have known it was too good to be true.'

'Leo, I'm so sorry—'

'Tom, I'm just on my way to the beach. Can this wait until later?' He had to say it, had to show he was making an effort. But he knew from Tom's voice what the answer would be.

'I'm sorry. It really can't.'

Of all the things Leo had imagined going wrong while he was away this summer, this wasn't one of them – his oldest client, a personal friend, suddenly deciding to pull his business and go elsewhere for his marketing strategy and needs. Some new start-up who'd arrived with flashy new suggestions and impossible, budget-stretching moves.

'What do you mean they cancelled the meeting? They can't! They've been with us from the start. Wait, I'll call Harry now, straighten all this out.'

He'd left the girls standing at the door, buckets and spades in hand, and climbed back up the stairs to the study to make the call. And then another call. And another, when it turned out that Harry wasn't the only client this new company had approached.

'We're not going to the beach, are we?' Mia had said, less of a question than a complaint, when she arrived in his doorway, halfway through the third call.

'Sorry, sweetheart, not right now. Can you guys entertain yourselves for a bit? No Tom, not you. Now, who else can we call?'

When he looked up again, she was gone.

He didn't know how much later it was when Christabel arrived, but she'd suddenly appeared, sitting on his desk when he hung up his latest call, playing with one of those eighties executive toys he'd bought for Dad one Christmas as a joke.

'Your daughters are waiting for you downstairs,' she told him. 'Much like I was waiting on the beach. For an hour.'

He'd winced. 'Sorry. Something came up.' This, from his past experience, was the moment that the yelling started.

'So I see. It's important?' Her voice was too calm. Too dangerous.

'Very.' He put as much emphasis on the word as he could, and hoped she wouldn't respond with Emily's favourite retort: *More important than me? More important than your family?*

She didn't. 'And are you making a difference?'

That had made him pause. Was he? Really?

So far, nothing had really changed. All they knew was that some new kid on the block had contacted a few clients. Harry was the only one to defect as of yet – and getting him on the phone to explain his decision was still a work in progress, as so far Leo had spoken to almost everyone in his office, down to the janitor, except Harry himself.

'I have to try,' he'd said.

Christabel had nodded. 'OK, then. Just remember what your priorities are here. The path you've chosen.'

'I will.' He'd picked up the phone again, and hadn't watched her go.

And now, before he knew it, it was late afternoon. Mia arrived in the doorway again, this time with a plate of sandwiches he recognised from the picnic basket he'd packed that morning.

'Christabel said I should bring you these.' She dumped them on the table and walked away again, making it obvious that, left to her own devices, she'd have let him starve.

'Mia, wait.' She paused in the doorway, but didn't turn around. He searched for something, anything to say to make her less angry. 'Are you and Abby OK down there?'

'We're fine. Christabel stayed for lunch and we played in the garden and had a game of Monopoly after, before she had to go. Auntie Juliet went out on the horse and carriage ride with Rory a while ago – Abby saw them – and Auntie

Miri went into town with the band this morning and hasn't come back. So Abby and I are playing weddings.'

'Good, good.' That sounded safe, happy. 'And I'm sure Juliet and Miranda will be back soon too; they'll watch a movie with you or something.' A small part of his brain questioned Juliet and Rory's carriage ride, but he dismissed it. Whatever was going on in his sisters' love lives, he didn't have the brain space to think about it right now.

'Great,' Mia said, with a complete lack of enthusiasm.

Then the phone rang again, and he took it. 'Tom? What's the latest?'

His assistant sounded weary. 'Still nothing more than we knew at eleven this morning, Leo. I told you, Harry's email just said it was time for a fresh approach. I don't think this is the huge coup you seem to believe it is—'

'Which one of us has a decade's experience of running this business?' Leo asked, sharply. 'And which one of us has been doing it for eighteen months?'

'I know that, Leo. I get it. I'm new and untested. But I'm the one who is here dealing with the actual work this summer and—'

'Exactly! And if I was there this wouldn't have happened!' he yelled.

Silence on the other end. 'You don't know that. Harry said—'

'I don't care what Harry said. I know my clients; I know my business. You presented to Harry on Monday and it obviously wasn't good enough. If I'd been there, it would have been.'

'You're being unreasonable, Leo.' Tom was obviously trying to keep his cool, but there was a frayed edge that Leo couldn't help but pick at until it felt apart, until someone else felt as bad as he did right now.

'Am I? Is it unreasonable to expect my employee to *do his job right?*'

'We went through that proposal together! I presented it exactly the same way you would have.'

'Except I'd have got the business!' He was being unreasonable; he knew he was. But who else did he have to blame? Except himself.

'Daddy! Stop shouting. We're having a wedding downstairs and you need to come and give the bride away!' Abby bounced through the doorway over to his desk, tugging on his arm.

'Not now, Abby,' he snapped. 'This is important.'

'Lucy's wedding is important too!' Abby replied. 'Come *on,* Daddy.'

'Look, why don't you go deal with that,' Tom said, down the phone. 'There's nothing else we can do here anyway—'

'Yes there is. There are more people we need to speak to.'

'Leo, it's gone five on a Friday. People don't want to talk to us now, they want to go home. Or to a bar, where they can get very, very drunk.'

'You mean that's what *you* want,' Leo replied. 'Real professionals—'

'Daddy! The wedding!'

'Not *now,* Abby! I don't care about some stupid llama wedding! And I don't care if you want to skive off and go to the pub, Tom, I want to get this fixed! Now! So let's start at the beginning again.'

There was a sob from the doorway, then the sound of running feet. On the other end of the phone, Tom sighed.

'Leo, we're getting nowhere. Isn't it better to wait until—'

'No. Now read me Harry's email again.' He couldn't think about Abby and Mia, or Christabel, or the bloody llama wedding. He had to fix his business first.

That was the thing he was good at. If he couldn't do that right, he had no chance at the rest of it anyway.

Suddenly, another sound cut through the air – the old dial phone his father kept on his desk, which Leo had assumed was more decorative than functional. 'Hang on, Tom.'

He picked up the heavy black receiver and held it to his ear. 'Hello? The Lighthouse B&B?'

'Mr Waters?' The voice on the other end was cultured, and just a little bit smarmy. 'It's Timothy here from Coastal Properties. I just wanted to let you know that we've had some interest from a buyer who'd like to come and view the Lighthouse.'

MESSAGES

Mum (to the Waters Wanderers group): Hey kids! Sorry we've been out of touch the last week. Been off exploring a wonderfully remote island network on the boat. Glorious sunshine, fresh seafood for dinner every day, and the best cocktails you'll ever taste. Juliet – you'd love them! Hope all is OK back on our island. Miss you all. Love, Mum xxx

Dad (to the Waters Wanderers group): As you can probably tell, your mother has been enjoying many of the aforementioned cocktails tonight. Let me know that our B&B is still standing when you get the chance? Here's a photo of the fish I caught this morning (with your mother for scale).

JULIET

'Where are we going?' Juliet held onto the side of the carriage, mostly to avoid grabbing Rory's hand and giving him the wrong idea. Ohhh, she had a very bad feeling about this.

'We're going to all the places that matter,' Rory replied, enigmatically.

But she knew this island. She knew these paths, these places. And Harriet was leading the carriage right down towards Gull Bay – the place they'd spent the night together one summer evening, right before she walked out on Rory and left Seashell Island for good. At least, so she'd thought.

It was a place loaded with meaning. Like this whole carriage ride.

Oh God. Look at those flowers, those ribbons. This was a romantic horse-drawn carriage ride around the island she'd spent years waiting to escape. He was going to ask her to stay. Again.

Didn't he remember how badly this had gone last time?

He'd taken her down to Gull Bay, wooed her as best as a teenage boy could – with warm fizzy wine and chocolates – and made love to her on a picnic blanket on the sand. Then, afterwards, he'd asked her to stay with him. *Just until my dad gets better. Then we can leave together, like we planned all along.*

But she'd known it wouldn't happen. She'd seen it with Miranda and Paul, not to mention so many girls in the years above her at school. Everyone talked about leaving, but hardly anyone ever did. If they left now, at eighteen, for university, like she wanted to, then they had a chance. If they put it off for any reason . . . they were still on the island years later, popping out babies or working at the Crab Leg Cafe.

She hadn't wanted that future. And now it seemed to have found her anyway, just ten years later.

She stared out at the familiar landscape as the horse trotted along, dragging her towards whatever doom Rory had planned for her. What had she been thinking, agreeing to this? Probably, she'd been thinking about how he'd been so conspicuously 'just friends' all week, even though every inch of her had been desperate to kiss him. He'd been so hands-off she'd had no clue he might be feeling similarly. In fact, she'd put it all down to her stupid hormones, like so many other things. Or perhaps the fact he'd been so kind, so understanding, that she'd just wanted to let him take care of everything.

But he'd not even hinted at them revisiting the romance, not once.

Clearly it had all been part of a cunning plan, all leading to this moment.

Because as much as she wanted him, liked him, cared about him, and remembered how desperately she'd loved him as a teenager – hell, could probably fall in love with him again in seconds, if she let herself – it just wasn't as easy as all that. It wasn't 'romantic carriage ride equals happily ever after' simple.

It wasn't a movie. It was her life.

Harriet brought the carriage to a halt, studiously looking straight ahead and paying them no attention at all as Rory turned to Juliet.

'Do you remember what happened here?' he asked.

She nodded, scared to open her mouth and find out what words might come out. She didn't want to remember that last night they were together.

But Rory was remembering something else. 'It was the first place I kissed you, the night of that party on the beach, remember?'

'I remember you practically falling over your own feet when I kissed *you,*' she corrected him, automatically. But his magical mystery tour was already having what she assumed was his desired effect – bringing their past to life again.

She remembered the smoke from the bonfire on the beach, the sound of guitars as a few guys drunkenly tried to warble their way through some songs, the laughter and the taste of vodka and Coke. Remembered seeing Rory in the firelight, and knowing he wasn't just a friend any more, and hadn't been for a long time. Knowing that she just had to kiss him.

So she had.

'Next stop please, Harriet,' Rory said, before she could deal with the feelings coursing through her, and then the carriage was moving again.

'What are you doing?' she asked in a whisper.

'Remembering,' was all Rory said.

When the carriage paused again, they were outside the Ice House ice-cream parlour, and people were staring at them.

God, she hated this. The tourists were one thing; they probably thought this was romantic, a proposal tour or something equally corny. But the locals . . . they knew. They knew what she and Rory had been, what he'd been like when she left. Knew that she'd come back with her tail between her legs, even if Mrs Hibbert hadn't spilled exactly why yet.

She stared impassively ahead, and tried not to imagine what people were saying about her.

'Remember the Ice House?' Rory asked, softly.

'I had ice cream here with Abby and Mia last week,' she pointed out. 'Of course I remember it.'

'Remember what happened here for us, was more the point.' Rory sounded faintly exasperated. She couldn't even blame him. Here he was, trying to do something meaningful and romantic and lovely, and she was being a stonehearted bitch about it because, hey, that's who she was.

Who she'd had to be to leave him in the first place. Who she'd need to be to look out for her child on her own and not let the world get her down.

'We . . . this is where we planned our big escape,' she said, haltingly. She'd been working there all summer, the year before she turned eighteen. Rory had come in every evening for a single scoop and to talk to her, whenever she wasn't busy serving or bussing tables. He'd sat there at the counter making one ball of ice cream last for hours, and they'd talked.

They'd talked about the world outside Seashell Island. About moving to London and following their dreams. How Rory would go to culinary school, become a chef at one of the big-name restaurants. How Juliet would study psychology or something and learn how people worked and charge exorbitant amounts to listen to people talk about themselves.

Except Rory's dad had got sick that winter, and he'd told her he had to stay. And when summer rolled around . . . she'd gone anyway. Without him.

He'd never tried to stop her, she realised. Never begged her to stay on the island with him. He just asked her that once, and when she hadn't answered, told her he wouldn't be able to go with her.

She'd have begged, she knew. She wasn't as good a person as Rory.

She'd never even told him she was going, not officially. Too much of a coward. Or perhaps she'd been too afraid that if he asked her again, she'd say yes.

They'd just carried on as if everything was normal, as if it was just one more summer. Maybe their kisses had been a little more desperate, and they'd stopped talking about the future altogether.

And then she'd left. She hadn't even said goodbye.

She'd thought that was a kindness, at the time. She knew better now.

The carriage was moving again, all the way to the far end of the beach, and the ramshackle old holiday park where they'd broken in one winter night and made love for the first time, in a fold-down bed in a freezing caravan. Then past the crazy golf where she'd beaten him three times and he'd told her he loved her. All the way around the back of the island, through the woods where they'd played as children, back past the Lighthouse and Gull Bay – the site of their final night – again, then down into town and coming to a halt in front of the Flying Fish.

She blinked. 'Why are we here?' Every other stop had something to do with their past, their relationship, and the moment she left it behind. Nostalgia and guilt all mingled together inside her, tying her stomach in knots.

'Because this is where you walked into my life again.' Rory took her hand, and panic flared through her.

She couldn't do this. Whatever he was about to suggest, she couldn't do it.

She was Juliet Waters – screw-up extraordinaire. She'd always vowed she'd get out of this place, live a real, grown-up life, away from all the people who'd watched her and gossiped about her since reception class, when she had pushed Iain French into a muddy puddle.

Yes, she was back, for now. But if she let Rory finish whatever he was about to say, she knew, deep inside, that she'd be stuck here forever. She wasn't strong enough to leave him a second time. It would be so *easy*, just to give in, to let Rory take care of her, to give *up*.

But she couldn't do it.

She was an adult now. She couldn't let anyone swoop in and save her. She needed to save herself.

She needed to figure out her own future, what she needed, what she wanted, before she let Rory anywhere near it.

'Juliet. I've spent ten years missing you. Now you're back in my life, and I know why. I want to be there for you, support you, be what you need.'

If he kissed her now, she'd kiss him back. And then she'd look up in a year's time, five years' time, whenever, and she'd resent him for making her stay. And he'd hate her for being so bitter about it.

Rory slipped from the bench seat onto one knee on the floor of the carriage, and Juliet's heart stopped.

Last time, he'd let her go. This time . . .

She could see it all happening like a movie behind her eyes, her whole future. And she had to get out before the credits rolled.

'Juliet. Will you—'

'I'm sorry, I can't.' Snatching her hand back from him, she jumped down out of the carriage, ignoring the stunned looks from tourists who'd stopped to watch, and ran. Straight back home to the Lighthouse – and safety.

Juliet was panting for breath by the time home came in sight. There were lights on inside, in the kitchen, the study, the bedrooms – and suddenly she couldn't go in. She'd come here for safety, for support, but she couldn't take it.

Because she still hadn't told them.

She'd told precisely two people she was pregnant. One had abandoned her and one had tried to propose – neither of which was the response she was looking for. Maybe her family would do better.

Or perhaps their reaction would be even worse.

She could hear Abby and Mia playing weddings on the terrace, but she didn't go towards them. Instead, swerving away from the house, she headed towards the small stall they'd set up for Lucy on the edge of the field behind the house.

The llama gave Juliet her usual impassive stare as she walked inside. Reaching into the bucket of feed they'd hidden behind a high barrier even Lucy's long neck couldn't reach, Juliet pulled out a handful to hold out for the llama.

Lucy dipped her head instantly to gobble up the food, then nudged against Juliet's side to ask for more.

'Oh, Lucy.' Juliet grabbed another handful of feed. 'What am I supposed to do? Rory is going to hate me again and . . . I hate that. And I know I should be concentrating on the bigger picture, not fretting about my ridiculous love life. I need to be thinking about the future, for me and the baby. Do I go back to London? Do I force Callum to acknowledge the baby, to play a part in its life? I haven't even properly registered at the GP here or anything, because you know it'll be all over the island the moment I do – if Mrs Hibbert hasn't told everyone already. I have seriously big problems to deal with, and instead . . .'

She sighed, as Lucy finished off the food and started nudging again.

'Yes, OK, fine.' Juliet grabbed another handful. 'You'll get as big as I will, though, and you won't have my excuse.'

Sighing again, she moved away from the feed bucket, and

over to a bench in the corner of the stall. Sitting heavily on the wooden bench, she smiled as Lucy followed her, head ducked to press against her shoulder in support.

'I need to think about the baby, first and foremost, I know that. But I can't stop thinking about Rory – what was he thinking? Was he proposing because he loves me? Or because he thinks I need saving? Because I'm damn sure he wouldn't have done it if it wasn't for the baby. But most of all . . . most of all, I'm obsessing about what Miranda will say when she finds out.'

'When I find out what?' Miranda asked from the entrance, and Juliet jumped so hard she fell off the bench.

MIRANDA

Miranda batted Lucy aside as she reached down to help her little sister up.

'Juliet,' she said, as soon as she was seated again. 'What's going on?'

She'd known something was wrong. She'd known that Juliet wouldn't have just come home for the summer because she fancied a break. Juliet had spent years counting down to when she could escape Seashell Island. It had to be something huge to bring her back now.

And Miranda had ignored it. Because she'd been tied up in her own stuff — with Paul, with her parents, with the Lighthouse, with the festival, and with Owain. She'd just hoped that whatever it was would go away, the same way she was hoping that the incredible pull she felt with Owain would fade away eventually, before he left for good.

Obviously neither of the problems had gone anywhere at all.

And it was past time that she put on her big sister hat and started doing her job again. Being wild and free Miranda with Owain was one thing — one incredible, brilliant thing. But it was only ever a holiday from being the real her.

Responsible, sensible, big sister Miranda. Who always arrived in time to fix whatever mess Juliet had got herself into.

Maybe Paul was right, in a way. She couldn't change who she was, not at her core.

If she'd gone with Owain today, she wouldn't have been here now, to help her sister. Just like last time.

She took a breath, nudged Lucy out of the way again, and sat down beside Juliet.

'Do you want to tell me why you came home to Seashell Island this summer?' she asked, softly.

'Not really,' Juliet replied.

Miranda clenched her jaw. No wonder she needed a holiday from that Miranda. That Miranda had to deal with *this* Juliet – sulky and difficult and unable to accept help even when it was offered.

'I mean, you're going to be really, really disappointed in me, and I kind of wanted to put that off for as long as possible, if I'm honest,' Juliet continued, and Miranda felt her frustration dissipate.

The Juliet she remembered as a teenager had never once worried about disappointing her, or anyone else. She'd just gone her own way and done what she wanted without thinking about anyone else at all.

She's an adult. Maybe she doesn't need me to save her at all. Miranda shook away the thought and focused on her sister.

'Why would I be disappointed in you? You're here, doing an incredible job with the B&B. You stuck by your word that you'd take it seriously, and you have. Plus . . . you're an adult, Juliet. You get to make your own choices, now. What does it matter if I'm disappointed in the ones you choose to make?'

Juliet looked up from her hands at last, her expression sceptical. 'You really think *you* wouldn't be bothered if Mum and Dad, or Leo, or the whole damn island knew you'd done something really stupid?'

Like swimming naked in Gull Bay. Or falling for a musician who'll walk out of my life once the summer is over.

No. She wasn't thinking about those things either. This was about Juliet, not her disaster of a sex life.

Except the sex life is pretty perfect. It's the what comes next that's screwed up. The part where he leaves and I realise I've fallen too far too fast and there's nothing I can do about it because he's not even here.

Rebound sex. That was all it was. That was the promise they'd made each other that first night. She had to remember that.

And right now, she had to help her sister, most of all.

'Juliet. Tell me what's going on.'

Her baby sister's big green eyes filled with tears. 'I'm pregnant.'

Miranda refused to have the conversation that would follow in the llama stall, so she led a shaky Juliet towards the kitchen where they could both have some tea and biscuits and deal with things in a proper manner. They passed Abby and Mia on the terrace, setting up for another of Abby's pretend weddings in which some teddy bear got the happy ever after Miranda was never going to.

Paul was right. There was no one else on this island she would fall for, and the odds of anyone remotely suitable for her – let alone her soulmate – deciding to move there were infinitesimal. *And even if they did, I'd probably still be mooning over Owain . . .*

Focus, Miranda.

Juliet. That was who mattered here.

Mia jumped in front of some part of their set up, hiding it from view; Abby, hurrying alongside her a moment later had the stuffed llama Juliet had bought her tucked under her arm.

'Do I want to know what you're doing here?' Miranda

asked, wondering where the hell Leo was anyway.

'It's a surprise,' Mia said quickly. 'Dad . . . he's working, and he yelled at Abby, so we're planning an extra, extra-special wedding to make her feel better.'

Abby nodded. 'You're all invited. When we're ready.'

Miranda spent a second or two deciding how much she cared about whatever it was they were hiding, and concluded that it couldn't be all that bad. And if it was, it was Leo's problem anyway.

'OK. Let us know when the bride arrives,' she said, and ushered Juliet into the kitchen, the girls chorusing 'We will!' behind them.

Miranda put the kettle on, dumped the whole biscuit tin on the kitchen table – although someone had eaten all the chocolate ones, she realised, and mentally blamed Leo – then turned to Juliet.

'OK. Tell me everything.'

It wasn't a pretty story, and it took a full pot of tea and far too many biscuits to tell. Juliet's voice was so soft Miranda had to lean right across the table to make sure she didn't miss any of it. She forced herself to stay silent until the very end, knowing that if she spoke it would give Juliet a reason to stop.

She needed to know everything if she was going to help her.

'So I came home,' Juliet finished, tugging the sleeves of her cardigan over her fingers. It looked like one of their mum's. Miranda figured it was probably a comfort thing. 'But Mum and Dad weren't here and I didn't know how to tell you and Leo.'

'You told Rory, though?' That shouldn't have hurt, knowing how close those two had always been, as friends long before they were a couple. But it did anyway.

'The night of Leo's llama party,' Juliet confirmed. 'And since then . . . I don't know what's going on with us. First he pulled away, then he started fussing about everything and baby books – like some sort of demented midwife. Then today . . .' She took a deep breath before continuing, pausing long enough to allow Miranda to imagine all the horrible possibilities of what Rory might have done. 'Today, he took me on some magical-mystery carriage ride of the island, hitting all the places on the map of our relationship. And then he tried to propose to me.'

'Oh.' Well, that was . . . predictable, for Rory, she supposed. 'What did you do?'

'I ran.' And that was just as predictable for Juliet.

Miranda sighed, and ran a hand over her forehead. Suddenly, she missed the days when cleaning up after Juliet just meant hose-piping vomit from the plants by the front door.

'So since you came back, you two have been . . . together?' she asked. How was she this out of touch with her own sister's life?

But Juliet shook her head. 'Not at all. Not even a kiss. Not even a hint that he *wanted* a kiss.'

'But did you? Want a kiss, I mean?'

Colour sprung to Juliet's cheeks. 'That's not the point. The point is, we're not even together, I'm pregnant with another man's child, and he just *proposed* to me. In front of the whole town!'

Miranda winced. Put like that, it didn't sound too great. But she was certain that Rory wouldn't have been thinking of it that way.

'Or, you came home, lost and afraid, and turned to your old friend – and the only man you ever truly loved, right? – for help. And this is what he came up with.'

'How would a random proposal of marriage help?' Juliet asked, sounding completely bemused. 'As if I didn't already have enough to worry about.'

'Juliet . . . ever since the two of you were little, Rory's been looking out for you. He protected you in junior school, he covered for you in secondary school, and then he fell madly in love with you. He fell apart when you left, like, completely. And now you're back . . . it seems to me, he's trying to look after you all over again. Maybe even cover for you. Because people will talk a lot less if they think you came back here for Rory, and now the two of you are having a baby together.'

'But that's . . . that's a lie.'

Miranda laughed. 'You say it like you've never told one.'

'No, but I wouldn't ever ask Rory to live one like that.' Juliet shook her head, obviously repulsed by the very idea. Miranda supposed that however many white lies she might have told as a teenager – about where she was going, when she'd be home, whether she'd been drinking – she'd never actually been a deceitful person. She was just herself, plain and simple.

And watching her now, Miranda rather admired that.

'I don't care what people say about me,' Juliet said, sitting up straighter in her chair. 'I thought I would – thought I'd hate all the locals gossiping about me the way they always used to. That was one of the reasons I left, to get away from everybody knowing my business. But now . . . this is who I am. It's my life. And I'll live it wherever I choose, and however I want.'

'I never thought you wouldn't,' Miranda said, smiling. 'So, tell me. If you don't want to marry Rory, what *do* you want?'

Juliet slumped down again. 'That's the problem. Beyond

having this baby, I have absolutely no idea.' She bit her lip as she looked up at Miranda. 'So, are you?'

'Am I what?'

'Disappointed in me?' She looked so worried. Miranda had never imagined that her opinion might actually *matter* to Juliet.

'I thought you didn't care what people said or thought about you?'

'You're not people,' Juliet replied. 'You're family.'

That sent a warm and fuzzy feeling through Miranda as she considered her answer.

'The way I see it,' she said, slowly, thinking through everything her sister had told her. 'Your sleazebag boss lied to you, took advantage of you, abandoned you, left you holding the literal baby, and forced you into a situation where you felt you had to give up your job and your home, too. And in response you found the strength to come home − even though you always said you wouldn't − you decided to keep your baby, and to find a way to raise it yourself. You took over running the Lighthouse when Mum and Dad extended their trip, and you mended your friendship with Rory, as well as helping Leo out with the girls and looking after the damn llama. Through it all, *you've* been the grown-up, even if it hasn't felt like it. Juliet, I'm not disappointed in you. I'm proud as all hell of the woman you are today.'

Tears welled up in Juliet's eyes, and Miranda grabbed for the tissue box behind her.

'Really?'

'Of course.' They'd never really been hugging siblings, but Miranda figured that if there was ever a time to start it was probably now. Perching on the chair beside her, she wrapped her arms around Juliet and hugged her. Tight.

'You got screwed over, and you're not letting it stop you.'

'Like you and Paul.' Juliet sniffed, and wiped her eyes. 'He dumped you horribly, and you took up with a sexy musician who looks at you like you're the only woman in the world.'

'And who will be leaving soon. Again.' Miranda sat back and sighed. 'Paul tried to get us back together today. Said he could come home at weekends. He pointed out that there's literally no one else on this island I'd want to marry and, well, he's not wrong.'

Juliet stared at her in horror. 'You said no, right?'

'Of course I said no. But . . . it means deciding that I'm OK with being on my own here for the rest of my life. Which before I met Owain, I might have been. But now . . .'

'You could always leave the island,' Juliet said, eyebrows raised.

Miranda laughed, but it felt cold and dead in her throat. 'Yeah. Anyway. We're not talking about me tonight. We're going to get Leo, and we're going to have a family meeting.'

'Without Mum and Dad?' Juliet sounded horrified.

'We're adults now,' Miranda pointed out. 'And they're not here. We can do this on our own.'

'Do what, exactly?'

'Help you figure out what's next,' Miranda said, firmly. 'And then we'll help you do it.'

Juliet threw her arms back round her neck and hugged her tight. 'I take back all the awful things I ever said about big sisters. You get the kettle back on, and I'll go get Leo.'

But before either of them could move, the back door flew open and Abby and Mia appeared.

'We're ready!' Abby shouted, with far too much excitement. 'Lucy's getting married! Come and see her in her dress!'

Miranda and Juliet shared a look, then crossed to the kitchen door and looked out beyond the terrace, to where Lucy the Llama stood, all in white, with a circlet of oxeye daisies around her head.

They stared.

Then Miranda realised something, and horror rose up her throat.

'Wait. Is that my *wedding dress?*'

LEO

Tom had long since hung up on him leaving Leo staring at his screen, wondering what he'd missed. He couldn't even think about the call from the estate agents right now – not until he'd figured out where he'd screwed up at work. The one thing he was supposed to be good at. How could he fix anything else – his family, the Lighthouse – when he couldn't even manage his business?

What had it been about that presentation that made Harry decide to go with someone else? When they'd worked so well together for so many years? He still hadn't been able to get him on the phone, and the lack of answers was driving him crazy.

'Are you seriously still up here?' Leo looked up and found Christabel leaning against the doorframe.

He rubbed a hand across his forehead. 'I thought Mia said you went home.'

'I did. And then I came back again, to see if you'd wised up yet. Apparently not.'

'Look, I appreciate your help with the girls and everything over the last few weeks. But I have an actual job to do, you know, and sometimes that requires working during office hours, not taking bike rides and picnics.' He knew he was taking his frustration out on her, knew it wasn't fair, but that didn't seem to be stopping him doing it.

'Actual office hours like seven o'clock on a Friday night?' Christabel asked mildly.

He blinked at the clock on the corner of his screen. No wonder Tom had hung up. 'When did it get so late?'

'Around the time you were obsessing about whatever it was I'm assuming you couldn't fix?' She leaned against the edge of his desk, and pushed his laptop screen closed. 'Tell me honestly, have you achieved anything since I left you that has actually made a tangible difference to your business?'

Leo thought about it. 'I've properly pissed off my assistant, if that counts?'

Everything else had just been noise. He had been playing the blame game, trying to make himself feel better about something he couldn't change. To try and make up for not being there this summer.

He should probably send Tom flowers. Or whisky.

'Well done you.' The sarcasm was strong in her voice. 'God, I don't even know why I came back. I'd like to pretend that it was just to make sure the girls hadn't starved, but it wasn't. I came because I wanted to believe that this summer had made a difference to you. That *I* had made a difference to you. Pathetic, huh?'

Leo's eyes widened. Had he ever heard Christabel talk herself down before? God, how much of a let-down must he be if he'd knocked even her unshakeable confidence?

'You made a huge difference this summer.' He pushed away from his desk, rolling the chair backwards, and got to his feet, crossing the room to her. 'You think I've made a mess of things now? I guarantee you it would have been a hundred times worse if you hadn't been here, steering me in the right direction.'

Every time he'd screwed up, or felt lost, or out of control, or just overwhelmed by it all, Christabel had been there to ask him the questions that guided him back to his path. As long as he'd been listening.

Today, he'd closed his ears.

'Normally it's easier than this,' she admitted, her voice smaller than he was used to hearing. In the dim light of his father's study, he felt like he was finally seeing underneath the positive exterior Christabel showed the world every day. He'd spent so much time with this woman – kissed her, made love to her, laughed with her, shared his feelings with her – and yet it felt like this was the first time he was seeing all of her.

That shook him.

'Easier, how?' He perched on the desk beside her, reaching tentatively for her hand. He was used to touching her now, but this wasn't the Christabel he was used to, and suddenly he felt like he needed to be more careful.

'Normally, I see it as a kind of a challenge. Like a mutually beneficial experiment. I find someone I like, we flirt, we have fun, and I help them find what they're really looking for in life. And I know it's never going to be me and that's fine, because that's the deal. There's always a time limit. I get to feel good for helping them, for putting some positivity out in the world. Plus we have fun together. Then, when it's time, we each move on towards what we really want. But you . . .' she shook her head ruefully. 'You are a much harder nut to crack. Our time is nearly up, and I'm no more confident about your path than I was when we met.'

Leo nudged her with his shoulder. 'I might just be a hopeless case, you realise.'

'I don't believe that,' she replied, fiercely. 'I've always found that the most worthwhile things are the ones that take the most work – as long as you're working for something you believe in.'

'And you believe in me?' Leo asked, surprised.

'I'd like to. I'd like to believe that you love your daughters more than your job. That your family, your life, matters to you at least as much as your business does. I hope you're just still scared and trying to find the right balance. I just don't know what else I can do to help you.'

'I'd like to believe all that too,' Leo said, slowly, thinking about the girls, and the call from the estate agent. He needed to talk to his sisters. But first he needed to fix things with his daughters. Again. 'I *want* to be the man you hope I can be, the dad my daughters need – even the brother that Miranda and Juliet deserve. But I think that becoming that person might be a longer path than you'd like. I might not be a quick fix, but I hope to keep getting closer to where I'm going, every day. And it's not up to you to hold my hand and get me there. It's up to me to keep working for it.'

She smiled at that. 'Well, working is the one thing we know you're good at.'

'The only thing?' he asked.

'Maybe not the only thing.' Reaching up, she kissed him, slow and sweet. 'Come on. I don't know what your daughters are up to down there, but I heard some shouting about a wedding dress on my way up here, so I suspect we'd better get down there pronto.'

'Wedding dress?' Leo asked, as they hurried down the stairs. 'I know the girls mentioned something about a . . . a llama wedding, I think?'

'That's right,' Juliet said, meeting them in the hallway, visibly biting the inside of her cheek to keep from laughing. 'I think they're marrying Lucy off to the old rocking horse from the sunroom. And they've dressed Lucy in the wedding dress Miranda bought to marry Paul . . .'

Leo's eyes widened. 'Shit. I'd better go save them from the wrath of Randa.'

Juliet laughed. 'Actually, it's OK. She said it was a sign she *really* wasn't meant to marry Paul. Then she fetched them the veil to go with it.'

'Wow.' That did *not* sound like the Miranda he remembered, growing up.

'I think it helped that Paul was a total arse to her today,' Juliet added. Then her face grew more sombre. 'Um, they're waiting for us outside for the wedding ceremony – I was told it was my turn to get yelled at by you. And then afterwards . . . Miranda wants a family meeting.'

'Without Mum and Dad?'

'Yep.' That was weird, but that didn't mean it wasn't a good idea – one he should have had. Maybe he would have, if he hadn't been distracted by his work disaster. They all needed to talk about the sale of the Lighthouse, after all.

'Well . . . good.' Then he frowned. Miranda didn't know about the phone call from the estate agent. So why was *she* calling a meeting? 'Wait. What's the meeting about?' He didn't like this. This had the feeling of a disaster.

'Oh, nothing much.' Juliet turned and started to walk outside. 'Just the fact I'm pregnant and unemployed. We'll talk about it later.'

Leo stared after her, then turned to Christabel. 'Did she say—'

Christabel patted his arm. 'That you'll talk about it later. Llama wedding first.'

The wedding went off without a hitch. Well, apart from Lucy trying to eat the veil, Juliet actually crying as Abby asked Lucy if she'd take Rocking Horse to be her husband, Misty the cat bridesmaid screeching and racing away the moment Abby tried to put a flower crown on her head, and Mia pointing out that Rocking Horse was a girl, so they'd be wives. Leo was pointedly *not* asked to give either of the brides away, and when, after the wedding breakfast of chocolate biscuits – brought by Christabel to make up for the ones they'd eaten earlier in the week – and glasses of milk, Leo suggested it was bedtime, Mia dragged Abby straight up the stairs declaring they didn't need tucking in tonight.

'I'll go,' Christabel whispered to him, as they disappeared up the stairs. 'I'll make sure they're settled, then let myself out. You get on with your family meeting.'

But Leo shook his head. 'No. I need to make up with them both. Their mother always says, "never go to bed angry". That might have been our problem, actually. I'd work so late that there was never time to make up. I can't make that mistake with my daughters.'

The smile Christabel gave him told him he'd got something right, at last.

Taking the stairs two at a time, he made it up to the top floor and found the girls brushing their teeth. Hanging back by the banister, he waited, knowing they hadn't heard him.

'Don't worry, Abs,' Mia said, around her toothbrush. 'Mum'll be back soon. And Dad can go back to just seeing us every other weekend, like normal.'

The words hit his heart like needles. Was that what they wanted? Well, why wouldn't they? Christabel had set him a challenge at the start of the summer; to be a father that his daughters could rely on to always listen, to be there when they needed him.

And he'd tried, he really had. But it wasn't enough.

He wasn't enough.

And maybe another day, another summer, he'd have decided that it was time to stop trying. To accept that there was nothing more he could do here, like he should have done hours earlier with the lost client.

He might have given up and accepted that he'd never be the father he wanted to be so he might as well focus on being the businessman he wanted to be instead.

But not this summer. He'd tasted how good it could feel when he got it right, and he knew now that he'd keep striving for that feeling, even if it took him a lifetime. Parenthood wasn't something he'd win crystal awards for, that he could line up on the shelf in his office. In fact, he was pretty sure he'd keep getting it wrong more often than he got it right.

But maybe all his girls needed to know was that he'd keep trying. That he was in this for ever, for them. And that even when he screwed up he was still trying his best.

As the girls finished up on the bathroom, he clunked loudly up the last few steps, making them both turn towards him.

'How about I tuck you both in, huh?'

Mia shrugged, as if to say she didn't care, but Leo persisted.

'I'm sorry about today,' he said, as he tucked the duvet around her. 'I made you a promise and I broke it. I shouldn't have.'

Mia stared at him for a moment, as if she were trying to find a hidden message in his words. Then, apparently convinced his apology was genuine, she burst out, 'You didn't even tell us what the problem was. We might have been able to help. But at least we would have understood what was going on. I'm not a baby any more you know. You can talk to me.'

'You're right. I should have explained. I'm sorry about that too. Next time, I'll talk to you about what's going on.' Which might mean talking to her about the Lighthouse being sold, sooner rather than later – something he *really* didn't relish.

She nodded. 'Then we can see When had his little girl grown up so much? And how did she already understand people and relationships so much better than he did? Probably from paying attention to her mother, he supposed. And Christabel, this summer.

Perhaps it was just his generation of the family that were totally screwed in that area.

Moving to the other bed, he tucked Abby in too, and pressed a kiss to her forehead.

'Goodnight, sweetheart. I'm so sorry I shouted at you.'

'Sorry means you won't do it again,' Abby told him. 'So that's OK.'

'It definitely means I'll try.' Leo knew his own limits.

'Did you enjoy the wedding, Daddy?' she whispered, her eyes already starting to close.

'I thought it was wonderful.' The lump in his throat hurt when he spoke, but Abby seemed happy, all the same. 'I was so happy to be there with you both. In fact, spending this summer with the pair of you has been the best thing I've done in years. I'm sorry if I let you doubt that today.'

Switching off the last lamp, Leo headed downstairs to find out what was going on with his sisters, hoping it was an easier fix than his relationship with his daughters.

'Goodnight, Daddy,' they chorused behind him, and Leo smiled.

MESSAGES

Juliet (to the 'Rents group): Hi Guys! Hope you're still having lots of fun on your travels. Um . . . I have some news for you both, but I'd rather tell you in person than by text. Do you know yet when you'll be home?
(Unread)

JULIET

Family meetings had always had a structure, a tradition about them – and it seemed that Miranda intended to follow it to the letter. Already, she'd lit the candles on the proper dining table – the kitchen table wasn't formal enough for a full-on family meeting – and set out the crystal whisky tumblers. Juliet's had sparkling water in it, but still, it was the thought that counted.

'The girls settled?' Miranda asked, as Leo appeared in the dining room.

'Yeah.' He slumped into his seat and reached for his whisky. 'What's going on?'

Juliet scooted her chair closer to her brother's. 'What's going on with *you*? What happened today? I thought you guys were going for a beach picnic?'

'We were.' He sighed. 'But then we lost a client at work, and I yelled at Tom, and the girls, and told them a llama wedding was stupid, and now they can't wait for Emily to come home so they can go back to seeing me once a fort-night at most.'

Juliet winced. 'Well, I'm pregnant by my married ex-boss, I quit my job, I'm basically in hiding, and I ran away from a proposal on a romantic carriage ride around the island with the only man I've ever really loved, because I don't know what the hell I'm doing with my life. If that makes you feel any better.'

He stared at her. 'Not really.'

'Well, maybe this will do it then.' Miranda dropped into the seat at the head of the table, the one their father always sat in, and poured herself a very large whisky. 'The man I planned to marry, who dumped me for a new job, told me today that we should get back together anyway to keep his mother happy, and because it wasn't like I was ever going to find anyone else on Seashell Island to marry me.'

'Yeah, but you can't marry him now anyway,' Juliet pointed out helpfully. 'The girls used your wedding dress for Lucy.'

'Sorry about that,' Leo mumbled.

Miranda shrugged. 'It's fine. I already told him no. Even if he's right.'

'He's not!' Juliet couldn't bear thinking about him being right. Miranda – strong, annoying, perfect Miranda – deserved someone far better than Paul. Someone like Owain, perhaps. 'Maybe Owain will stay?'

'And maybe I'll leave Seashell Island to stay with him,' Miranda shot back. They were all silent at that. Even Juliet had to agree, they seemed equally unlikely.

'The point is,' Juliet said, trying to get them back on track, 'And the reason we're having this family meeting—'

'We're all screwed up,' Leo put in for her.

'And we can't rely on Mum and Dad to help us fix it,' Miranda added.

'So we need to work together,' Juliet finished. 'To help each other figure out what we *really* want from life, and how to get it.'

'Plus we need to save the Lighthouse from being sold—' Miranda said.

'What?' Juliet interrupted, but Miranda ignored her.

'And hold the Lighthouse Festival to stop Seashell Island

dropping off the tourist map altogether and collapsing in on itself.'

They all looked at each other, taking in the magnitude of the tasks ahead of them.

'The Lighthouse is up for sale?' Juliet asked, finally, figuring that might be the easiest place to start.

Leo and Miranda exchanged a glance. It looked like she wasn't the only one who'd been keeping secrets this summer.

'We found an estate-agent brief for the house,' Leo admitted. 'We think Mum and Dad are getting ready to sell. In fact, I know they are. I had a call from the estate agent today, with a buyer wanting to arrange a viewing. I stalled them, said we needed to talk to Mum and Dad first.'

Shock reverberated through Juliet, along with a huge sense of loss. All those years spent trying to get away from here, and suddenly the idea of losing the Lighthouse made her want to cry.

Stupid hormones.

'Because it's not making enough money?' Juliet guessed. 'You said there were no guests booked until Owain and the others showed up.'

'That's what we're thinking,' Miranda admitted.

No. She'd only just found this place again. Juliet wasn't willing to lose it now.

Which meant they had to *do* something.

'The festival,' she said, thinking aloud. 'If the festival is a success, if we can bring enough new people to the island, and they see how great it is here, they'll want to come back. So we just have to show them the Lighthouse too so they know where to stay!'

'That could work,' Leo said, but Miranda was wincing. 'What?'

'I had a call earlier. The three food stalls I'd finally

managed to book – all from the same parent company – have cancelled. Food poisoning outbreak, apparently, which suggests we had a narrow escape. But as of right now, we only have the Flying Fish, the island craft collective and the Seashell WI holding stalls at the festival, plus Owain and the guys playing, I hope. We need more – lots more. And honestly? I don't know where to start.'

'With a list,' Juliet said. 'And a rota. Same as we always used to do when we were kids – except this time, Leo, you actually have to do your jobs, OK?'

He rolled his eyes. 'Fine, fine. So. What do we need?'

Juliet pulled out the notebook she'd been using to keep track of everything from her prenatal vitamins and what food didn't make her vomit to how many sausages and rashers of bacon she needed to order for the breakfasts. Turning to a clear double-page spread, she wrote a heading at the top of each of the pages. The first read *The Lighthouse,* the second *The Festival.*

She turned it around to show the others. 'So. What do we need to do. Let's get everything down in writing, then we'll start divvying up the jobs.'

'I need to find more food stalls for the festival,' Miranda started. 'Assuming we have enough other stalls to attract any visitors in the first place.'

'*We* need to,' Juliet corrected her, writing it down on the list. 'We're working together now, remember. And actually . . .'

She trailed off, thinking. *She* knew food vendors. She'd organised a dozen or more street-food events while she was working for Callum. But those contacts were part of her life *off* the island, and she'd promised Callum she wouldn't cause any trouble at the company. Would this count?

Miranda's eyes widened as she leapt to the same conclusion

that Juliet had. 'You must know some people, right? Your job was literally working with street-food stands.'

'I mean, maybe?' Juliet replied. What was it about bringing her London life and her Seashell Island life together that felt so wrong? 'I'd probably need to check my contract though. I'm not sure using company contacts for personal stuff is allowed . . .'

Miranda gave her a look. 'I'm pretty sure your boss knocking you up then essentially firing you wasn't in his contract either, Juliet.'

'You could probably take him to an employment tribunal,' Leo put in.

'Or I could just live my best life and call his best food vendors,' Juliet agreed. 'I'll log into my emails later and get some contacts. Plus, actually, there are some great suppliers from the local farmers' market. I've been there a few weeks now, made some connections. I'll see if I can call in some favours there, too. Now, what else?'

'Music,' Miranda said. 'Owain offered to help with that, and I . . . I guess I held back. I wanted the Lighthouse Festival to be the same as it always was, so I kept trying to find the same old stalls and such. But maybe he's right. Maybe it's time for something bigger and better.'

'I think we need it,' Juliet said.

Miranda nodded. 'I'll call him, and the band. See what they can come up with on short notice.'

'And we need entertainment for the kids,' Leo added. 'I bet Christabel will have some ideas about that.'

'And we could talk to Dafydd and Max about linking up with their glamping site for the visitors,' Miranda suggested.

'Ooh, and maybe a petting zoo! With Lucy as the star attraction, of course,' Juliet said, scribbling down all their ideas.

'We need a way to get people here, too,' Leo said. 'We've only got a week.'

'I put a flyer up on the noticeboard in town,' Miranda said. 'I've had lots of interest from the locals, but we really do need a last push. Plus I haven't been able to tell people anything much about what was going on, because I didn't know myself.'

'Then we pitch it as a flash festival.' Leo grabbed Juliet's notebook and started adding some scribbles of his own. 'Exclusive, secretive, if you know the kind of thing. Make people excited about it on social media, highlight the saving-the-island aspect . . . I reckon we can get the crowds here with a little bit of marketing know-how.'

'That can be your job, then,' Juliet told him, taking back her notebook. 'Now, what else?'

Once they'd finished listing possibilities for the festival, they moved onto the Lighthouse itself, and Juliet's other list grew too.

'Repainting the front door, decorating the two back bedrooms, oh, what about the cottage, Miranda?' she asked, as she wrote.

'Once the band leave, that'll be up for grabs I'm sure,' she said, her voice a little subdued.

Juliet put down her pen. 'I'm sorry. We got so caught up in fixing the festival and the B&B . . .'

'But we're ignoring our bigger problems again,' Leo finished, with a sigh. 'It's just the practical ones are so much easier to solve.'

Glancing once more at her list, Juliet closed her notebook. 'OK. Tomorrow morning we'll make plans and lists and figure out who is going to do what. But for now . . . we should talk. All three of us. About our lives and what matters to us and what we're going to do next. Like siblings do.'

And they never had. But maybe they could, if they tried.

Miranda nodded. 'OK. Let's start with you. Are you still in love with Callum?'

'Who's Callum?' Leo asked.

'The baby's father,' Miranda told him. 'Keep up.'

Juliet considered Miranda's question. It seemed absurd now that, only a month ago, she'd been planning their future together as a London couple as soon as his divorce had come through . . . a divorce it was now obvious he never intended to ask for in the first place.

'No,' she said, slowly. 'After everything he did, and everything I've learned about him because of it . . . no, I don't love him. I can't believe I ever did.'

'What *exactly* did he do?' Leo asked. 'I need to know how much we hate him, and whether it's worth calling my employment lawyer friend.'

With an impatient huff, Miranda turned to him and explained. 'He used his position of power as her boss to seduce her, while he was separated from his wife, promising her he'd get a divorce soon. Then, when she told him she was pregnant, he told him no one can ever know, that he's going back to his wife, and he doesn't want anything to do with the baby.'

'So I left my job and came here.' It felt funny, hearing Miranda describe the events of her life over the last six months. It wasn't how she would have put it, exactly, but it made her feel her sister was one hundred per cent on her side. She liked it.

'And now what are you going to do?' Leo asked, and Juliet deflated a little.

'That's the million-dollar question.'

'Rory wants to marry her,' Miranda said.

'He proposed. That's not the same thing.' Juliet sat up

straight, the same panic spiking as it had in the carriage.

'It kind of is.'

'No. Besides, I ran away before he could finish asking.'

Leo chuckled at that. 'Of course you did. Would it be so bad, marrying Rory?'

'If he was proposing purely because I was pregnant and he wanted to make an honest woman of me? Yes.' The very idea made her shudder. 'I need to stand on my own two feet for once. Figure out my life without relying on anyone else to swoop in and save me.'

'But what if it was because he loved you and wanted to spend his life with you?' Miranda's question was softer, more curious, and stopped Juliet in her tracks.

Would it be that bad? Not a rushed wedding or anything, but the possibility of being with Rory again.

She thought about the carriage ride that afternoon, about that trip back through their history and everything they'd shared as teenagers. It had been wonderful, then. But she didn't want to go backwards.

'I think it would depend,' she said, slowly. 'If he wanted us to go back and be who we were when I left, and just carry on as if it never happened, then I couldn't do that.'

But if he wanted to start a new relationship, fresh, the people they were now and see where that went . . . if he was willing to do that even with the baby coming, not because she needed him to, but because they both *wanted* to . . . then that might not be so bad.

It could even be wonderful. If she let herself believe it.

'Seems to me you need to talk to Rory,' Leo said, topping up his whisky glass.

'And what about you?' Juliet asked. She was done having them analyse her mistakes. It was definitely someone else's turn.

But Leo just shrugged. 'Like the girls say, Emily will be back soon. Everything can go back to normal. I can get back to work properly, and they can get on with their lovely family life with Emily and *Mark*.'

Juliet and Miranda shared a look at the bitterness in his voice. His divorce from Emily had been so amicable, and they'd both worked so hard at staying as a family, even when she met Mark . . . what had changed this summer to make him feel differently? Was it just Emily remarrying? Or was there something more going on here?

'Is that what you want to happen?' Juliet asked.

Leo slumped further down in his seat and took another sip of whisky. 'No. It *was*. At the start of the summer, I was looking forward to everything going back to normal again in September. But then . . . the day we met Christabel. She asked me if I wanted to be one of those dads who wasn't really a part of his daughters' lives as they grew up, or if I wanted to be the dad they could come to with anything, who they'd trust, who they'd talk to when they were in trouble. And I thought about Dad with us growing up and I realised . . . I wanted that.'

'So that's what you've been trying to do this summer?' Miranda shook her head. 'Leo, I love that you've been spending time with the girls, and I get that it's really important. But Dad never did any of that stuff with us, you realise? I mean, yes, we'd go out on bike rides and beach days, but it wasn't every day all summer. Because he was working too – either at the B&B or writing. Mostly, the three of us entertained ourselves in the summer, or ran around with our friends. But I never felt we couldn't talk to him – or Mum – if we needed to. Well, almost never.'

What was the exception, Juliet wondered? But it wasn't

the time to ask. Because Miranda was right. But, she had to admit, it was different for Leo.

'But Dad was here every evening, every day,' she pointed out. 'Leo doesn't have that.'

'*Mark* has that,' Leo added darkly.

'Leo, you *like* Mark,' Miranda reminded him. 'He's a nice guy, and he loves Emily and the girls. That doesn't mean he's going to try and be their dad, though. That's always going to be you.'

'As long as you want the job,' Juliet added. Because it was something she'd had a lot of cause to think about recently; what it meant to be a parent. She still didn't know if she'd be any good at it, but she *did* know she'd give it everything she'd got, because she was the only parent her baby would have who was willing to do that. 'Do you?'

'What if I can't do it?' Leo whispered. 'What if they still love Mark more anyway?'

'Some days they probably will,' Juliet admitted, remembering her own tumultuous teenage years. 'Some days they'll hate you, some days they'll try and use you to get back at Emily or Mark, some days they'll ignore you completely. Because they're children, and then adolescents, and they're still learning everything they need to know about the world.'

'I mean, in fairness, it sounds pretty dreadful to me,' Miranda admitted. 'But then, I never really wanted kids.'

Leo and Juliet both looked at her in surprise. 'You don't?'

'How did I not know that?' Juliet demanded.

Miranda shrugged. 'I guess it turns out that there's a lot we don't know about each other.'

'Like why you won't leave this island,' Leo said, but Miranda deflected it away.

'Let's focus on the here and now first. Leo, do you want

to be a dad to your girls? Not just someone they see every now and then?'

'Yes,' he said, a firmness entering his voice that they hadn't heard before.

'Juliet, do you want to go back to London to have this baby?'

'No.' The word was out before she could even think about it. Her eyes widened. She'd always assumed she'd go back to the city eventually, once she had a plan. 'No. I don't think I do.'

'Well, that's progress,' Miranda said, with a gentle smile. 'Now we just need to figure out what you *do* want.'

'And what you want,' Juliet pointed out. A thought occurred to her. Miranda had helped her find the start of her truth by surprising her with a question. Maybe she could do the same for her. 'Miranda, do you want to marry Paul?'

'No.'

'Do you want to persuade Owain to give up the band and stay here on the island?'

'No. He'd hate me for that, in the end.'

'Do you want to stay happily single for ever?'

'No.'

Now for the real question. The one she hopefully wouldn't see coming. 'Do you want to leave Seashell Island?'

'Yes.'

The word echoed around the dining room, even as Miranda brought her hand to her mouth, too late to hold it in.

'Oh God,' she mumbled against her fingers, after a long, stunned silence. 'I want to leave the island.'

Juliet looked at Leo, who stared back in shock.

'OK,' Juliet said. 'I'm going to put the kettle on. Because between the three of us, it looks like we've got a lot more talking to do, and I need a peppermint tea.'

But as she headed towards the kitchen, she realised she felt better, lighter, than she had in weeks. Because finally she had two things she'd been missing.

Hope and faith.

Faith that between the three of them, the Waters siblings could figure this all out, and get the futures they all wanted. For themselves, for each other, for the Lighthouse – and for Seashell Island.

MIRANDA

One week later, on the last day of August, in the early hours of Friday morning, Miranda woke to the sound of her bedroom door opening.

She peered through bleary eyes in the darkness, and made out just enough details of the person entering to smile.

'You're late,' she murmured, as Owain climbed into bed beside her. 'We were expecting you back last night.'

'Sorry.' He kissed her shoulder, her neck, up towards her ear, and Miranda squirmed with pleasure. 'There were some meetings that ran long yesterday. The rest of the band will be here later today, but I couldn't wait to get back to you.'

That made her smile. And made her want to kiss him. So she did. Then his words caught up with her. 'Meetings?'

'I'll tell you later,' he mumbled, between more kisses, and Miranda decided she could wait for that information.

But not for everything. 'Mmm.' She pulled away. 'Wait. Tell me how it went with the other bands. Did you persuade anyone else to come over and play for the festival?' They'd been in contact all week, with Owain twisting arms and calling in favours from everyone he'd ever worked with, it seemed — all to make her festival happen. Their line-up wasn't bad, but they could do with a few more acts to fill out the programme.

Owain groaned, but obviously realised his kisses weren't going any further until she had *some* answers. 'Yes. Three more definites, and one more who is trying to move some things around to make it.'

'That's fantastic! We've got a few local amateur bands – from the island and just over on the mainland – for the second stage too. What about the sound engineers?'

'Ryan and Robyn can do a lot of it like we planned, and they're bringing the last of the equipment we've hired with them when they come later – better have Rory's van on standby for that, actually. But I got another couple of mates to agree to come too. Did the speakers and boards arrive?'

'Yesterday,' Miranda confirmed. 'And all the staging. Plus a lot of people.'

'Then everything's ready?'

'As ready as it can be right now.' Which didn't stop the nervous excitement racing through her. She'd never get back to sleep now, there was too much to do, too much to think about – too much that could still go wrong . . .

'Good.' Owain kissed her again, deep and long. 'Because I have really, really missed you.'

And suddenly, miraculously, all of Miranda's worries melted away for a while.

But not for too long. With just twenty-four hours left before the festival, there was far too much to do to linger in bed all day.

Miranda led Owain down the stairs, amused to see the astonishment on his face as he took in their little hive of activity.

The dining table had been taken over by Leo and his assistant Tom – who'd arrived on the ferry the day after their family meeting, after a very apologetic call from Leo – as Festival HQ. Josie's best tablecloth had been cleared away and replaced by laptops, flyers, print-outs and empty coffee mugs. Juliet bustled through with a plate of bacon butties for all, handing one to Owain with a 'welcome home', and a kiss on the cheek.

'Home?' Owain mouthed at Miranda. She just shrugged. Filling him in on everything that had occurred around here in the last week had seemed less important in the early hours than welcoming him back properly, and now there was too much to do before the festival. She smiled a secret smile to herself. She hoped Owain would be pleased with all the changes and decisions she and her siblings had made. But she also wanted to find exactly the right moment to tell him about the biggest one of all . . .

'Where's Leo?' she asked Tom, just as he took a huge bite of his bacon butty.

'He and Christabel took the girls out for one last leafleting effort in town,' Tom replied, spraying crumbs. 'Those two munchkins are better than any advert I can buy on Facebook.'

'They're cuter, for a start,' Miranda agreed.

But Tom shook his head. 'Mia is a marketing mastermind. And even Abby has got the selling down pat. I heard Mia telling her sister not to make the poster she was drawing too perfect, because it would be more endearing if it looked more childish.'

Miranda grinned, even as Owain looked slightly shocked. 'They're Leo's daughters, all right. I had a call from my ex-boss yesterday complaining about them.'

Tom raised his eyebrows. 'I thought everyone on Seashell Island was behind this whole festival idea.'

'Oh, they are,' Miranda said. 'But the girls had been out putting up flyers and talking to all the tourists who stopped to ask them about the festival, and suddenly Seashell Holiday Cottages was inundated by visitors asking if they could

322

extend their stays just two more days so they could be here for the festival!'

'That explains the sudden surge in ticket sales from our stock at the Crab Leg Cafe then,' Tom said, sounding satisfied. 'Maybe we should send them over to the mainland to leaflet there . . . I'm going to suggest it to Leo.' He picked up the phone to call his boss, and Miranda turned away, leading Owain towards the kitchen, where Juliet was updating her ever-present list.

'How's it looking?' Miranda asked.

Juliet, pencil stuck in her hair holding up her blonde curls, frowned at her notebook. 'I *think* we're almost there. But then I keep thinking that must mean we're missing something.'

'Want to talk through it with me?' Miranda asked. 'I mean, I'm sure you have everything in hand, but sometimes it helps to have a fresh eye?' She turned to Owain. 'Juliet has been a marvel organising the festival,' she explained. 'Without her connections for the food stalls, local and from the mainland, I don't know what we'd have done. And her experience of organising street-food fairs and stuff was invaluable.'

Juliet was almost glowing at the praise – or maybe that was the pregnancy. Either way, Miranda was glad. She'd spent too many years not appreciating the talents her sister had, and now she was done focusing on her faults she found they were getting on much better.

'I think I've got it, thanks,' Juliet said. 'But I'll come find you if I think of anything we're missing. Why don't you go show Owain the festival site?'

'Good idea.' Looping a hand through Owain's arm, she dragged him through the back door and out towards the fields they'd spent so many mornings tramping through together with a recalcitrant llama.

'I'm guessing I missed some stuff this week?' he said, as they approached the fields.

'Just a bit,' Miranda admitted. 'Don't worry. You'll catch up.'

And then the festival site came into view, and he was too distracted to ask any more questions.

'Wow.' Owain looked around the field, taking everything in. 'I knew you'd been working hard while I was away, but still. When did you find time to do all this?'

Miranda grinned. 'It wasn't just me – I had a *lot* of help. And we were lucky with the weather – clear skies all week, so we could set stuff up early.' Most of the vendors from the mainland were arriving today to set up, and already the fields were buzzing with activity.

'It looks incredible.' He squeezed her waist, and pressed a kiss to the top of her head. 'I knew you could do it.'

It did look pretty good, Miranda had to admit. Bunting hung from the trees, with Leo's lights still in place for later. The vintage fairground Christabel had sourced was setting up on one side of the field, ready for the kids, and the food stalls had taken over the other side, nearest Lucy's stall. The llama was looking very intrigued by candyfloss, Miranda noticed.

'There'll be craft stalls from the local clubs over there,' she said, motioning to an empty area. 'There's going to be work-shops and tutorials as well as selling things. And Christabel's organising the kids' entertainment area. Apparently, she's offering circus skills lessons, as well as some giant garden games and, a little worryingly, archery.'

'Sounds like fun. Dangerous fun, but still fun.'

'That's what I thought.'

The biggest change from previous years, though, was the large stage at the far end of the field, ready to be set up with speakers and microphones and screens. Owain's friends had come through in large enough numbers that bands had been arriving all week, ready to play the festival – and there'd be more today, she knew.

Miranda had assumed that, being so last minute, they'd struggle to get people there, so she'd focused on any holiday-goers on the island who might be tempted to extend their trip by a day or two. Leo, it turned out, had bigger ideas. After a quick discussion with Tom, they'd had a website set up, with band bios and entertainment pages, ticket sales and a booking page for the glamping site Max and Dafydd had agreed could be set up in their field next door.

And it had *worked*.

Every band on the bill had put out notices on their social media, email lists, and websites – plus the strategic advertising Tom had managed on their very limited budget – and within hours of the site going up the bookings started coming in. And that was on top of Abby and Mia winning over every tourist already on Seashell Island.

Celebrate the end of summer at the Lighthouse Festival.

They'd had to put extra ferries on to deal with the sudden influx of people. The campsite was already full, and Nigel and Gwen had rented every cottage on the Seashell Holiday Cottages books. She couldn't believe it.

Now, all they had to do was pull the whole thing off.

'Come on,' Owain said. 'Let's see what we can do to help.'

By the time they all fell into bed that night – exhausted, happy, and full – Miranda thought they might *almost* be ready for when the gates opened at midday the following day.

Juliet had cooked up a vat of chilli and freshly baked jacket potatoes and served it to anyone who was hungry. Miranda had never seen the Lighthouse so busy as musicians, food sellers, technicians and islanders traipsed through the kitchen to grab a bite to eat and a bottle of beer to go with it, in most cases. And then, of course, because they had a field full of camping musicians – or glamping, actually, as most of them were staying over on Max and Dafydd's farm – there was music late into the night, played by firelight and starlight as everyone laughed and joked and enjoyed being together.

Miranda had watched Owain play and sing, watched Leo dancing with his girls in the firelight, watched Juliet swirling around chatting to everyone about the plans for tomorrow, confident and vibrant and happier than she'd seen her in years. She'd seen locals chatting with visitors, sharing jokes and drinks and song, and she'd known. They were all OK.

She could go, and they'd all be OK.

Whatever happened tomorrow, tonight, the festival already seemed like a success.

'Are you nervous about tomorrow?' Owain asked, as they snuggled under the duvet together, and she found herself automatically gravitating into his arms.

'A little,' she admitted. But it wasn't about the festival, not really. She trusted her siblings and the work the three of them had done together – everything was going to be fine.

It was that everything was going to change after it.

She should talk to Owain about her decision, she knew. Now was the perfect time.

Except then Owain's mouth met hers and he murmured, 'Maybe I can take your mind off that,' against her lips, and suddenly she had far more important things to focus on . . .

Miranda woke the next morning with a start, sun streaming through her window and Juliet banging on her door.

'Are you getting up? Only there's something I'm sure we're supposed to be doing today . . .'

'The festival!' Miranda elbowed Owain, who blinked up at her.

'That's today?' he joked, blearily.

'That's today,' Juliet confirmed from outside the door. 'The vendors are already arriving. I'm going to go take them all a cup of tea.'

There was no time for conversation, or anything beyond a quick good morning kiss and a rapid shower. In record time, Owain and Miranda were downstairs, dressed and ready to work.

There were plenty of last-minute tasks to be done, and they both threw themselves into them with everything they had – although Miranda's attempts were somewhat hampered by the number of people wanting to talk to her. Many had questions about festival logistics, or expected numbers. But most of them wanted to say some variation on the same thing.

'You've done a good thing here, Miranda,' Albert Tuna said, as he passed by with Abby and Mia. In his arms were two piglets for the petting zoo. Miranda didn't like to ask where the fisherman had found them. 'You're doing a great thing for our island. Thank you.'

Miranda swallowed around a lump in her throat, and just nodded to show she'd heard him. She'd heard it so many times today she didn't know what else to say.

She loved this island, and it loved her. But somehow, she was going to have to tell them all she was leaving.

'OK?' Owain asked, stopping by and pressing a kiss to her temple.

'Fine,' she replied, thinking once more that she was going to have to tell him too. When things were a little quieter. 'What's next?

The festival was due to kick off at midday, and by eleven thirty they were almost ready.

'Are you going to say something to all the volunteers?' Leo asked, as he and the girls joined them after helping set up the petting zoo and Christabel's family area.

'Like what?' Miranda asked.

'Thanking them for their help, that sort of thing.'

Miranda looked around. That *did* sound like the sort of thing she should do, even if she hadn't planned it. 'Right. OK.'

Dafydd, who had agreed to compère the music section of the festival, was already up on the stage testing mics for the last time. He handed one over happily when she explained what she wanted.

And then it was just her, standing in the middle of a huge stage. Across the way she could see the queues of people already waiting at the gates, eager to get in. Suddenly, she realised how much bigger this was than she'd ever intended or imagined it could be.

And she smiled.

This, everything she'd done, would help Seashell Island. It would benefit from more tourists, more possibilities.

It wouldn't need her any more. And maybe, just maybe, she wouldn't need it either. Not every day. Not as the limits of her existence, of her own potential and possibility.

Just as somewhere to come home to, whenever she wanted.

'Everybody?' she said into the mic, pulling it back a little as it squealed. 'If I could have your attention?'

Not everyone turned to listen, but enough people did that Miranda figured she should just say what she wanted to say and get off the stage.

'Before we get started and let the crowds through the

gates, I just wanted to say a huge thank you to everyone who has come together to make today possible. As many of you know, my parents, Josie and Iestyn Waters, have held a small party here for islanders and the few remaining visitors at the end of every summer, ever since we arrived at the Lighthouse over twenty years ago now. It's always been a way to bring the island together, to celebrate the turning of the seasons, and prepare ourselves for the longer nights ahead.

'This year, my siblings and I decided to do something a little bit different. We decided to open up the Lighthouse Festival so the rest of the world can see how fantastic our island is, too. We want *everybody* to celebrate with us – and come back and visit us again and again in the future.'

A cheer went up at that, and Miranda smiled.

'So, thank you to everyone who has helped pull this festival together, in such record time. And . . .' She caught Juliet's eye in the audience, and her sister nodded. Now was the time. To make the decision, so publicly that she'd never be able to go back on it and still show her face in town again.

To take that terrifying step into strange waters.

So much for finding a quiet moment to tell Owain privately. She just hoped he'd be happy with her decision.

'On a personal level, this festival has been the cornerstone of my year. This island has been my home, after years of not having one. Seashell Island is where I feel safe and content and secure. But I've realised this summer that secure sometimes means stuck. That staying with something or someone who feels safe sometimes means not going after your heart's desire. And it's time for me to find out what my heart's desire is. So, once the summer is over, I'll be leaving the island. Seashell Island will always be my home, but as a very wise man told me recently, that only means it'll be here waiting for me when I return.'

Before she handed the microphone back to Dafydd, she took a moment to look out at her community – all cheering for her. And then she found the one face she really needed to see.

She met Owain's gaze and watched as a warm, true smile spread across his face, his eyes lighting up, and she knew, soul deep, that she'd made exactly the right decision.

LEO

With the festival ready to start, Leo listened to his sister's speech with pride. She'd really done it – no going back now. Which meant it was his turn to be brave.

They'd talked a lot over the last week, the three of them. About what the island meant to them, about family, and most of all about the future. What they each wanted and how to get it. There had been more surprises there than he'd anticipated, Leo had to admit. It turned out he was even less in tune with his sisters than he'd thought, although he hoped the last week had gone some way to changing that.

Listening to Miranda talk about their nomadic life before they moved to the Lighthouse, he'd finally started to understand something of the draw that had kept her on Seashell Island for so long. And started to wonder about his own need for security.

'I barely remember it,' he'd admitted. 'I remember things being tight once we were here, how Mum had to stretch things to keep everyone fed and clothed, plus getting the Lighthouse up to scratch. But before that it's all a bit fuzzy. Did we really move around that much?'

'Twice in one term, once,' Miranda had said. 'But in the end, I told Mum and Dad how unhappy I was, and I think they realised they needed something more stable for the two of you as you were starting school.'

'So they bought the Lighthouse,' Juliet shook her head.

'Well, at least we know where I got my itchy feet from.'

'And the whole extended vacation makes a bit more sense now,' Leo had added. 'I mean, they stayed in one place for so long, for us, and now they had the chance to go and explore the world again . . . I guess it isn't such a huge surprise they decided to keep doing it.'

And now it was Miranda's turn to let go of the security of Seashell Island and find her own adventures, for a while at least.

The girls had been more interested in adjusting Lucy's costume for the festival than listening to their aunt talk. They'd even enlisted Tom's help, much to Leo's amusement. His assistant might claim to be rubbish with kids, but he handled the girls well enough. Plus he had a feeling Tom had a soft spot for Lucy.

'What do you think, Dad?' Mia asked. There was still a little distance there, he could feel, but he realised now that wasn't something he could fix with one perfect summer. They'd made progress since the llama wedding, and he'd worked hard on being really there with them when they were together, and putting the same focus on his work when they were busy doing something else. But building a relationship with them, one that would last, well. That was the work of a lifetime. One summer couldn't achieve it – and one mistake wouldn't ruin it either. As long as he kept trying.

'She looks beautiful.' He took in the full effect of Lucy's flower crown and lacy tutu, and turned away. 'Now, why don't you let Tom go and enjoy the festival?' Tom gave him a grateful thumbs-up, and made a swift exit, towards the beer tent, Leo suspected.

'We need to head to the gates, anyway,' Leo went on. 'There are some guests arriving you'll want to see.' He'd had a long, frank talk with Emily, too. It hadn't been too difficult to persuade her and Mark to join them for the festival, and he knew the girls would be excited to see them and show them all the hard work they'd put in, helping make the Lighthouse Festival a success.

'Grandma and Grandad!' Abby guessed, as Leo grabbed her hand and led her the other way, Mia following behind.

Damn. He hadn't thought of that. Of course they'd assume it was his parents.

'Ah, no. Sorry, sweetheart.'

'No, there!' Abby pointed and, turning around, Leo blinked, twice, to make sure he wasn't imagining things. Because there, walking up the path from the gates, were his parents.

Across Gull Bay, back in the town, the church clock chimed midday, the bells carrying on the breeze, faint but audible, and the festival gates opened at last. The crowds flooded in, and Leo hurried after his daughters to get them and his parents out of the way.

'Mum! Dad! You didn't tell us you were coming home this weekend!'

In fact, they hadn't answered any texts for days. Miranda had been starting to panic about them, although Leo and Juliet had been more relaxed. Probably because they were used to going weeks without speaking to their parents, unlike their big sister.

'Did you really think we'd miss the Lighthouse Festival?' Josie asked, hugging Mia and Abby tightly. 'Besides, we have presents for my two favourite grandchildren, so we had to bring them before you headed back to London.'

'I have to say, I don't remember the festival looking like this last year,' Iestyn joked, as he surveyed the field. 'Miranda's really pulled it out of the bag. But what was she saying up there about leaving the island? I can't imagine Paul's very happy about that – or rather, his mother won't be.'

Leo winced. 'Um, there's actually quite a lot to catch you up on. It's been a bit of a busy summer. It was too much to put in text messages. And we have a few questions for you guys too. But first . . .' he looked past them, and spotted the guests he was expecting walking towards them. 'Girls, look who it is.'

Abby and Mia let go of their grandma's arms, and looked. 'Mum!' Abby yelled. 'It's Mum and Mark!'

And then they were running again, and there were more hugs and shouts and Abby demanding that they all come and meet Lucy immediately . . .

'Are you OK?' his mum asked, as she hugged him gently.

'I'm fine.' He put his own arm around her though, so she didn't move away too fast. What was it about parents that however long they'd been away or apart, no matter how old he got, sometimes they were the only people he needed at his side? He wanted to share everything he'd learned this summer with them. Wanted to ask their advice, hear their perspective, their stories.

He hoped he could be that for his girls, too. Someone who would always listen, always help, but never judge.

That was the sort of father he wanted to be. He knew that now, thanks to this summer, and Seashell Island, and his parents. And Christabel.

'I know it can't be easy seeing her married to someone else,' his mum went on, studying his face as Emily greeted the girls with huge hugs. 'Or watching him with the girls, for that matter.'

'It's not,' Leo admitted. 'But you know, I think it will be OK. The girls will have more people to love them. That can't be a bad thing.'

'No it's not,' Josie agreed. 'And I'm very proud of you for realising that. Now, come on. I want to meet a llama.'

Lucy was completely ambivalent to meeting them, as always. Everyone admired her flower crown, and nobody seemed to notice that her tutu used to be a wedding dress. As Mia dragged them all over to the family area to see Christabel juggle, Leo caught Emily's arm. 'Can I have a word?'

Emily exchanged glances with Mark, and Leo felt his heart pang just a little at the easy communication between them. 'Mark too, if that's OK?' he added, to make it simpler for them.

God, this hurt. This was hard. But it was also the right thing. And he and his sisters had made a pact. They were all going to do the hard, right things they needed to for their future. They were going to fix the relationships they'd spent too long ignoring. They were going to be brave, and step outside the comfortable barriers they'd built for themselves in their lives – whether that was their own expectations of who they could be, or other people's.

If Miranda could leave Seashell Island, if Juliet could remake her life and become a mother, then he could ask his ex-wife for what he needed.

'What's up? Is it the girls?' Emily asked, as they perched on the bench by the family area. Across the grass, Christabel looked over and met his gaze, giving him an encouraging smile.

'In a way.' Leo took a breath, deep and centring – just like Christabel had taught him, when they'd worked on what he wanted to say this week. 'This summer, having this time with them . . . it hasn't always been easy. But it has been important. And it's made me realise some things.'

'Like what?' Emily's shoulders were tense, like she was preparing for the worst. Mark moved behind her and placed his hands on them, rubbing them gently. Leo looked away.

'My relationship with the girls matters to me,' he said, staring down at his hands. 'And until this summer I didn't realise how close I was to letting it slip away. I don't want to be a weekends-only dad, or the dad who swoops in and takes them to the cinema or whatever, but isn't ever there for homework or long talks when it matters.'

'What are you saying, Leo?' He wasn't explaining himself right. Emily sounded defensive, like she expected him to announce some court battle for their children's hearts, when that was the last thing he wanted.

He looked up, into her eyes, and willed her to understand. 'I want to work with you both to find a way for us all to be important parts of the girls' lives,' he said, finally remembering the phrase he and Christabel had come up with late the other night, curled up together in her ambulance bed after a few glasses of her elderflower brandy. 'I'm glad that they have you as their mother, Emily, and Mark, I know you're going to be a great stepdad. But I want to be part of their family too. Someone they can trust and turn to and talk to – not just the guy who shows up with presents at Christmas. I want to help with homework, I want to know who their friends are. And I want to bring them here to Seashell Island every summer, if that's possible. Even if it's just for a week.'

Biting her lip, Emily broke away from his gaze and met Mark's, and Leo waited, heart thumping, to see what she said next. He knew that, whatever happened, he'd find a way to be important in his daughters' lives. But if they could work *together* to make it happen, it would be easier for everyone.

Which was why, however much it hurt his pride and his heart, he had to ask.

'I think . . . I think that would be great for the girls,'

Emily said, at last, and Leo felt his heart start beating again. 'What did you have in mind?'

Across the field, Leo spotted the beer tent. 'Why don't we talk about it over a drink?'

He'd done the hardest part, for today. And he knew now he could keep doing the hard things, over and over, as long as it was what his girls needed him to do.

JULIET

The last week had been so full, so busy and so chaotic, that Juliet had known she couldn't risk talking to Rory. Not when her feelings were still all over the place, and she was panicking about food stalls. But in between all the emails, calls and hard work – plus redecorating the back bedrooms and painting the front door of the Lighthouse – when she lay down to sleep at night, she thought about him.

She thought about why she'd run, again. About why he'd done what he'd done, what he'd been trying to achieve. And she thought about how, ten years later, she still imagined kissing him, one last time.

Just like she'd been encouraging Miranda and Leo to do, she thought about what she wanted from the world, from her life. And by the day of the festival, she was sure.

The Flying Fish had been booked to have a stall at the festival since the first day of planning, so Juliet knew that Rory would at least have to show up for that. If she hadn't been avoiding him anyway, he'd definitely been conspicuous by his absence this week. But this would be the perfect opportunity for them to talk – if she could just persuade him to leave the stall in someone else's capable hands for a while.

Luckily, she found an ally early on.

'Oh, thank goodness.' Rory's colleague, Debbie, grinned as Juliet approached the stall. 'He's been like a bear with a sore head all week. Please, for the love of all that is holy, take him away from here and make up, or whatever you guys need to do. I want my cool boss back, please.'

'I'll see what I can do,' Juliet promised, just as Rory appeared from the van. 'I'm missing your Welsh rarebit, anyway.'

'Juliet.'

'Hi, Rory. Um, can we talk?'

'I am absolutely fine here with the stall,' Debbie said. 'No need to worry about me. And look! Here comes Kieran to take his shift too. You are absolutely surplus to requirements, boss.'

'Apparently you haven't been a lot of fun to work with this week,' Juliet added, in a stage whisper.

Rory didn't even crack a smile. But he followed her back towards the Lighthouse all the same.

'Where are we going?' he asked, as they passed the house. 'Because I really don't want to leave Debbie and Kieran on their own for too long—'

'Just trust me on this one?' she asked. 'I promise, I'm going to get to all the apologising and the explaining any minute now. OK?'

He nodded, but he didn't look happy about it. God, she hoped this worked.

Finally, they crested the rise that brought them to the base of the old lighthouse itself. And there, surrounded by fairy lights that shone pointlessly in the sunlight, because she really hadn't thought this through as well as she should have, was the sign she'd made.

It was just a slice of wood, found out in the wood pile, but with enough good, smooth area to write on with Mia's sharpies. And it read, *The Lighthouse Restaurant.*

Rory stared at it. Then he turned to her. 'What's going on, Juliet?'

She took a deep breath. 'Miranda and Leo and I, we've been doing a lot of thinking the last few days. A lot of talking too, more than we've ever managed before without an argument.'

Rory raised his eyebrows at that. 'Talking about what?'

'About what we all want from our lives. Each of us . . . we'd reached a sort of . . .'

'Crossroads?' He sank down to sit on the step of the lighthouse, and Juliet took his lead, settling beside him.

'More of an impasse, I think,' she said, with a small smile. 'Like we'd reached the end of the roads on our plans for our lives, and didn't know where to go next. Miranda . . . she's leaving the island, probably with Owain, I expect. And Leo, he's rebuilding his family relationships, trying to focus on a more balanced life than just obsessing about work. And I . . . it took me a while to admit it, even to myself. But London didn't give me what I'd hoped it would. I didn't feel any more grown up or in charge of my life. In fact, I didn't feel in control of my future at all . . . until I came back to Seashell Island.'

Rory stilled beside her, and she could feel the tension radiating off him. 'What are you saying, Juliet?'

'This island has given me everything I needed this summer – and a lot of things I didn't even know I needed. It's given me support, it's given me purpose, it's given me hope for the kind of future I can offer my baby. It's given me my family back. And most of all . . . it's given me you. I hope.'

Rory stayed silent, just watching her. Juliet, trying not to panic as the adrenalin flooded her body, finally laid her plans out in front of the person who mattered the most.

'Running the Lighthouse B&B this summer has been a lot more satisfying than I could have imagined as a child. I want to keep doing it. I want to stay here on Seashell Island, raise my baby with sunshine and beaches and llamas, and a community who cares a lot more than I ever realised. I want to make the Lighthouse the best place to stay on the island.'

'And you want to open a restaurant and you called me here for pointers?' Rory nodded towards her makeshift sign.

'Actually, I was kind of hoping *you* might want to open a second restaurant,' Juliet explained, her fingers firmly crossed beside her thigh. 'I mean, I need to talk it all through with Mum and Dad, except they've gone radio silent the last few days. But with Miranda leaving, and summer coming to an end . . . there are no bookings at the B&B from here on in. And I don't know what Mum and Dad have planned for it, but I'm placing bets that they're ready for someone else to take responsibility around here. And for the first time in my life, I think I might be ready for it to be me. So I want to turn the B&B into more of a boutique hotel, and transform the lighthouse itself into a phenomenal restaurant that will bring in people from miles around, but I need you to run it because I don't know anything about restaurants and I'm still learning about B&Bs.'

Rory didn't answer. And when she turned to ask him what he thought, she found him just looking at her, a small smile on his face.

'What?'

'I think that sounds brilliant.' He shook his head. 'I just can't believe you're staying on Seashell Island. When you ran the other day—'

Juliet winced. 'Sorry. I meant to apologise for that first. Running out on you on the carriage ride, when you, you know.'

'When I asked you to marry me.'

'Yeah. That was rude.'

'Just a little bit.' With a sigh, Rory stretched his legs out in front of him in the sunshine. 'Of course, it probably wasn't my best idea. I just thought . . .' He trailed off.

'What exactly *were* you thinking?' She had her own ideas, but she'd like to hear it from him.

Rory sighed again. 'When you walked back into my life this summer, it was almost as if the last ten years never happened. I tried to keep my distance, but there's not a hell of a lot of distance to keep on an island like this. But I knew that if I spent too much time with you, let you get too close . . . I'd fall in love with you all over again.'

Juliet's breath caught in her throat. She wanted to ask *And did you?* But Rory wasn't done.

'And I didn't want to love you, because I knew you'd leave me again and break my heart. But then you told me about the baby . . .' He shook his head. 'Part of me was angry – irrationally, I know. Not at you being pregnant, or being with another man – well, a bit. But not really. I was mostly angry because the only reason you'd come back here was because you were desperate. It wasn't about *wanting* to be here at all. And I should have realised that already, I know, but I don't think I had, quite. Even when you said point blank to Leo that you weren't here for me, there was a part of me that still hoped.'

'I came back here because it was the only place I ever felt safe and loved,' Juliet said, softly. 'I don't know if I fully realised that when I made the decision, but I do now. And I know that a large part of that feeling was down to you.'

That earned her a small smile. 'I got over myself, obviously. Realised that if you were here for help then I'd need to give it to you, because what else could I do? I loved you, Juliet. I've always loved you, ever since we were kids and didn't even know what that meant. So if you needed help, I'd help. It was as simple as that.'

Loved her. As a friend, like they'd always been. Not *in* love with her. She had to focus on that distinction and not get carried away here. 'And you did. There were vitamins and books and advice about bras . . . but what I don't fully get is where the marriage proposal came in.'

He winced. 'Yeah. You can blame Mrs Hillier in the pharmacy for that, if you like.'

'Why, exactly?'

'Because I was buying you more vitamins and ginger chews and she said to me, "Doesn't that friend of yours have a good husband to buy these for her?" and I thought . . . no, but she could have.'

Juliet blinked. 'So, basically the regressive social norms of this island – which I spent years plotting to escape – led you to believe that if I was married everything would be OK?'

Rory rubbed a hand across his forehead. 'It sounds bad when you put it like that. And, no. Not exactly. I just . . . I wanted to look after you. And if I was going to be stuck in love with you for the rest of my life I figured . . . why not? Why not make it official that I took care of you?'

'And you thought that was what I wanted? Someone else to fix my problems, as usual.' She sighed. 'I can see where you got that idea. But actually . . . I like to think I've grown up at least a little bit since those days. I want to fix my own problems. And this baby? It's not a problem at all. It's a little miracle. An opportunity that's given me back something I thought I could never have – my home. Coming back here this summer . . . I feel like I've grown up enough to appreciate Seashell Island at last. And to value everything it has to offer.'

'I'm glad. This place . . . it's more than just an island. It's home.' Rory twisted round to look at her. 'So, if I sign on

343

for this restaurant thing, how is it going to work? Between you and me, I mean.'

'Well, we'll be business partners. And friends, I hope.' She'd given this a lot of thought. She'd already turned down his offer of marriage, because she knew his reasons for asking weren't the right ones. She might still have feelings for him, but there were a dozen reasons why starting a new relationship with him right now was a bad idea.

'Just friends.' He sighed. 'OK. I can live with that.'

Juliet paused. Was that . . . disappointment? Did he want something more, too?

Something tickled at the back of her brain. Something he'd said. She'd been concentrating on the fact he'd been trying to marry her to save her reputation, in some Jane Austen sort of way, and she'd missed the most important thing.

Wait.

If I was going to be stuck in love with you for the rest of my life . . .

'Wait. Did you say you're in love with me?'

'Very. Did you miss that part?'

'Of course not.'

'That's a yes.'

Hard to lie to someone who knew her better than she knew herself, most of the time.

'Just to be completely clear,' he said, turning to meet her gaze head on and taking her hands in his. 'I'm in love with you. I've always been in love with you. And if there's even a chance of you feeling the same way, I'd like us to explore that. Together.'

Her heart seemed to stop inside her chest. A chance? There was a hell of a lot more than that. But . . .

'But I'm going to be a *mother*, Rory!'

344

'I know.'

'To someone else's child!'

'I know that too.'

She shook her head. 'You don't get it. I have to focus on that before everything else. You'd never matter more than the baby will.'

'I understand that.'

'And if I'm going to stay on the island I need to find a way to make sure the Lighthouse stays profitable. Which means I'll be working, a lot, so I'd be a rubbish girlfriend.'

'I'm used to that.'

She elbowed him in the ribs. 'And at some point I'm going to have to go back to London and deal with my stuff and my flat and my housemate and my ex-boss who's also the father of my baby. Which you'll hate.'

'I know.'

'And you still want to do this anyway?' she asked, incredulously.

'Yes.' He reached up a hand and brushed a lock of hair behind her ear, leaving his fingers lingering against her cheek. 'I'll love the baby because it's a part of you, and I love every part of you. And the rest of it . . . Juliet, I've waited ten years to have another chance with you. If you think that any of those things are enough to make me wait a second longer, then you are seriously underestimating how in love with you I really am.'

His gaze was locked on hers now, and she could feel herself moving closer to him without even trying. Like magnets were drawing them together.

'You're sure?' she asked, giving him one last chance to pull away. 'We'll be business partners, friends *and* lovers and, I guess, parents? You want *all* of that with me?'

'Juliet, I want every single part of you. I want to build that

345

life, here on Seashell Island, with you. If you'll have me.'

She kissed him, then, because how could she not?

Relief flowed through her like sea air in her lungs, a feeling of home and rightness and forever that she'd never felt in London.

After long moments, she pulled back, resting her forehead against his. 'When you proposed, I thought . . . the whole island tour thing, I thought you wanted me to go backwards. To be the Juliet I was when I left. And while I had no idea what I wanted to do with my life next just then, I knew in my heart I needed to move forward. But . . . I think moving forward with you could be pretty wonderful. Building that life you talked about, together . . . I want that too. More than anything.'

He kissed her again, then slipped an arm around her shoulder and pulled her close. With the lighthouse at her back, Juliet looked out over the sea towards the mainland, her head resting against his shoulder.

She knew herself well enough to know that she'd still need to escape the confines of Seashell Island again from time to time, and she'd want her baby to know the rest of the world too. And that was fine.

Because she could always come home to Seashell Island. And Rory.

'Happy?' he murmured against her hair.

'Happiest,' she replied.

They sat in companionable silence for a while, watching the waves and the sunlight playing on the water. It wasn't until they heard Owain's voice through the speakers on the festival field that they realised how late it must have grown.

'Come on,' Juliet said, tugging Rory to his feet. 'We need to get back down there.'

They were almost back to the festival when something

caught Juliet's eye in the family area. 'Wait. Is that . . . ?'

'Your mum juggling fire sticks?' Rory finished, his voice faint. 'Um, yeah. I think it is.'

Juliet grabbed his hand and set off for the festival at a run.

MIRANDA

Miranda had intended to go straight from the stage to finding Owain, to talk to him at last about her plans. Unfortunately, the crowds of locals waiting to congratulate her and wish her luck had other ideas. By the time she'd made it through, Owain was nowhere to be seen.

Heart thumping, Miranda tried not to take that as a bad sign.

Her phone buzzed in her pocket and she grabbed for it, hoping it would be Owain, and was disappointed when the screen revealed a text message from her brother.

Mum and Dad are here! Come find us! We're in the kids' area.

She read it twice, blinking hard between readings, just to make sure she had it right.

Her parents were home? Now? Why?

And then she was running, racing across the festival site, weaving between vendors and stalls and the occasional loose animal, heading for the kids' zone.

She slowed at last as her parents came into view. Dad, tanned and relaxed, leaned against the fence surrounding the petting zoo, watching as Mum juggled batons and Christabel tried to teach Abby and Mia some juggling basics with some simpler bean balls.

'Auntie Miri! Did you know Grandma can juggle?' Abby asked, as Miranda approached. With a smile, Josie caught all five sticks and placed them on the bench, as Iestyn pushed away from the fence to join them.

'I didn't even know Grandma was back in the country!' Miranda hugged her mother, then her father. 'Why didn't you tell us you were coming back?'

'We thought it would be a surprise,' Josie explained. 'And actually . . .' She glanced over at her husband.

'We don't think we'll be staying long,' Iestyn finished for her.

'You're going travelling again?' Miranda asked, surprised to find that she wasn't surprised at all.

'As are you, we understand,' Josie said. 'But yes. We've been invited out to stay with some friends we met on our travels, who live out on the west coast of America and, well, your dad has always wanted to do a road trip along that coast so we thought, well, why not? We'll be home for Christmas, I'm sure.'

'And then I can feel Japan beckoning me,' Iestyn said. 'I've always wanted to go to Japan.'

'But you'll come home again, right, Grandad?' Mia asked. 'We will still see you, won't we?'

'Of course!' Iestyn flung his arms around both his granddaughters' shoulders, although he had to kneel almost in the grass to get down that low. 'We'll always come home again, because how else could we bore you with all our stories about the places we've been?'

'And because we'll miss you,' Josie added. 'But we'll send postcards, and we can still Skype. It won't be very different from you two being in London and us being here!'

That seemed to satisfy them, as they ran back off to where Christabel was blowing enormous bubbles with a rope hoop.

'Wait,' Miranda said, because those sorts of assurances might work for nine- and six-year-olds, but she was going to need a little more. 'You're leaving again? Because there are some things we need to talk about before you decide that.'

Josie and Iestyn shared a look that didn't look unlike the ones that Leo and Juliet used to share when Miranda tried to instil some sort of order and control over them as kids.

'Of course,' Josie said. 'Do you want to wait for your brother and sister?'

She should, Miranda knew. But she needed *some* answers straight away, just for her own peace of mind. 'We'll talk to them too, later. But first . . . the Lighthouse. There are no bookings for the rest of the year. And Leo and I found the sales brochure from the estate agents . . .'

'That was just a draft,' Iestyn said, motioning for them all to sit down on the bench by the fence to talk. 'We wanted to know what it would be worth as it was, if we decided to sell it.'

'And have you?'

'Not yet,' Josie said, as she sat. 'But with you leaving—'

'I think Juliet might want to stay.' Miranda blurted out, then grinned at the confused astonishment on her parents' faces. 'I know, I know. I was as surprised as you. But things have changed. *We've* all changed this summer. And it's up to her to tell you all about it, but . . . talk to her first.'

'We will,' Iestyn promised. 'And as for our plans . . . I think we've been rather bitten by the adventure bug again.'

'We saved for decades to be able to take a big trip, once you were all grown up and settled,' Josie added. 'And it's brilliant to be able to do that at last.'

'So it's not because, well, either of you are sick?'

Her parents both laughed at that. 'Why would you think that?' Josie asked. 'We're both in better health now than we've been in years. All that sunshine, sea air, and morning yoga on deck.'

'And you're not . . . in financial difficulty?' Miranda thought she'd better check, since they were having all the awkward conversations right now.

Iestyn shrugged. 'No more than anyone else on the island,' he said. 'My writing might not have ever made us rich, but together with the paintings your mum sold in the gallery in town, as well as the income from the Lighthouse . . . we're doing fine. As long as you lot aren't expecting some windfall inheritance.'

'No! No, nothing like that. We were just . . . worried.'

Iestyn patted her arm. 'Miranda, we're grown adults. We can take care of ourselves, you know.'

'I know.' They all could, it seemed. And the only person Miranda really had to worry about was herself.

That was sort of freeing, in a way.

'Now, I want a turn with those juggling fire sticks,' Josie said, jumping to her feet and heading towards the circus skills area. 'Much more exciting than the boring normal ones!' She gave Iestyn a meaningful look before she went, which Miranda interpreted as it being his turn to find out what was going on with her.

It usually was his turn. She loved her mother very much, but she'd always been better with Leo and Juliet's problems. When Miranda was worried, even as a child, she turned to her dad.

'So. Quite the party you've pulled off here,' Iestyn said, when it was just the two of them again. 'How about we leave your mum with the girls and you show me around a bit.'

'OK. And don't forget, we need you to light the light-house lamp, once it gets dark.'

'Of course.' Iestyn smiled, the smile he'd always seemed to keep just for her, and Miranda felt warm and safe all over again. More proof, if she'd needed it, that security and happiness came more from the people she loved, than from where she stayed. Seashell Island was precious and home, but the people on it mattered more to her than the land itself.

They wandered together around the festival field, locals stopping Iestyn to welcome him home, and stallholders stopping Miranda to check some detail or another. Rory wasn't on the Flying Fish stand, she noticed as they passed. Hopefully that meant that Juliet was holding up her side of the bravery pact, too.

As they walked, Miranda filled her dad in on everything that had happened while they'd been away – starting with Paul dumping her, Leo and Juliet coming home, the band staying at the Lighthouse, the festival planning . . . everything except Juliet and Leo's secrets and decisions, which were their own to tell, and the exact nature of her relationship with the lead singer of that aforementioned band.

Some things, a father just didn't need to know.

'And now you're ready to leave at last?' he asked. 'I always wondered if you would. All those maps and adventure stories, I felt sure you were bound for a great adventure one day. But then you never seemed to be ready to go.'

'I think I am, now,' she said. 'I was . . . I was scared, before. That if I left, something would go wrong here. Like the time I went to Cardiff University for the open day and Juliet nearly drowned. I just felt—'

'You felt responsible for the family, and the Lighthouse. For all of us.' Iestyn sighed. 'I always knew that you thought you were the only grown-up in the family. That we'd all fall apart without you. And maybe you were right. But Miranda . . . sometimes, you need to let others find their own way. Make their own mistakes. Figure out their own futures.'

'Like you did with us, this summer,' she replied. 'If you

and Mum had been here this summer, none of this would have happened. And I'd probably never have decided to leave.'

'Then it's a good thing we went,' Iestyn decided. 'Because I think you're going to have the most marvellous adventures, my girl. And I can't wait to hear all about them.'

They smiled at each other and, Iestyn's arm around her shoulder, they made their way across the rest of the site. Finally, they reached the stage, and Miranda slipped them around to the side through the security ropes – manned by an understanding Dafydd.

Owain and the others were just preparing to go onstage, but he put down his guitar and crossed over to them, kissing Miranda hello as if by habit. 'I've been looking for you all afternoon. I heard your speech before. Does this mean—'

Definitely time to interrupt. 'Owain, this is my dad, Iestyn. He and Mum have popped home for a brief break in their travels.'

'Nice to meet you, Mr Waters.' Owain shook Iestyn's hand, but then turned straight back to Miranda. 'You're leaving Seashell Island. For real?'

'I . . . am. Yes. Terrifying as that still sounds.'

Owain placed a hand against her cheek. 'I'm so proud of you.'

'I'm pretty proud of myself, to be honest.'

'Have you thought about where you're going?' Owain asked.

'I think I'd like to see some more of the world,' Miranda said. 'I have all this money saved up for the wedding that never happened, and I think . . . I think I just want to spend it exploring. Finding myself, if we're going to be clichéd about it. I want to drink coffee in Paris and eat sauerkraut in Berlin and visit the salt mines in Poland . . . everything, really.'

'All the places on those maps on the cottage walls, huh?'

'Apparently the itchy feet gene didn't skip a generation after all.'

'Did you think you might like some company, for any of this travelling?' Owain asked. 'Only . . . that meeting I mentioned? It was about a last-minute slot supporting another band on their European tour. I could give you the itinerary, just in case any of your stops happened to coincide with ours?'

Miranda beamed. 'I would like that a lot.'

Getting off the island was something she needed to do for herself. But getting to share some of that journey with the man who'd made her realise she needed to leave in the first place could only be a good thing.

'So would I.'

They held each other's gaze for a long moment, until Miranda heard her father clearing his throat, and realised that Dafydd was introducing Birchwood onstage.

'You'd better go,' she told Owain.

Swearing, he kissed her again, then ran to catch up to the others. 'We'll talk properly later though,' he called back to Miranda, and she nodded.

Talking with Owain was definitely on her list for tonight. Along with doing lots of other things with Owain. Not entirely limited to planning the travel itinerary.

'So,' Iestyn asked, as they headed back out front to watch. 'Should I be worried about my daughter running off with a rock star?'

'Folk-rock,' she corrected him. 'And no, not really.'

She wasn't running off with Owain. She was stepping out into the world on her own, at last.

Owain being with her was just an added bonus.

The gig was electric. All the bands today had been great,

but Owain and the guys blew the rest of them out of the water. The energy, the musicality, all of it had the whole field of people vibrating in time. She'd thought she'd known how good they were from their impromptu performances on the terrace, but those had nothing on this.

Even her dad was tapping his feet. 'OK,' he said, between songs. 'Maybe I'll let you run away with this one. Just for a little while. As long as you promise to come home again, now and then, to tell me about your adventures.'

'Always,' she promised. 'As long as you do too! You and Mum, the Lighthouse, Juliet and Leo, Seashell Island . . . this is home, and it always will be. I could never stay away for too long.'

Miranda smiled, and let her dad put his arm around her while they listened.

'So, I can tell your mother you're not heartbroken about Paul then?'

'You can definitely tell her that,' Miranda replied. 'In fact, you can tell her that I'm happy. And I'm heading out into the world to find out what can make me even happier.'

'Good for you, my girl.' Iestyn kissed the top of her head. 'Good for you.'

By the time Owain and the band reached the last song of their set, the others had all made their way from the corners of the festival to join them. Juliet was there, her hand clasped in Rory's, which made Miranda smile. Abby and Mia were right up by the stage, dancing their hearts out, while Mark and Emily stood nearby watching them. Leo and Christabel stood on the other side, whispering – or probably shouting – into each other's ears to be heard that close to the stage. Josie and Iestyn stayed a little further back, but Miranda knew they were watching all of them, checking in on them all.

She wondered if they saw what she saw. Three siblings, all

355

finding their right paths again after too many wrong turns.

She looked up at the stage and saw Owain singing down at her, his eyes focused on her own.

Maybe he was her right path. At the very least, she wanted to walk it a while to be sure.

For a moment, she let the music carry her away, on a wave of energy and fun and possibility. And then she smiled.

Because it was all out there waiting for her.

LEO

As night started to fall, Leo gathered up Abby and Mia, and led them away from the stage where they'd been dancing to the music. Owain's band had been the last official act to play, but now makeshift combinations of musicians from all the bands were creating new tunes and playing old favourites up on the stage, much to the crowd's delight. It seemed that no one wanted to go home just yet.

The sun hadn't fully set yet, and the moon was still on its way up – the magic hour between the day and the night.

And time for something really special.

'Where are we going?' Mia asked, testily.

'You'll see,' Leo told her.

'Can Lucy come?' Abby pointed to where the llama was grazing, far away from the rest of the petting zoo, uncontainable as always, her tutu fluttering in the breeze.

He shrugged. 'Why not?'

Llama in tow, he led the girls up the winding path, past the B&B, to the old lighthouse on the crest of the cliff. His parents, sisters, Emily and Mark, Christabel, Owain, Rory and even Tom were all already there, watching and waiting. The fairy lights Juliet had twisted around the fence beside it twinkled in the fading light. Lucy trotted over towards them and grazed happily on the fresh grass there.

'Are we ready?' Iestyn asked.

'For what, Grandad?' Abby asked.

Mia gasped. 'It's time to light the lamp, isn't it!'

Iestyn beamed. 'That's right! You two girls want to come up and help me?'

They both nodded, and raced through the lighthouse door before their grandfather.

Leo wandered over to the fence, where Christabel had joined Lucy, and hopped up to sit on it, the way he always had as a boy.

'Will you come join us up at the house after?' he asked Christabel, as they waited for the lamp to spill its brightness into the gloom. 'There's bound to be at least one or two nightcaps, and Dad will want to tell all sorts of stories about their travels.'

Christabel smiled, but shook her head. 'I'd love to, but I've got an early ferry to catch tomorrow. Need to go pack up the ambulance.'

Leo froze. 'You're leaving?'

'So are you,' she reminded him. 'Tomorrow or the next day. You're going back to London, and I'm going wherever the wind takes me next.'

'Like Mary Poppins.' She'd blown into his life and made him look at it differently, and now she was leaving again. She'd told him that they had a time limit, that at the end of the summer it would be over between them. And now it was September. The wind had changed and she was on her way.

He'd known it was coming. He just still didn't feel ready for it.

'If Mary Poppins drove an ambulance, I suppose.' Head tilted to one side, she bit her lip as she looked at him. 'You know, normally at this point I'm desperate to get on with the next new thing. I spent so long stuck in a life that didn't suit me, that these days I just want to keep hunting to find something that does.'

Was she suggesting that she *didn't* want to leave? Except, as she said, he wouldn't be here anyway. So it wasn't exactly a ringing endorsement of their romance.

They'd both known, from that first night they fell into bed together, that this thing between them wasn't for ever. The end had just crept up rather quicker than Leo would like. In the back of his mind, he supposed he'd been imagining coming back to visit Seashell Island next summer and finding Christabel here waiting for him.

Which was half his problem. Imagining that other people would just wait for him to have time for them, rather than getting on with their own lives.

'You don't feel ready to leave Seashell Island?' he asked, as neutrally as he could.

She rolled her eyes. 'Yes, I think I've got everything from the island that I can. And with Miranda leaving . . . it's time for me to move on too.' Moving a little closer, she whispered close to his ear, 'But I will regret not getting at least one more night with you.'

Blood rushed through his body, and Leo hoped he wasn't blushing as the lighthouse lamp suddenly flared to life and illuminated the whole sky. A cheer went up – first from the family gathered around them then, a fraction of a second later, from the festival field below.

Abby and Mia came racing back down the lighthouse stairs and shot out the door into his arms. 'Did you see! We turned on the light!'

'I saw!' He gathered them close and held them to him, grateful for everything this summer had given him. Over their shoulders he saw Emily smiling too, and knew that between them they were going to make all this work. Somehow.

'Let's get back up to the house,' his mum said, clapping

her hands together. 'I think it's time for a nightcap, don't you?'

No one disagreed with that.

The festival had most definitely been a success – one he suspected would carry on late into the night on the camping field, and one that would start early again the next morning with the clean-up. But as the moon rose high over the waves out beyond Gull Bay, Leo watched his family wending their way back to the B&B, and knew that the biggest successes today had been the personal ones.

Juliet had her head on Rory's shoulder as they walked. He didn't know if she'd told their parents about the baby yet, but he thought she would, soon. Miranda and Owain, meanwhile, had snuck away together – he was betting back to the cottage – for some time alone.

Everything had gone to plan.

Well, almost everything.

He hung back a little to say a final goodbye to Christabel as they reached the crossroads with the path down towards St Mary's.

Christabel reached up on her tiptoes, and placed a kiss against his cheek, her hand reaching round to rest in the back pocket of his jeans for a moment. 'I'll see you around, Leo Waters.'

'I hope so,' he said, with feeling. 'I mean, it's a big world out there, and I know you want to explore it. But I would love to see you again.'

The smile she gave him was half mysterious, half pleased.

'Then I imagine you will,' she said. 'I mean, even an explorer has to come home for supplies, right? And there is that bike shop in London that I still technically own half of. I should probably stop by there sometime soon and check in, don't you think?'

'Wait, what bike shop?' he asked, confused, but then she was gone, off into the crowds heading back through the gates, onto the road into town.

Out of his life. But maybe just for now.

He stuck a hand into his back pocket and pulled out a card that definitely hadn't been there when he got dressed that morning.

Aphrodite Bikes, he read, smiling as he realised that the address on it was only a short way from his flat.

Then, still grinning, Leo turned back towards the house, and followed his family home.

He had plenty else to be getting on with, until Christabel blew back into his life again.

JULIET

'So, you and Rory are an item again are you?' Josie asked, as she and Juliet made the tea in the kitchen. Everyone else had retired to the sunroom, apart from Leo and Emily, who had gone upstairs together to put the girls to bed. 'I always liked him. Seems like you've all been making some big changes while we've been away.'

'It's . . . a possibility,' Juliet admitted. 'Things are a little complicated right now.'

'Because you live in London and he's here?' Josie guessed, reaching for the biscuits. 'Although Miranda did mention you might want to stay here for a while . . . ?'

Juliet took a breath. Now or never. She just hoped she hadn't used up all her brave for one day.

'Because I'm pregnant with another man's child and I've decided to move home to Seashell Island to raise the baby and hopefully run the Lighthouse and a new restaurant with Rory and please God don't disown me or anything.' The words came out like a babbling stream, an unstoppable force of nature.

Josie put the biscuits back and took down the emergency bottle of vodka.

'Right. Let's start from the beginning, shall we?' she said, after she'd poured one shot and drunk it. 'And no more of that silly disowning talk. You're my daughter, and that's all there is to it. Now, tell me what happened.'

362

It was easier this time. Juliet tried to imagine having this conversation with her mother at the start of the summer and, even though that's exactly what she'd intended when she came home, she couldn't picture it. But having already been through it with Miranda and Leo, and with Rory; having already learned that it wasn't the end of everything, but only the beginning . . . that made it all easier.

'Oh, my baby girl.' Josie put her arms around Juliet as she finished the story. 'I'm so sorry that happened to you. But I'm not sorry that I get to be a grandmother again, however it happened. Only . . .' she trailed off, and Juliet looked up to see a pensive expression on her mother's face.

'What is it?'

'Are you really sure you want to stay on Seashell Island? You were always so adamant about leaving . . . I'd hate for you to feel you had to come back just because you're having a baby. Being a mother doesn't mean giving up all your dreams, you know, or your *you-ness*. You can raise this baby in London if that's what you want. You know we'll support you however we can—'

'Mum. I want to come home. I . . . I don't think I appreciated this place the first time around. Now, this summer, maybe I'm starting to.'

'Because of Rory?' Josie asked, a little sceptically Juliet thought, especially since she'd just said how much she liked him.

'Actually, because of the Lighthouse,' Juliet replied. 'I've been running it while you were away – I know you didn't have any bookings, but we couldn't bear the idea of the place sitting empty, so that's how Owain and the band ended up staying here. And I was thinking about some ideas to maybe bring the place up to date, if you didn't mind . . .'

Josie beamed. 'Love, if you really want to take over this

place, you'd be doing your dad and me a favour. We've done our time here, and it's been the most wonderful home for us and for you kids. But now it's our turn to get back out in the world and explore again. We'd thought we'd have to sell it, which would break our hearts. You make this place your own. Just make sure there's always a room for us, when we come home.'

Relief, and gratitude, and love, and happiness all swelled up in her at the same time.

The Lighthouse was hers. Her future, hers and her baby's. 'I promise.'

'And don't forget, if you ever need us, we'll be on the next plane back. You only have to call.'

'I will.' Juliet looked up, and saw Rory standing in the doorway, waiting for her, that patient smile on his dear face. 'But you know, I think everything is going to be all right.'

Maybe not straight away, maybe not always. She knew there'd be obstacles to clear to get the Lighthouse to how she saw it in her mind's eye. She knew things wouldn't always be easy with Rory – and knew for certain that people would talk.

But this was her right path. And she was ready to walk it, at last.

Josie followed Juliet's gaze, and smiled. 'You know, I think it will too, love.'

Festival clear-up took the whole of the next day, and then, impossibly, it was the third of September, and summer was over.

Emily and Mark had headed back to London the day before, and now Leo and the girls wheeled their cases out to Harriet's horse and carriage, ready for the journey back to the ferry. Tom was travelling with them; apparently, he'd be driving Leo's car back to London, while her brother took the girls back on the train, ready to start school again the next day. Tom was looking positively gleeful at the opportunity, and to her surprise, Leo barely looked nervous at all.

'You will look after Lucy for us, won't you?' Abby asked, as they said their goodbyes.

'I promise,' Juliet said, solemnly. 'After all, she's part of the family, now she's married in.'

'I'll come and visit again soon,' Leo said, as he hugged her goodbye. 'Make sure you're doing OK.'

'I'd like that,' Juliet admitted. 'I'm going to miss our monthly dinners in London.'

Next up was Miranda, who hugged Leo goodbye as well. 'Maybe I'll stop by and see you for dinner instead,' she suggested, and Leo grinned.

'I'd really like that,' he replied. Then the girls were dragging him away to Harriet's carriage – although Harriet was rather busy enthusiastically kissing Suzi goodbye, too.

Owain and the rest of the band were loading their bags and equipment into Rory's van again, and Miranda turned to Juliet.

'I can't believe you're going off to become a groupie,' Juliet said, as she hugged her sister goodbye. The morning air was fresh, with just the tiniest hint of autumn in it.

'I am not!' Miranda objected. 'Well. Maybe just a little bit.'

'I want postcards from every single place you go.' It was hard to imagine Miranda being the one out in the world, while Juliet stayed home on the island. But for right now, it felt exactly as it should be.

'I'll be home for Christmas,' Miranda promised. 'And when the baby is born. And definitely for the Lighthouse Festival next year. I want to see how you top this summer.'

Juliet stood on the driveway to the Lighthouse, and looked around her at the family she loved, all scattering to the winds again. Mum and Dad were already packing, ready for their next adventure. Leo and the girls were still waving from the back of the carriage as it headed down the hill, Suzi blowing kisses behind them. Owain was waiting for Miranda by the van, the others already inside. Lucy the Llama was munching the flowers in the beds by the front door.

And Rory was smiling at her, her whole future waiting to happen.

'Top this summer? I'm not sure I could,' Juliet said.

Miranda's smile was soft and mysterious. 'Oh, I'm pretty sure you will. And I can't wait to see it. Oh, and this is for you.' She pushed an envelope into Juliet's hand, and then she was gone. Rory put his arm around her shoulder as they all waved them off, Josie and Iestyn walking halfway down the hill behind them, still waving.

'What's that?' Rory asked, as she opened it.

Juliet blinked at the figure on the paper in front of her, and the scrawled note from her sister. 'It's . . . all the money we made at the festival. Miranda wants us to use it set up the Lighthouse restaurant.'

'Really? Wow.' Rory kissed her. 'So. Are you ready?'

'For what?'

'The future.'

A smile spread across Juliet's face. 'You know what? I think I am.'

And even Lucy hummed her agreement.

MESSAGES

Tom (to Leo): Boss, if you get a notice about a speeding ticket on the M4, just know that the tunes were pumping and the road was clear and I'm very, very sorry.

Juliet (to the 'Rents group): Um, some guy just showed up here with a parrot in a cage and said it was for me. This is your idea of a joke, right?
Josie: We just thought the new baby would like a pet!
Juliet: He or she already has a llama!!!

Miranda (to Owain): You're still in Rome tonight, right? Meet me at the Colosseum and I'll take you for pizza. I can stay a couple of days, then I'm off to Venice. Fancy a trip on the canals between gigs?

Leo (to Christabel): So, I'm looking at buying a city bike for cycling to work. Don't suppose you could recommend a good bike shop in London . . . ?

ONE YEAR LATER
MIRANDA

As she stepped off the ferry, Miranda took a deep lungful of sea air, and smiled. Down by the harbour, she could hear Albert Tuna singing to himself as he cleaned his boat. The candy-coloured houses lined the edge of Long Beach like always, and there was a scent of ice cream and chips in the air. Puffy white clouds bobbed overhead, as the waves lapped gently against the shore.

Ferry passengers pushed past her, all keen to get onto Seashell Island, ready for the Lighthouse Festival tomorrow night. Miranda didn't know what Juliet had planned exactly, but the excited chatter from festival goers on the boat over suggested great things. Plus she knew from Juliet's messages that the B&B had been booked solid all summer – as had most of the island's holiday cottages, apparently. Nigel and Gwen had needed to hire another two staff members to cope with the demand, and were still run off their feet. 'Which is good,' Juliet had said when she called, 'Since Paul hasn't been home *once* since he left. Takes their mind off it.'

Juliet, now a staple of the island community, always had all the gossip.

And Miranda *had* been home – for a couple of days at Christmas, and then in the early spring when baby Noah was born. But coming back to the island in summer . . . that was seeing Seashell Island as it was meant to be.

'Good to be home?' Owain asked, moving to stand behind her, as the final passengers disembarked and pushed past them.

'Always.' She turned to kiss him, happy to take their time. 'It's hard to believe that it's over a year ago that I was chasing Lucy across that beach, though. So much has happened since then.'

'And you've been to many places,' Owain replied. 'But right now, I think there are some people waiting for you.' He nudged her around to face the far end of the jetty, and her smile widened as she saw what he was talking about.

There, waiting by the harbour wall, was her family. Josie and Iestyn, waving madly, both wearing sombreros they must have picked up on their latest trip to Mexico. Juliet and Rory, the latter holding a squirming Noah, both looking tired but happy. Leo and – ooh, that *was* a surprise – Christabel too, not standing too close but clearly together, with Abby and Mia in front of them waving as well. And even Leo's long-suffering assistant Tom had made the journey back for the festival. He, Miranda was amused to note, was holding the end of the lead attached to the harness that someone had managed to fasten around Lucy's body.

For a second, Miranda just took in the view, content to see them all together again, and all happy. Then, as Owain took her hand, she stepped forward to greet them all, her heart overflowing. She wondered how long it would take one of them to notice the sparkling engagement ring on her left finger . . .

They wouldn't stay more than a week, Miranda knew, before it was time to move on again – Owain had recording planned this autumn, so she'd be running her VA business from his cottage in North Wales for a while, until the gigs started up again. The best thing about having a job she could do from anywhere, she'd found, was all the places she got to travel while doing it.

But for now, she was home on Seashell Island for the end-of-summer Lighthouse Festival, with all her family around her.

And there was nowhere she would rather be.

ACKNOWLEDGEMENTS

No book is an island . . .

A huge thank you to everyone who helped make *Summer on Seashell Island* a reality, most especially:

• My parents, Steve and Janet Cannon. If you hadn't disappeared to Australia for months on end, I'd never have had the idea to write this book. Not to mention all those cruises you keep going on . . .
• My brothers, Kip and Mike Cannon. It's good to know we can just about survive without them being in the country, right? Still, Kip, maybe hide the passports next time you're at the old homestead?
• My husband, Simon, and my kids, Holly and Sam. Without the three of you, Lucifer the Llama would never exist. And I think that would be a shame.
• My agent, Gemma Cooper, always.
• My editor, Victoria Oundjian, for answering 'of course!' when I asked if there could be a llama. And, you know, everything else she did for this book . . .
• Everyone at Orion, for all the support and hard work that's gone into making this book happen, even in difficult times.

And, above all, thank you to YOU – my readers. Messages

from you, photos of you reading my books, emails and comments and questions – they all make my day, every day. Come find me on social media and stay in touch, please?

Facebook: @SophiePembrokeAuthor
Instagram: @sophie_pembroke
Twitter: @Sophie_Pembroke

CREDITS

We would like to thank everyone at Orion who worked on the publication of *Summer on Seashell Island* in the UK.

Editorial
Victoria Oundjian
Olivia Barber

Copy editor
Justine Taylor

Proof reader
Kate Shearma

Audio
Paul Stark
Amber Bates

Contracts
Anne Goddard
Paul Bulos
Jake Alderson

Design
Debbie Holmes
Joanna Ridley

Nick May
Helen Ewing

Editorial Management
Charlie Panayiotou
Jane Hughes
Alice Davis

Finance
Jasdip Nandra
Afeera Ahmed
Elizabeth Beaumont
Sue Baker

Marketing
Tanjiah Islam

Production
Ruth Sharvell

Publicity
Kate Moreton

Sales
Jen Wilson
Esther Waters
Victoria Laws
Rachael Hum
Ellie Kyrke-Smith
Frances Doyle
Georgina Cutler

Operations
Jo Jacobs
Sharon Willis
Lisa Pryde
Lucy Brem

If you loved *Summer on Seashell Island*, don't miss Sophie Pembroke's heartwarming winter romance . . .

Welcome to Mistletoe Island,
where dreams can come true . . .

The snow is falling and Fliss's friends have arrived to celebrate her wedding for a week at Holly Cottage. It's the perfect way to kick off her brand-new life, isn't it?

Except Ruth wishes she was anywhere other than a remote Scottish island, Caitlin is keeping a secret from her friends, Lara is suddenly facing her ex a decade after turning down his proposal and even the bride has something to hide . . .

But as the friends prepare for a week to remember, will Fliss's dream wedding go off without a hitch, or will the secrets they've been hiding change everything?

Available now in paperback, ebook and audio